MYSTERY

The Rockingdown Mystery

The Rilloby Fair Mystery

The Ragamuffin Mystery

Armada
An Imprint of HarperCollinsPublishers

More titles by Enid Blyton in Armada

The Rilloby Fair Mystery
The Ring O'Bells Mystery
The Rubadub Mystery
The Rat-A-Tat Mystery
The Ragamuffin Mystery
The Secret Island
The Secret of Spiggy Holes
The Secret Mountain
The Secret of Killimooin
The Secret of Moon Castle
The Mystery That Never Was
Mystery Stories
Adventure Stories
The Treasure Hunters
Shadow the Sheepdog
The Boy Next Door
More Adventures on Willow Farm
The Children at Green Meadows
Six Cousins at Mistletoe Farm
Six Cousins Again

Enid Blyton

THE ROCKINGDOWN
MYSTERY

The Rockingdown Mystery, The Rilloby Fair Mystery and
The Ragamuffin Mystery were first published in
Great Britain in 1949, 1950 and 1951 by
William Collins Sons & Co Ltd.

First published in Armada 1967, 1967 and 1969
First published in this edition in 1994
1 3 5 7 9 10 8 6 4 2

Armada is an imprint of
HarperCollins Children's Books,
a division of HarperCollins Publishers Ltd,
77-85 Fulham Palace Road,
Hammersmith, London W6 8JB

Printed and bound in Great Britain
by HarperCollins Manufacturing Ltd, Glasgow

Contents

Chapter One

The Beginning of the Holidays

'Hallo, Roger!'

'Hallo, Diana! Had a good term?'

The boy and girl grinned at one another, half-shy as they always were when they met again at the end of the school term. They were brother and sister, and rather alike to look at – sturdy, dark-haired with determined chins and wide smiles.

'My train came in twenty minutes before yours,' said Roger. 'Bit of luck, breaking up on the same day – we usually don't. I waited about for you. Now we've got to wait for Miss Pepper.'

Diana groaned. She dragged her night-case, her tennis racket and a large brown parcel along with her. Roger had a racket and a case too.

'These aren't going to be very nice hols,' said Diana, 'with Mummy and Daddy away, and us poked down in the country somewhere with Miss Pepper. Whatever made Mummy ask her to look after us? Why couldn't we have gone to Auntie Pam?'

'Because her kids have got measles,' said Roger. 'Miss Pepper isn't so bad, really – I mean she does understand how hungry we always are, and she does know we like things like sausages and salad and cold meat and potatoes in their jackets and ice cream and gingerbeer . . .'

'Oh, don't go on – you make me feel hungry already,' said Diana. 'What are the plans for today, Roger? I only know you were going to meet me and then we were to see Miss Pepper somewhere.'

7

'I had a letter from Dad yesterday,' said Roger, as they pushed their way through the crowds on the platform. 'He and Mummy sail today for America. They *had* fixed up for us to go to Aunt Pam, but the measles knocked that on the head, so Mummy wired to her old governess, Miss Pepper, and got her to fix up to spend the hols with us – and we're to go to a little cottage somewhere that Dad managed to get hold of in Rockingdown – goodness knows where that is!'

'Where we're to moulder all the hols, I suppose,' said Diana sulkily. 'I think it's too bad.'

'Well, there's a riding school not far off and we can ride,' said Roger, 'and I believe there's a river near. We might get a boat. And it's jolly good country all round Rockingdown for birds and flowers.'

'All very nice for you because you're so mad on nature,' said Diana. 'I shall feel buried alive – no tennis, no parties – and I suppose that horrid little Snubby is coming too.'

'Of course,' said Roger, digging somebody hard with his tennis racket. 'Oh, sorry! Did I hurt you? Do let's get out of this awful crowd, Di. We seem to be going round and round in it.'

'We've got into one that's rushing for a train,' said Diana. 'Let them go by, for goodness' sake. Look, here's a seat – let's sit down for a bit. When do we meet Miss Pepper?'

'Not for twenty-four minutes,' said Roger, looking at the station clock. 'Shall we go and see if we can get an ice cream somewhere nearby?'

Diana immediately got up from the seat. 'Oh, yes – what a brainwave! Look, there's the exit. There'll be a tea shop or something nearby. We'll get ices there.'

Over the ices the chatter went on. 'You said Snubby was coming, didn't you?' said Diana as she ate her strawberry ice. 'Little pest!'

'Well, he hasn't got any parents,' said Roger. 'That's pretty awful, you know, Di. He gets kicked about from one aunt to another, poor kid – and he likes coming to us better than anywhere else. He's not so bad, if only he wouldn't play the fool so much.'

'Just our luck to have an idiotic cousin with an idiotic dog,' said Diana.

'Oh, I like Loony,' said Roger at once. 'He *is* quite potty, of course – but he's a lovely spaniel, he really is! Loony's a wonderful name for him – he's an absolute lunatic, but honestly he's wizard, the things he does. I bet he plays Miss Pepper up!'

'Yes. He'll go off with all her shoes and hide them under a bush, and fight her Sunday hat, and get himself cleverly locked up in the larder,' said Diana. 'What about another ice?'

'If Snubby was more our age, it wouldn't be so bad,' said Roger. 'After all, I'm fourteen and you're thirteen – and he's only eleven – quite a baby.'

'Well, he doesn't behave like one,' said Diana, beginning on her second ice. 'He behaves like a horrible little imp or goblin or something – always up to mischief of some sort – and thinking he can tag along with us. Oh dear – what with Miss Pepper and Snubby these hols look as if they'll be awful.'

'Gosh, look at the time,' said Roger. 'We shall miss Miss Pepper if we don't look out. I must get the bill and we'll go.'

The girl brought him the bill, and he got up with Diana to go to the desk and pay. As they were going out of the door Roger glanced at Diana's hands. 'Idiot! You've left your racket and bag at the table. I knew you would. You always do! It's a marvel to me you ever manage to bring anything home safely!'

'Blow!' said Diana, and went back to get her things,

9

knocking over a chair in her impatience. Roger waited for her patiently, a grin on his good-looking face. Harum-scarum, untidy, impatient Di! He laughed at her, kept her in order, and was very fond of her indeed. He was fond of his cousin Snubby too, with his impudence, sense of fun, and his habit of doing the most surprising and annoying things.

Both Diana and Snubby would have to be kept in order these holidays, Roger was certain. Diana was cross and disappointed at being sent off with Miss Pepper to some place she had never heard of – she would be annoying and perhaps sulky. Snubby would be more irritating still, because he wouldn't have Roger's father to jump on him and yell at him. He would only have Miss Pepper, and Snubby hadn't much opinion of women.

Loony the dog was, of course, another problem, but a very nice problem indeed. He was a dog who only obeyed one person and that was Snubby. He had never outgrown his habit of chewing things, hiding them and burying them. He went mad quite regularly, racing up and down the stairs, in and out of every room, barking his head off with excitement, and thoroughly upsetting every grown-up within miles.

But he was so beautiful! Roger thought of the little black spaniel with his silky, shining coat, his long drooping ears that always went into his dinner dish, and his melting, mournful eyes. How lucky Snubby was to have a dog like that! Roger had often smacked Loony hard for being wicked, but he had never ceased to love him. He was glad that Loony was to share the holidays with them, even though it meant having his cousin Snubby too.

'We've go to meet Miss Pepper under the station clock,' said Roger. 'We've go a minute to spare. Look – isn't that her?'

It was. The children took a good look at their mother's

10

old governess as they hurried up to her. She was tall, thin, trim, with straight grey hair brushed back under a small black hat. Her eyes behind their glasses were sharp and twinkling. She had a very nice smile as she saw the children hurrying up to her.

'Roger! Diana! Here you are at last – and punctual to the minute too. It's a year since I saw you, but you haven't changed a scrap.'

She kissed Diana and shook hands with Roger. 'Now,' she said, 'we've a little time before we have to leave for our train at another station – what about a couple of ices – or have you grown out of your liking for them?'

Roger and Diana brightened up at once. Neither of them said that they had just had two ices each. Diana nudged Roger and grinned. Miss Pepper certainly was good at remembering to provide ice cream and gingerbeer and the rest. She never failed in that.

'Now – I wonder where we can get ice creams without going too far,' said Miss Pepper, looking round the station.

'Er – let me see – isn't there a little tea shop just outside the station?' said Roger.

'Yes – where they have lovely ices,' said Diana. 'Do you remember the way, Roger?'

Roger did, of course, and promptly led the way back to the little tea shop they had left only a few minutes before. Miss Pepper's eyes twinkled. She wondered how many ices the two had already had whilst waiting for her.

Roger led his sister and Miss Pepper to a different table this time. He didn't want the girl to make some remark that would give them away. They ordered ices.

'When is Snubby coming?' asked Diana.

'By train tomorrow,' said Miss Pepper. 'With Loony, I fear. I don't like dogs, as you know, and I like Loony even less than most dogs. It means I shall have to lock

11

up all my slippers and hats and gloves. I never knew such a dog for smelling out things! Never! Last time I stayed with your mother, Roger, I began to think that Loony could undo suitcases, because things I had put in disappeared regularly – and I always found Loony with them sooner or later.'

'I expect Snubby had something to do with that,' said Roger. 'He was awful those hols you were there, Miss Pepper. As loony as his dog.'

'Well, I hope Mr Young will be able to keep Snubby in order,' said Miss Pepper.

There was a sudden startled silence. Roger and Diana looked at Miss Pepper in alarm.

'Mr *Young*,' said Roger. 'What's he coming for?'

'To coach you all,' said Miss Pepper, in surprise. 'Didn't you know? I expect you'll get a letter soon, if you haven't heard. Your father rang up your schools, you know, to find out what kind of a report you both had, because he knew he wouldn't get it before he left for America – and you've got to have coaching in Latin and maths, Roger, and you in French and English, Diana.'

'*Well!*' said both children together. 'How absolutely foul!'

'Oh, no,' said Miss Pepper. 'Mr Young is very nice – and a very good coach. You've had him before.'

'He's as dry as dust,' said Diana angrily. 'Oh, I do think it's hateful – holidays without Mummy and Daddy, at a place we don't know anything about – with Mr Young and lessons – and . . .'

'Shut up, Di,' said Roger, afraid that his angry sister would say something about Miss Pepper too. 'You know we missed the whole of the Easter term because of scarlet fever – we're behind in a good many things. I meant to do some work anyhow these hols.'

'Yes – but Mr *Young* – with his beard and his sniffs

and his "My dear young lady!" ' cried Diana. 'I hate him. I'll jolly well write and tell Daddy what I think of him for – '

'That's enough Diana,' said Miss Pepper in a sharp voice.

'Is Snubby having coaching too?' asked Roger, kicking the furious Diana under the table to make her stop working herself into a rage.

'Yes. Unfortunately he had a very bad report from the headmaster,' said Miss Pepper.

'That's nothing new,' growled Diana. 'And I ask you – *can* Mr Young do anything at all with Snubby? Snubby will lead him a frightful dance.'

'Shall we have another ice?' said Miss Pepper, looking at her watch. 'We've just time. Or do you feel too upset to have another?'

They certainly didn't feel to upset to have another ice and a gingerbeer on top of it. Roger began to talk cheerfully about the happenings of the last term, and Diana gloomed over her ice for a minute or two and then cheered up too. After all, it was holidays – and it would be fun to explore a new place – and there would be riding and perhaps boating. Things might be worse!

'Time to go,' said Miss Pepper. 'We're having dinner on the train. I hope you'll enjoy that. We shall be at Rockingdown by tea-time. Well, come along – and cheer up, Diana dear – I expect you'll enjoy the holidays just as you usually do!'

Chapter Two

Rockingdown Cottage

Rockingdown Village was a tiny little place with a butcher's shop, a baker's and a general store, and plenty of farms and cottages around. The church tower showed above the trees, and the church bell could be heard quite clearly in the cottage where the children were to stay for the holidays.

This proved to be a very exciting little place. 'It's more than a cottage,' said Diana approvingly. 'It's a jolly nice old house, with lots of rooms.'

'It used to belong to a big mansion about half a mile off – this cottage is actually in the grounds of the mansion,' said Miss Pepper. 'It was what is called the Dower House.'

'What's that?' asked Diana.

'It was a house set aside for the mistress of the big mansion when her husband died and her son and his wife came to take over the mansion,' said Miss Pepper. 'She was then called the dowager mother, and came to live here, in this house, with her own servants.'

'It's very old, isn't it?' said Diana, looking at the oak panelling of the dining room in which they were having tea. 'And I like the wide staircase – and the tiny little back staircase that winds up from the kitchen. We could have wizard games of hide-and-seek here.'

'I like my bedroom,' said Roger. 'It's got a ceiling that slants almost to the floor, and I've had to break away strands of ivy across one of the windows, Miss Pepper – it was so overgrown!'

'And I like the way the floor goes up and down,' said Diana. 'And the funny little steps down to this dining room and up to the kitchen.'

They were just what Miss Pepper didn't like. She was rather short-sighted, and in this old house she seemed to stumble everywhere. Still, no doubt she would get used to it!

'This tea is wizard,' said Roger approvingly. 'Did you make the scones, Miss Pepper?'

'Dear me, no – I'm afraid I'm no cook,' said Miss Pepper. 'Mrs Round made them. She's a village woman who comes in each day to do the cleaning and cooking.'

'Is she like her name?' said Diana at once. Miss Pepper considered.

'Well, yes,' she said. 'She *is* rather plumpish – and her face certainly is very round. Yes – Mrs Round seems a good name for her.'

The children explored the house after they had had tea – and a very good tea it was, with home-made jam, home-produced honey, scones, and a big fruit cake.

'This is the kind of fruit cake I like,' said Diana, taking a third slice. 'You don't have to look and see if you've got any fruit in your slice – there's plenty all over the cake.'

'You're a pig, Di,' said Roger.

'People are always pigs at your age,' said Miss Pepper. 'Some are worse than others, of course,'

'Am I a worse pig?' demanded Diana.

'Sometimes,' said Miss Pepper, her eyes twinkling behind their glasses. Roger roared at Diana's indignant face.

'Miss Pepper, Di can eat a whole tin of Nestlé's milk by herself,' he began, and got a kick under the table.

'So could I, once,' said Miss Pepper, surprisingly. The children stared at her. It was quite impossible to imagine the thin, prim Miss Pepper ever having been greedy enough to devour a whole tin of Nestlé's milk by herself.

'Go on, now, finish your tea,' said Miss Pepper. 'I want to do your unpacking.'

They explored, whilst Miss Pepper unpacked their school trunks, exclaiming over the dirty clothes, and looking with horror at the rents and tears in most of Diana's things. Anyone would think that the girl spent all her time climbing thorn trees, judging by the state of her clothes. Miss Pepper thought of having to unpack Snubby's trunk the next day, and shuddered. Really, children nowadays were quite impossible!

'Is the old mansion empty?' asked Roger that evening. 'We saw it from a distance. There was no smoke coming from the chimneys. It looked a dead place.'

'Yes. I believe it is,' said Miss Pepper. 'Roger, *where* are all the socks you took back to school with you? It says you took back eight on this list, but I can only find one pair, very holey and dirty.'

'I've got one pair on,' said Roger helpfully. 'That makes two.'

'Miss Pepper, can we go and look over the mansion if it's empty?' asked Diana.

'No, I shouldn't think so,' said Miss Pepper. 'Diana, it says on your list that you took four blouses back to . . .'

Diana fled. It was dreadful the way grown-ups always put you through a cross-examination about clothes as soon as you got back from school. She and Roger rushed upstairs – and then tiptoed down the little back-stair and out into the garden.

Miss Pepper followed them upstairs in a moment or two, with another list of questions – but they had mysteriously disappeared. She looked round Diana's room and groaned. How could any girl make a perfectly neat room into such a terrible mess one hour after she had taken possession of it?

Roger was pleased that night when the two of them went up to bed. 'It's going to be a wizard place for birds, this,' he told Diana. 'And there are badgers here too – in these very grounds. That old fellow we met told me. One of these nights I'm going to get up and watch for them.'

'Well, don't badger me to come with you!' said Diana, and shrieked as Roger aimed a punch at her for her pun.

'You sound like Snubby,' he said. 'He's always making silly puns and jokes. For goodness' sake leave it to him!'

Their bedrooms were side by side under the slanting roof. Snubby's bedroom was across the landing, a tiny one looking to the back of the house, across the grounds. Miss Pepper slept on the first floor. Tucked away in another corner of the first floor were two other rooms.

'We'll have to meet Snubby tomorrow,' said Roger, calling from his bedroom as he undressed, 'And Loony.'

'Yes. We'll walk over to the station,' said Diana, flinging all her clothes on the floor one by one, although she knew perfectly well she would have to get out of bed and pick them up as soon as Miss Pepper arrived to say good night. 'It's only about two miles. I could do with a good long walk. We can bus back if Snubby's got a lot of things.'

The next day was brilliantly fine. Snubby's train was due in at half-past twelve.

'We'll go and meet him,' said Roger to Miss Pepper. 'You needn't come unless you want to, Miss Pepper. I expect there are lots of things you want to do.'

They set off at twelve o'clock to walk to the station. They decided that the shortest way would be to go through the grounds of the old mansion. They were horrified to see how overgrown everything was. Even the paths

17

were almost lost in the nettles and brambles that spread all round. Only one broad drive seemed to be at all well-kept, and that was now beginning to show signs of being covered with weeds.

'Funny,' said Diana. 'You'd think that whoever owned this place would want to keep it up decently, so that he could sell it at a good price, even if he didn't have any intention of living in it himself. Golly, how are we going to get through these brambles! I'll scratch my legs to pieces.'

Here and there as they walked through the large grounds, they caught sight of the old mansion through gaps in the trees. It certainly looked a desolate place. Diana didn't like it.

'Well, I don't much feel as if I what to explore that,' she said. 'It would be full of spiders and creepy things and horrid noises and draughts from nowhere. A nasty spooky place.'

They were out of the grounds at last and came to the village. They stopped for an ice cream at the little general store.

'Ah – you're the new people in Rockingdown Cottage,' said the old woman who served them. 'That's a nice old place. I remember old Lady Rockingdown going there when her son brought his wife home from Italy. Those were grand days – parties and balls and hunts and such goings-on! Now it's all dead and done with.'

The children ate their ices and listened with interest. 'Where did the family go, then?' asked Roger.

'Lady Rockingdown's son was killed in a war and his wife died of a broken heart,' said the old woman, remembering. 'The place went to a cousin, but he never lived there. He just let it. Then it was taken over in the last war, and some kind of secret work was done there – we never knew what. Now that's finished, of course – and the place had been empty ever since. Nobody wants it – it's so big and cumbersome. Ah – but it was a fine place once – and many's the time I've been up to it to help with a party!'

'We must go,' said Roger to Diana. 'Else we shall be late for the train. Come on!'

He paid for the ices and they ran off to the station. They got there just as the train was coming in. They stood on the platform waiting for Snubby and Loony to appear from a carriage. Usually they both fell out together!

An old market-woman got down. A farmer and his wife appeared. But nobody else at all. The train gave itself a little shake, preparing to start off again. Roger ran all down it, looking into the carriages for Snubby. Had he fallen asleep?

There was no one in the carriages except another farmer and a young woman with a baby.

The train steamed off importantly, and its one porter went off to his dinner. There was no other train for two hours.

It took the children a little time to find this out, because there didn't seem to be anyone else at the station once the ported had gone. No one in the tiny booking office. No one in the stationmaster's room or in the waiting room.

'Blow Snubby! He's missed the train,' said Diana. 'Just like him! He might have phoned to say so – then we needn't have fagged all the way to meet him!'

They found a time-table that told them what trains there were. It took Roger a good ten minutes to discover that there were no more trains till the afternoon.

He looked at the station clock which now said a quarter past one. 'We've wasted nearly an hour here,' he said in disgust. 'Messing about looking for Snubby and hunting for someone to ask about trains and trying to find out what the time-table says. Come on – let's go home. We'll catch the bus and perhaps we shan't be awfully late. Miss Pepper said she'd make lunch at one o'clock – we should be back by half-past.'

But there was no bus for an hour so they had to walk. The sun was hot and they were hungry and thirsty. Blow Snubby!

They arrived back at the cottage at two o'clock – and there, sitting at the table, looking very full indeed, was their cousin Snubby!

'Hallo!' he said. 'You *are* late! Whatever happened?'

Chapter Three

Snubby – And Loony

Diana and Roger had no wish to fling themselves joyfully on Snubby; but Loony flung himself on them so violently that he almost knocked Diana over. He appeared from under the table, barking madly, and threw himself at them.

'Hey – wait a bit!' said Roger, very pleased to see Loony. The spaniel licked him lavishly, whining joyfully. Miss Pepper looked crossly at them.

'Diana! Roger! You are very late.'

'*Well!*' said Diana indignantly. 'Snubby wasn't on the train – and we waited and waited, and tried to find out when the next train was. It wasn't *our* fault!'

'We've had lunch already,' said Snubby. 'I was so hungry I couldn't wait.'

'Sit down, Roger and Diana,' said Miss Pepper. 'Snubby, call Loony to you, for goodness' sake!'

Roger and Diana sat down. Loony tore back to Snubby and began to fawn on him as if he too had been away for some time.

'Still the same old lunatic,' said Diana, holding out her plate for some cold meat-pie. 'Snubby, what *happened* to you?'

'I suppose you were late for the train, and missed Snubby, and didn't see him or Loony on the road,' said Miss Pepper. 'I ought to have gone to meet him myself.'

'They're not very observant,' said Snubby, accepting another helping of tinned peaches and cream. 'I mean –

I could walk right past them with Loony, under their noses and they wouldn't see me.'

Diana looked at him scornfully. 'Don't be an idiot. You can't make out you passed us and we didn't see you.'

'Well, but what else could have happened?' said Miss Pepper. 'Snubby, I will not have Loony fed at meal times. If you give him any more titbits I shall say he's to remain out of the room when we have a meal.'

'He'd only scratch the door down,' said Snubby. 'As I said, my two cousins are not very observant, Miss Pepper. Fancy not even seeing Loony.'

Loony jumped up in excitement whenever his name was mentioned. Miss Pepper made a resolve that she would never mention his name at all – only refer to him as 'the dog'. Oh dear – things were going to be twice as difficult with this mischievous boy and his excitable little dog.

'Snubby, you didn't come by that train,' said Roger quietly. 'What did you do? Go on – tell us, or we'll never go to meet you again.'

'I got out at the station four miles before Rocking-down,' said Snubby. 'The train had to wait three-quarters of an hour there for a connection – so out I got, hopped on to a bus and here I was at quarter to one! Easy!'

'Oh, Snubby!' said Miss Pepper. 'Why couldn't you have said so before? It was so nice of your cousins to meet you – and all you did was to make them late for their lunch, and arrive cross and hot and hungry.'

Diana glared at Snubby. 'He's just the same horrid little boy,' she said to Roger, speaking as if Snubby wasn't there. 'Same old ginger hair, same old green eyes, same old freckles, same old snub-nose, and same old cheek. I'm sure I don't know why we put up with him.'

'Well, I put up with you,' said Snubby, wrinkling his turned-up nose and grinning, so that his face appeared to

22

be made of rubber, and his eyes almost disappeared under his sandy eyebrows. 'Sorry to upset you, cousins. Honestly, I didn't know you were going to meet me. I'm not used to kind attentions of that sort from you. Are we, Loony?'

Loony leapt up madly and pawed violently at Snubby's knees, knocking his head against the table. He whined and yapped.

'Loony wants to go out,' said Snubby, who used Loony as an excuse whenever he wanted to go wandering off by himself. 'Can we go, Miss Pepper?'

'Yes,' said Miss Pepper, thankful to be rid of them both. 'Leave him outside in the garden when you come in again, and then go upstairs to help me to unpack your trunk. It came this morning.'

Diana and Roger finished their meal in peace. Roger grinned to himself. What an idiot Snubby was – but it would certainly liven things up a bit to have him there – and Loony too. Diana mooned over her peaches and cream. She wasn't pleased. She would rather have had Roger to herself. She knew that Snubby admired Roger and wanted to be with him, and this always made her want to push Snubby away.

Except that Snubby found an outsize stag-beetle in the garden, which he insisted on displaying on the tea table, and that he had arrived with another boy's trunk instead of his own, things passed off peacefully the first day.

He and Loony explored everywhere thoroughly by themselves. Snubby hated being 'shown round'. He liked to size things up for himself and go his own way. He was a most intelligent and sharp-witted boy, very clever at hiding his brains under a constant stream of tricks, jokes and general idiocies. He was adored by all the boys in his form, and was their natural leader – but the despair of all the masters who seemed to vie with one another in making biting remarks about his work and character in his reports.

His jokes and tricks were endless. All his pocket money was spent on ice creams, chocolate, or the latest trick. It was Snubby who tried out all the trick pencils on the various masters – the pencil whose point wobbled because it was made of rubber – the one whose point disappeared inside the pencil as soon as the unsuspecting master tried to write – the pencil that could be nailed to the floor and couldn't be picked up.

It was Snubby who experimented with stink pills which, when thrown on the fire, at once gave out a smell like bad fish, and Snubby who climbed to the top of the school tower without falling. Everything was always Snubby – even when it really wasn't! But Snubby didn't mind. He accepted his punishments, rightful ones or wrongful, with pluck and resignation, and always owned up when tackled.

'A bad boy with a lot of good in him,' said the head-master. 'It's a pity he has no parents. If he had he would behave better because he wouldn't like to let them down. He'll turn out all right – but in the meantime he's a pest.'

Snubby was pleased with Rockingdown Cottage and the garden and grounds of the old mansion. He could make plenty of good hidey-holes in the grounds for Loony and himself. They could play pirates, wrecked sailors, and Red Indians to their hearts' content under the thick bushes, and up in the tall trees – because Loony didn't mind being dragged up trees by the scruff of the neck. In fact, he didn't mind where he went as long as he was with his beloved master. He had even been know to crouch in a smelly dustbin with Snubby for an hour whilst Snubby waited to play a trick on the unsuspecting butcher's boy.

Snubby made up his mind to explore the old mansion. It would be locked and bolted and barred, but he's get in somewhere all right. If Di and Roger would come, that would be fun – if not, he'd go by himself. He hoped Roger would come, though. He would like to be in Roger's good books – Roger was fine. Diana was a nuisance – but then, in Snubby's opinion all girls were a nuisance. Always in the way.

It was a terrible shock for Snubby to hear that he was to have coaching those holidays. Diana broke the news to him that night.

'You know you're to have lessons these hols, don't you, Snubby?' she said. 'Mr Young's coming to coach you.'

Snubby stared at her in horror. 'I don't believe you,' he said at last. 'Nobody could do that to me – make me learn things in the *summer hols*! I've never heard of such a thing.'

'Well, you'll have to believe it,' said Diana. 'Daddy's arranged it. Roger is to have coaching in Latin and maths, I'm to be coached in French and English.'

'What am I to be coached in?' said Snubby gloomily.

'Oh, I should think you want coaching in everything,' said Diana. 'I don't suppose you know your tables properly yet, do you, Snubby? And can you spell yet?'

'All right. I'll pay you out for that,' said Snubby. 'What about a worm or two under your pillow?'

'If you start doing that kind of babyish thing again I'll sit on you and bounce up and down till you cry for mercy,' said Diana. 'I'm much bigger than you are, baby-boy!'

This was quite true. Snubby was not big for his age and hadn't really begun to grow yet. Diana was a sturdy girl, and quite able to do what she threatened.

Loony appeared and rolled himself over and over on the floor. Snubby tickled him with his foot. The spaniel leapt up and fetched something from the hall. Diana gave a shriek.

'Oh – he's got my hairbush. Snubby, get it from him. Quick!'

'Why? You never use it, do you?' said Snubby, neatly getting back at his cousin for her jibes of a minute or two ago. 'What good is it to you? You might as well let Loony play with it.'

The brush was rescued and Loony got a few spanks with it from Diana. He retired under the table, and looked at her mournfully with big brown eyes.

'Now you've hurt his feelings,' said Snubby.

'I'd like to hurt a lot more of him than that,' said Diana. 'Now I shall have to wash this chewed-up brush. Blow Loony!'

'Blow everything!' said Snubby dismally. 'Fancy – coaching with Mr Young. I can't think of anything worse!'

Chapter Four

Changed Plans

But after all Mr Young didn't come to coach the three children. Two days later, when Roger, Diana and Snubby had put out their school books neatly on the study table, and had gloomily sharpened their pencils and found their pens, the telephone bell rang shrilly.

'I'll answer it, Miss Pepper, I'll answer it!' yelled Snubby, who adored answering the phone and pretending that he was one of the grown-ups in the house. He rushed to answer.

The others listened, bored. Probably it was the butcher saying he couldn't send the meat, and one of them would have to fetch it.

'Yes. This is Rockingdown Cottage,' they heard Snubby say. 'Oh – who? Oh, Mrs Young. Oh, yes, certainly. Yes. I can give any message you like. Certainly. Dear, dear, how very very sad. I'm *so* sorry to hear that. Well, well, to think how suddenly these things happen! And is he getting on all right? That's *wonderful*, isn't it? You have my deepest sympathy, Mrs Young – such a terrible time for you. Yes, yes, I'll give your message. Certainly. *Good-bye.*'

By this time both Diana and Roger were out in the hall, amazed at Snubby's telephoning.

'What is it? What are you saying? Who on earth are you pretending to *be*, Snubby?' demanded Diana.

'Nobody. I'm just being polite and helpful,' said Snubby, beaming. 'I *say* – Mr Young's gone and got

27

appendicitis and he's NOT COMING! What do you think of that?'

The others stared at him. 'Gosh – we couldn't think what you were doing, talking in that idiotic way over the phone!' said Diana.

'It wasn't idiotic. It was only like grown-ups talk,' said Snubby. 'I can tell you I felt very sorry for poor Mr Young – you know, having to go to hospital and everything.'

'You didn't,' said Roger. 'You know you're always saying appendicitis is nothing, and telling us how you had it and enjoyed it. But I say – does this mean no coaching then? Of course, it's upsetting for Mrs Young – but it does solve a problem for us. We can enjoy ourselves now.'

Loony was barking round their ankles, sensing their excitement. Miss Pepper came down the stairs.

'What's all the excitement about? Who was that on the telephone? I hope it wasn't the butcher again.'

'No. It was Mrs Young,' said Snubby. 'Mr Young is in hospital with appendicitis, Miss Pepper. He's not coming here to coach us.'

'Dear, dear! I *am* sorry for poor Mrs Young,' said Miss Pepper in exactly the same voice that Snubby had used over the telephone. 'Well – that does put us into a difficulty.'

'*Does* it?' said Diana, astonished. 'It seems to us that we've got out of one.'

'Oh, dear me, no!' said Miss Pepper at once. 'I shall get someone else to coach you. I can't imagine who, though. I shall have to go through my list of tutors. Snubby, stop Loony eating that rug. He's had more than half of it since he arrived and I should like a *little* bit left.'

'He thinks it's a rabbit – it's a fur rug, you see,' said Snubby.

'I don't care what he thinks it is,' said Miss Pepper. 'You heard what I said. Take Loony out of the hall at

28

once. I'm getting tired of him already. I'm thinking of buying a whip – a nice strong whip.'

Snubby stared at her in horror. What, whip Loony! Surely nobody could think of doing that! Smacking, yes – but whipping with a whip!

'He's run off with Mrs Round's hearthbrush and left it somewhere. He's been in the larder twice. He's pulled every mat into a heap on the landing. And if I catch him under my bed again I shall BUY THAT WHIP,' said poor Miss Pepper.

Loony suddenly sneezed and looked very surprised at himself. He was always surprised when he sneezed. He sneezed again.

'Now what's the matter with him?' said Miss Pepper. 'Sneezing all over the place.'

'He's had too much pepper,' said Snubby at once. 'That's what it is – too much pepper – it's got up his nose. There's a lot of it about these days.'

Miss Pepper looked at him coldly. 'Don't be rude, Snubby,' she said, and went into the dining room. Roger roared and Snubby grinned.

'Let's all sneeze when Miss Pepper gets peppery,' he said. 'She'll stop rowing us then. Loony, clear out. You really *will* get into trouble if you go off with any more of Mrs Round's brushes. Besides, you're not to, anyway. She's nice.'

Mrs Round appeared at this minute. She was certainly like her name, and her face shone like the harvest moon, it was so red and round.

'That dog of yours,' she began, 'if he hasn't got my hearthbrush somewhere now! And if I chase him off with my broom what does he do but think I'm playing a game with him. Loony by name and Loony by nature that dog is.'

'What's for pudding today, Mrs Round?' asked Snubby,

changing the subject in his clever way. 'Are you going to make us one of your smashing treacle puddings again? Honestly, I wish you'd come and be cook at our school. The boys would cheer you every day.'

Mrs Round beamed and patted the bun of hair at the back of her head. 'Oh, go on with you now!' she said in her pleasant country drawl. 'You keep that dog of yours out of my kitchen, and I might make you pancakes with raspberry jam.'

'Loony! Don't you dare go into Mrs Round's kitchen today,' said Snubby sternly, and Loony wagged his little black stump of a tail. He crawled humbly on his tummy to Snubby and lay quite flat in front of him.

'All humbug,' said Diana. 'He's as good at pretending as you are, Snubby!'

Miss Pepper came out into the hall. 'Are you *still* here?' she said to Loony, who promptly went out of the front door at top speed. She turned to the children. 'I'm going to telephone one or two coaches I know to see if one is free to come. Go and clear away your books now. There certainly won't be any lessons today.'

They cleared away their books thankfully. Miss Pepper telephoned for some time and then came into the study. 'It's no use,' she said. 'Everyone is either already fixed up, or is away. I'll have to put an advertisement in the newspapers.'

'Oh, don't bother to do that, Miss Pepper,' said Roger. 'All this trouble for you! It's dreadful! I'm sure Daddy wouldn't want you to bother like this.'

'Then you think wrong, Roger,' said Miss Pepper, and began to draft out an advertisement. It went off by the next post, much to the children's annoyance.

'Goodness knows who we'll get now,' said Diana gloomily. 'At least we *knew* Mr Young – and we *know* how to get him talking so that we didn't have to do much work ourselves. Blow!'

For the next three days the children were quite free to do what they liked. They found the riding school, and Miss Pepper arranged for one whole-day ride, and two hour-rides. That was fun. Loony was the only one who disapproved of it. He hated Snubby and the others to go off on horses, because sooner or later he couldn't keep up with them and dropped back. The stable dog, a big airedale, kept up with the whole ride easily and was very scornful of the little spaniel.

They found the river and hired a boat. They could all swim like fishes, so Miss Pepper didn't worry about them on the river. They explored the countryside, and enjoyed looking for uncommon flowers, unusual birds and queer beetles. At least the two boys did – Diana didn't do much seeking for birds and flowers – she 'mooned along', as the boys called it, enjoying the smells, the sounds and the sights of the countryside – the smell of the meadow-sweet, the blue of the chicory, the queer little trill of the yellow-hammer, and the blue flash of the kingfisher as he flew past them crying 'tee-tee-tee!'

On the third day Snubby roused the scorn of the others. Diana was sitting beside the bank of the river, watching for the kingfisher again. Roger was lying on his back with his hat tilted over his eyes, listening to the high twitter of the swallows as they darted over the water, skimming the surface for flies.

Snubby was nowhere to be seen. He had crawled off to see if he could watch a few young rabbits who had unexpectedly come out to play in the daylight. Suddenly he came back.

'I say! Do you know what I've just seen?'

'A cabbage butterfly,' suggested Diana.

'A dandelion,' said Roger, not moving.

31

'A *monkey*!' said Snubby. 'Yes, go on, laugh. But I tell you it *was* a monkey!'

'Don't try and stuff us up with one of your tall stories,' said Roger. 'we're not in the lower third with you.'

'Look here – I tell you I *did* see a monkey,' repeated Snubby. 'It isn't a tall story. It was at the top of a tree and it swung itself down half-way, saw me – and disappeared. Loony didn't see it – but he smelt it. I could see his nose twitching like anything.'

Diana and Roger stopped listening. Snubby had too many marvels to tell – wonderful things always seemed to be happening to him – this must be one of them! Diana shushed him.

'Sh! I think I can hear the kingfisher. He may come and sit on this branch.'

'You are a disbelieving lot,' said Snubby bitterly. 'Here I come and tell you, absolutely solemnly and truthfully, that I've just seen a wizard monkey, and all you do is talk about kingfishers.'

Nobody said anything. Snubby sniffed scornfully. 'All right – I'm going off by myself. And I shan't come back and tell you if I see a *chimpanzee* this time!'

He went off with Loony. Roger gave a gentle little snore – he was asleep. Diana sat with her chin on her knees, and was at last rewarded for her long wait. The kingfisher flashed down, sat on the branch just in front of her, and waited for a fish to swim along in the water beneath.

Snubby went gloomily through the wood behind. Loony trotted along at his heels, pondering over the inexplicable ways of rabbits that lived down holes too small for dogs to get into.

Then he stopped and growled deep down in his throat. 'What's up?' said Snubby. 'Oh – somebody coming? I can hear them now. Wish I had ears like yours, Loony, though

32

how you hear at all with those big ears flapping over your ear-holes, I really don't know!'

Somebody came through the woods, whistling softly, and Loony growled again. Then Snubby saw the new-comer. He was a boy of about fourteen or fifteen, burnt very brown. His hair was corn-coloured and he had eyes so blue that they were quite startling to look at. They were set curiously wide apart and were fringed with thick dark lashes. He had a very wide mouth that grinned in a friendly fashion at Snubby.

'Hallo!' said the boy. 'Have you seen a monkey?'

Chapter Five

Barney and Miranda

That was the first time any of the three children saw the strange boy they were to know so well. Snubby stared at him, at his brilliant, wide-set blue eyes and friendly grin. He like this boy immensely, but he didn't know why.

'Lost your tongue?' said the boy. 'Well, I've lost my monkey. Have you seen one anywhere?'

The boy did not talk quite like anyone Snubby had ever heard. He had a slight American twang, and yet he sounded foreign? Spanish – Italian – what could it be? Nor did he look English, for all his blue eyes and fair hair.

Snubby found his tongue. 'Yes!' he said. 'I *have* seen a monkey. I saw one about five minutes ago. 'I'll take you to where I saw him.'

'Her,' said the boy. 'It's a she-monkey. She's called Miranda.'

'Is she really yours?' said Snubby. 'I've always wanted a monkey. I've only got a dog.'

'Lovely dog, though,' said the boy, and he gave Loony a pat. Loony at once rolled over on his back and put all his legs into the air, doing a kind of bicycling movement upside down.

'Clever dog,' said the boy. 'Why don't you get him a little bicycle?' he said, turning to Snubby. 'See how well he pedals upside down. Get him a bike with four pedals and you could make a fortune out of him. The only bicycling dog in the world!'

'Do you really mean it?' said Snubby eagerly. He was

ready to believe anything wonderful about Loony. The boy laughed.

'No. 'Course not. Come on, where's this tree? I must find Miranda – she's been gone an hour!'

Miranda was in the tree next to the one that Snubby had first seen her in. The boy gave his soft little whistle and the monkey leapt down like a squirrel, landing in his arms. He fondled her and scolded her.

'You know,' said Snubby, trying to keep the excited Loony away from the monkey. 'You know, I told my two cousins about the monkey and they absolutely refused to believe me. I suppose you wouldn't play a little trick on them for me?'

'If you like,' said the boy, turning his blue eyes on Snubby with an amused look in them. 'What do you want me to do?'

'Well – do you think you could make Miranda walk all round my cousins, or something like that, and then come back to you?' said Snubby eagerly. 'Then I could go up and they'd tell me they'd seen the monkey too and I'd disbelieve them like they disbelieved *me*!'

'Not much of trick,' said the boy. 'I'll tell Miranda to drop on them from the tree and then leap off again. Give them a bit of a fright.'

'*Could* you make her do that?' said Snubby.

'You bet!' said the boy. 'Where are these cousins of yours? Come on – we'll liven them up a bit. We won't show ourselves, though.'

They crept towards the river. Snubby made Loony crouch down quietly. He pointed out Diana to the boy, and then Roger. The boy nodded. He said a few quiet words to the monkey who answered him in a funny little chattering voice and then sped up into the trees. The two boys watched. Loony looked most surprised to see the

35

monkey disappear into the tree above him. Cats did that, but this creature didn't look or smell like a cat.

Miranda made her way to the tree immediately above Roger, who was still lying asleep with his hat over his face. The monkey leapt down and then jumped full on top of Roger. Diana turned in astonishment, her eyes almost falling out of her head when she saw Miranda leaping down on Roger and then leaping up into the tree again and disappearing.

Roger woke with a start and sat up hurriedly.

'What fell on me?' he said to Diana.

'A monkey,' said Diana. 'A little brown one.'

'Oh, don't *you* start about monkeys,' said Roger crossly. 'Anyone would think this place was full of monkeys the way you and Snubby go on about them.'

'But, Roger – honestly, it *was* a monkey,' said Diana.

'You and Snubby can go on telling me all day long that you keep seeing monkeys, but I shan't believe there's a monkey about even if I see one!' said Roger.

And at that very moment he saw Miranda! He saw her sitting on the strange boy's shoulder, as he came along with Snubby, both of them grinning widely.

Roger had to believe in the monkey then. He was very astonished. 'Is that your monkey?' he said to the boy. 'Is it a pet?'

'Sure,' said the boy. 'You a pet, Miranda?'

Miranda chattered and put a little brown paw down the boy's neck. 'Don't tickle,' he said. 'Shake hands with these people, and show your manners.'

Loony sat by open-mouthed whilst Miranda gravely held out a little paw and allowed Roger, Diana and Snubby to shake it. The boy sat down beside them. Loony at once made a rush for Miranda. He was jealous.

Quick as lightning the monkey leapt off the boy's shoulder and on to Loony's back. She held on tightly and

36

he couldn't get her off till he rolled on the ground. The children roared.

'Poor old Loony – nobody's ever tried to ride him before,' said Diana. 'What did you say her name was – Miranda? What a queer name for a monkey.'

'Why?' said the boy. 'I thought it was a mighty pretty name when I first read it, and it just suits Miranda – *she's* pretty too.'

None of the three children thought Miranda was pretty, though they all thought she was sweet and amusing. Still, they were used to people thinking their pets pretty and marvellous even though they mostly weren't.

'She's cute, isn't she?' said the boy, as Miranda began to turn head over heels very fast indeed. 'She can do no end of tricks. Turn cartwheels, Miranda.'

Miranda turned dozens of cartwheels, going over and over on hands and feet without stopping. Loony regarded her solemnly. No – this couldn't be a cat. No cat he had ever seen behaved like this.

'What's your name?' asked Roger, liking this strange boy just as much as Snubby did.

'Barney – short for Barnabas,' said the boy.

'Where do you live?' asked Snubby.

The boy hesitated. 'Nowhere at present,' he said. 'I'm just tramping around.'

This was puzzling. 'What do you mean? Are you on a hiking trip, or something?' asked Diana.

'You might call it that,' said the boy.

'Well, where's your *real home*?' persisted Snubby. 'You must have a *home*!'

'Don't pester Barney,' said Roger, seeing the boy hesitate again. 'You're always so inquisitive, Snubby.'

'It's all right,' said Barney, and he rubbed Miranda's fur gently. 'Actually I'm looking for my father.'

This sounded queer. 'Doesn't your mother know where he is?' demanded Snubby.

'My mother's dead,' said Barney. 'She died last year. I don't want to talk about that, see? I don't know much about her myself or about myself either, but I'm trying to find out. My mother was in the show business – you know, travelling around in a circus, and attending fairs and things like that. She was wonderful with animals. I thought my father was dead – but just before she died my mother told me she didn't think he was. He was an actor – acted in Shakespeare plays, she said – and she ran away from him after she'd been married three months. He doesn't know anything about me.'

'Don't tell us all this,' said Roger awkwardly. 'It's your own private business.'

'I want to talk to somebody,' said Barney, looking at them with his startling blue eyes. 'But there's been no one to talk to. Well, when my mother died I felt sort of lonely, and I couldn't settle to anything. So I thought I'd go off on my own – with Miranda, of course – and see if I could find my father. I'd like to know there was *some*body belonging to me, even if he turned out to be a disappointment.'

'I haven't any father *or* mother,' said Snubby. 'But I'm lucky. I've heaps of other relations and they're jolly decent to me. I'd hate to have no one – only just Loony.'

Diana couldn't imagine what things would be like without her mother. She was sorry for Barney. 'What do you do for a living, then?' she asked him.

'Oh, just scrounge around,' said the boy. 'I can always go to a circus or a fair, you know, and earn some money there. There's not much I can't do. I've often been in the circus ring with Miranda here. I've just left the fair over at Northcotling. I'm at a loose end now, wandering about with Miranda. What I want to do is to get hold of some of Shakespeare's plays and read them. I suppose you can't lend me any?'

Snubby couldn't imagine why anyone should want to borrow Shakespeare's plays. Diana tumbled to it at once.

'You want to know the plays that your father acts in – or used to act in!' she said. 'You want to know the things he liked and the parts he could play!'

'That's right,' said Barney, pleased. 'I've only read one of them – about a storm and a shipwreck, it was. It's where I got Miranda's name from.'

'Oh, yes – *The Tempest*,' said Roger. 'That's quite a good one to start off with. Do you *really* want to read the plays? They'll be jolly difficult for you. If you really do, I'll lend you some.'

'Thanks,' said the boy. 'Where do you live?'

'Over at Rockingdown Cottage,' said Roger. 'Do you know it?' Barney nodded.

'Where are you living just at present?' said Diana curiously. It seemed odd to think of somebody without a bed at night.

'Oh – this weather I can sleep anywhere,' said Barney. 'Under a haystack – in a barn – even up a tree with Miranda so long as I tie myself on.'

Diana glanced at her watch and gave an exclamation. 'Do you know what the time is, boys? It's quarter of an hour past tea-time already. Miss Pepper will be all hot and bothered!'

They scrambled up. 'If you come and whistle outside Rockingdown Cottage any time, we'll hear you and come out,' said Roger. 'I'll look out those plays for you.'

'I'll see you tomorrow,' said Barney, and stood watching them go, his blue eyes looking very far apart as he smiled and waved. Miranda waved a tiny paw too.

'I like him most awfully,' said Snubby. 'Do you, Roger? And hasn't he got amazing eyes? Like somebody belonging to the Little Folk, not to us. That sounds silly – but you know what I mean.'

They did know. There was something strange about Barney, something lonely and lost – and yet he was fun and had a most uproarious laugh, and the most natural manners in the world. 'I hope we see a lot of him,' said Roger.

He needn't have worried about that – they were going to see far more of Barney than any of them guessed!

Chapter Six

Mr King – and an Exciting Idea

The next thing that happened was that Miss Pepper found a tutor for the three of them. They were helping Mrs Round to clear away breakfast when he arrived. He knocked and rang, and Mrs Round scurried to open the door.

'Gentleman to see Miss Pepper,' she announced to the children. 'Name of King.'

Diana hurried to fetch Miss Pepper, who took Mr King into the study and remained there with him for some time. Then she opened the door and called the three children.

'Mr King, these are the three I told you about – they are cousins – this is Roger, this is Diana, this is Peter.'

Roger and Diana looked surprised to hear Snubby called Peter. They had quite forgotten that that was really his name. Mr King grinned at them all. He was a stocky, well-built man about thirty-five or forty, with hair going a little grey, and a mouth that looked distinctly firm.

'They don't look too bad,' he told Miss Pepper. She smiled.

'Appearances don't always tell the truth,' she said. 'Children, this is Mr King. Subject to final arrangements, he is going to come and give you the coaching your parents want you to have.'

This wasn't so good. The children's smiles faded away. They looked more carefully at Mr King. He looked back. Did they like him – or didn't they? Snubby decided that he didn't. Diana wasn't sure. Roger felt that he might like him when he knew him better. Their hearts all sank when they thought of lessons morning after morning, just when they had got used to nice free days.

'Mr King will start with you on Monday next,' said Miss Pepper.

'Can Loony be in the room too?' said Snubby.

Mr King looked a little startled. 'Er – who is Loony?' he asked, wondering if it was another child, not quite so bright as these appeared.

'My spaniel,' said Snubby, and at that moment Loony made one of his usual hurricane-like appearances. He came in at the door like a rocket, and hurled himself at everyone as if he hadn't seen them for a year. He even rolled over Mr King's feet, too, before he realised that they were the feet of a stranger, and then he leapt to his own feet and growled.

'Oh – so this is Loony.' said Mr King. 'Well – I don't see why he shouldn't be in the room, if he doesn't disturb us.'

Snubby immediately decided that he liked Mr King very much after all. Miss Pepper spoke hurriedly.

'I shouldn't make any rash promises if I were you,' she said, trying to give Mr King a warning look. He saw it.

'Ah – yes – I won't *promise*,' he said, and then as Loony tore at his shoe and got his shoelaces undone, he firmly added a few more words. 'In fact, we'll put Loony on trial first.'

'I wish Miranda could come too,' said Snubby. 'She's a monkey, Mr King – really a pet!'

Mr King thought it was time to go before he was asked to put a monkey on trial too.

He went, and Miss Pepper spoke to the three children.

'He has the most excellent testimonials, and I think he should be a very fine coach. You'll begin on Monday – and if I hear of you misbehaving, Snubby, I shall put

Loony into a kennel at night instead of letting him sleep in the house.'

This was a very alarming threat, and one that Miss Pepper was quite capable of carrying out. Snubby slept with Loony on his bed all night long, and the spaniel would be broken-hearted if he had to sleep anywhere else. Snubby didn't dare to argue with Miss Pepper about this. He sneezed violently, and then sneezed twice more, fishing for his handkerchief with a most concerned expression. 'Whoooosh-oo! Oh dear – I'm so sorry – Whhoooooooooo . . .'

'Have you got a cold, Snubby?' said Miss Pepper. 'I told you to take your coat yesterday evening.'

'No – no cold, Miss Pepper,' said Snubby, finding an extremely dirty handkerchief and sneezing into that. 'Just – whooosh-oo – sorry just a little pepper up my nose. Whoooooooo . . .'

Miss Pepper made an impatient noise and went out. Diana and Roger roared with laughter. Loony joined in the excitement and tore round the table six times without stopping.

'Racehorse trick being performed,' said Snubby, putting away his hanky. 'All right, Loony – you've passed the winning-post about three times. Woa!'

'What shall we do today?' asked Diana, as she stacked up the breakfast dishes to take out to Mrs Round.

'Let's go and peep in at the old mansion,' said Roger. 'Ask Mrs Round if there's any way of getting in. I'd just love to poke round it, and imagine what it was like in the old days.'

Mrs Round didn't know very much. 'You keep away from it,' she said. 'Folks do say that once a young fellow managed to get in there, and he couldn't never get out again. That might happen to you too. There's doors there that shut of themselves, yes, and lock themselves too.

And there's rooms there still full of furniture, left by the last owner – my, they'll be full of moths and spiders! A strange, creepy, place I wouldn't go into, not if you paid me a thousand pounds!'

This sounded pleasantly eerie. The three children at once made up their minds to do a bit of snooping that very day. They would meet Barney and take him too.

So, when they heard Barney's soft whistle they went out to see him. He had Miranda on his shoulder. She leapt into a tree and peered into a window nearby. Mrs Round was in the room, sweeping. The monkey made a soft chattering noise.

Mrs Round looked up, and was extremely astonished to see Miranda apparently about to jump in at the open window. She shut it at once, almost catching the monkey's nose.

Mrs Round stood at the window, shaking her fist at the surprised monkey. She called to Miss Pepper. 'You come here, Miss, and see what those children have collected now!'

Miss Pepper hurried in, wondering what caterpillar or beetle or mouse Mrs Round had found. She was always finding something in Roger's bedroom. She was startled to see the monkey. Miranda disappeared down the tree.

'All I say is – if they starts bringing in monkeys I'm going,' said Mrs Round. 'Loony dogs I can put up with, beetles and such I can deal with – but monkeys, no. It'll be elephants next, trampling up the stairs and down.'

Miss Pepper hurried downstairs to solve the monkey mystery. She saw Barney with the others; Miranda was on his shoulder. He nodded his head politely to her when the children introduced him. 'Miss Pepper, this is Barnabas, and this is Miranda, his monkey. Isn't she sweet?'

Miss Pepper wasn't going to go so far as to say that. In

her experience, monkeys were full of fleas and apt to bite people. She eyed Miranda mistrustfully.

'I'd rather you didn't bring that animal indoors,' said Miss Pepper firmly. 'Sweet or not, I'd rather she stayed outside.'

'Yes, certainly, Mam,' said Barney. 'It isn't everyone that likes monkeys.'

Miranda looked at Miss Pepper just as mournfully and pathetically as Loony sometimes looked at her. Oh dear – these animals! Why did they look at you like that? Miss Pepper ran to the kitchen, got a cucumber end and sliced it up. She ran out with the little slices on a plate.

'Monkeys like cucumber,' she said. 'Here's some for her. But please take her down the garden. Oh, do be careful Loony doesn't chew her tail!'

Miranda's tail hung down and Loony was eyeing it hopefully. It did look nice and chewy. He made a snap at it and Miranda gave a leap off Barney's shoulder and sat on his head, chattering.

'Loony! If you dare to chew Miranda's tail I'll let her chew yours.' said Snubby. Loony promptly sat down on his as if he understood every word. Barney gave one of his uproarious laughs, and set everyone else laughing too. Even Mrs Round opened the bedroom window and looked out to see what the joke was.

'Come on,' said Roger to Barney. 'Let's go down the garden. Oh, wait a bit. I say, Miss Pepper – Barney's keen on reading Shakespeare's plays. He's read *The Tempest* and he wants me to lend him another. What would be a good one for him to read next?'

Miss Pepper was most surprised. What with his monkey, and his strange blue eyes, and now his liking for plays, this boy was puzzling. He looked quite a nice boy, and Miss Pepper wondered where he came from. She would have to ask Roger about him when he had gone.

'Well – he could try *Midsummer Night's Dream*,' she said.

'Oh, yes – that's a lovely play,' said Diana. 'We did it once at school. I was Titania.'

They went down the garden to a tumbledown summer-house and sat there, with Loony on the floor trying to get another chew at Miranda's tail, and Miranda first on Snubby's shoulder and then Barney's – always swinging her tail just a *little* out of Loony's reach. She was very naughty. She took Diana's hanky out of her pocket and produced a horrible sticky mass of toffee from Snubby's shorts, which she proceeded to lick with great enjoyment before she threw the rest down to Loony.

'You're not to eat it, Loony,' ordered Snubby. 'You know what happened last time you ate toffee.'

'What happened?' asked Barney with interest.

'He got his top and bottom teeth stuck together,' said Snubby. 'And he was in such a fright that he rushed straight out-of-doors and down the street and didn't come back for hours, till the toffee had melted and gone. For a whole day after that he was scared. It's the only day I've ever known him be really good from morning to night.'

'Miranda only licks it,' said Barney.

'She's sensible,' said Diana. 'Loony isn't.'

'Let's tell Barney what we want to do this morning,' said Roger. 'Barney we want to go and walk round that big old mansion whose chimneys you can just see from here. It's empty now – nobody lives there – and there are all kinds of strange stories about it. We thought it would be fun to snoop round it.'

They all got up, Loony too, his tail wagging. Were they going for a walk? He didn't like this sitting about. It was boring. They made their way through the overgrown paths, working their way steadily towards the old house.

46

'You almost have to hack your way through,' said Roger. 'We'll come to the drive soon – that's fairly clear. Look – now you can see the house – enormous, isn't it?'

It certainly was. Great chimneys stood up from the roof, scores of windows peered out dimly, half-covered with ivy creeper, and there was an air of desolation and decay about the place.

'Come on,' said Roger. 'We'll explore – and I say – wouldn't it be fun if we managed to get inside!'

Chapter Seven

A Little Exploring

The four children and Loony came right up to the old house. A sparrow darted out of the thick ivy nearby and made them jump.

'It's so jolly quiet,' said Roger. 'Even the wind seems to have deserted the old mansion!'

'I don't like it at all,' said Diana. 'It's a horrid place.'

They came to the great flight of steps that led up to the front door. The stone steps were cracked in places and weeds sprouted through the cracks. One step wobbled when Roger stood on it. The foundations had rotted away.

'It would need an absolute fortune spent on it to make it liveable in,' said Diana. 'Still – I can quite well imagine how cheerful and lovely it all was when it was properly kept up and a jolly family lived in it.'

They came to the great front door. It was a double one, and had a lot of ironwork about it, which had rusted. There was no knocker, but a great iron bell-pull hung down beside the door.

Of course Snubby had to pull it. He found it very heavy and stiff to pull down and he almost hung on it to pull it. And suddenly a tremendous jangling broke out somewhere in the old house. It startled the children and Snubby let go of the bell-pull. Loony barked madly and scraped at the front door.

'Gosh – that made me jump,' said Diana. 'Who would have thought the bell rang after all these years! I guess it gave a fright to any rats and mice in the house. You are an idiot, Snubby. For goodness' sake don't go ringing all the bells you see. You might break one.'

'I don't see that that would matter,' said Snubby. 'I'm the only person ever likely to ring the bells here!'

There was no letter box so the children could not peep through that. But there was a crack in the door and by putting their eye to it the children could see into the vast, dim hall.

It was not a pleasant sight. It was covered in grey dust, and the walls were festooned with cobwebs. It looked lost and forgotten and dead. A great staircase loomed up dimly in the distance, at the back of the hall.

Roger shook the door hard, but he couldn't open it or budge it an inch, of course. Not that he really hoped to! Barney laughed at him.

'It would need a giant to force that door open!' he said. 'Come on – let's look in through the windows. There are plenty of them!'

They went down the flight of stone steps and made their way round the east side of the house. They came to some large french windows. The glass was dirty and streaked, but they were able to see in. It must once have been a ballroom, with a beautiful floor. Built-in mirrors still had their places on the walls. Most of them were now cracked. The children saw their ghostly faces reflected in the mirror opposite the window through which they were peeping. It made them jump.

'I really thought it was somebody looking at us,' said Diana, scared, 'but it's only our reflections in that cracked mirror. What a lovely room this must have been! What are those broken things in that corner?'

Roger squinted at them. 'Broken chairs, I think,' he said. 'You know we heard this place was used in the last war for something or other. I expect this was one of the rooms used. Those look like office chairs or something.'

They went on round the house, peeping into window after window, peering into dim, dusty rooms that had a look of utter forlornness. It made the children feel quite depressed. Even Miranda and Loony were quiet and subdued.

They came right round the house back to the front door again. Not one window had been found unfastened, nor even cracked or broken. One or two had had shutters fastened across them and these windows might have been broken. The children couldn't see.

They looked at the upstairs windows. They seemed tight-shut too – and again some had shutters fastened across them.

'Look!' said Diana, pointing. 'There are two rooms there with bars across. They must have been the children's nurseries. When Roger and I were small we had bars like that across our windows too. We used to hate them.'

Snubby was squinting up at the windows, blinking in his efforts to focus them clearly, for they were rather high up. 'You know – it almost looks to me as if there are *curtains* at those windows,' he said. 'Can any of you see?'

Barney had the best eyesight of them all. His bright blue eyes fastened on the nursery windows. 'Yes!' he said in surprise. 'There *are* curtains there – almost falling to bits, I think!'

They all stared up at the barred nursery windows, Loony too. Miranda suddenly left Barney's shoulder, leapt up the ivy, bounded on to a window-sill, flung herself upwards again to a little balcony, and then there she was, sitting on the window-sill of the old nursery window, peering in!

'Golly – I wish I could do that!' said Snubby in admiration.

'I'm surprised you can't!' said Roger.

They were all watching Miranda. She sat on the window-sill, and then she suddenly got between the bars and disappeared! Everyone gaped.

'Where's she gone?' said Diana, amazed.

'Into the room behind!' said Barney.

'But – isn't there any window-glass there?' said Roger.

'Apparently not,' said Diana. 'Or she wouldn't have been able to go in! How peculiar!'

'Wait a bit,' said Barney, squinting up at the window. 'I think I can see where it's broken – just at one side, look. There's a hole there as if a stone's been thrown through it or something. That's where Miranda went through.'

She appeared again and looked down at the interested children below. She chattered and waved her tiny paw.

'She's found something interesting up there,' said Barney at once. 'There – she's gone into the room again. Whatever can she have found?'

Miranda appeared once more – and this time she was holding something. She held it out and they all tried to see what it was.

'Throw it down, Miranda!' shouted Barney. And down through the air came the thing Miranda was holding. It fell beside Diana's foot. Loony pounced on it at once and Diana had to wrench it from him. She held it out to the others.

'A doll! A funny old-fashioned rag doll! Would you believe it! Fancy Miranda finding it in the old nursery!'

'She loves dolls,' said Barney, and he took it and examined it. He shook it and dust flew from it in a cloud. He looked thoughtfully. 'I wonder if there's anything else there?' he said. And as if Miranda could read his thoughts she appeared again at the window with something else in her paws. She held it out, chattering – then down it came, turning over and over in the air. Barney caught it. He gave an exclamation and showed it to the others.

'A soldier on horseback – carved most beautifully!' said Roger, taking it. 'It's simply lovely. The colour's still showing. What lovely soldiers children must have had in the old days – I never had ones like this.'

'Must be part of a hand-made set,' said Diana. They all looked at the beautiful model and then gazed upwards again. And Miranda threw down yet another thing!

This time it was a book. It fell to pieces as Miranda threw it and the pages fluttered in the air. Diana picked some of them up. 'What a funny old book!' she said. 'It's rather like one Granny has, in her special bookshelf – she keeps a collection of children's books that are very precious because they are more than a hundred years old. I say – it's strange, isn't it, that there are still curtains to that room – and toys there? What do you make of it, Roger?'

'I don't know,' said Roger. 'Except that perhaps when the house was let, the nurseries were locked up – because of memories, or something – you know how grown-ups sometimes feel about those things. Think how Mummy keeps the first shoes you ever wore, Di – and the first tooth of mine that came out. She just won't part with them.'

'Mothers seem to be like that,' said Diana. 'Perhaps the mother of the children who had these toys couldn't bear to let strangers use her nurseries – couldn't bear to part with the toys and things – and locked them up. Perhaps the rooms were forgotten. It's such a big house they might quite well have been.'

Miranda appeared again. Barney called up to her. 'No, Miranda. No more.'

But one more thing came floating down, spreading itself out in the air. It was a small handkerchief. Diana caught it as it floated by her head. In the corner, beautifully embroidered, was a name in what once had been pale blue silk.

'Bob.' Just that and nothing more. The children looked at the name. Who was Bob? Was he grown-up now – or was he dead long ago? They didn't know. They pictured a tiny boy being told to use his hanky – the one with his name on. Diana could almost hear his nurse speaking to him.

'Don't sniff, Bob, dear. Use your hanky – the one with your name on. I gave it to you this morning.'

'Come down, Miranda!' called Barney. He turned to the others. 'She'll throw down everything in the room if I don't stop her,' he said. 'And goodness knows how much more there is up there. I wouldn't be surprised if the nurseries are still furnished – with cots and things. Odd, isn't it?'

Miranda came leaping down. It was astonishing how she could come safely down the walls, by just clutching lightly at the ivy here and there.

Loony greeted her with a mad series of barks. He was jealous because she could do so many things that he couldn't. She settled on Barney's shoulder, and took hold of his right ear with her tiny paw. She made a funny whispering sound in his ear. He shook his head like a dog.

'Don't! You tickle!'

'What are we going to do with these things?' said Diana. 'They don't belong to us.'

'Well – we can't possibly put them back,' said Snubby. 'Unless we tell Miranda to – and surely she wouldn't have the sense to take them all back.'

'Oh, yes, she would,' said Barney. 'She'll do anything I tell her. You don't know how clever she is. I should think she's just about the cleverest monkey in the world.

53

If people knew how clever she was they'd offer me a thousand pounds for her – and I wouldn't take it.'

They all gazed at Miranda with respect. A thousand pounds! 'Why, that's more than *I'm* worth!' said Snubby.

'I should think so! About nine hundred and ninety-nine pounds, nineteen shillings and eleven pence three farthings more,' said Roger at once. 'Work that out, Snubby.'

Snubby couldn't. He changed the subject and looked longingly up at the barred windows. 'I wish *we* could get up there!' he said.

'Well,' said Barney surprisingly. 'That's easy – if you really want to.'

Chapter Eight

Barney has an Idea

'What do you mean?' said Roger, staring at Barney in surprise. 'We can't possibly get up there – why, it's three storeys up – and jolly high storeys at that. No ladder we've got would reach there – even if we'd got one, which we haven't.'

'And it would be too heavy to carry if we had,' said Diana, remembering how heavy the longest ladder at home had been when she had tried to carry it with Roger.

'I'm not thinking of a ladder,' said Barney. 'I'm thinking of a rope.'

They all stared at him. 'A rope?' repeated Roger. 'But how in the world are you going to get a rope up there? You'd want a ladder to take up the rope!'

Barney laughed one of his loud laughs. 'No, no – I'd just send Miranda up with a rope. She'll do anything like that.'

Still they didn't understand. Barney grinned at them.

'It's plain you've never lived in a circus or a fair,' he said. 'You get used to puzzles of this sort there. Now look – if we get a rope, we give one end to Miranda – and up she goes to the nursery windows with it. She sits on the window sill and twists the rope over the bars – then she throws the rope down to us. It comes slithering down the walls – and down to us. We catch it – and we've got a double rope then, haven't we, with the middle held by those bars up there! And it's easy enough to test the bars by pulling on the rope.'

'And then up we go to the window-sill!' cried Roger,

55

seeing light. 'Gosh – that's an idea. All the same, I don't think I could climb a rope all that way. I'm pretty good at gym, and one of the best on the ropes at school – but it's a terrific way up to those windows.'

'I shall be able to manage it all right,' said Barney. 'I've been on the ropes at the circus many a time – on the tightrope too. You should see me walk along it backwards!'

The others looked at Barney with a new respect. Could he really walk on a rope or a wire? Snubby made up his mind to get him to teach him during those holidays. He imagined himself setting up a rope across the gym and walking airily along it. That would make the others stare!

'Climbing up a rope's nothing,' said Barney. 'It's just a question whether those bars will still hold. Now the thing is – where is there a rope? I haven't got one – have you?'

Roger didn't know. His exploration of Rockingdown Cottage hadn't shown him any ropes or ladders.

'Even if there isn't a rope at home we can buy one,' he said. 'I say – this is exciting, isn't it? Do you think you really could get into that window, Barney?'

'Sure of it,' said Barney. 'Miranda can easily take up the rope. She knows how to put it over the bars – she's done that often enough in the circus. Then I'll go up and see what I can see. If there's a hole big enough for Miranda to get through, it will be big enough for me to put my hand in to slip the catch of the window – and in I'll go!'

'Let's go and buy the rope at once,' said Diana eagerly.

With Loony rushing ahead like a mad thing, the four of them made their way back through the grounds. They went down the overgrown drive, as that was the shortest way to the village. They had decided that it wouldn't be much use looking for a rope at Rockingdown Cottage.

Miss Pepper would be sure to ask what they were looking for and why they wanted a rope and a hundred other things.

'Grown-ups are terribly inquisitive,' said Snubby plaintively. 'Even if I'm doing absolutely nothing at all people come and ask me what I'm up to.'

'I don't blame them,' said Diana. 'You're always up to some kind of mischief as far as I can see. By the way, was it you who put my bedroom slippers on the top of the cupboard last night? I couldn't find them for ages.'

'I expect I put them there out of Loony's way,' said Snubby.

'Well, don't. Just shut my bedroom door if it happens to be open – then Loony can't go in,' said Diana. 'I'm not going to hunt all over the place for my slippers every single night!'

They decided to have an ice cream at the little general store when they got there. They sat down at the one and only table and ordered vanilla ices. The old lady came bustling out with them.

'And how do you like Rockingdown Cottage?' she said. 'Nice little place, isn't it? No strange stories about it, like there are about the big house.'

'What strange stories are there?' said Roger, paying for the ice creams.

'Oh, I wouldn't scare you with such tales,' said the old woman, beaming. 'That old place has fallen on evil days. Seems as if a curse was on it, somehow, the things that happened.'

This sounded interesting. 'What happened?' asked Roger.

'Oh – folks were killed – and two children died – and . . .'

'What two children?' asked Diana. 'Was one called Bob?'

'Well, there now – fancy you knowing that!' said the old woman in surprise. 'Yes – that was Master Robert. His sister, little Arabella, fell out of the nursery window and was killed – then only Master Robert was left. So they barred the windows up. And then if he didn't go and get scarlet fever and pass away too.'

'What happened then?' asked Diana, after a pause. Poor little Bob! She actually had his small hanky in her pocket. He hadn't lived to grow up – but his hanky was still there. And his soldier and book.

'The nurseries were shut up just as they were,' said the old woman, trying to remember. 'The nurse was given orders to leave everything as it was – everything! She was so upset, poor creature – she loved those two children like her own.'

'What happened to the father and mother?' asked Roger.

'Lord Rockingdown was killed,' said the old woman. 'Yes, and his lady died of a broken heart – no husband, no child left. Wasn't I telling you this the other day? I'll be boring you, repeating myself like this! The place went to a cousin after that, but he never came near it.'

The children now had a picture of what had happened to the unlucky house and family. Diana felt sad. She pictured the big house happy and lively, with Lord and Lady Rockingdown giving parties, going off to hunt, choosing ponies for their two small children, Arabella and Bob – planning all sorts of things for them as they grew up.

But they didn't grow up. The time came when the happy family was no more – the house was empty and unloved. Only the nurseries with their toys, and goodness knew what else, were left to guard the memories of the little family.

Diana's eyes had been wandering round the crowded

little shop. It really was a most interesting place and Diana felt sure that there was practically nothing that couldn't be bought there. Pails, deck-chairs, lengths of garden hose, saucepans, kettles, rugs, crockery – everything seemed to be there, muddled up together. Things hung down from the ceiling, and were piled on shelves round the walls.

'Do you know exactly what you've got in your shop?' asked Diana curiously. 'There are so many things – surely you don't know them all.'

'Ah, indeed I do,' said the old woman, beaming all over her wrinkled pink face. 'There's not a thing I don't know, and I could put my hand on anything you like to mention!'

'Well – could you put your hand on a good, long, strong rope?' said Roger at once.

'A rope? Now, let's see,' said the old dame, frowning. 'Yes – second shelf to the right, near the end. That's where it should be.'

'I'll look for you,' said Barney, getting up. 'Don't you go climbing about on those shelves!'

The second shelf was near the ceiling. Barney leapt up like a cat, found the rope, and leapt back again.

'What it is to be young!' said the old woman admiringly. 'You ought to be in a circus, you ought!'

Everyone grinned, but nobody said anything. The old woman looked at the price on the rope. 'Do you really want a rope?' she said. 'Don't you go doing nothing dangerous now. This rope's expensive – but then it's good and strong. Perhaps a cheaper one would do for you. What do you want it for?'

'Oh, this and that,' said Diana quickly. 'I think this strong one would be best. Pay for it, Roger.'

Roger paid, thinking it was a good thing it was the beginning of the holidays and he had plenty of money!

They said good day and went off with the rope. As they went down the street the church clock struck loudly.

'Half-past twelve already,' said Diana. 'We shan't have time to do any more exploring this morning. We'd better meet you this afternoon, Barney.'

'Right,' said Barney.

'What are you going to do about lunch?' asked Snubby, suddenly realising that Barney had no nice-smelling meal to go home to – in fact, not even a home.

'I'll buy myself some bread and cheese,' said Barney. 'And I'll get Miranda an orange. She loves oranges.'

He went off with Miranda on his shoulder, after arranging to call for the children at half-past two. Diana made up her mind to ask Miss Pepper to give them a picnic tea – one they could share with Barney.

She was worried about Barney. Was it comfortable to sleep under a haystack at night? Did he have enough money to buy himself the food he wanted? Suppose it rained? What did he do then? He didn't seem to have any clothes except those he had on. What a strange life he must lead with Miranda – just the two of them, wandering about together. She looked up.

'It's going to pour,' she said to the others. 'I hope Miss Pepper won't say we're to keep indoors this afternoon.'

'It'll hold off until the evening,' said Roger, looking at the clouds. 'We'll be all right this afternoon, I think. There may be a storm tonight.'

Miss Pepper was pleased to see them punctual for once. An appetising smell filled the house as they went in.

'Sausages – and onions,' said Roger. 'I hope there are chip potatoes.'

There were – and fried tomatoes too. The children were hungry and soon cleared the big dish. Diana wished that Barney could have shared such a meal. She pictured him sitting on a grassy bank somewhere, munching bread and cheese, with Miranda beside him, eating an orange.

'Never mind – he'll be with us this afternoon – sharing our tea – and a jolly fine adventure!' she thought.

Chapter Nine

Barney was outside at half-past two, whistling. 'There's that boy with the monkey again,' said Miss Pepper. 'I do hope he's a *nice* boy, Roger. I don't want you to make friends with anyone who will lead you into bad ways.'

Roger grinned. 'It's much more likely that *Snubby* will teach *him* bad ways,' he said. 'Barney's all right, Miss Pepper. Shall I ask him in for a meal sometime, then you can judge for yourself?'

'Yes. That would be a good idea,' said Miss Pepper. 'Well, you'd better go, if he's waiting for you. I've got your picnic ready for you. It's on the kitchen window-sill. Ask Mrs Round for it.'

Snubby went racing out to the kitchen, Loony at his heels. 'Roundy, Roundy, where are you? Have you got our tea for us?'

Mrs Round looked up from her after-dinner cup of tea. 'Now, don't you be cheeky,' she said. 'Calling me Roundy like that! I've told you of that before, Master Sauce-Box!'

'Roundy's a lovely name for you,' said Snubby, and gave the plump Mrs Round a sudden squeeze. 'I can't help calling you Roundy. It's a pet name. You needn't mind.'

Mrs Round didn't. She thought Snubby was what she called a 'caution', and she didn't seem to mind what he said or did. She was even putting up with Loony a bit better now, in spite of his habit of taking all her brushes out into the garden.

'That dog and you are a pair,' she said, putting her hair straight after Snubby's sudden squeeze. 'Get down, Loony. Where did you put my carpet brush, I'd like to know? Wait till I find it and I'll give you such a hiding with it.'

Loony picked up a duster and ran off with it, shaking it as if it were a rat. Snubby yelled at him and Miss Pepper appeared in the doorway.

'Snubby! Stop that noise. What's the dog got now? Drop it, Loony. I'm so sorry, Mrs Round – that dog is completely mad.'

'That's all right, Miss,' said Mrs Round graciously. 'I'm getting used to him now. He's not so bad, take him all round. Just puppy-like.'

Miss Pepper was relieved to hear Mrs Round taking things so calmly. She gave Snubby the basket of tea things and sent him off. He tore into the garden with Loony.

Loony greeted Barney riotously, and Miranda sat on her master's shoulder and watched. She suddenly slid down and caught hold of Loony's ear. She gave it a good tug and leapt back again to Barney's shoulder almost before the dog knew what had happened. He yelped.

The children laughed. They always enjoyed these bits of by-play between Loony and Miranda. 'We've got the tea,' said Diana. 'And the rope. Come on!'

Feeling rather excited the children made their way once more through the grounds to the old mansion. Miranda made a little chattering noise when they came near. She remembered her adventure of the morning.

'Blow! It's beginning to rain!' said Roger. 'Just as we've got a picnic tea too!'

'We can have it on that veranda place,' said Snubby, pointing to where a veranda showed on the south side of the house, almost hidden by hanging creepers. 'We could drag away some of those creepers to let a bit of light and air in.'

They put the teabasket on the veranda. It certainly was a dismal place. Diana felt sure it would be full of spiders

63

and earwigs, and very damp. She hoped they wouldn't have to have tea there.

The boys were longing to get on with the exploring. They were already walking round to the part of the house where the nurseries were. They looked up at the barred windows. Miranda was off Barney's shoulder and away to the nursery window-sill immediately. Barney called her back.

'Here, Miranda! Come back. We've got a job for you to do!'

Snubby and Roger undid the rope. It certainly was a good strong one. 'I believe it will be too heavy for Miranda to pull up behind her,' said Roger weighing it in his hand. It certainly was very heavy.

'I thought of that,' said Barney, and he took some string from his pocket. 'We'll play the old trick of letting a string pull the rope!'

The others watched whilst he tied some string to the rope-end. Then he found a stone with a hole in it and tied the other end of string to it.

'What's that for?' said Diana.

'You'll soon see,' said Barney. 'Now, Miranda – are you ready? Take the string up – twist it over the bars just as you do when you go up to one of the trapeze swings in the circus – and let the other end of the string drop!'

Miranda listened, her brown eyes gleaming intelligently. She chattered softly back. She really was a remarkable little monkey.

She took the stone in her tiny paw, and leapt off Barney's shoulder. She bounded to the little balcony, the string pulling up behind her. Up the ivy, on to another window-sill, and up the ivy again to the barred windows. The string unravelled swiftly behind her.

Miranda sat on the window-sill, peering in at the

window again. Barney called to her, 'Go on, Miranda. Do your stuff!'

The others watched breathlessly. Would Miranda really 'do her stuff'?

She did! She slipped the stone over the top bar, and let it drop down the other side of the bars – the window side. The stone fell, dragging the string behind it. More string unravelled and ran up the wall, as the stone with its tail of string dropped down to the ground.

Barney caught the stone as it fell and pulled the string. 'Now, watch,' he said to Diana. 'You'll soon see the rope go up.'

He pulled hard at the string, and it travelled over the bars of the window and down the wall to his hand – dragging behind it the rope that was tied to it. Up went the rope after the string, round the bars, and down to Barney's hand, as he pulled.

'It's very, very clever,' said Diana, much impressed. 'Barney, I should never have thought of that.'

'Oh, there's nothing at all in that,' said Barney, smiling. 'Any circus kid could do that from the age of two. Hallo – Miranda's gone into the room again. I'd better go up before she starts showering us with all kinds of things!'

He twisted the rope as the two strands hung from the bars to the ground. He twisted it so thoroughly that the two strands looked like one. They would be very strong, and give him a good hold.

'Now let's hope the bars will hold all right,' said Barney. He put all his weight suddenly on the rope and pulled hard. There was an ominous grating noise.

'Oh dear – the top bar's giving way,' said Diana in alarm. 'Look out – it may fall!'

Barney put his weight on the rope again. The top bar came out of the wall at one side, and hung down crookedly. The rope slid down to the next bar. There were five bars altogether.

'Well – that's one bar gone,' said Barney. 'Perhaps the next one will hold.' Again he put all his weight on the rope. The second bar gave a very little bit, and then held.

'I'll try going up now,' said Barney. 'Don't worry if this bar breaks. The rope will just slide down to the next one – and if that one breaks it'll go down to the fourth one.'

'Yes – but, Barney, suppose they all break?' said Diana in a panic.

'By the time that happens I'll be on the window-sill,' grinned Barney. 'Don't worry. I'm like a cat, I always fall on my feet.'

He suddenly swung on the rope, slid up his legs, holding the rope between his feet, and then hauled himself up strongly. 'He's going up!' said Snubby, and Loony leapt at the rope in excitement, barking.

'The bar's breaking!' screamed Diana. 'Look out, Barney – it's breaking!'

Sure enough, it suddenly gave way and dropped out from the wall, striking the stone sill as it fell, and just missing hitting Loony on the head. He jumped away in fright and went to hide under a bush. Barney felt the rope drop a little and got a jerk as it came to rest on the next bar. He hung still for a moment. What about this bar?

That held for a few seconds only, and then it too broke from its place. It didn't fall but hung down to one side and the rope slid down to the fourth bar.

'Barney, come down! All the bars will break and you'll hurt yourself!' shrieked Diana, really frightened. Barney took no notice. He went on hauling himself up the rope, intent on reaching the window-sill before the last bar broke. Once the fourth one broke, there was only one bar left.

The fourth one broke just as he reached the window-sill. With a light catlike motion he was over the last bar and on to the broad sill. He sat there, grinning down at the others, the rope swinging below him. Diana was pale with fright.

'Well, I'm here!' called Barney, getting his breath back after his long climb. He glanced into the window behind him to look for Miranda. He looked into the room there for what seemed a long, long time to the children below.

'Barney! What can you see?' called Snubby impatiently, longing to see everything himself.

'It's weird!' called down Barney at last. 'The room in here is a proper nursery – rocking-horse and all and there's a meal laid on the table. Gives me a funny feeling!'

Diana shivered a little. It certainly did sound strange. 'Can we come up the rope too?' she called. 'Can you tie it to something in the room?'

'You're none of you coming up the rope,' said Barney. 'You can't climb like me. You'd kill yourselves.'

He put his arm in at the hole in the glass of the window – the hole Miranda used when she went in and out. He felt about for the window-catch. Would it be too old and rusty to move? He didn't want to have to break the window much more.

He found the catch. It certainly was stiff – but he moved it at last. Then the window stuck, of course! It took a lot of shoving and pushing to make it move a little way. Barney almost fell off the window-sill in his efforts to open it.

But at last it was open far enough for him to squeeze in. He disappeared, whilst the children below watched eagerly and impatiently.

Barney looked round the room. It had a carpet on the floor, almost eaten away by moths. The window curtains were also in holes, destroyed by moths. A nursery table, covered by what had once been a pretty patterned cloth, stood in the middle of the room. Coloured nursery chairs stood about. A big rocking-horse stood near the window. Barney touched it with his foot. It rocked, creaking to and fro. It sent a cold shiver down his back.

A big doll's house stood on a low shelf. A box of bricks was upset on the floor nearby. Books stood on a bookshelf, mostly picture books. Bob and Arabella apparently had not been very old, dead embers of a coal fire still showed.

'It must have been left and shut up very suddenly,' thought Barney. 'Nothing tidied up – nothing cleared away – just left exactly as it was when Bob was taken ill.'

He saw another door leading out of the nursery and went to it. It was half open. There was another room beyond. In this room were two small beds – evidently one for each child. A low dressingtable and two little chests of drawers stood near the window. Yet another door opened out from this middle room.

Barney looked into that. This must have been the nurse's room. It was neat and tidy, covered with dust, and not so much eaten up by clothes moths. The bed stood in the corner with its once-white cover now grey with dust. It was all very strange indeed. Barney felt as if he had stepped back years and years.

A voice came up from below. 'Barney! BARNEY! What are you doing? You might come and tell us what's up there!'

Chapter Ten

In The Old Forgotten House

Barney went back to the window through which he had climbed. He leaned out.

'It's all jolly peculiar,' he said. 'There are three rooms up here – still furnished. Wait – I'll come down and tell you all about it. Somehow I don't feel as if I want to shout.'

'Barney! There's only one bar left!' shouted Diana in a panic. 'Don't risk that. Tie the rope to something else in the room.'

Barney tried the last bar with his hand. It broke at once. It was the rottenest one of all. Thank goodness he hadn't had to trust his weight to that one. Then he looked sharply at the rope. It was almost in two! It had pulled against something jagged on one of the bars and was cut practically to the last thread. Even as he took it up it fell in half. He made a grab at it – but down it went.

There was a dismayed silence. 'Now what's going to happen?' asked Diana. 'The rope's in two!'

'We can knot it, silly,' said Roger. Barney leaned out of the window and pointed up to the sky.

'Look there – there's a rainstorm just about to pour down. You'll all get soaked if you mess about knotting the rope and sending Miranda up with it. I think I'd better see if I can get out of this room and into the main part of the building. Then I can open a door or something from inside and let you in.'

'Right,' said Roger. 'We'll go and wait on that veranda, Barney. It's beginning to pour now.'

Roger, Snubby, Diana and Loony ran round the house to the horrible veranda. As Diana had feared, there were spiders and earwigs, and many other insects she felt she had never seen anywhere else. The floor was slimy and the place felt very damp. It was quite impossible to think of having tea there.

'I hope Barney will find some way of letting us in,' said Snubby with a shiver. 'It's jolly cold now.'

He sneezed.

'Pepper up your nose,' said Roger, trying to raise a laugh. But the veranda was too gloomy a place for a joke or a laugh.

What was Barney doing in the old house? Was he finding a way to let them in? He was certainly doing his best.

He went to the outer door of the first nursery. It was not locked. In fact, the key was in the keyhole inside the room. He opened the door and looked out on a long dark passage. Surely these rooms had been locked – not left open for anyone to come into?

He went down the passage, disturbing the dust on the floor. It rose in a light cloud. One or two long cobwebby strands hanging from the ceiling brushed against his face and made him jump. They felt like soft fingers. He didn't like it at all, and wished he had a torch with him. The passage was so very dark.

He came to a stout door at the end of the passage. He tried it, turning the big handle this way and that. No use. The door wouldn't open. It was well and truly locked on the other side. Of course – that was how they had sealed off the nurseries – by locking the door that led to all three rooms. Nobody could go near them.

How could he get into the main part of the house? He considered the matter carefully. He could not possibly kick this stout door down, and the lock was strong. It looked as if he couldn't leave this passage at all.

A thought struck him. What about the key he had seen in one of the nursery doors? Would that by any chance fit this door? It was worth trying.

He went back quickly, almost choking as he kicked up the dust. Miranda clung to his shoulder in silence. She didn't like this. It was strange and dark. She held on tightly to Barney's shoulder.

He looked at the three doors in the other rooms. Each had a key in it. He looked at the keys. They seemed more or less the same to him, but perhaps they weren't. He took them back to the passage door.

The first key slid in easily, but wouldn't turn. However he tried, it wouldn't turn more than half-way. He was afraid of forcing it in case the key broke in the lock. He tried the second one. That would only turn half-way too. Without much hope he tried the third key.

And it turned! True, it was stiff, and grated protestingly as he turned it slowly and carefully – but it suddenly clicked back the old lock. He could open the door!

He turned the handle and pulled at the door. It came open and a cloud of dust arose again, making him cough. He was looking out at a broad landing. Doors opened on either side of it. Barney went to them, walking on tiptoe, he didn't quite know why.

He pushed open the doors, one by one, and looked into the rooms. They were completely empty. Not a chair, not a book, not a rug, remained in any of them. Only dust covered the bare floors, and cobwebs hung everywhere. Large spiders scuttled over the ceilings as he opened the doors, terrified to be disturbed in the midst of their long dark peace.

Most of the rooms were dark, or at least dim, because of the ivy that grew across the windows, allowing only a small amount of daylight in. The rooms smelt musty and old.

Barney went down the bare stairs. Dust rose from each stair, fine dust, like grey flour, that made him choke whenever it reached his nose. He didn't touch the banister rail as he went down, for fear of disturbing even more dust.

Down to the first floor. Here there were more doors that opened on to miserable dark rooms, dusty and silent. From the first floor down to the ground floor the staircase descended from each side of the great landing, and then joined its two flights together to sweep down in one huge curve to the enormous hall.

Now Barney was in the hall, which he had seen through the crack in the front door. He tiptoed into a big room to the right. It was the ballroom. The mirrors gave back a dozen reflections of his dim, shadowy figure and made him feel uncomfortable. He left the ballroom and went into another room. This must have been used by people during the last war, as well as the ballroom, for here, again, there was broken furniture, old papers strewn about and the remains of a broken telephone receiver. It was dusty but the dust was not so thick as in the upper floors.

He went into another room, and saw that it was the room leading out on the veranda. He made out the figures of the three children and Loony, standing patiently outside, waiting for him. Perhaps he could open the veranda door. He went over to it and knocked on the glass with his knuckles. All three children jumped violently and then turned to see what the noise was.

'It's Barney!' cried Diana gladly. 'Oh, Barney – you were able to get out of the rooms upstairs, then!'

Barney could just make out what she said. He struggled with the veranda door-bolts and managed at last to push each one back. He unlocked the door, and forced it open. The children outside rushed in, and Diana caught hold of his arm.

'Barney! You *are* clever! We were getting so cold out there, and the rain comes sweeping in on the veranda.'

Loony tore round and round the room, kicking up dust as he went. 'Shut up, Loony,' said Roger sharply. 'You'll choke us all – and yourself too.'

Miranda still clung to Barney's shoulder. She was very glad to see the other children. They all looked round at the silent, dusty room. Diana took a few steps forward and then screamed, making the others jump.

She had walked into a cobweb, which had swung softly against her face. 'Someone touched me,' she yelled.

'No. It's only a hanging cobweb,' said Barney with a laugh. 'There are plenty of those. Has anyone got a torch?'

Snubby had. He usually had everything. It was really amazing what his pockets could hold. He fished out a torch and switched it on. Immediately a horde of spiders went this way and that and Diana screamed again. She couldn't bear spiders. The children saw the big webs everywhere and the long strands of web hanging down from the ceiling.

'I don't like this much,' said Roger. 'It's an awful place to have our tea in. What's the place upstairs like, Barney? You haven't told us anything yet.'

Barney told them quickly what he had found, and how he had got out of the rooms and downstairs. 'I think we'd be better up in the nurseries really,' he said. 'They are frightfully dusty too, but at least there are chairs to sit on – and it seems lighter up there. Let's go up.'

So they all went up, climbing first the two-branched stairway to the first floor and then the smaller one to the

73

second floor. They came to the passage door and went through it.

'This must have been the nursery wing, all on its own,' said Barney. 'A very nice place it was too, with a wonderful view over the countryside. Look!'

He swung open the nursery door and the children peered in. They fell silent when they saw the rocking-horse standing motionless as if waiting for some child to ride it – the toy cupboard door open to show the toys still sitting there – the dolls' house on the shelf – and the plates and dishes on the table, set out ready for a meal.

'Weird,' said Diana. 'Weird to look at and weird to feel. I'm not sure I like it. Still, the house feels a bit happier here than it did downstairs.'

'We'll have tea here,' said Roger. 'That's if nobody minds sitting down in dust inches thick! Come on! Where's the basket? I'll feel a lot better when I've got a few slices of cake inside me.'

Chapter Eleven

A Very Good Idea

The storm came whilst they sat eating their tea. Thunder suddenly rolled over the sky and lightning forked across, dazzling the children for a moment and making them jump and blink.

'Well – I'm glad we're not out-of-doors picnicking!' said Roger, trying to be cheerful. But nobody felt terribly happy. Still, they felt a lot better when they had eaten every sandwich, every cake and biscuit, and drunk the gingerbeer too. Loony had his share. Actually he was a real nuisance in that dusty room, because his four feet scraped the dust up so much. Miranda stayed sedately on her master's shoulder, nibbling slices of cucumber sandwich.

The children explored the three rooms again after tea. It seemed sad to think that they had never been used since little Bob had been taken away with the fever so many, many years ago. 'I suppose the mother couldn't bear to come into the empty room again,' said Diana. 'Poor thing! She couldn't even bear to have them touched. I wonder if anyone knows about them but us. They might quite easily have been forgotten by now. I mean, people might have thought that door in the passage outside, that was locked, was only a door to a boxroom or something.'

'I think you're probably right,' said Barney. 'My word, hark at the rain pelting down!'

It certainly was pouring hard. The thunder rolled still, but sounded farther away, and the lightning flashed but not so vividly. Diana glanced at Barney. Where would he sleep that night? Surely not under a haystack.

'Barney – you won't sleep out in the open tonight, surely?' she asked him at last, putting away the gingerbeer bottles in the empty basket. 'Everywhere will be so wet.'

'No, I shan't,' said Barney. 'As a matter of fact, I had thought of sleeping here.'

The others looked at him in amazement.

'What, *here*! By yourself! In this awful old empty house, with its spiders and dust!' cried Diana horrified. 'How could you *dare* to? All alone too!'

'I shall have Miranda,' said Barney. 'And I'm not easily scared, you know. I've slept in much worse places.'

Diana couldn't think of any worse place to sleep. She shuddered. Miranda put her little arms round Barney's neck and chattered to him.

'She says it's all right, she'll be with me and chase any spider away,' said Barney with a grin.

'I think it's a good idea,' said Snubby. 'After all, the beds are still good, even if the bedclothes fall to bits! The nurse's room didn't look too bad. Why don't you take that for your own room, Barney? You'd be quite comfortable there.'

'I know!' cried Diana, getting up and looking in various cupboards. 'I'll see if there's a brush and a dustpan some-where – and I could perhaps clear up some of the dust in the nurse's room.'

It was Loony who found the brush, of course! He darted into the bottom of a cupboard and brought out a carpet brush, whose bristles had gone soft. 'Just the thing!' said Diana, wrenching the brush away from Loony. 'Thanks, Loony. I'll have it. Snubby, keep him away from me – he's kicking dust up all over the place.'

'Better put something round your hair, Di,' said Roger, seeing how the dust flew up round Diana's head as she began brushing dust into the pan. 'Here's my hanky. It's a big one. Tie it round your head.'

So, whilst the boys amused themselves by looking through the old toy cupboard and picking out more of the beautifully carved old soldiers, and Miranda tried on various dolls' bonnets, Diana got very busy.

She took the bedclothes off the nurse's bed and carried them down the passage to the landing. She shook them well. They were full of dust, of course. The bedspread and one of the blankets fell to pieces and were no use – but one blanket seemed quite good. Diana carried it back to the bed and laid it on the mattress. There were no sheets. Perhaps those had been removed by the nurse. The pillow was full of moths. They flew out as she punched it. Grubs had eaten the pillow almost to nothing.

'Barney will have to do without a pillow,' she thought. 'We must bring him an old coat or something, to roll up under his head. Or perhaps an old cushion.'

She swept the dust off the dressing table, the washstand and the chest of drawers. It choked her and she began to cough. She had to wait for the dust to settle a little before she went on. She went to the window and struggled to open it. The room was so musty and dusty – a little fresh air would be good. She got the window open at last and a shower of raindrops came over her as she pushed back the thick sprays of ivy.

That gave her an idea. She picked some of the rain-wet sprays and sprinkled the dusty floor with the raindrops. 'That will help to lay the dust a bit,' she thought, rather pleased with herself. It certainly did. She was able to sweep the floor carefully without raising too much dust now.

In the end she took up the moth-eaten carpet and stuffed it into a cupboard. It fell to pieces in places as she brushed it. It was easier to brush the bare boards beneath.

77

She called Barney when she had finished. 'It's the best I can do,' she said. 'It's not nearly so dusty now – and you've got one fairly decent blanket to sleep on – or under. I don't know what you'll do for water though.'

'There's probably an old well somewhere – or a pump in the kitchen,' said Barney cheerfully. Things like that didn't worry him at all. 'Anyway, I always swim in the river each morning.'

'There's a bottle of gingerbeer left,' said Roger. 'We'll leave you that. Well – I hope you'll be all right, Barney – sleeping here all by yourself!'

'It's fine,' said Barney. 'Better than a wet barn or a dripping haystack any day!'

'Will you leave the veranda door unlocked and unbolted?' said Roger. 'Then we can get in and out as we like. So long as the door is shut no one will guess anything. We could use these rooms up here as playrooms in wet weather.'

'I'm glad Barney's got somewhere sheltered to sleep,' said Diana. 'And Miranda too, of course. Where is she?'

They went to look for her. She had watched Barney stretching himself on the bed and had considered him carefully and then bounded out of the room. Now she had disappeared!

It was Loony who smelt her out. He rushed over to the wall opposite the window in the day nursery and barked madly. There was a doll's bed there, with a doll in it.

Beside the doll lay Miranda, her big brown eyes looking wickedly up at Loony. She was in bed too! If Barney had a bed, she would have one as well!

'Oh, Miranda!' cried Diana. 'You really look a darling there. Barney, isn't she sweet? Don't, Loony. You've pulled the covers off Miranda. That's unkind.'

'I think we'd better go now,' said Roger, 'or Miss Pepper will be ringing up the village policeman.'

'I'll come down with you,' said Barney. 'Then I'll leave the veranda door unlocked and unbolted as you suggested, Roger. Nobody will know it's open. It's obvious that no one ever comes here.'

He saw them safely through the veranda door, Miranda sitting on his shoulder, wearing a doll's hat she had found. She fancied herself in it very much, and wore it back to front. Diana ran across the spidery veranda and down the steps to the wet grass.

The three of them got very wet going home through the thick undergrowth. Everything was dripping with silvery raindrops. The sun was trying to struggle out now. It might be quite a nice evening.

Miss Pepper was very concerned about them when they came in. 'Oh, dear – how wet you are!' she said. 'Go and put on something dry at once. I do hope you sheltered during the storm.'

'Oh, yes,' said Roger. But they didn't tell her where! No – that was their own very private secret. Nobody was going to know what they had been up to that afternoon.

When they went to bed that night the three called cautiously to one another, with Loony rushing as usual out of one bedroom and into another, sending all the mats sliding this way and that.

'Do you suppose Barney's in bed? Do you think he's all right?'

'*I* wouldn't like to sleep in that awful old deserted house at night!' That was Diana, of course.

'I bet he's in that bed and sound asleep! I bet he'll sleep sound till the morning!'

Barney *was* in bed and asleep. Miranda was in her little dolls' bed. She usually slept with Barney, cuddled up to him, but the bed appealed to her funny little monkey mind very much. She was there, under the blanket, hugging the old doll.

Barney slept soundly till half-past two in the morning – and then he awoke with a jump! Miranda had leapt on top of him, and was cuddling into his neck, trembling, chattering in a tiny voice in his ear.

Barney sat up.

'What's the matter, Miranda? What's frightened you? You're shivering all over. Were you lonely?'

Miranda clung to him and showed no signs of going back to her own little bed. Barney came to the conclusion that something had frightened her badly. But what? Was it a noise? It couldn't have been anybody coming into the nursery, because there was nobody to come!

He thought he heard a far-away sound then. He sat there on the bed, and listened, feeling his ears pricking like a dog's. Was that a sound? Or was it his imagination?

It must be his imagination! He lay down again, with Miranda still cuddled into his neck – and then he sat up straight in one quick movement.

He *had* heard a sound! Quite a loud one. Bang! He listened intently, and heard it again.

Bang! Then the wind blew in at the window, and the ivy rustled against the glass. It made Barney jump. He realised what the rustling noise was at once – the wind in the ivy. Could the other noise have been caused by the wind too? Was it a door banging somewhere? Or was it perhaps the veranda door that had swung open in the wind and was banging?

Barney debated whether to go and see. He wasn't afraid, but he definitely didn't want to get up in the middle of a dark night, and go wandering down dark stairs and along dusty passages without a light.

'If I hear the noise again I'll go down,' he decided. 'If I don't, I won't. I bet it's that beastly veranda door banging. I can't have shut it tightly enough.'

He heard no more noises at all, except that the wind

blew an old ivy leaf into the room and made it shuffle along the floor in a very hair-raising manner. For a moment poor Barney thought somebody was in the room – but Miranda knew it was only a leaf, and didn't move. So Barney decided it was just something being blown along the floor.

He lay down again and shut his eyes. He listened for a few minutes longer, but all he heard was the monkey's little heart pattering fast against his neck.

Then he fell asleep and didn't wake till the sun pushed through the ivy leaves in the morning.

Chapter Twelve

Mr King Arrives

Immediately after breakfast the next morning Diana wanted to go and see if Barney was all right.

'You've got to help make the beds and clear away the breakfast,' said Roger. 'We'll let Snubby go with Loony. I'm just about fed up with Snubby this morning. He put a worm in each of my shoes and put treacle or something on my sponge. If it's going to be one of his tiresome days we'd be better off without him. Let him go and plague Barney. Barney will know how to deal with him.'

So Snubby was told to take some bread and butter and tomatoes and a bottle of milk to Barney. He set off in glee. Loony running at his heels. He had got half-way over the grounds when he discovered that Loony was carrying Miss Pepper's hairbrush. So back he went and stood beneath Miss Pepper's bedroom window. He threw the brush up and it went straight in at the window.

There was an agonised yell and Snubby took to his heels. 'Well, how was I to know she was standing in the way?' he argued to himself. 'Just like a woman.'

He looked down at Loony, who was again at his heels. This time he was carrying Mrs Round's old shoe-cleaning brush. Snubby stopped and addressed Loony fiercely.

'What do you think you're doing? Do you suppose I'm going to spend half the day taking back your silly brushes? You're a very bad dog. Take it back! Grrrrrr!'

Loony stared up at Snubby out of melting brown eyes, his tail down.

'Take it back! Don't you understand plain English when it's spoken?' yelled Snubby. 'TAKE – IT – BACK!'

Loony wagged his tail and darted off. Snubby was pleased. 'Clever dog that,' he said to a couple of sparrows nearby. 'Understands every word I say.'

He petted Loony when the dog came back. 'Good dog. Took it all the way back to the kitchen and dropped it at Roundy's feet, I bet! Cleverest dog in the world.'

Loony was very pleased. He had just dropped the brush down the nearest rabbit-hole. Well – if Snubby was so delighted with him, he'd drop plenty of other things down the rabbit-hole too.

The two went on together, Loony making a dart at anything that dared to move – a leaf, a swirl of dust, a bit of paper. Grrrrrr! He darted at Snubby's shoe-laces, tripping him up. He behaved, in fact, just like the lunatic dog he was, and pleased Snubby very much indeed.

Snubby got to the old house at last and made his way round to the veranda. The door was fast shut. He pushed against it. It was so hard to open the he had to put down the basket that he was carrying, and push against the door with all his might. It obliged him by suddenly flying open and sending him headlong into the room. He sat down abruptly. Loony flung himself on him and licked him wildly.

'Hallo! It's you, is it?' said Barney's voice. 'I heard an awful row and came to see what it was. You're early. But why sit on that dusty floor?'

'Get off, Loony,' said Snubby, pushing the excited spaniel away. He looked up at Barney and grinned. 'I found the door shut so hard I couldn't get in. So I had to barge against it with all my might – and it flew open unexpectedly. And I flew in!'

'I see,' said Barney. He spotted the basket outside. 'I

say – anything to eat? How super! Bread and butter and tomatoes! Are they for me?'

'Of course,' said Snubby, brushing himself down. Barney took the basket into the room and shut the door. He pulled at it when he had shut it. It certainly did shut very tightly indeed. He looked puzzled.

'What's up?' said Snubby, noticing Barney's looks. 'Anything wrong with the door?'

Barney told Snubby about how frightened Miranda had been the night before, and how he had heard noises.

'I thought it must be the wind blowing open this door and banging it again,' he said. 'But I don't think it was now. The door fits so tightly.'

They went up to the top rooms together. Snubby felt a little nervous. 'I'd have hated that,' he said to Barney. 'Lying up there in the dark, hearing noises – and not able to put a light on. Brrrrrr!'

'You might lend me your torch for tonight,' Barney said. 'I could do a little snooping round then, if I hear any more noises.'

Snubby handed out his torch at once. He sat and watched Barney eat. 'It's a gorgeous day,' he said.

'What about going to the river and getting a boat?'

'Yes, I'd like that,' said Barney. 'When do you start this coaching of yours? Monday? We'd better make the most of out time then. I've been reading that play Roger lent me, this morning, up there in bed. It's grand.'

'Well, better you than me,' said Snubby, making a face. 'I never could make out why Shakespeare wanted to write in such a funny way – you know, all the lines the same length. Seems a strange idea.'

Barney laughed. 'I wish I could come and listen to you all being coached,' he said. 'I bet I would enjoy it! I bet I'd learn a lot.'

'Well!' Snubby looked at Barney as if he were quite

mad. 'You must be crazy. Fancy wanting to come and be coached! Well – I don't see why you shouldn't come and listen if you want to. But fancy *wanting* to! Do you hear that, Loony? Here's a chap madder than you are!'

They walked to the door, their footsteps showing clearly in the dust. All their footsteps were there, Loony's as well. Snubby pointed them out.

'There's Loony's marks – and mine – and these must be yours. Those are Di's, they're small. And there are Roger's – he's got the biggest feet of the lot.'

They went out of the veranda door and Barney pulled it fast behind him. He pushed at it. It didn't open. He had to barge against it hard before it flew open. It couldn't have been this door banging last night. He must find out which door it was – if it was a door. It was a bit of a mystery!

Barney didn't sleep in the old house for a night or two after that. It was suddenly very hot weather again and the children hired a boat for a day or so. Barney had the idea of sleeping in the boat, with a rug over him, and the boat-cushions for a bed.

'Do you mind if I do!' he asked the others. 'It will save you the bother of taking it back to the boatman and I should love to bob about all night long on the water.'

'Right,' said Roger, pleased. 'You do that. It's very stuffy up in those dusty old rooms in this weather – much better sleep out if it's going to be hot and dry.'

Monday came all too soon, and with it came Mr King, armed with textbooks and a suitcase. He was apparently going to stay at Rockingdown Cottage! The children hadn't realised this. They were shocked.

'Gracious! Have we got to have him for meals and everything?' said Snubby, dismally, seeing him go upstairs to one of the rooms on the first floor, accompanied by Mrs Round and Loony.

'Oh, don't be silly, Snubby,' said Miss Pepper, impatiently. 'He lives too far away to come over every day. And I may have to go away for a day or two, so I shall be glad to know there's someone responsible in the house to see to you.'

A gloom settled on the children. Barney peeped in at the window and raised his eyebrows.

'Yes. He's come,' said Diana. '*And* he's living here. Isn't that frightful? We shall have to behave more than ever.'

'Well, I shan't,' said Snubby.

'You never do,' said Diana. 'Barney, do you really want to come in and listen to us being coached? Honestly, you'll be bored stiff. Honestly!'

Barney nodded. He had a real thirst for book knowledge, and thought the three children very lucky in their education, and their possession of so many books.

'All right. You come and knock at the door in about ten minutes' time,' said Diana. 'Then when you come in you can be surprised to see us all working so quietly and . . .'

'He can apologise and back out,' said Roger, enjoying this little plan. 'And I'll say, "Oh Mr King, would you mind if Barney sits here and waits for us?" And everything will be O.K.'

'Right,' said Barney, and disappeared with Miranda just as Miss Pepper came into the study with Mr King.

'Ha! All ready and waiting, I see,' said Mr King. 'Very good. We'll just see what standard you've all reached and then I can tell how to proceed with you.'

In about a quarter of an hour's time Barney passed the window. He walked in at the open hall door and came to the study door. He knocked.

'Come in,' yelled all the children at once, before Mr King could say a word. In came Barney, looking unexpectedly tidy, his hair wet and brushed back , and his hands and face clean.

'Oh – er? I'm sorry,' he said, as he saw the three children sitting with Mr King at the table. 'I don't want to interrupt. So sorry, sir.'

He began to back out of the room, looking hot and bothered. Diana thought he was doing it all very well! Snubby choked back a giggle. Roger spoke earnestly to Mr King.

'Oh, Mr King – would you very much mind if our friend Barnabas sits down and waits for us?' he said. 'He won't be any trouble.'

'Certainly,' said Mr King graciously. 'By all means. Sit down by the window, Barnabas. Have you a book to read?'

Mr King was pleasantly surprised to see that Barney had a book of Shakespeare's plays. He turned his back on the boy and went on with his coaching. Loony was lying quietly at Snubby's feet, rather exhausted by a mad race he had had up and down the stairs. Mr King congratulated himself on a nice quiet class. Miss Pepper had warned him he might not find things too easy – but nothing could be easier than this.

Snubby wondered where Miranda was. Barney hadn't brought her in. He must have shut her up somewhere – probably in the shed. He yawned. Things were getting boring. Even Loony was subdued.

Then things happened quickly! The door was slightly ajar and Miranda came shuffling in quietly. She saw Loony lying under the table asleep. Unseen by anyone, she went under Snubby's chair and came to the spaniel. Ha – her enemy was asleep! She took hold of both his long floppy ears and pulled them hard, making a loud squawk as she did so. Loony woke up in a hurry and yelped madly. He leapt out from under the table, and snapped at Miranda, who hung on to the tablecloth to get out of his way. The cloth slid to the side and books fell off with a crash. Then a battle royal developed under and round the table, and Mr King leapt up in alarm, his chair falling on Miranda, who happened to be chasing round it. She gave a howl and leapt on to his shoulder, pulling his ear hard.

Snubby rushed after Loony, who had fallen into the fireplace, bringing the tongs and the shovel down on himself with a clatter. He almost leapt up the chimney in fright. Barney yelled at Miranda.

Snubby knocked a vase over as he tore after Loony, and Miss Pepper and Mrs Round, talking about meals in the kitchen, looked at each in amazement.

'What can they be doing?' said Miss Pepper and rushed to the study door, to be met by a crazy spaniel and an equally crazy monkey, both intent on devouring one another if they possibly could.

Miranda disappeared upstairs and hid. Loony crept back to Snubby, who had yelled at him without ceasing, partly to get him to come, and partly to make as much noise as he could.

'Well!' said Miss Pepper, annoyed. 'I suppose this is what comes of letting Loony be in the room with you, Snubby.'

'It was nothing to do with Loony,' said Snubby indignantly. 'He was asleep under the table. It was Miranda.'

'Er – I think – I think you must take the dog out of the room,' said Mr King, trying to recover himself under the prim disapproving eye of Miss Pepper.

'But, I tell you, it wasn't Loony's fault,' almost yelled Snubby. 'That's not fair.'

'I cannot have either a dog or a monkey in my class,' said Mr King with great dignity and sudden firmness. 'They've both had a trial. It was not successful.'

'But Mr King – Loony was fast asleep,' wailed Snubby. 'Didn't you hear his little snores?'

'No, I didn't,' said Mr King. 'Take the dog out, Peter.'

Snubby took Loony by the collar to lead him out. He faced Mr King, his face as red as a beetroot.

'All right,' he said, in a choking voice. 'If you don't like my dog, I don't like you. You'll be sorry you didn't give him a chance – when he was fast asleep too!'

He went outside with Loony, who was quite scared now. Miss Pepper took him from Snubby. 'Now don't be so *silly*, Snubby,' she said. 'Acting like a seven-year-old. I'll take Loony to the kitchen with Mrs Round.'

'I'll pay Mr King out,' said Snubby, darkly. 'See if I don't. He'll be sorry, Miss Pepper. He will, really!'

Chapter Thirteen

Snubby Gets a Surprise

Mr King didn't like the next few days very much. Snubby produced his vast collection of tricks and became a perfect nightmare to the coach.

Poor Mr King was given a rubber that wouldn't rub out but made strange yellow marks on the paper. He was provided with a ruler that was mysteriously wrong in its measurements and astonished him considerably. This ruler was one of Snubby's pet tricks and had been confiscated at school, times without number, by irritated masters. But somehow or other its always found its way back to Snubby.

Books fell suddenly to the floor in a cascade, though Snubby was quite a long way from them. Mr King did not see the cunningly laid string that tipped up the bottom book when pulled, and sent the whole pile crashing down near him. The wall blackboard continually fell down in a most amazing way, and when Snubby was sent to clean it, at any time a thick cloud of horrible-smelling dust appeared. It would have been a good thing if Mr King had examined Snubby's duster occasionally, but he didn't seem to think of things like that.

'Considering he has been a master in a boys' school he's pretty innocent,' said Roger, who was very amused at all Snubby's idiotic tricks. As for Barney, he couldn't contain himself when Snubby perpetrated yet another foolish joke, and his uproarious laugh sounded all over the house.

Barney seemed to be the only one who really enjoyed

the morning lessons. He didn't actually join the class but sat in the window, apparently reading. Mr King's back was to him, so he was unaware that the boy was absorbing everything that went on – listening to the explanations of mathematical problems, taking in the French lessons, enjoying the readings of English literature. There was nothing that Barney didn't enjoy. He had an extraordinary memory, and quite annoyed Roger by the way he could repeat the Latin phrases and declensions, when poor Roger himself was struggling to do the prep that Mr King gave him.

Mr King was not really a good teacher, Diana thought. He didn't seem interested enough. Nor could he keep Snubby in his place, but often seemed inclined to be amused at his silly tricks. Snubby sulked. He hated Loony being kept away from him, and he was determined not to have Miranda sneaking in at any time. The little monkey was shut up in the shed whilst lessons were going on, but she sometimes managed to escape. She would find some crack or crevice and squeeze miraculously out of it – then she would appear silently at the window.

She would look for Loony, and then cuddle down with Barney. But at once Snubby would point her out to Mr King. 'There's Miranda, Mr King. Can I get Loony in here?'

And Miranda would then have to go. Barney didn't bear any resentment toward Snubby for this. He liked the red-haired, freckled little pest, and always watched for his next trick.

Mr King was with the children in the mornings, and had all his meals with them – but he disappeared for the rest of the time.

'You're awfully fond of walks, aren't you?' Roger said, one afternoon, when Mr King set off with his stick and a book. 'Where do you go?'

'Oh, anywhere,' said Mr King vaguely. 'Down to the river – through the village – and yesterday I visited that strange old mansion.'

The children pricked up their ears at once. Blow! Would he discover their secret? Would he see the curtained windows they had seen, and notice the marks of their feet on the ground below?

'It's a very desolate place, I believe,' said Diana, after a pause. 'Not worth looking at!'

'I though it was very interesting,' said Mr King. 'It's very old – has quite a history. I wish I could go over it.'

This was worse than ever. Had they better lock and bolt the veranda door in case Mr King found that it could be opened? What a nuisance he was!

But if they did that they wouldn't be able to go in and out themselves if they wanted to – and as Barney was once more sleeping up in the nursery at the top of the old house it was useful to have that door left unlocked, so that they could use it if they wanted to.

Barney was quite used to sleeping in the old bed up in the little bedroom now. Diana had provided him with a garden cushion for a pillow, and an old rug. He had taken some of the nursery crockery for himself.

Diana had managed to get rid of most of the dust and Barney enjoyed his little hiding-place. Nobody would ever guess he was there! On wet days the children went up to the three rooms and amused themselves there. They had once thought of playing hide-and-seek, using the front stairs and the back ones – but somehow it didn't work. Nobody liked hiding in the gloomy old place, and it was horrid tiptoeing along to find the hiders!

'I feel as if somebody is going to jump out and grab me all the time!' said Diana, with a shiver.

Barney had not heard any more noises. Miranda would not sleep in the doll's bed any more since she had been frightened the first night, but cuddled up with him. She only went into the doll's bed in the daytime when she got bored with the children's games. Then she would leap in, draw the bedclothes over her, and apparently sleep soundly with the old doll!

The only one who had really thoroughly explored the house and gone into every cupboard and corner was Loony, of course. His paw-marks were everywhere! He sniffed here and snuffled there, choking with the dust, and scraping madly at doors to make them open.

One night Snubby thought of going to sleep at the old house with Barney. The idea just came into his head. 'But why?' said Diana. 'What a horrible idea! In that dark old place – I wouldn't sleep there for anything.'

'I'd like to,' said Snubby obstinately. 'Anything for a bit of change. I call these hols too dull for words.'

So that night, when he was supposed to be in bed and asleep, Snubby dressed again, and went out on the landing and listened. Downstairs the clock struck half-past eleven. Was Mr King in bed? He usually went up at eleven, about the same time as Miss Pepper. Mrs Round didn't sleep in the house. She came in from the village each day.

Diana and Roger knew that Snubby was going to go to Barney for the night of course – but they hadn't bothered to keep awake to see him go. Snubby had borrowed Roger's torch, because he had lent Barney his. He switched it on and off, whilst he stood on the landing, to see if it worked all right. Yes, it did. It was a good torch, better than Snubby's.

Loony was at the boy's heels, his tail-stump wagging. He liked this kind of thing. He pressed against Snubby's legs, and didn't make a sound. He could be quiet and good if he wanted to – and he wanted to now, in case Snubby left him behind.

Snubby decided that Mr King was safely in bed.

Anyway, in case he wasn't he'd go down the little back stairs. Then nobody would hear him. He crept to where they began and went down on tiptoe. He knew that the third and the seventh and the thirteenth stairs creaked, so he counted carefully, and missed those out. He had his hand on Loony's collar to stop him tearing downstairs as he usually did.

Now he was at the bottom. Good. He cautiously opened the back door and looked out. It was a fine starry night. There was no moon, but the stairs were so bright that it was possible to see the trees outlined against the sky. Now for the walk across to Rockingdown Hall. The children had made quite a path of their own now by hacking away branches and bushes.

Silently Snubby shut the door behind him and then he and Loony began their walk across the grounds. He could soon see the black mass of the old mansion looming up against the starry sky. It looked much bigger than it did in the daytime.

Loony made several little excursions into the under-growth, and scared a good many rabbits who were not expecting him at all. He would have liked to chase them, but he wanted to keep with Snubby. It was night-time, and his master must be protected – against what, Loony didn't know. He just felt that he must keep close to him.

Snubby whistled softly. He wasn't scared but he felt it would be nice to whistle a little tune. He came out on to what had once been a great lawn – and then he stopped very suddenly indeed, and his hand closed over Loony's collar.

He could see a light moving near the house! He screwed up his eyes and tried to see what the light was. It must be the light of a torch! It moved here and there as if the owner were looking for something. Was it Barney?

Snubby didn't like to whistle and find out, in case it wasn't.

And then Loony told him quite plainly that it wasn't Barney. He growled ominously, deep down in his throat.. Snubby shook him a little to make him stop. He didn't want the person with the torch to know he was there with the spaniel. Loony would never growl at Barney. Snubby knew that. This was a stranger then. Whatever could be be doing? Or was he a tramp, seeking a way in to get a night's shelter?

Snubby crept nearer with Loony. The dog now knew he was to keep quiet, and Snubby relaxed his hold on his collar. He had switched off his own torch. He followed the light of the other torch. Whoever held it was going systematically round the house, examining doors and windows. Suppose he came to the veranda door and found it open? Would he go in?

The man went round a corner of the house and Snubby saw his outline clearly. He gazed in real amazement. Why – he knew who this night prowler was – surely it was Mr King!

Chapter Fourteen

A Mysterious Night

Snubby was full of astonishment. What in the world was Mr King doing prowling round the old house in the middle of the night, when he was supposed to be in bed? He stood still in the shadow of a big bush and thought about it. He couldn't make head or tail of it at all.

He made up his mind to make his way to the veranda door, go in as quietly as he could and run upstairs to warn Barney. He would lock the door behind him, so that Mr King couldn't get in. The man was now on the opposite side of the house to the veranda, the north side. If Snubby was quick he could get in without being seen or heard. He set off quietly for the house with Loony padding at his heels.

On to the veranda he crept, and had to put on his torch to see the handle of the door. He turned it and pushed. The door was easier to open now that the children had used it a good deal, and it swung inwards without much noise. Snubby went in with Loony and shut the door behind him. He shot the bolts and locked the door as well. Now Mr King wouldn't be able to get in!

He tiptoed into the hall and across into another room, standing by the door to see if he could spot Mr King's torch shining on the opposite side of the house. Yes, there it was!

Snubby shot upstairs to the first landing, then up again to the second. He went to the door that led into the passage to the nurseries. He turned the handle.

The door was locked! Snubby was puzzled. Why was

the door locked? Barney left it unlocked usually, so that the children could go in and out as they pleased. He rattled the door gently. Then he heard Miranda chattering softly on the other side.

'Miranda!' he said, in a low voice. 'Where's Barney? Fetch Barney.'

The door was unlocked immediately and Barney stood there with Miranda on his shoulder. He pulled Snubby into the passage and locked the door. In silence he led the way to the room where he slept.

'Why did you lock the door?' whispered Snubby.

'Because there's somebody about,' said Barney in a low voice. 'Didn't you bump into him?'

'Yes, almost! I know who it is, too,' said Snubby.

'Who?' said Barney.

'Mr King!' said Snubby. 'Yes – that's surprising isn't it? But it is. He's snooping all round the house trying to get in, I should think.'

'Miranda woke me up a few minutes ago,' said Barney. 'I knew there was something up the way she was chattering, and pawing at me, patting me on the cheek and putting her paw down my neck. So I got up and looked out of the window – and I saw somebody down below, using a torch!'

'Why didn't you rush down and lock the veranda door?' asked Snubby.

'Because I thought this fellow would have been at the door just about the same time as I would,' said Barney.

'So I locked the passage door instead. Then you came along, and I got a bit of a fright. I thought you must be the man – or another man perhaps. It was only when Miranda began her friendly little chatter that I guessed it was one of you three. Are the others here? Why have you come tonight?'

Snubby explained in whispers. 'I just had a sudden idea

I'd like a bit of an adventure so I came along to spend the night with you – and I saw this man just as I came up to the house. I was awfully surprised when I saw who it was. The others aren't here. They're in bed'

'What do you suppose he's doing?' said Barney, puzzled. 'What's he after?'

'Can't imagine,' said Snubby. 'By the way – have you heard any more noises in the night, Barney?'

'None,' said Barney. 'I think it must just have been the wind banging the door, that's all.'

He went to the window and looked out cautiously. There was nothing to be seen. 'He may be at the other side of the house,' said Barney. 'Well, now that the veranda door is safely locked we know he can't get in. Let's go down the passage, unlock the door there, and see if we can find out where Mr King is now.'

Off they went, very quietly. Miranda was on Barney's shoulder, chattering softly in a whispery voice. Loony trotted along with them, enjoying himself.

They unlocked the passage door and went down the stairs quietly to the rooms on the next floor. There was one with a bay window that jutted out – they would stand in the bay and see if they could spot Mr King's torchlight.

They spotted it at once – moving slowly along below, as if he were examining every window catch. What *was* he doing? Why did he want to get in?

And then – just as they stood there quietly watching, they heard a noise.

Bang! Thud! Thud! Bang!

They almost jumped out of their skins. Evidently, Mr King heard the noise too, for he switched off his torch at once. Snubby clutched Barney in a fright. Loony growled loudly and Miranda sat quite still, listening.

'That's the noise I heard the first night,' said Barney in a low voice. 'Is it a door banging, do you think?'

'Well – it *might* be,' said Snubby, listening.

Bang!

'There it is again,' said Barney. 'Where is the noise coming from?'

'Downstairs,' said Snubby, his teeth beginning to chatter. He was ashamed of himself for being afraid, and tried to shut his mouth firmly to stop his teeth from behaving in such an idiotic way. He badly wanted to go upstairs again, and lock the passage door and go into the nurseries and lock their doors too! He was shocked to find that he wasn't nearly as brave as he had always thought he was.

Barney was quite calm and didn't seem afraid at all. He stood there listening. The noises came again. Yes – they were definitely from downstairs.

There was no sign of Mr King's torch. Either he was in hiding or he had gone – or had he joined the persons who were making the noise? Barney thought it was very likely that that was the reason he had come along that night – to join friends of his somewhere about here!

He stood there, puzzling it out, waiting for more noises. There came a curious whining, half-screeching noise that made all Snubby's hair slowly stand upright on his head, much to his surprise – and then dead silence. Not a bang or a thud came again.

'Well,' said Barney at last, moving from the window, 'I think the show's over for tonight, whatever it was! Mr King's disappeared, and the noises off have stopped. Let's go and explore downstairs and see if we can find out what made them.'

Snubby was horrified. What! Go down in the dark and snoop about to see what made those terrifying noises? Barney must be mad. He clutched at his arm.

'No, Barney! Let's go upstairs and lock ourselves in!'

'You go,' said Barney. 'Take Loony with you. I'll go and explore myself.'

But poor Snubby didn't dare to go upstairs by himself – no, not even with Loony at his heels! He thought that of the two evils, going with Barney was the lesser – he couldn't possibly go anywhere by himself at the moment!

Feeling very panicky Snubby went down the stairs with Barney. Loony pressed against his heels, and that was comforting. Snubby wished he were a dog too. Dogs never seemed really afraid!

'I think the noises came from the kitchen part,' said Barney, in a whisper. 'Let's just stand here in the hall and listen once more.'

They stood there – and then, to Snubby's horror something touched his hair! He almost yelled in fright. Then the something *pulled* his hair – and Snubby nearly died with relief. It was only Miranda putting out her paw from where she sat on Barney's shoulder, and being affectionate!

They went into the great kitchens. Barney switched on his torch, and the beam played over the room in front of them. Shadows seemed to flee into the corners as the beam of light moved round the room. Snubby trembled and Barney felt him.

'You frightened?' he said in surprise. 'Don't worry, Snubby. Miranda and Loony would soon let us know if there was anyone near. There can't be anyone about now or Miranda would chatter and Loony would growl.'

That was true. Snubby felt relieved at once. There was nothing to be seen in the great kitchens at all. The beam of light travelled over the floor and showed footmarks – but only those of the children and the dog, where they had once gone across the rooms. No other footsteps showed at all.

'Nobody has been here,' whispered Barney and he went into the scullery. This was a big room with a pump for water as well as taps in a sink. Nobody had been there either. Not even the children's footsteps showed here in the dust on the floor. They had never been into the scullery.

It was very puzzling. How could people make loud noises downstairs and yet leave no footmarks or any sign of having been there?

'It's a bit spooky, isn't it?' said Snubby at last. Barney laughed.

'Don't you believe it! Those noises were made by people – there was nothing spooky about them. Surely you don't believe in spooks! What a baby you are!'

'Well – it's all jolly funny,' said Snubby. 'All those noises – and nothing to show for it. Not even a footmark! Can you tell me how anyone could make such a row down here, and yet not leave the dust disturbed?'

'No, I can't,' said Barney. 'But I'm going to find out! That's quite certain. There's something strange about all this – very strange – and I'm going to solve the mystery!'

'Do you think Mr King's in it, whatever it is?' asked Snubby.

Barney considered. 'I shouldn't be surprised,' he said. 'Ask him a few questions tomorrow, Snubby, and see what he says. Ask him if he slept well – ask him if he heard any noises in the night – ask him if he ever walks in his sleep!'

Snubby grinned in the dark. 'Right! I'll just see what he says! I say, is the show really over now, Barney? I'm frightfully sleepy.'

'Yes – it seems to be over,' said Barney. 'Come on, Miranda – to bed! Are you really going to sleep here tonight, Snubby?'

'Well, nothing would make me go back to Rockingdown Cottage in the dark tonight,' said Snubby. 'Can you make room on your bed for me?'

'I suppose that means Loony too!' said Barney. 'Yes, I expect the bed will take four of us. Come on!'

They went upstairs again, carefully locking the passage door and the nursery doors, and went into the little third room. Snubby felt sure it would take him ages to go to sleep – but his eyes shut tight as soon as his head was on the pillow. And there the four of them slept soundly till the morning – Miranda cuddled in Barney's neck and Loony on Snubby's feet – what a bedful!

Chapter Fifteen

Snubby is a Nuisance

Snubby was up and about very early, anxious to be back at the cottage before anyone else was up. Barney went with him and sat in the tumbledown summer-house. Snubby promised to see if he could manage to smuggle him out some breakfast.

But Mrs Round caught sight of Miranda outside the summer-house as she hurried to the cottage to do her morning work and get breakfast. She peeped in and saw Barney.

'Ah – another one to breakfast, I suppose!' she said. Barney grinned. He and Mrs Round understood one another. He often did little odd jobs for her – unstopping her sink when it got stopped up, putting up a new clothes-line for her and so on. She thought, he was a very handy, obliging boy, though she couldn't bear Miranda.

Barney had breakfast with everyone else. Miss Pepper didn't mind. One more didn't make much difference, and Barney seemed a nice boy, if a little strange. Mr King was there too, looking a little tired. He came in very late for breakfast.

Snubby was ready and waiting for him. He had told Diana and Roger the happenings of the night before, and they had listened, thrilled and astonished.

'Lucky fellow – having all that fun with Barney in the middle of the night!' said Roger. Snubby didn't tell him how frightened he had been – now that it was daylight and the sun was shining brilliantly he quite forgot how his teeth had chattered and his hair had stood on end.

He was boastful and brave now – aha, he had had a marvellous night whilst the others had been fast asleep in bed!

They had been amazed to hear that Mr King had been on the prowl in the night too. Roger whistled. 'What on earth was he up to? He's a dark horse, isn't he? Why didn't he say anything about it?'

Mr King made his apologies for coming late to breakfast and helped himself to cornflakes. Snubby began at once.

'Did you have a bad night, Mr King?'

Mr King looked surprised at this concern on Snubby's part. 'No,' he said. 'I had a very good one, thank you.'

'I didn't,' said Snubby. 'I was awake a lot. Didn't you hear noises in the night?'

Mr King looked rather startled. He glanced at the innocent-looking Snubby.

'What noises?' he said, cautiously.

'Oh – just noises,' said Snubby. 'Perhaps you slept too well to hear anything, Mr King.'

'I certainly slept very well – in fact, as you know, I *over*-slept,' said Mr King. 'Miss Pepper, will you have the mustard?'

Snubby wasn't going to have the subject changed like that. He persisted with his questions.

'I thought I heard somebody about last night. It might have been somebody walking in their sleep. Do *you* ever walk in your sleep, Mr King?'

'Never,' said Mr King, shortly. 'These are very nice sausages Miss Pepper.'

'I wonder who it was getting up in the night,' said Snubby, innocently. 'Did you, Roger? Did you, Diana?'

'*We* didn't,' said Roger and Diana, enjoying all this baiting of poor Mr King.

'And you didn't either, did you, Mr King?' said Snubby,

turning to him. 'Unless you were walking in your sleep, of course.'

'I've already told you I don't walk in my sleep,' said Mr King, exasperated. 'Now, will you kindly let me talk to Miss Pepper? If this is your latest idea of being funny, think of something else. It's puerile.'

'What's puerile?' asked Snubby at once.

'I'll tell you in your Latin lesson,' said Mr King, in a voice that promised a very harassing lesson for Snubby that morning. 'Though I should have thought you already knew what "puer" meant. It's a pity you're so backward.'

Snubby winked at the others. He had found out what he wanted to know. Mr King wasn't going to admit that he had been out last night – that was his own business evidently. He was going to keep it a secret – which probably meant he was going snooping again sometime. It would be fun to keep an eye on him in that case.

'Are you going for a walk today?' asked Snubby, addressing himself to Mr King again. 'Can I come with you?'

'I *am* going for a walk – but I certainly don't want you with me in your present tiresome mood,' said Mr King. Snubby at once made up his mind to follow him on his walk. Loony, who was under the table, quietly began to chew Mr King's shoelace. Miranda had been left in the shed in case she and Loony started one of their mad games with one another.

Snubby was even more tiresome in lessons than he had been at breakfast. He was told to make up three sentences and write them down in French. He produced the following sentences and read them out gleefully.

'Ils étaient de bruits dans la nuit – There were noises in the night.'

'Je me promene dans mon sommeil – I walk in my sleep.'

'Je ne parle toujours le vrai – I do not always speak the truth.'

Mr King listened to these peculiar sentences in silence. He looked consideringly at Snubby and seemed about to break out angrily. Then he apparently changed his mind.

'Full of the most elementary mistakes,' he said coldly. 'Please write three more. If those are also full of mistakes you can write yet another three.'

Snubby decided not to bait Mr King any more. He wrote three innocent French sentences which were perfectly correct in every way. This was not surprising as he had taken them from his French book. Mr King did not seem to be up to little tricks of this sort. Snubby wished fervently that his French master at school could be taken in so easily. Unfortunately Monsieur Rieu was apt to smell out a trick before it was even played.

After dinner the children met together in the summer-house. They giggled when they talked about Snubby's cheekiness that morning. 'All the same, Mr King's pretty peculiar,' said Roger. 'Why all the secrecy about his prowling? He could easily have said that he couldn't sleep and went for a walk.'

'I'm going to track him this afternoon,' said Snubby. 'Aren't we, Loony, old chap?'

Loony agreed eagerly, leaping up on Snubby's knee and licking his nose lavishly. He then tried to lie on his back, fell off with a bump, saw Miranda and raced after her till she bounded up a tree and sat there chattering at him.

'The names Miranda calls him!' said Barney, pretending to be shocked. 'Wherever did she learn them!'

Mr King set off on his walk at half-past two, taking with him a map and a stick. Snubby, who was on the watch, let him get a good way ahead and then went quietly after him. Loony, having been told to keep quiet, nosed along at his heels.

Mr King struck across country towards the river. Snubby was a little disappointed. He had hoped that he would go snooping round the old mansion again. If so he might possibly get in, as the veranda door was not locked. Most unfortunately the key would not lock it from the outside.

Snubby followed Mr King carefully, occasionally sinking down flat with Loony if the tutor stopped, or looked round. This caused great astonishment to an old lady who was near Snubby when he did one of his disappearing acts. He lay down flat, hissing to Loony to lie down too. The old lady went up in concern.

'Are you all right, little boy?' she said. 'Do you feel ill?'

'Sssssst!' said Snubby, annoyed. He crawled sideways into the hedge like a crab and the old lady looked at him in alarm. The boy must be mad. Then an idea came to her.

'Are you playing Red Indians?' she asked.

Mr King had now walked on. Snubby got up cautiously and stalked down the other side of the hedge. 'I'm Chief Redfeather,' he said to the relieved old lady. 'Be careful of my men. Don't let them scalp you, whatever you do!'

He left the old lady looking out for his 'men', and went on after Mr King, frightening several cows by suddenly flattening himself out on the ground whenever Mr King stopped again to consider his way. Snubby thoroughly enjoyed himself. He was getting his own back nicely on Mr King.

They came to the river eventually. Mr King glanced at his map again and then made his way up the river. There was a very wild part just there, and both Mr King and his pupil found the going difficult. In fact Snubby, having

107

fallen into a marshy piece two or three times, and having had to haul poor Loony out of the mud at least six times, almost gave up.

Steep hills now rose up on one side of the river. A stream came into it from the east, and to Snubby's surprise Mr King now left the main river and began to follow the stream. Poor Snubby groaned. This was much worse than he had imagined. It must already be nearly tea-time – and there was all that way to go back!

To make matters worse, Mr King suddenly sat down on a nice dry spot, pulled out a packet from his pocket, and opened it, displaying a very fine array of sandwiches and cake! Snubby could have cried! Why hadn't he had the sense to find out if Mr King meant to get back to tea or not?

He had to lie under a rather prickly bush and watch Mr King devour every sandwich and two pieces of Mrs Round's fruit cake. Loony whined when the smell wafted towards him on the wind. He thought his little master was extremely foolish not to have brought something to eat too. Snubby saw Mr King raise his head when he heard the whine, and he hissed at the surprised spaniel.

'Shut up, idiot! Not a word!'

Loony looked at his master for a moment, made up his mind that Snubby was temporarily mad, and curled himself up in disgust to go to sleep. Snubby was very glad when Mr King folded up his sandwich papers and put them back into his pocket. Now perhaps he would go home!

But he didn't. He followed the stream instead, and Snubby had to give up the chase because the country was now too bare for him to follow without being seen. All that way for nothing!

Wait a minute, though. Mr King was standing still now, looking with great interest at something. What was it?

Snubby was full of curiosity. He saw Mr King bend down to the stream and touch something. Then he bent very low, almost disappeared, and remained practically out of sight for a few minutes. He then reappeared again, and took out some field glasses. He swept the countryside with them. What could he be looking for? And what had he found in the stream? Snubby made up his mind to go and see, even if it made him hours late for supper!

Chapter Sixteen

Snubby is Not Very Clever

Mr King at last went off in another direction altogether, much to Snubby's surprise. He took a look at his map and set off to the south, across rough country – hilly country too. Snubby who hadn't the faintest idea where he was, and felt that he was miles from home, looked after Mr King with exasperation.

'Now where's he going? What a wild goose chase this is!'

He waited till Mr King was out of sight behind a small clump of trees and then went as quickly as he could to where he had seen him stop by the stream. There was a tiny creek there – a little backwater, with trees and bushes overhanging. Pulled right back in the creek, almost hidden under a bush was a boat. It had no name. A couple of oars lay in it, and a coil of rope. Nothing else. How mysterious!

Snubby gazed at the lonely little boat. Who owned it? There didn't appear to be a house within miles. What a strange thing to leave a boat here, on this stream, hidden like that. Why? Who used it? And where did the owner live? Snubby wished he had field glasses like Mr King. Then he could have swept the countryside with them and found out if any cottage or house was hidden in a corner of the hills.

By the time he had finished examining the boat, which told him absolutely nothing, Mr King had completely disappeared. Snubby couldn't see a sign of him anywhere. He looked down at the patient spaniel.

'Could you track him, Loony, do you think?' he asked. 'Then we could follow him without getting lost.'

Loony looked up intelligently and wagged his tail. 'All right – track him then,' said Snubby, waving his hand vaguely in the direction in which Mr King had gone.

Loony started off eagerly, for all the world as if he knew exactly what Snubby meant. Snubby was delighted.

'He's the cleverest dog that was ever born,' he said to himself, as he followed after the pattering spaniel. But when Loony had led him to eight rabbit-holes in succession, he began to change his mind.

'You're daft,' he said to Loony, gloomily. 'Do you really think I said "find rabbit-holes"? Do use a little common sense, Loony.'

Loony barked and wagged his tail, and started off to find yet another hole. But Snubby had had enough. He was tired, muddy, hungry and thirsty. In addition he felt most annoyed with Mr King. His tracking had taught him nothing except that Mr King liked long and apparently aimless walks – and he had seen a hidden boat which didn't seem to belong to anyone at all. Mr King had enjoyed a jolly good tea and had now completely disappeared into the blue. Snubby would get lost if he tried to follow his trail. He must go back to the stream, follow it to the river, then follow the river to the part he knew, and so get home.

It seemed a long long way to poor Snubby and even Loony's heart sank as they began to stumble back down the marshy banks of the little stream.

Snubby didn't arrive home till eight o'clock. He found everyone in a terrible state about him, even Mr King. He glared at the tutor, feeling that it was all his fault he had had such a terrible afternoon and evening.

'How long have you been back?' he asked.

'Oh – since about half-past five,' said Mr King, to

Snubby's intense astonishment. Half-past five! Why, Mr King had got back from the stream in about half an hour then – or less. But how had he done it? Snubby couldn't make it out at all. He was almost in tears with tiredness and hunger.

Miss Pepper suddenly took pity on him and forgot her worry and anger over his being so late. She hustled him up to a hot bath, and got him to bed – then she brought up a dish of Mrs Round's delicious tomato soup, a plate of corned beef and salad and another plate of fresh peaches and cream. Snubby was in the seventh heaven of delight. What a feast! Honestly, it was worth going through those awful hours of hunger and thirst to get all this!

He said very little to Miss Pepper about his long absence. 'I went for a walk and lost my way,' he said. 'That's all.'

'Where did you go?' asked Mr King, curiously.

'I really don't know,' said Snubby, politely. 'Where did *you* go?'

'Oh, round and about,' said Mr King. 'But I was sensible – I took my tea with me. Pity you didn't come across me, I could have shared it with you.'

Snubby grinned to himself. Little did Mr King know that he had been hidden under a bush near enough to him to see what he ate! Not until Miss Pepper and Mr King had gone downstairs did Snubby tell the others exactly what had happened. They were very interested indeed.

'Fancy a boat there, hidden under the trees, with no visible owner anywhere,' said Roger. 'A mystery!'

'Yes. But what seems to be much *more* mysterious is how did Mr King get back here so quickly?' said Snubby. 'I mean – it took hours to *get* to that boat, you know –

and yet it seems only to have taken Mr King under half an hour to get back home!'

'Well – he must have taken a short cut back,' said Roger. 'Let's have a squint at a map and find out.'

He went downstairs, found a big map of the district, and put his finger on Rockingdown Village. 'Here we are – here's the village, see – and there's the way to the river. Now you went *up* the river, you say – like that.'

'Yes. And we came to a stream – quite a big one where it entered the river,' said Snubby, stabbing a piece of corned beef with his fork. 'Is the stream shown?'

'Yes, here it is – Rockingham Stream,' said Roger. 'You say you went up it a good way – right, here we go,' and he ran his finger up the stream.

Diana gave an exclamation. 'Well! It's quite easy to see how Mr King got home so quickly! Look – he had walked almost round in a circle – and by taking a short cut across this hill, he came out quite near Rockingdown Cottage. See – it's hardly any distance.'

Diana was right. Because of the way the river curved, Snubby had walked in a half circle, and then up the stream, which made a three-quarter circle – and the other quarter of the circle lay over the hill to Rockingdown Cottage. Easy!

Snubby let out a long sigh. 'Gosh! I was certainly a prize idiot! There I was, only a little way from here, and I go and walk miles and miles the long way round. But I didn't know.'

'You want to take a compass with you,' said Roger. 'Anyway, if you want us to see the boat, it won't take long to get there – we'll take this path here, and go over the hill, across this bit of marsh to the stream – and the boat will be somewhere there!'

It all looked very easy and simple, when the map lay before them. Snubby felt really exasperated when he saw what a long and unnecessary walk home he had had. What a lover of walks Mr King must be to struggle along through marshy ground and overgrown paths, up the stream! Well, it was the last time he would ever do any tracking. Mr King could go walking every day if he wanted to – but as far as Snubby was concerned he would go alone!

Snubby fell asleep immediately after he had finished his supper. What with his disturbed night, and his long and tiresome walk, he was tired out. There were going to be no excursions for him tonight!

Barney played a game with Roger and Diana till it was time for them to go to bed. The map they had all been looking at lay unheeded on a nearby table.

Barney, who was out of the game for one or two turns, glanced idly at the map. His eye followed the river – then followed the stream – and he looked at it, puzzled.

'Here's a funny thing!' he said to the others, suddenly. 'Look!'

'What?' said Diana, throwing the dice out of the shaker. 'A six – good! Just what I wanted.'

'Look,' went on Barney. 'See this stream? The one where Snubby found the boat. Look where it goes.'

They all looked. 'Well, I don't see anything wonderful about it,' said Roger. 'It just runs close by Rockingdown Manor – then goes off northwards to those hills – where it apparently has its source.'

'Yes – but don't you *see*,' said Barney. 'Have you ever seen any stream in the grounds at all? The old house is set right in the middle of very big grounds. Well, this map apparently shows the stream very close to the house indeed – but you know as well as I do that there is no stream to be found here in these grounds.'

The others stopped their game and looked more closely. Yes – it certainly seemed as if the stream ran very

114

close to the house indeed. The map was on a large scale and the stream was shown, or seemed to be shown, actually in the grounds.

And yet what Barney said was quite true. None of them had seen any stream in the grounds at all, and yet they had explored them very thoroughly indeed.

Miranda dropped down on the map and they pushed her off. They were interested now. Where was the stream? They tried to figure it out.

'It's not near our cottage, that's certain. It's not anywhere near the village itself, or we'd have had to cross over a bridge or something. It must be on the other side of the old house. We'll look and see.'

'If it isn't it must simply have dried up or altered its course or something,' said Roger.

'We can easily find out,' said Barney.

'How?' asked Diana.

'Use your brains!' said Roger.

'Oh, of course, we can follow the stream all the way up from the river!' said Diana. 'I never thought of that. How stupid of me!'

'Yes. We can easily follow it and see what its course is,' said Barney. 'Not that it matters really. I was just suddenly interested to notice how near it came to the old house, when I was looking at the map.'

The subject was dropped and a new game begun. Miss Pepper put her head in at the study after a while. 'Barney, it's time you went. It's raining hard. Is it far for you to go to your lodgings?'

Miss Pepper thought Barney had lodgings somewhere. He had told her he had a room to sleep in and she imagined it was one in the village. Nobody undeceived her. They couldn't possibly tell her where Barney really slept.

'No. Not far, Miss Pepper,' said Barney, rising to go.

He really had very good manners. 'I'll be seeing you tomorrow,' he said to Diana and Roger. 'So long!'

He went off with Miranda as usual on his shoulder, Loony escorting him to the door, sending a few barks after him, which were really meant for Miranda. 'Good riddance to bad rubbish!' was what his barks meant. Then back he trotted to the others, pleased with himself.

Barney went cautiously through the grounds, wondering if Mr King – or anyone else – was about. But he saw no one. All the same, he locked the veranda door *and* the passage door too – he didn't mean to be disturbed in the middle of the night again!

Chapter Seventeen

Barney Does Some Exploring

All the same, it was a very disturbing night for Barney. He was awakened suddenly by Miranda chattering to him in fright, pulling at his hair and ears. He took her in his arms and sat up in bed.

Bang! Thud!

There were the noises again. Blow! What *was* going on in this empty old house? Should he get up and see, or should he lie down and sleep again? Apparently nothing happened except noises. There was nobody actually *in* the house, otherwise there would be strange footprints as well as their own.

The noises came again, and then the strange whining, half-screeching sound. Miranda was absolutely terrified. She tried to get inside Barney's shirt, and made little whining noises of fear. He comforted her automatically, listening hard. What was making those noises? And where were they being made? They simply *must* be inside the house!

Barney sighed. He was tired after his disturbed night the night before, and he dearly wanted to go to sleep. But he felt intensely curious about all this. He was not in the least frightened, and he threw off the blanket and went across the room feeling for the door. He did not put on his torch for fear of the light being seen by anyone who might perhaps be outside.

Miranda tried to pull him back. She leapt down to the floor and pulled at his legs, chattering wildly. Barney laughed. 'You'll be all right with me, Miranda. I'm not afraid! Don't be a little idiot. Now – be quiet, or you'll be heard.'

He went down the passage and unlocked the door there quietly. He wondered how the person or persons who made those noises could possibly get into the house – and if they did where were the footmarks they made? He gave it up. It was a real puzzle.

'I'll solve it somehow though,' thought Barney. 'I don't know what's going on, but something is! And what's more I believe that Mr King's in it too, whatever it is. Maybe he can get into the house somewhere we haven't found – and it's he who makes those extraordinary noises.'

Thud! Thud! There it went again, deep down in the house. One thud was so loud that Barney was really startled.

He went right down to the kitchen, feeling his way cautiously, not daring to put on his torch. All was quiet there. Barney switched his torch on and off very swiftly, gazing at the floor as he did so. No fresh footprints were there, nobody had been in the kitchen.

He went to the scullery. No footprints there either. And yet it honestly seemed as if the noises came from this direction. As he stood there, waiting, a noise came again.

Thud! Thud! And then the whining sound, and an odd guttural noise that Barney hadn't heard before. He felt a moment's fear. That was a strange noise – what could it be? It didn't sound at all human. Could there be dungeons or something under the scullery floor? Was the house old enough for those? What about cellars? Where were they? There must be plenty in an old house of this kind.

Barney wondered why he hadn't thought of cellars before. They ought to be explored! Probably the explanation of the noises lay in the cellars.

He went through the scullery and came to some stone-paved outhouses – one was a washhouse, the other must have been a dairy at one time. It had shelves of marble all round to hold pans of cream.

His torch swung over the floor and the beam showed up dust again. Not a footprint anywhere! Not even Loony's. The doors to the outhouses had been shut, so Loony hadn't gone through them. Barney looked carefully over the floor. He found what he was seeking – a square place where a trap door lay, its handle sunk into a groove of the wood, so that no one would trip over it.

That's where the cellars would be – under there. Well, he wasn't going down there tonight. Whatever was going on could go on without him. Fearless as Barney was he had no wish to explore dark cellars at that moment – especially cellars that gave out such peculiar noises!

He would tell the children in the morning and they would all do a little more exploring. It would be exciting! Barney went back to bed, yawning. A few more noises came up to him as he lay in bed, but he took no notice of them. Miranda didn't either. She was cuddled up to him half asleep, her tiny front paws round his neck.

In the morning Barney told the children what he had heard, and how he had gone into the outhouses and seen the trap door.

'The washhouse and the dairy open out of one side of the scullery,' he said. 'We've never been into them. There's a trapdoor in the dairy – I bet it leads down to cellars. We'll explore there this afternoon. I'm sure there's something peculiar going on in there, though I can't for the life of me imagine what it is!'

This was so thrilling that nobody could pay much attention to their coaching that morning. Fortunately Mr King seemed a little bored with it too, and appeared to be working out calculations of his own on a sheet of paper.

Loony crept in unnoticed and lay at Snubby's feet. He

119

began to gnaw the edge of the tablecloth that hung just by his nose. He made a chewy kind of noise and Mr King looked up.

'Stop making that silly noise, Snubby,' he said. Snubby hastily kicked Loony to stop him chewing, and there was peace again. Everyone was thankful when the morning came to an end. Mr King noticed with a start that Loony had apparently suddenly materialised under the table, and was just about to make a stern remark about it, when Snubby fell on Loony and fondled him extravagantly.

'How did you know we'd just finished! How clever of you to come in just at the right moment! Mr King, wasn't he clever to know it was the right minute to come in?'

Mr King said nothing. He just looked sternly at Loony and even more sternly at Snubby. Before he could make up his mind exactly how to answer Snubby, the boy rushed from the room with Loony, yelling like a Red Indian. 'Come on, Loony, walkie-walks!'

The other three children grinned at one another. They had known perfectly well that Loony was under the table all the morning, and had wondered when Mr King would find it out.

'Can Barney stay to lunch, Miss Pepper, can he, can he?' shouted Snubby, was always yelled at the top of his voice for about ten minutes after finishing his coaching. 'It's cold chicken and salad and Roundy says there is enough.'

'All right, all right,' said Miss Pepper, putting her hands over her ears. 'Why must you shout so? And didn't I tell you to go upstairs after breakfast and change out of that disgustingly dirty shirt?'

'Oh – so you did,' said Snubby. 'Well, need I now? I shall probably get awfully dirty this afternoon.'

'Why? What are you going to do?' asked Miss Pepper.

'You came home filthy yesterday too. Is it *necessary* to do all the dirty things you seem to do?'

'Yes – it's absolutely necessary,' Snubby assured her cheerfully. 'Well, I won't change my shirt then. I don't want Roundy to have any more washing to do. I wish I was like Loony, and just wore my own coat of hair and nothing else.'

'You wouldn't manage to keep yourself as clean as Loony does, even then,' said Miss Pepper. 'I really do think you are the most filthy dirty child I have ever . . .'

'Dear old Pep!' said the irrepressible Snubby and swung her round, trying to do a foxtrot with her.

She was half cross, half amused.

Mr King came in suddenly, looking as black as thunder. 'Snubby! Did you tie that bit of string between the gateposts in the garden? I've almost broken my ankle over it. Miss Pepper, I'm going to buy a cane this afternoon – a nice thin one that goes wheeeee in the air.'

'Do,' said Miss Pepper. 'Lend it to me to use some time will, you?'

Snubby didn't like this. It wasn't good when Miss Pepper and Mr King both sided against him. He looked pained. 'I'm sorry, Mr King. I was practising jumping. You must have fallen over my jumping-string.'

'Snubby, that kind of thing is stupid and dangerous,' said Miss Pepper. 'I shall make you go without your pudding at dinner today. I've told you before about dangerous tricks. I will not have them played.'

'Aha – no pudding for you then,' said Mr King, pleased. 'Serves you right, you little pest.'

Snubby lost his high spirits and looked sulky. He couldn't do anything if both Mr King and Miss Pepper were in league against him. There were all sorts of nasty punishments they could think up. He scowled at their retreating backs.

121

'I'll have to set them against one another,' he thought and sat down to worry out a plan. It didn't take him long. He went into the kitchen and got the kitchen pepper-pot when Mrs Round's back was turned. He slipped it into his pocket. He tiptoed out again, Loony sniffing at his pocket. Then the spaniel suddenly sneezed.

'Pepper up your nose?' said Snubby, loudly, so that Miss Pepper could hear. 'Poor little dog. Pepper's awful, isn't it?'

Dinner was soon ready. There were big bowls of steaming pea soup. Mrs Round was good at making soup, and she knew the children liked it. It filled them up too, when there wasn't much meat to go round, like today.

Snubby had a few words with Roger, who grinned and nodded. They all sat down. Roger tasted his soup.

'Wants salt and pepper,' he said. 'Pass the pepper, Di. Mr King, will you have some?'

Just as Mr King took up the pepper pot to sprinkle a little on his soup, Snubby left his place and went to pick up his table napkin ring. As he passed behind the unsuspecting Mr King he whipped the kitchen pepper pot from his pocket and tossed pepper round Mr King's head.

Miss Pepper didn't notice anything. Nor did poor Mr King. He finished sprinkling pepper and salt on his soup, and was about to take up his spoon when he felt an enormous sneeze coming. He got out his handkerchief hastily.

'Whooooosh – oo! I beg your pardon, Miss Pepper. A – Whooooosh – oo! Oh dear me! Here's another one coming. Really – I – whooooosh – oo!'

Miss Pepper looked at him. What an extraordinary paroxysm of sneezing! Mr King was now purple in the face, wondering whether to leave the room or not.

'A – whooooosh – ooosh – oo!' he began again. 'I do apologise. It must be a little pepper up my nose!'

The children roared with laughter. Good old Mr King! He had said the exact words that Miss Pepper hated.

Miss Pepper looked at Mr King coldly. How dare he make fun of her like this – in front of the children too. She didn't believe in his sneezes at all, now that he had said the fatal words. 'Perhaps you would like to leave the room till your er – indisposition is over?' she said, in an icy voice.

Mr King got up and went. The children heard him still coping with his sneezes in the bedroom above, and Diana was almost helpless with laughter. Every time she ate a spoonful of soup she laughed and choked. Miss Pepper got really angry.

'Now stop it, Diana. It's an old joke now and a silly one, this pepper joke. It's not even funny.'

Snubby made his face solemn. 'I think it was rude of Mr King to say that in front of you,' he said, righteously.

'I mean – it's all very well for *us* to say silly things like that, Miss Pepper – but Mr King shouldn't forget his manners, should he?'

'That's enough,' said Miss Pepper. 'Not a word more from you. And when Mr King comes back we shall not refer to this again.'

Mr King came back shortly looking very sheepish, not understanding his fit of sneezing at all. He was upset to find Miss Pepper so cold to him. Was she cross because of his sneezing at table? Well, anybody might do that! Sneezes were like hiccups – you just couldn't stop them.

The meat course came in and then the pudding. Snubby was supposed to go without – but because Miss Pepper was still annoyed with Mr King she quite forgot to leave Snubby out when she served the pudding – and he got his usual big helping.

And poor Mr King, who remembered about it, didn't

dare to remind Miss Pepper! Snubby grinned. He had got
on top as usual.

Chapter Eighteen

A Very Exciting Afternoon

The exploration that afternoon proved very interesting indeed. They all arrived at Rockingdown Manor at just after half-past two, full of anticipation. What would they find in the cellar?

Snubby had forgotten his fears of a night or two ago. He was once again brave and fearless, entering the old house first of all, and even shouting loudly in it to make the echoes come.

Barney laughed at him. Snubby always amused him with his silly tricks and ridiculous ways. They all went to the big kitchens and out into the scullery. Then through the door that let into the outhouses. The washhouse first and then the dairy with its marble shelves.

'Here we are,' said Barney. 'And look, there's the trap-door. I bet that leads down into the cellars. And I bet they're pretty big ones too.'

Roger took the iron handle and gave it a tug. Nothing happened at all.

'It'll be stiff,' said Barney. 'It can't have been used for years. Let me try.'

He couldn't budge the trapdoor either. Loony went and scraped madly at it as if he could open it that way. They all sat back and panted after their exertions.

'Where's that rope we had?' said Barney, suddenly. 'Let me see – what did I do with it? I believe it's upstairs in the nurseries, Snubby. Go and get it.'

Snubby shot off with Loony – but when he got to the passage door, he heard noises beyond. He stopped, frightened. Who was it? He tore down the stairs again and into the dairy. 'There's somebody upstairs. I heard them.'

'Don't be silly,' said Barney. 'You're a little coward, Snubby! There's nobody there.'

'There *is* I tell you – I heard them,' said Snubby. Barney got up.

'I'll go,' he said, and up he went. He came down with the rope – and with Miranda too. He was grinning.

'It was Miranda up there,' he said. 'She'd got a box of skittles and was throwing them all over the place. That's what you heard. Baby!'

Snubby went very red. The others laughed at him whilst Barney slid the rope through the handle of the trap door. He twisted the two strands into one.

'Here you are,' he said to the other three. 'Take hold, all of you, and we'll pull together. Miranda, you pull too!'

So, with Miranda pulling as well, and looking extremely proud, the children pulled together with all their might.

And, of course, the trap door opened so very suddenly that they all sat down in a heap, and Roger, who was last, got a terrific bump that shook all the breath out of him!

They got up and went to peer into the dark hole under the trapdoor.

'Steps,' said Roger. 'Stone steps. They go down to the cellars, no doubt about that. Got the torch, Barney?'

'I'll go first,' said Barney, and down he went, flashing the torch carefully in front of him. The steps curved a little towards the bottom and ended in a stone floor. Barney felt it with his feet to see if it were slimy. No, it was quite dry.

A musty smell of old casks and barrels came to his nose. He flashed his torch round. It was, as he had suspected, a most enormous cellar. Boxes, casks, barrels, old cobwebbed bottles lay about everywhere. Wooden shelves showed where wine had once been stored.

Everyone was now down the steps. Miranda would not leave Barney's shoulder, and held on to his hair as he made his way into the depths of the cellar. The others followed, flashing their torches too. Loony, surprised at this new place so unexpectedly opened in the depths of the earth, ran about sniffing. Any rabbits down here? Not even a smell of one!

The children explored the old cellars from end to end. They opened the old boxes but found nothing in any of them. They knocked on the casks and barrels and decided they were absolutely empty. 'Not even a full bottle of gingerbeer,' said Snubby, mournfully. 'Very dull.'

Mice or rats scurried away into corners as the torches lighted them up. Loony had a lovely time chasing them, and got a bite on the ear. Miranda wouldn't chase rats. Loony got a rat in a corner behind a cask, and began to scrape there after it. The cask fell, and three more fell too, making a terrific noise in the old cellars. Everyone jumped.

'It's only Loony,' said Roger, relieved. 'I say, Barney – I wish we could hear those strange noises now. We should know what part of the cellar they came from.'

'I think it's very strange,' came Barney's voice from another corner. 'There doesn't seem to be anything here to account for those noises at all – and honestly I can't see any signs of people being here – there's dust in quite a lot of places, but no footprints again – no cigarette ends – nothing!'

'Well – how can we solve the mystery?' demanded Snubby.

'I think I shall come down here one night when I hear the noises and watch,' said Barney. 'Or better still I could hide myself *before* the noises begin.'

'Would you *dare*?' said Snubby, in horror. 'Gracious, you must be brave.'

'Yes, I certainly wouldn't dare to do that,' said Diana, soberly. 'Would you, Roger?'

Roger thought about it. 'No, I don't think I would,' he said. 'And what's more I don't think you'd better, Barney.'

'Well, I'm going to,' said Barney. 'I can't make all this out. I'm going to find out what's going on.'

They sat silent for a few minutes on one or two old boxes whilst Loony snuffled round them. Barney pricked up his ears. 'Can you hear anything?' he asked the others.

They listened. 'Well,' said Diana doubtfully, 'I *think* I can hear a little noise occasionally – but I don't quite know how to describe it – rather a *gurgly* sort of noise!'

This didn't please Snubby at all. He got up. He had no wish to hear any noises, least of all 'gurgly' ones. Anyway he was tired of this awful dark, musty cellar. He wanted to be out in the daylight again.

'Come on – don't let's listen for gurgles or gobbles or guzzles,' he said. 'Let's go.'

The others laughed and got up too. Barney listened for a moment or two more and gave it up. 'Probably my imagination,' he said.

They went up the stone steps, chattering, with Loony bounding in front. At the top he stopped and growled. The children ceased talking at once and Diana clutched Barney. Now what?

There was the sound of men's voices! 'Did we lock that veranda door?' whispered Roger. 'Gosh – we didn't! What idiots! Now someone has got in!'

'I'll go and see,' whispered Barney. 'Keep Loony back and don't let him growl or bark, or he'll give us away.'

Snubby put a hand on Loony's collar and the dog stopped his low growling. Barney went quietly through the outhouse and into the scullery. He stopped and listened. Nobody was in the kitchen beyond. He went to the kitchen door and peered through the crack of the door' there into the hall.

What he saw surprised him very much! Mr King was there with two other men. Both were strong, burly men, and had their backs to Barney. They were talking together.

'See all these footprints?' Mr King was saying. 'That tells you something, doesn't it! We'll have to find out whose they are. And who left the veranda door ajar too? Look at the footmarks going up the stairs. Crowds of them! Looks as if there are troops of people using this place for their own purposes! And yet there's never anyone to be found here when I come – and not a light to be seen anywhere. Where do they go?'

'Beats me,' said one of the men. 'Anyway this is the place all right. We'll get going now, no doubt about that.'

Barney had heard enough. He slipped back to the others. 'It's Mr King – with two others,' he whispered. 'I don't believe they're up to any good here, really. There's some strange plan or something going on – and Mr King's in it. I don't believe he's a tutor at all. He's a fraud!'

This was amazing news. Diana clutched at Barney. 'Will they find us down here? What shall we do?'

'We'll get out, shut the trapdoor, and steal out of the kitchen door,' said Barney. 'We can take the kitchen key, so that we can get in again if we want to. You can bet anything you like that those fellows will search the house now to find out who's made those footprints everywhere – and when they go they will see that every door and window's fastened so that we can't get in again.'

'But we'll have the kitchen door key, so we can if we

129

want to!' said Snubby, trembling with excitement. 'Is it safe to go now?'

Barney went to see. He came back in half a minute. 'They've gone upstairs. I wonder if they know about those nurseries. Anyway the passage door is locked and I've got the key. They may think it's only boxrooms or something.'

'We'll steal out now then,' said Diana, who was very anxious to go. They all got out of the opening in the floor, and then quietly shut the trap door. They made their way into the kitchen, Loony as quiet as the others.

Over to the kitchen door they went – and Barney unlocked it. He took the key from the lock and opened the door. It creaked a little but not much. They all went out into an overgrown yard, where an old dustbin still stood. A dog kennel stood nearby, almost falling to bits. Loony went over to it and sniffed in it inquisitively. But there was no dog smell left.

Barney locked the door behind them. He put the key in his pocket. He looked up at the windows. Could anyone see them if they made a dash for it now? No. Trees overhung the backyard and screened it from overhead.

'Come on,' he said. 'We'll run for it now. Keep under bushes and trees and don't show yourselves at all.'

They ran from the back door, across the yard and into the bushes. There had once been a kitchen garden on the other side of the yard, but it was so overgrown with weeds that it would have been impossible to know what it was now, if it had not been for the apple trees showing here and there, struggling against the ivy that was slowly choking everything.

The children soon found a part of the grounds they knew and quickly made their way home, astonished and puzzled. Was Mr King really a fraud? Ought they to tell Miss Pepper? What was he doing here? And what had

Rockingdown Manor and the peculiar noises to do with everything? It was all very puzzling indeed.

'I think we ought to tell Miss Pepper,' said Roger, at last. 'We'll sleep on it first – and then tell her in the morning.'

Chapter Nineteen

Mr King in Charge

But that night something happened which upset all their plans. A telephone call came to Miss Pepper and after she had answered it she came into the study, looking very upset.

'Children – I have to leave you for a few days. My sister is very ill – dangerously ill – and I must go to her. I must leave you in Mr King's charge. You will be quite all right, and I shall put you on your honour to be as good as you can.'

'Oh, Miss Pepper – I'm so sorry about your sister!' cried Diana. 'Is there anything we can do? Are you leaving to-night – or tomorrow morning?'

'Tonight, I think. Oh dear, I *can't* make up my mind what to do. Can I catch the last night-train, or not? There is my packing to do – and I must see Mrs Round before I go.'

'You can give me any messages for Mrs Round,' said Diana. 'You know I'll help her all I can. And I can do your packing for you too, if you'll put out the things you want. The boys can ring up for a taxi. You will easily be able to catch the night-train.'

'What a kind, good child you are!' said Miss Pepper, almost in tears. 'Very well. I'll go tonight. Come up and help me to pack whilst I tell you what I want you to say to Mrs Round.

Roger rang up for a taxi. Diana did the packing and listened to the instructions for Mrs Round. 'I'll telephone her tomorrow to tell her how things are getting on,' said

Miss Pepper. 'Did I pack my hairbrush? And a clean blouse? Now what have I done with those shoes?'

'They're in your hands, Miss Pepper,' said Diana, taking them from her. 'Now, do take things easily. You've plenty of time for your train – and I expect your sister will feel much better as soon as she sees you.'

'I must talk to Mr King too,' said Miss Pepper. 'Thank goodness I can leave him in charge of you. He seems very dependable and responsible.'

Diana said nothing to that. Because of what she now suspected about Mr King there didn't seem anything to say except things that would upset miss Pepper and probably upset her plans too! So she went on packing and made no remark.

Mr King came up to condole with Miss Pepper. He had been out for one of his walks. He was very sweet to her and she felt comforted.

'I feel quite safe to leave the children with you and Mrs Round,' she said. 'I only hope they'll behave themselves – but I think they will, Mr King. They always come out well in an emergency and are really very trustworthy.'

She went off in the taxi, still looking very worried. Everyone waved cheerily to her.

'Well!' said Mr King, shutting the door. 'Poor Miss Pepper! I hope everything goes all right for her. Now children – we've got to make the best of one another! You'll have to put up with me in charge of you!'

He beamed round at them. They looked away. 'Er – we shall do our best, Mr King,' said Roger, feeling that somebody certainly ought to say something. Mr King looked faintly surprised at the children's lack of response, but put it down to their being upset at Miss Pepper's sudden going.

He looked at his watch. 'My word – we *are* all late tonight!' he said. 'I think we ought to go to bed. Off with you! Lights out in ten minutes, please.'

The three of them had their lights out in ten minutes. They wondered about Barney. He wasn't going to sleep in the old house tonight. They had taken cushions and a rug to the old summer-house for him, hoping that it would not rain. The summer-house was not very weatherproof nowadays.

When they were sure that Mr King was in bed they stole down the back stairs to find Barney in the summer-house, and tell him the news about Miss Pepper's leaving.

'We haven't been able to tell Miss Pepper what we suspect,' finished Roger. 'That must wait till she comes back. In the meantime – we must keep our eyes and ears open!'

'I wonder if I ought to go back and sleep in the old house tonight,' said Barney. 'Just in case there's something being planned there by Mr King and the other men.'

'No don't,' said Roger. 'Mr King is indoors now – look, you can see his light through the curtains of his bedroom window. If he has any idea of wandering over to the mansion again tonight, he will have to pass near the summer-house – and then you can follow him.'

'Yes. There's something in that,' said Barney, snuggling down in his rug. 'I don't really feel like scrambling through the grounds again at the moment. I feel jolly sleepy.'

'Well, we'll go back now,' said the others. 'Good night Barney. See you tomorrow.'

It seemed strange without Miss Pepper the next day. Mrs Round arrived and heard the news. 'Dear, dear – she's so fond of her sister too,' she said. 'Well, we must hope for the best. Now you don't need to bother your heads about anything except just to do a bit of shopping for me now and again, and make your own beds and give a hand at times.'

They all had their coaching as usual, though Mr King seemed lost in thought. If they hadn't been on their honour to behave themselves they could have played any amount of tricks on the absent-minded tutor. But not even Snubby thought out any. Barney sat as usual in the window, listening. He looked earnestly at the back of Mr King's head and thought about him. What was he doing at Rockingdown Manor? What was he interested in there? It must be something important or he wouldn't have gone to the trouble of taking the job here as coach – which meant that he could live near the Manor, and find it easier to carry out his plans.

Barney couldn't imagine what those plans were. He wondered if by any chance the three men had done anything in the house after the children had escaped in such a hurry – had they hidden something there, perhaps? Or found something they were looking for?

He slipped out of the room before the end of the lesson.

He felt that he wanted to go and see if anything had been done at the old house – the men certainly hadn't got in for nothing.

He saw nothing at all on the ground floor except for the footmarks of the three men in every room. He took the trouble of going into the outhouses to see if the trap door had been discovered.

It was wide open! The wooden trap door was swung back, and the flight of stone steps was plainly to be seen.

Barney went to the open trap door. He listened. All was quiet below. There was no one down there now. But obviously the three men had been down to search for something.

He went up to the first floor and saw the prints of the men there, in every room. They had walked to every cupboard. Some of the doors were left open. What *could* they be looking for? A secret hiding-place?

Up the stairs to the second floor went the boy, feeling certain that the locked door at the end of the passage would have been opened.

It had been burst open! Somebody had either kicked it or flung himself hard against it. The old lock had given way, and the door was swinging wide open.

'Now my hiding-place is discovered!' thought Barney. He went into the nurseries. The three beds had been stripped and the covers thrown to the ground. The chests had been looked through, the cupboards opened. Even the linoleum in the day nursery had been taken up.

The rooms were in a dreadful state now. It would need a good morning's work from Diana to get them straight again. Barney wondered if it was safe for him to sleep there any more. Well, as long as the good weather lasted he could sleep comfortably in the old summer-house at Rockingdown Cottage.

It was all very puzzling. Barney made up his mind about one thing straight away. He would certainly go down into the cellars and wait for those noises that night! He meant to get to the bottom of those. Had the three men anything to do with them?

He went back to the children after he had bought himself some bread and cheese at the village shop. He gave Miranda some plums to eat. She liked those. She pulled each plum in half, took out the stone, threw it away, joined the halves together, and then nibbled the plum in delight.

'You want a bib, Miranda,' said Barney, with a laugh. 'Those plums are so juicy that you're getting sticky all down your chest!'

After his meal Barney went to see the children. He told them what he had discovered in the old house – the open trap door, the footmarks everywhere, the burst-open door, and the rifled nurseries. They listened in amazement.

'How *dare* Mr King do all that!' said Diana. 'After I'd made everything so tidy for you too. It's too bad. I've a good mind to tick him off.'

'No. Don't you say a word,' said Barney, quickly. 'Don't put him on his guard at all. As long as he thinks we don't suspect anything wrong about him he won't try to hide his doings. If he guesses what we know, he may go off – and whilst he is here we have at least got him under our eyes!'

'Yes, that's true,' said Diana. 'Well, I won't say a word. Barney, I hate the idea of your going to watch down in the cellars tonight. Wouldn't you like one of us with you?'

'Of course not!' said Barney with a laugh. 'What do you think could happen to me down there? Nothing, of course!'

But for once in a way Barney was wrong.

Chapter Twenty

Down in the Cellars

None of the three children at Rockingdown Cottage felt
very friendly towards Mr King, and he was puzzled. Even
Loony sat with his back to him whenever he could! The
spaniel always knew when Snubby was doubtful about
anyone, and if his master would not be friendly towards
someone, then Loony behaved in the same way.

Mr King looked at the children three or four times
during their midday meal. How odd they were all of a
sudden! Anyone would think he had offended them in
some way, he thought. They wouldn't look at him, and
hardly smiled at all. They hardly spoke to him either.

'Anything the matter?' he said at last. 'You seem to be
a very gloomy lot today. Are you worried about
something?'

'Well – yes,' said Diana. 'We're worried about Miss
Pepper's sister, of course.'

'Dear me – I didn't think you even knew her,' said Mr
King in astonishment. 'Well, do cheer up. I'm sure you'll
hear things are all right.'

Miss Pepper did ring up shortly after that, but the news
was not very good. Her sister was still very ill and Miss
Pepper didn't know when she would be back. 'But I'm
sure you'll be all right with Mr King,' she said. 'And Mrs
Round is very good too.'

Mr King kept trying to cheer the children up. He
offered to take them for a walk. He offered to fix up a
riding lesson for them. He even suggested going down to
the river to bathe as it was a hot day. In the ordinary way

the last two suggestions would have been hailed with glee – but nobody felt that they wanted to take any favours from Mr King at the moment. He was a fraud. They weren't going to like him any more. He was 'up to something,' and they wanted to know what!

Mr King gave up his efforts at last, decided that the children were sulky and cross, and could jolly well look after themselves. Loony annoyed him most. He couldn't believe that a dog would sit with his back to him on purpose, but it really did look as if Loony meant to!

Barney stayed to tea. The children had it out in the garden, hoping to get away from Mr King. But he most annoyingly came and had it with them. He seemed to feel that he must look after them every minute, now Miss Pepper was away. So the children couldn't talk freely at all, and Diana grew very sulky. She was the worst of them all at hiding her feelings.

'You really are a set of miseries!' said Mr King. 'Take that sulky look off your face, Diana – it doesn't suit you at all!'

Diana immediately looked twice as sulky. Barney felt that Mr King would really begin to suspect something if they all behaved like this, so he began to talk to the coach, relating all kinds of tales, and livening things up considerably. Miranda also did her best by behaving very badly with Loony – snatching away a biscuit Diana was giving him, and throwing plum stones at him.

Everyone laughed at her ridiculous antics except Loony, who was very hurt. Mr King felt quite relieved to find that they *could* laugh!

They escaped from the coach after tea, and went to the village to buy ice creams. The old lady in the general store seemed to keep her shop open till all hours at night, and it was possible to get ice creams from dawn to dark at her exciting little shop.

'Don't let's go back to supper till we've got to,' said Diana. 'I just can't bear Mr King now that I know he's a fraud. Let's go over the grounds and see if we can find that stream.'

'Oh yes – that's a good idea,' said Roger. 'I've been puzzling my head where it is. It's shown so very close to the old house on the map.'

They explored the grounds very thoroughly indeed, north, south, east and west – but there was no sign of a stream at all!

'There's not even a dried-up bed, or ditch,' said Roger, puzzled. 'The map must be wrong.'

'I suppose it must be,' said Barney. 'Anyway, as I said, we can always trace where it goes by following its course up from the river. Still – it's not important.'

'I don't like to think of you down in those cellars to-night,' began Diana again, as they made their way back to the cottage. 'I really don't. You'll take your rug and cushion down there with you, won't you? You may as well be comfortable. That floor will be hard and cold.'

'Yes. I'll take them,' said Barney. 'And look – I've bought myself a new torch – grand, isn't it!'

He showed his torch to them. It certainly was a nice one and gave out a very good light. 'I shall be all right with this!' he said.

Mrs Round had left enough supper for Barney, so he stayed. He always enjoyed his meals with the children. Afterwards they played a game, whilst Mr King read.

'I'd better be going,' said Barney at last. Mr King looked up.

'Where do you sleep at night?' he asked, and he spoke the words in such a pointed way that the children felt sure he suspected Barney of sleeping up in the nurseries of Rockingdown Manor.

'I slept in the summer house last night, sir,' said Barney,

140

politely. 'And last week I slept in the boat with a rug and a cushion. I haven't a proper home, and lodgings are expensive.'

'I see,' said Mr King. 'Well – so long as you don't get into mischief! I suppose you're sleeping in the summer-house again tonight as it's a hot night – well, look out for a storm, if so!'

'Yes, sir, I will,' said Barney. His eyes gleamed as he looked at Mr King. What would the coach say if he knew he was sleeping in the cellars of the old house?

Barney went off with Miranda. The children went with him to the gate, Loony too. He was always glad to see the back of Miranda!

Diana watched Barney out of sight. She was worried. 'I do hope he'll be all right,' she said.

''Course he will!' said Roger. 'Nothing will happen to old Barney. Anyway, he's like a cat – he'll always fall on his feet. He'll look after himself all right.'

Barney unlocked the kitchen door of the old house when he got there, and let himself in. He took a quick glance round the ground floor. Nothing had altered since the morning. He went upstairs to get his rug and cushion. The nurseries were just the same as when he had seen them that morning – untidy and higgledy-piggledy, drawers and cupboards open everywhere.

Barney picked up his rug and the cushion. He went downstairs with Miranda, yawning. He thought he would get a little sleep straight away, then if the noises began he would be wide awake and fresh.

Miranda was astonished to find that Barney was going to sleep down in the dark cellars. She was not at all pleased. She chattered angrily and pulled at the rug as if to say 'No, no – come upstairs! This is all wrong!'

'Sorry, Miranda – but this is where we sleep tonight!'

141

said Barney, firmly. 'Now – where do you think would be a good corner?'

All the corners were equally dirty. In the end Barney thought it would be quite a good idea to lie on one of the wooden shelves that had once held bottles. Wood was not as cold or hard as stone.

He climbed up on a shelf, put the cushion down for his head, and wrapped himself up in the thick rug. The cellars were cold, but it was a very warm night. Barney thought he would be all right in the rug, with Miranda cuddled to him like a hot-water bottle! She snuggled down protestingly.

Barney fell asleep at once, hard though his bed was. A spider ran over his face but didn't disturb him. When it ran over Miranda's hairy little face she put up a quick paw and caught it. Then she too went to sleep.

Barney slept on peacefully. Half-past ten came, eleven o'clock, half-past eleven, midnight. Then Barney was awakened by the hardness of his bed. One of his arms was aching through being bent underneath him on the hard board. He shifted his position, remembered where he was, and sat up to listen. Were there any noises at all?

The cellars were very, very quiet – and in the silence Barney again thought he caught the faint noise he had heard once before, with Diana. Was it a kind of gurgle? It had gone before he had made up his mind. Well – it was so faint and far-off that it was quite impossible to tell what it was, if it was anything.

He switched on his torch and shone it round. Nothing to be seen except a pair of frightened rat's eyes gleaming. Then the rat scampered away to a corner and disappeared.

Barney lay down again and Miranda snuggled into his neck, putting her paws inside his shirt for warmth. Barney liked the feel of the tiny monkey-hands. He patted

142

Miranda affectionately, and she nibbled the skin of his neck, also affectionately. She had some funny little ways!

Barney soon fell asleep again. One o'clock came – two o'clock – and then Barney was awakened suddenly.

Thud! Bang!

He shot up straight and Miranda fell off the shelf. The boy listened intently.

BANG!

The noises were very much louder down here. But they couldn't be in the cellars! They sounded too far away for that.

Barney listened hard. When he was sure that the noises were not in the cellars he switched on his torch. He flashed it all round – no, there was absolutely nothing to be seen. But the noises went on!

Bang! Thud! And then there came the whining noise, and after that a curious grating sound, guttural and harsh. Then Barney felt sure he could hear voices. But they were muffled voices – as if there was a wall or two between them and Barney.

'Well! This is certainly where we do a spot of exploring,' said Barney to Miranda, and he threw aside his rug. He jumped down from the wooden shelf and stood listening. He must go in the direction of the noises.

They came from the right. He went in that direction and came up against a stone wall. The noises seemed to be on the other side. But how could they be? There was no way of getting through to the other side.

Barney ran his torch along the stone wall on his right. It was just the same as the rest of the cellar walls, except that it was glistening with damp.

Thud! That noise really did sound as if it were behind the wall. Well then, there must be some place behind there! Barney shone his torch again.

And then he found what he was looking for! He

wouldn't have seen it but for Miranda – it was really she who found it for him.

Chapter Twenty-One

Strange Happenings

An old box stood against the wall. Miranda saw something moving there – was it a spider – a moth? In a trice she was after it! She slid down behind the box, and Barney moved it out to see what she was after.

And there in the wall he saw an iron handle. It was low down, and very rusty. He had to kneel down to look at it closely.

Why was there an iron handle so low down in the wall? Surely it wasn't meant to be used for anything? Perhaps in the old far-off days this cellar was used as a dungeon and prisoners had been tied to the iron ring.

Barney looked at it. He set down his torch, put both hands to the ring and tugged. It was very fast in the wall and would not move. He pushed. No result. He tugged again whilst Miranda sat close by and watched with great interest.

It was quite by accident that he found the secret of the iron handle. He discovered that it turned round and round. So he turned it with a screwing motion – and something happened!

Barney never found out quite what did happen. The screwing round of the handle seemed to work some kind of lever – and suddenly the stone next to the one in which the iron ring was set began to move, very very slowly! It moved inwards, towards Barney, grating a little as it ran over hidden grooves. He stopped twisting the handle in surprise, and the stone stopped moving. It was half in, half out of the thick wall. Shaking with excitement Barney twisted the iron handle again and once more the stone next to it began to move.

It came right out from its place, leaving a small gap between itself and the wall. Barney looked at the gap. It would take him easily, or a small man. A big man would have difficulty in squeezing through. He flashed his torch to the gap, but it was impossible to see what lay behind it.

'Shall we get through?' said he to Miranda. She did not wait to answer, but slipped neatly through herself! She came back at once, chattering.

She was not frightened, so Barney decided there couldn't be much behind the sliding stone. He would go and see. The noises might have their origin behind it somewhere.

So he squeezed in through the gap. On the other side of the wall was pitch darkness! Barney shone his torch round to see what was what.

He was in a very curious place indeed. It was very small, not much bigger than a boxroom, and the ceiling or roof was so low that Barney could not stand upright. The walls were running with damp, and there was a very damp smell there too.

Barney looked round this strange little place in surprise. What in the world was it? There was nothing there at all, as far as he could see.

And then he heard one of the 'noises'. My goodness, it was so loud that he almost jumped out of his skin! It sounded almost in the little room, but not quite.

It seemed to come from under the ground. Barney flashed his torch on the floor – and how he stared!

Not far from him was a dark hole, quite round and very narrow. It went down for some way because his torch could not pick out the bottom of it. He could see the remains of an old iron ladder going down this curious shaft – and it was up this hole that the noises came!

They sounded very loud indeed when he stood at the top of the hole. Miranda was terrified. She bounded back to the gap in the wall and shot through it, gibbering with fright. Barney called her back, but it was a long time before she would come. He had to go to the gap and coax her gently.

She came through again at last, and then something really dreadful happened! Barney must have touched some hidden lever, or pressed on some spring – because the stone that had moved out to make the gap, began slowly to move back again. At first Barney did not realise what was happening. He was fondling Miranda and trying to make her less frightened.

Then a small noise made him look up – and to his horror he saw that the gap was almost closed! He tried to catch hold of the moving stone and push it out again – but it was heavy and he couldn't stop it going right back into its place.

Barney got into a panic then. He was cold and damp in that horrid little space with its streaming walls. He hunted frantically for any iron ring or lever that would set the stone moving again, so that he might squeeze through the gap. He was a prisoner if he couldn't find it! There must be some way of getting the stone to move from this side – or wasn't there? Surely this could not be a horrible little dungeon where unwanted prisoners were hidden long ago?

Another noise boomed up through the strange hole. Warm now with his exertions at trying to find some way of moving the stone out again, Barney stopped to listen.

If men were causing that noise, then there must be a way of escape down that hole! But where in the world did it lead to? Barney didn't want to go down it at all. It was so black and narrow and the iron ladder was not safe.

He made some more frantic efforts to find a way to move the stone, but it was no use. It couldn't be done. He walked the three steps to the hole and looked down it. Again he thought he heard voices. Were they really voices? If there were men down there they might help him – except that whatever they were doing must be very secret, and probably against the law. They would certainly not be pleased to see him!

Supposing Mr King was down there too! That would be a funny state of affairs! Well – not funny. Things were far from funny at the moment – in fact they were horribly serious.

There was nothing for it but to begin climbing down that fearsome shaft. Barney knelt down on the stone floor and gingerly put one leg down into the hole. His foot felt about for the ladder. He found a bar and let his weight go down on it.

It broke at once! Well – this was going to be very difficult indeed if the ladder wasn't going to hold him!

He felt for the next rung. His weight pressed down on it – and that broke too! Barney began to feel panic-stricken again. Miranda chattered in fright, clinging on his shoulder.

Then Barney felt for the sides of the rungs. Were there staples there, or nails – or even bits of broken rung?

He found a sharp piece of iron, the bit of rung that was driven into the wall of the shaft. He decided that it would be best to tread on the ends of the rungs, because then possibly they would not break. They would certainly break if he trod in the middle of them. So, very carefully indeed Barney felt about for another rung and trod gingerly at the very edge of it, where it was driven into the shaft wall. Each one held now, and Barney breathed more easily.

Soon his whole body was in the hole, his feet feeling for the edges of the rungs, his hands holding on to the ones above his head. Down he went and down. Where did the hole lead to? One of the noises came up as he descended and Miranda nearly fell off his shoulder in fright.

The hole was about twelve feet long. It came to an end at last. Barney felt his feet on solid ground. He let go and turned himself round. There was a kind of doorway in the shaft wall behind him, low and narrow. Barney stooped and went through it.

Now he could plainly hear the voices of men, shouting and calling to one another. Then he jumped. He heard that screeching, whining sound. He guessed what it was now. It was some machine – a winch perhaps being worked.

He squinted round, not yet daring to put on his torch again. He had switched it off as soon as he found his feet on solid ground. He stood there in the dark, listening, not wanting to take a step forward or backwards in case he fell down yet another hole!

Then he became conscious of another sound – a sound that went on and on all the time – a quiet sound that occasionally became louder. The sound of water!

'Yes – that's it – it's *water*!' said Barney to himself in amazement. 'Where is it? It sounds awfully near.'

He switched his torch on and off quickly for a moment. He was in a narrow passage that slanted down from the shaft-hole. At the end of the passage was the gleam of water!

'Well!' said Barney, in amazement. 'What is it? An underground pool?'

He walked cautiously down the narrow passage and

149

came to the water, shading his torch with his hand so that its light would not easily be seen. Yes – there was the water, black and gleaming – and flowing along!

Flowing along! Then it must be a river of some kind – no, a stream, because it wasn't wide enough for a river.

And then, in a flash Barney knew what it was! It was Rockingdown Stream – the stream shown on the map as flowing near, very near, Rockingdown Manor! Not only did it flow near – but it must flow practically *under* the old house! No wonder the wall near the shaft-hole was damp.

Forgetting to be cautious he flashed his torch on the stream. It flowed in a rocky bed, and there was an arched rocky roof to it, that was very low in places. Beside it, on the side that Barney stood, was a ledge, wide enough to walk on. There was no ledge at all on the other side.

What an extraordinary thing! A river flowing under the house – and men working by it in the tunnel, making weird noises underground that sounded up in the old house – muffled and distant, but still easy to hear!

Barney wondered if the men knew that their noises could be heard. Still, even if they knew, they wouldn't care, because they thought the old house was completely deserted – there would be no one there to hear!

From some way down to the left, the way the stream was flowing, a dim light showed. It was from there the sound of voices and other noises came. Barney made his way carefully along the rocky ledge beside the stream, crouching when the roof swept down low. He came out on the other side of the low roof, and saw that the stream curved to the left. Round the corner the light was brighter – that was evidently where the men where.

Barney began to feel more cheerful. If men knew a way in to this place, then there was a way out! And he would be able to find it and escape. But before he did that he was going to see what was happening down here!

He came to the place where the river curved to the left, and peeped cautiously round the corner. He was astounded at what he saw. The narrow tunnel, in which the stream ran, suddenly widened out into a great, low-roofed cave, and here men were at work with a winch, which was giving out the whining, screeching noise that Barney had so often heard. Another winch was at work nearby, and that had a harsh guttural sound, which was magnified very much in the tunnel.

Barney could make out three men. They were shouting above the noise of the winches. Whatever were they doing? If only he could find out!

Chapter Twenty-Two

Any Way of Escape?

Barney stood hidden by a rock that jutted out from the tunnel, and watched in astonishment all that was going on. The stream flowed quickly past him, gurgled along at one side of the big low cave, and disappeared again into another tunnel, leaving the cave behind.

Men were working at a couple of winches, which made loud harsh noises as the rope was wound up on each winch. One of the men gave a shout: 'Lights up!'

A bright glaring lamp was switched on near the stream. Another man appeared from the far tunnel with what looked like a pitchfork in his hand. The winches went on winding. And then a large object appeared, coming out from the far tunnel, bobbing about on the swift-flowing stream, whose current was against it.

Barney stared, his mouth open in surprise. The men were winding in big crates from the far tunnel where the stream disappeared on its swift course. Barney could not make out quite what these crate-like objects were – great boxes of something? Cases of something heavy? It was impossible to see.

The four men rushed to the crate and it was dragged right in to the cave. Bang! Thud! It was shifted into place, and was obviously very heavy indeed, judging by the thuds it made when it was turned over and over to be put into place.

Barney craned round as far as he dared to see where the crate was being put. He thought he could see other cases piled together. This must be a hiding place – or sorting place? It was obviously some very secret spot, used for very secret things.

The winches wound again and another crate came bobbing up the tunnel – and yet another. Barney guessed they must all be tied together in some way. There must be a long line of them down the far tunnel! The man who held what looked like a pitchfork disappeared into the tunnel each time a new crate appeared, guiding it deftly as it bobbed along. Barney guessed there was a narrow little rocky ledge by the side of the river there, just as there had been in his part of the underground tunnel.

'That's the lot!' shouted the man with the pitchfork, as the last crate was man-handled into place: 'Now let's clear off! I'm dead!'

Barney crouched back against the rocky side of the tunnel, hoping the men would not come near him. They didn't. They walked off the other way, clambering along the rocky ledge of the distant tunnel and disappearing in the dark, their torches shining out for a time and then vanishing.

The whole place was now in pitch darkness. Miranda, on Barney's shoulder, chattered into his ear. She was cold and tired. She didn't understand this curious adventure at all.

Barney switched on his own torch again, glad he had such a powerful one. He made his way to the low-roofed cave. It was even bigger than he had imagined! It was, in fact, a vast, underground cavern, its walls gleaming with phosphorus here and there.

Piled against one wall were crates of all kinds and sizes. There were names on them that Barney did not understand – were they names of places or people? He didn't know.

He wandered round the big cavern. Right at the end he found what was evidently a kind of workshop or sorting place. Here were empty crates that had been unpacked. There was nothing to show what had been in them except for a stack of dull leaden-looking bars. Barney picked one up.

It certainly was very heavy. He thought it must be a bar of silver – silver that had been melted down and made into a bar.

'Perhaps stolen silver articles are melted down into these bars,' thought the boy. 'Perhaps this is a kind of central receiving place for stolen or smuggled goods – what a wonderful hiding place! Nobody would ever guess where it was!'

He wandered all round the big cavern. He found something that pleased him very much – an old mattress with rugs and a pillow – and, even better, a ledge on which were stacked tins of meat and fruit!

The men evidently had meals down here sometimes in the middle of a big job – and maybe even slept here on occasion. Well – Barney would sleep here too, if he had to – *and* have a meal as well! If he couldn't find a way of escape at once, he could make himself comfortable till he did find one. In the meantime he would find out all he could.

He looked at the winches. They were powerful ones. They needed to be to drag those crates against the fast-flowing water – and how far did they have to be dragged? Barney began to wonder about that too.

He decided not to explore any more for the present. He was tired and cold and he had had enough adventures for the time being. He would lie down on the mattress and sleep. Miranda would wake him if she heard anyone coming.

He lay down and was soon asleep, Miranda cuddled up to him once more. He did not know how long he slept for he had no watch, and, as it was always dark in the underground cavern, he could not tell, on waking, if it was daytime or not.

But he felt as if it must be, when he awoke. He was hungry so he went to the collection of tins. Ah! – tins of ham. He would open one of those – if there was an opener! He saw a pile of tin plates and dishes nearby, with a little heap of cheap knives, forks and spoons. With them were two tin-openers.

Barney was soon enjoying a meal of tinned ham, and peaches from another tin. He hid the empty tins behind a rock so that if the men came back they wouldn't suspect anything.

He felt a good deal better after that – in fact he felt fit for anything! Miranda, who had gobbled up four half-peaches in delight, was also ready for anything. She bounded round the cave, examining this and that – and then, quite suddenly, the place was flooded with a dazzling light.

Barney leapt to his feet, blinking, expecting to see the men returning. But nobody appeared. Then how did the light come on so suddenly?

He laughed – of course, it was that monkey Miranda. She had come across the light switch and turned it on, flooding the cave with light! She loved meddling about with any switches she found, and had often got herself into trouble over this. He called to her.

'Naughty Miranda! Don't meddle! Turn it off again.'

Miranda made a chattering noise, full of glee. She switched the light on and off several times. Finally she switched it off and left the place in darkness again, except for Barney's torch.

'Come here, Miranda,' called Barney. 'It's time we got out of here. We're going down the river – if the men have a way of escape there, so have we!'

Miranda leapt to his shoulder and held on to his right

ear. Barney went to where the stream disappeared into the far tunnel, and flashed his torch down it. Beside the water ran a very narrow ledge of rock, much narrower than the ledge he had scrambled down before. Also at times it was not above the level of the stream, but below, which meant wading through the cold water for some way.

The tunnel did not run straight, but curved about, and the stream curved with it. It was a weird journey, walking beside the black water, on a terribly narrow ledge of rock. At one place the tunnel roof was so low that Barney was forced to go on his hands and knees, and Miranda screamed in terror. She didn't like water.

After about ten minutes of this Barney was quite fed up. But he had to go on. On he went for another fifteen minutes – and then he saw a dim light in front of him. What was it? He hurried along as fast as he could, hoping it was daylight.

He came to a great iron gate! Beyond the gate was daylight, obscured by enormous strands of greenery that hung down over the bars! This was where the stream flowed out from underground into the open. Barney stopped and stared at the iron gate. It was very old, very stout, very overgown. It could never have been meant to open. It had been built from the low roof of the tunnel right down to the bed of the stream, allowing the water to flow out between the bars.

Barney did not even try to shake the gate or move it in any way. It was quite plain that nobody had gone out that way – nobody could! It must have been built years and years ago, to stop people exploring up the underground stream, so curiously flowing out of the hill on which the old house stood.

The boy stood looking through the thick curtain of greenery that dimmed the daylight. Brambles, ferns, and creeping plants climbed across the iron gate. It was impossible to get out of this strange prison behind the bars! 'The men can't have escaped through this,' thought Barney. 'Well – where *did* they go, then? I must have missed their way of exit. I'll go back.'

So back he went, stumbling along the rocky ledge again. Looking carefully everywhere to see if he had missed the men's way of departure from the tunnel.

And then Miranda suddenly gave one of her little excited chatterings. She had seen something! It was about half-way up the tunnel. Barney flashed his torch all around but at first could see nothing but the rocky sides of the river tunnel, and the ledge he was standing on.

Then Miranda suddenly left his shoulder and swung herself over the water. She grasped something in mid-air and rocked to and fro! Barney flashed his torch on her. She was swinging on a rope!

'Gosh! A rope! Where does it come from?' said Barney in astonishment. His torch picked out the thick sturdy rope. It ran up to the roof of the tunnel – and there, in the roof, was what looded like flat pieces of board. Barney stared, puzzled. A rope – hanging down from boarding in the roof of the tunnel!

He puzzled it out. There must be a hole in the roof of the tunnel there – either a natural one, or man-made. It was possible that there was a dip in the ground above and that the surface was quite near the tunnel roof. A hole had been found – or made – the river below discovered and explored – and the cavern found.

'The men must have used this as their way of escape,' thought Barney. 'Once the boards are taken up, and they climb through the hole, they are above ground. I wonder if this is the place where the crates are brought, and lowered down to the water. It must be.'

He swarmed up the rope, hanging above the water. But

he could not move the boards lying in place across the hole in the roof. Something heavy must be put on top of them, to hide them. He dropped down disappointed.

He worked out what the men did. 'They bring the crates and boxes here at night – they remove the boards that hide the hole in the tunnel-roof. They drop the goods down into the water and fasten them to a wire rope that runs up the stream to those winches. Then it's just a question of dragging them up the water, guiding them as they go! What a very ingenious idea – nobody in the world would guess such a hiding-place!'

But working out the ingenious idea didn't help Barney to escape! There he was, a prisoner underground, and with no way out at all!

Chapter Twenty-Three

Where Can Barney Be?

Next day the children wondered what in the world had happened to Barney. He didn't appear for breakfast, though he had said he would. He didn't even appear when the time came for lessons, and that was very disturbing. Barney never missed his morning's listening!

'Where is he?' wondered Roger. 'I hope he's all right.'

Diana was very worried indeed. When Barney didn't appear at lunch time she was quite beside herself. 'I *know* something's happened to him!' she said. 'We must all go and look for him in the old house – we'll go down to the cellars and see if we can find out anything there.'

Mr King couldn't make the children out at all. They obviously had some worry, but they wouldn't tell him a thing, and when he came near they stopped talking at once.

'I must say I think your behaviour is peculiar,' he remarked to Diana. 'Why don't you tell me what's wrong? I might be able to do something. Where's Barney?'

'He'll probably turn up,' said Roger at once. Certainly they were not going to tell Mr King their worries. As for peculiar behaviour – well, what about his?

So they told him nothing, and he felt very cross. Miss Pepper telephoned to say that her sister was better. Perhaps it would not be very long before she could come back. Mr King was relieved. Maybe the children would behave in a more normal way when Miss Pepper was back.

After dinner they set off for the old house. Loony was

very pleased to be out. He didn't like it when the children stayed in the house and went into huddles over something, and talked earnestly and worriedly, never noticing him at all.

First of all the three went up to the nurseries with Loony. They had wondered at first how to get in, but had found that Barney had not locked the kitchen door, whether purposely or not, they didn't know. The untidy, dishevelled nurseries shocked Diana very much. How dare Mr King mess them up like this?

'Don't bother about putting them straight now, Di,' said Roger. 'We'd better go over the whole of the house and down into the cellars straight away – just in case Barney's ill or hurt, and wants help. You never know. It's so strange that he has not turned up today.'

They went all over the house. Nothing to be seen. Then they went down to the kitchen, through the scullery and into the outhouses. The trap door in the dairy was wide open.

'Well – down we go,' said Roger, switching on his torch, and down they went, carefully descending the steep, stone steps. Now they were in the dark cellars. They called Barney.

'Barney! Where are you? Are you here?'

Echoes answered them eerily. 'Here! Here! Here!'

'He's not here,' said Roger. 'Loony, go and look for him.'

Loony was soon sniffing into every corner. It was he who found the wooden shelf on which Barney had slept the night before. He stood by it and barked loudly. The others hurried up. They saw the rug and the cushion on the shelf at once.

'There! That's where he slept last night!' said Roger. 'But where is he now? And where's Miranda?'

160

The children sat down on a box to think what to do next.

Whilst they were sitting there Loony ran sniffing round the cellars, trying to smell where Barney had been. He came to the corner where the iron ring was, low in the wall. He scraped at it, whining, smelling Barney's smell there.

Snubby ran over to him. 'What is it, Loony? What have you found? I say, you others, what do you think this is?'

They all knelt down in the corner and examined the iron ring set in the wall. Just as Barney had done they pushed and pulled. But unfortunately nobody thought of turning it round and round, so they did not discover the secret of the moving stone. They gave it up after a time.

'It's nothing,' said Roger. 'It's not worth bothering about. I expect Loony's only excited because he can smell rats there or something.'

So they left the iron ring and went up the steps into the dairy. It was nice to be in the daylight again.

'Well – Barney's not here,' said Snubby, dolefully. 'Let's go. This house gives me the creeps today. It really does.'

'What shall we do about Barney?' said Diana to Roger. 'Do you think we ought to report that he's disappeared?'

'Not *yet*,' said Roger. 'We'd feel awfully silly if we did that and then Barney walked in with Miranda, grinning all over his face as usual!'

'All right,' said Diana. 'We won't then. But if he doesn't turn up by tomorrow I really think we ought to tell somebody. I wish Miss Pepper was at home. We can't possibly tell Mr King. And we don't know anyone else here.'

They went soberly out of the kitchen door and pulled it to. They began to make their way through the grounds.

'What shall we do for the rest of the afternoon?' said Roger.

'Well, we won't go riding or swimming,' said Diana. 'Just in case Barney comes in to tea. I want to be about when he does come, in case he's got any news for us.'

'I know,' said Snubby, suddenly. 'We could take the short cut to that stream I saw the other day when I was tracking Mr King – and we could follow it up and see where it does go to. We could find out where the map goes wrong.'

'It's not a very exciting thing to do – but we may as well do it,' said Roger. 'Come on, Loony – leave that rabbit-hole alone. You'll never get down it. You're too fat!'

Off they went with Loony at their heels. They went to Rockingdown Cottage for the map, and discovered that Mr King had gone out, Mrs Round told them.

'He went off over that way, with his stick,' she said, pointing down the hill. 'He said he'd be back for tea.'

'Blow! That's the way *we* want to go,' said Roger, looking at the map. 'See – we take this path – and then go down there, round that little wood – then on down the hill, till we come to the stream. This spot must be about where Snubby saw the hidden boat. We'll make for that and then follow the stream upwards and see where it goes.'

They set off with Loony, who was very pleased at the prospect of a second walk. Perhaps he would find rabbit-holes big enough to get down this time! That was always Loony's biggest hope.

It didn't take them long to find the stream. 'Where's the place where the boat was hidden, Snubby?' said Roger, standing beside the stream that flowed swiftly by.

'See that bunch of willows over there? That looks like the place,' said Snubby. They went on again over the

162

marshy fields, Loony cleverly leaping from tuft to tuft of wiry grass; the children, less clever, walked into sodden ground from which they had to pull their feet with a plop-plop-plop.

'I don't like this much,' said Diana. She stopped and surveyed the big flat field. 'It's rather a desolate sort of place – there are trees only where the stream runs. You can easily see its course by the willows and alders on its banks.'

'Look – this is the place where the boat was hidden,' said Snubby, when they came near to the clump of willows he had pointed out.

The boat was not there! The little backwater was empty.

'Now where's the boat gone?' wondered Snubby.

'Oh well – I suppose whoever owns it has gone for a row!' said Diana.

'But *who* owns it?' demanded Snubby. 'Look all round you – there isn't a single house or cottage in sight!'

There wasn't. What Snubby said was perfectly true. It was really very odd to think of a boat in a little hidden creek and nobody within miles to own it. Anyway the boat was gone now. It wasn't any good puzzling about it.

'Let's follow the stream upwards now,' said Roger. 'Come on, Loony. This way. Get him, Snubby, he'll fall into the water. He's seen a vole or something.'

Snubby rescued Loony from a watery bed and propelled him in front of him. Loony promptly rolled over on his back.

'Right,' said Snubby. 'If you want to spend the afternoon like that, do! Goodbye!'

Loony soon followed, forgetting his vole. The four of them went along the banks of the stream. It flowed downhill and the current was quite swift. The little stream twisted and curved about as all streams do, making the children walk twice as far as they need have done.

They followed it for about fifteen minutes, and then a steeper hill towered in front of them. 'If the stream flows down that it will come pretty fast,' said Roger. But it didn't flow down the hill. It suddenly disappeared behind a curtain of greenery. In fact, it went underground.

'Gosh – it's gone to ground!' said Roger. 'Well – *that* explains the map then, when it showed the stream so near the old house – it must flow almost underneath it, underground.'

'Yes – of course,' said Diana, quite excited. 'That's what the explanation is – it's an underground stream as far as here – and then it pops out and flows across the marshy fields.'

They clambered to where the stream came out from the hill. They could not see the iron gate that shut it off because of the thick curtains of brambles and fern and ivy. But Roger, thrusting his hand through the ivy, felt the iron bars.

'There's something here,' he said, and began to tear away the ivy strands. 'Yes – a gate or barrier of some sort. To stop people going up the stream, I suppose. Perhaps it's dangerous.'

'Oh, what a pity! I'd have loved to go up the stream underground and see where it goes,' said Snubby. 'What a pity Barney isn't here – he would have loved this.'

Not many hours before, Barney himself had stood only a yard or two away from where they were – but on the other side of the barrier! They didn't know that. They peered through the thick green curtain, but could see nothing but darkness there.

'Well – we've solved *that* mystery,' said Roger, climbing down from where he had clung to see through the ivy sprays. 'We'd better go back.'

'Look – is that a little backwater there?' said Diana, pointing to the other side of the stream a little way down from the iron gate. 'Let's see if it is.'

'Well – we really ought to go home,' said Roger, looking at his watch. 'Still – we'll just see if there's anything interesting there. We might even find the mysterious boat.'

They did! They followed the little backwater between a row of alder trees. It curved round very suddenly and entered a dip in the ground where it opened out into a pond. Ducks were on the pond and – the boat was there, tied to a tree! Snubby was sure it was the same boat because it had no name!

In a hollow was a farmhouse. Barns rose around it, mellow and with moss on the tiles. It was a lovely place.

'Well – what a surprise!' said Diana. 'A farmhouse up here, lost to the world! That's where the boat belongs. No mystery about it at all!'

They went towards the farmhouse. A man came out from a barn and saw them. He looked extremely disagreeable.

'You clear off!' he shouted. 'Do you hear? We don't allow hikers here. Be off at once, or I'll set the dogs on you.'

Three or four dogs now set up a terrific barking and Loony barked back. But he did not venture any nearer. He was afraid of so many dogs at once!

'All right!' called Roger indignantly. 'We're going! Don't worry.'

He and the others turned to go back. What a horrid fellow! They made their way back down the stream to the backwater – and there they had another surprise.

Mr King was there, gazing earnestly at the iron gate, the barrier covered with green!

Chapter Twenty-Four

A Very Great Surprise

Mr King was just as surprised to see the three children and Loony as they were to see him. Loony was so astonished that he quite forgot the feud that seemed to lie between Mr King and the children, and hurled himself at him to greet him.

'Well!' said Mr King, in surprise. 'Who would have thought of meeting *you* here!'

'Yes. Odd isn't it?' said Roger politely. *Now* what was Mr King up to? Had he followed them? What was he doing snooping round in that part of the world again – staring at the iron gate covered with greenery as if he knew some secret about it! Perhaps he knew where Barney was!

'Well, we might as well walk home together,' said Mr King, looking at his watch. 'We shall be a little late for tea, but I don't expect Mrs Round will mind.'

The children didn't want to walk home with him but there was nothing for it but to agree. So off they all went, Loony rather subdued. He had suddenly remembered that Snubby was not friendly towards Mr King, and he wished he hadn't given him such a welcome!

'Isn't Barney with you?' said Mr King, sounding surprised. 'Where's he got to today? Don't you know?'

'Oh, he's got all sorts of things to do,' said Roger. 'He's about somewhere, I expect. Haven't *you* seen him, Mr King?'

'You haven't quarrelled, I hope?' said the coach. This was too silly a suggestion to be answered. Snubby made a noise that sounded rather like 'Pooh' It would be difficult to quarrel with the good-tempered Barney.

Barney was not waiting for them at tea-time. Mrs Round said he hadn't called at all. They ate their tea with Mr King, and began to be really worried again about Barney. What could have happened to him?

'We'll wait till tomorrow morning and then we'll go to the police,' said Roger, desperately, when bed-time came and still Barney had not appeared. Diana was almost beside herself with worry. She was very fond of Barney. But Snubby looked the most miserable of them all.

That night Roger woke up with a jump. He had heard something. He sat up and thought for a minute. What had the sound been like? Could it have been made by Barney? What did it sound like – yes – it sounded like someone closing the front door very, very softly!

Roger was up in a trice. Without putting on slippers or dressing-gown he went quietly down the stairs. He ran out of the front door, leaving it open. He saw a figure moving down by the gate. There was a little moon that night, and Roger could make out who it was – Mr King!

Yes – Mr King on another of his mysterious night prowls. All right – Roger would follow him and see where he went – he might even lead him to Barney. Roger felt that Mr King was villain enough to keep him prisoner somewhere, for some secret reason of his own!

It was not nice walking in bare feet, especially as Mr King went through the grounds of the old house. He must be going there. Carefully – and painfully – Roger followed him, biting his lip as he trod on a thorn or stone with his bare feet.

Mr King stopped. Two men materialised out of the bushes. They began to talk in low voices. Roger strained his ears, but could only catch a few sentences.

'We got him all right – but he won't talk.' Then there was some conversation Roger couldn't catch.

'Oh yes – it makes a very good cover! I'll say it does – nobody would ever guess that.'

More low talk, and then a sentence from Mr King again. 'Well – if those kids I coach guessed what I'm really up to, they'd pass out!'

Roger froze into the bushes. Had they got hold of Barney then? What cover were they talking about – the old house? 'All right, Mr King, you think we don't know anything, but we know *you're* a bad lot all right!' thought Roger, grimly.

The men talked a little while longer, and then walked towards the old house. Roger had heard enough. He would go to the police tomorrow and tell them all he knew, and beg them to find Barney. He'd tell them to arrest Mr King too, the fraud! He didn't want to follow the men any farther. His feet were sore and bleeding. He must go back. Anyway he knew enough to spike Mr King's guns now, and stop his little game, whatever it was!

He went home to bed, but not to sleep. He puzzled things over in his mind, trying to make out what Mr King was doing, why he had captured Barney, and hundreds of other things that gradually slipped into dreams, and gave him nightmares. He awoke in the morning, anxious and exhausted with his worried sleep.

He told the others what he had planned to do. 'I'm off to the police,' he said. 'You sit down and begin lessons as usual with Mr King, so that he doesn't suspect anything. Just say I've gone to do some urgent shopping for Mrs Round. I know she wants some potatoes. I'll tell her I'll go and get those!'

So Snubby and Diana sat down alone with Mr King. No Barney, no Roger. Diana was pale and looked worried. Mr King looked at her and at the restless Snubby. What on *earth* was the matter with these three kids ever since Miss Pepper had been away?

At about eleven o'clock footsteps came up to the front door – *two* pairs of footsteps! Diana began to tremble. Had Roger brought back a policeman? She couldn't see who it was from the study window.

The door opened and in came Roger, looking extremely important. Behind him came a burly policeman. Diana gave a gasp. Mr King looked amazed.

'What's all this? he said, in astonishment. 'Roger – you haven't got into trouble, have you?'

'*I* haven't,' said Roger.

'It's like this, sir,' said the policeman, taking out a notebook and flicking over the pages. 'This boy here came and made a report to me, sir, this morning. Seems as if a friend of his has been missing for two days – name of Barnabus, surname not known. And Master Roger here seems to think you know something about his disappearance.'

'This is absurd,' said Mr King angrily. 'Roger, what do you mean by it?'

'Well, we know all about your night prowlings, and your mysterious walks, and your explorations of the old house,' said Roger boldly. 'You went into Rockingdown Manor and looked everywhere – you messed up the nurseries and threw everything all over the place. You meet with strange men at night – you're plotting something with them. We don't know what it is – but we're sure you've got something to do with Barney's disappearance – so I went to the police this morning and reported everything.'

'That's right, sir,' said the policeman, stolidly. 'It's a strange story, sir, and I'd like some kind of explanation, *if* you please – most particularly about this here breaking into Rockingdown Manor. Serious business that, sir.'

Mr King was frowning. He glared at Roger, who looked him straight in the face. 'Aha!' said Roger's look, 'what have you to say to all this, fraud of a Mr King!'

Mr King stood up. He looked rather taller and more imposing all of a sudden. He spoke in a crisp, commanding voice.

'Constable, take a look at this, will you?'

He held out something in his hand. The constable took a look, and his face slowly went red. He shut up his notebook and backed away hurriedly.

'I beg your pardon, sir. I'd no idea, sir, none at all. I never got any notification from headquarters, sir.'

'That's all right,' said Mr King, still in his new, crisp voice. 'It was thought better to say nothing locally. You can go. I'll deal with this matter now.'

The constable went. Even the back of his neck was red, Diana noticed. She was completely overcome with amazement. As for Roger and Snubby they couldn't make head or tail of anything. They stared at Mr King, bewildered. He sat down again.

'Sit down,' he said, and Roger sat. Mr King took out a cigarette from his case, tapped it on the table, and got out his lighter. Nobody said a word. Mr King looked round grimly at the three.

'So you were spying on me, were you? What for, I should like to know? And why not come to me straight away and tell me everything, instead of going to a village policeman? Exactly what do you know?'

Nobody answered at first. They felt completely in the dark.

'Mr King – what did you show to the constable, please?' said Diana, at last.

'I showed him something that told him I was somebody

considerably higher up in the police force than he was,' said Mr King, after a pause. 'I'm here on an important investigation. I'm sorry you thought I was the villain of the piece. I assure you I'm not.'

There was another silence. Roger felt more foolish and more embarrassed than he had ever felt in his life before. What was Mr King then – a detective – a secret agent – or what? Roger didn't even dare to ask him!

'I'm very sorry, sir,' he said at last. 'It – it was only because I was so worried about Barney disappearing that I went to the police – and – and – well – told them what I suspected about you. I'm very sorry.'

'I should think so,' said Mr King. 'But what *is* all this about Barney disappearing? I didn't know you were really worried about him. Look here – you've been snooping about just as much as I have, evidently – and maybe you know things I don't. We'd better pool our knowledge and help one another instead of working against each other – though I'm blessed if I knew anything about your secret activities at all! Little criminals, the lot of you!'

He smiled, and the children's hearts lightened. He had a nice smile. How could they have thought he was a fraud, a villain? He was somebody important, somebody intensely interesting, somebody unexpectedly commanding and altogether admirable.

'We've been idiots,' said Snubby, finding his voice suddenly. 'Absolute super-idiots.'

'Smashing ones,' agreed Mr King, with a wider smile. 'I've been a bit of a fraud though, I must confess. I'm not really a coach! I know enough to teach three ignoramuses like you, though it's not a job I like. I took it because I needed to be somewhere in this neighbourhood, as you have probably guessed by now.'

'Yes, we did guess your were a – fraud in that way,'

Diana agreed, blushing. 'Shall we tell you all we know, Mr King? Then perhaps you can help us with Barney.'

The three of them told everything. Mr King listened intently. 'Well – there's not much I don't know in all you tell me,' he said. 'Still, it all helps. Now, I'll tell *you* something – and you'll please keep your mouths shut about it.'

The three of them listened, thrilled.

'There's smuggling going on in this neighourhood,' said Mr King. 'It's been suspected for a long time. There's a mysterious aeroplane that lands somewhere at night and takes off almost immediately. There's a motor-launch, also mysterious, that appears at times in this neighbour-hood, on the river. We think there's a kind of receiving headquarters here – where the stuff is hidden till it's safe to dispose of it – or where it is sorted out into small bits for sale and disposed of immediately, somewhere, somehow. But where this hiding place is, and who are the chief men concerned we don't know. We've got one of the smaller men, but he won't talk. We had an idea that the old house, Rockingdown Manor, was the centre – but we've gone through it with a tooth-comb and there's nothing to show that it is. Nothing at all.'

'What about those noises?' said Roger, in excitement. 'The ones Barney was going to find out about?'

'Ah – those are very, very interesting,' said Mr King. 'And I think young Barney's disappearance is due to his curiosity about those noises! He's paying for his inquisi-tiveness, I fear.'

'Oh dear,' said Diana, going pale. 'What – what do you think has happened to him? Where is he?'

'I've no idea,' said Mr King. 'But we'll find him as soon as we can. There are such a lot of loose ends about all this – that Rockingdown Stream, which runs under-ground, might lead us to the heart of the mystery – but no, it's blocked up with a completely impassable barrier – so we have to rule *that* out!'

'It's a good thing Miss Pepper is away,' said Snubby suddenly. 'She'd have a blue fit about all this.'

'Yes – she'd certainly go up in smoke,' agreed Mr King. 'Now – will you leave me alone for a bit. I must think, and I must remake my plans. I'll see you at lunch time, and tell you what I'm going to do. So long till then – and cheer up, do, for goodness' sake!'

Chapter Twenty-Five

Everything Is Very Difficult

At lunch time Mr King told the children his plans.

'I'm pretty certain Barney's disappearance is the result of his poking his nose into this smuggling affair,' he said. 'We'll have to find him, or things will be serious for him. These men are rogues – real bad fellows who stick at nothing.'

Diana was frightened. She stared at Mr King with wide, scared eyes. 'What are you going to do then?' she asked.

'First of all go through Rockingdown Manor again, top to bottom – especially the bottom, where the cellars are,' said Mr King. 'I feel you're right when you say those strange noises have something to do with all this – and Barney must have stumbled on the cause, and now he's disappeared because of it. Though I must say it beats me how the noises are made, and where they come from. If they don't come from the cellars, where *can* they come from?'

Mr King went on explaining his plans. 'I must also find out who that boat belongs to, and have a look at the farmhouse you told me about – and I must examine that gate or barrier thoroughly. It certainly looks as if nobody has moved it for centuries – but we must see. And if *we* can't get up past the barrier, well, I'm pretty certain nobody else has been able to push by it!'

'We'll come and help,' said Roger eagerly. He looked hard at Mr King. It was puzzling to think how he and the others had been so certain he was a villain! He seemed such a very admirable person now – really a very thrilling person indeed. Roger felt quite proud to know him! And yet he had been so scornful of him a short time ago. It just showed how careful you had to be in judging people.

They all spent a very busy and exciting day, but without much result. Rockindown Manor was searched once more from top to bottom. Two men appeared from the grounds on the way over, and joined them. They were the two men Roger had heard Mr King talking to the night before. They turned out to be men under him, detailed to help him.

'Meet Jimmy and Fred,' said Mr King, introducing them to the children, 'The terrors of the police force – hunters of rogues and scoundrels and my very good friends!'

The children grinned. Jimmy and Fred were strong and well-built, but otherwise quite ordinary-looking except for their quick observant eyes. They were both dressed in plain clothes.

'And Jimmy, Fred – meet Roger, Diana, Snubby – and Loony,' said Mr King. 'Terrors too, all of them, especially this young limb, Snubby. Watch out for him, or he'll play one of his frightful tricks on you; he's a real pest. Actually, Loony is the best of the lot – and quite the most intelligent.'

This was the kind of foolery the children understood and liked. They laughed. They began to feel that things really must turn out all right if Jimmy, Fred – and Mr King – were all on the job. Barney would soon be back!

Down in the cellars at Rockingdown Manor Mr King looked at the rug and cushion on the wooden shelf. He also looked at the iron ring in the corner, but, like the children dismissed it as nothing. It did not occur to him to screw the great ring round and round.

'Nothing here,' he said at last. 'I think either Barney left the cellars and went up into the grounds and was captured – or else the men came down here for some reason and found him. In any case he can't be anywhere near us, or he would yell and we would hear him.'

Jimmy was sent to make enquiries about the boat, and Fred was sent to examine the iron gate barring the way to the underground stream. The children wanted to go too but Mr King said no – he didn't want a whole crowd of people about, in case the men got wind that something was up. Where they were he didn't know – but obviously they must be hidden somewhere about the countryside.

Jimmy came back and reported. 'I've been to the farm-house, sir. Said I wanted to buy some eggs. There was a boy there, in the boat, messing about on the backwater. He said the boat was his – he'd had it from his uncle for a present for his last birthday. Seemed quite honest, sir – I don't think there's any reason to disbelieve him.'

'Well – there goes the mystery of the boat, then,' said Mr King. 'It belongs to a small boy who plays about in it! Ah – here's Fred. Perhaps he has something more interesting to report.'

Fred hadn't. He had been to the iron gate and had done a lot of dragging-away of greenery, pulling off enormous strands of ivy.

'No one has entered that way sir,' he reported. 'It's impossible. Short of blasting out the gate by dynamite we'd never make an entry there. The solid earth has settled all round the gate, and it's absolutely immovable. I don't think that stream has got much to do with this case.'

Mr King rubbed his chin and frowned. 'It's a real mys-tery, this,' he said. 'We know a mysterious aeroplane lands somewhere in that field – probably in the dry, flat area in the middle of it. We know a strange motor-launch haunts the spot where that stream joins the river. We suspect smuggling on a large scale here – and yet we can't find out where the stuff goes, or how it comes out again from wherever its hiding-place is. And on top of all this a boy disappears into thin air – with a monkey – and we haven't the faintest notion where he's gone!'

'Do the men at the farmhouse know anything of this affair, do you think?' asked Roger.

'So far as we know, they don't,' said Mr King. 'The farm is run by an old farmer who has been there for years – man called Daws. His father had the farm before him, and they've a very good name. We've checked up on him all right – and we've had a quiet inspection made of the whole farm – sent a man there who was apparently a Food Inspector, you know – and old Daws took him unsuspectingly around the farm, showing him every nook and cranny, most indignant that anyone should think he didn't keep on the right side of the law in every way!'

'Well – we really are at a dead end,' said Roger. 'There doesn't seem anything else we can do at all.'

'I do wonder where Barney is,' said Diana. 'I keep thinking of him. What's he doing? I'm sure he must be very miserable and frightened.'

'Barney's never really frightened,' said Snubby. 'He's one of these naturally brave people – he doesn't turn a hair when everybody else is shivering with fright.'

All the same, Barney was not feeling very brave at the moment. He was not having a good time at all! He had spent the day before exploring everywhere, trying to find a way of escape, but without success.

As we know, he explored as far as the iron gate and gave that up. He discovered the rope hanging down from the hole in the rocky roof of the tunnel – and gave that up too as a way of escape. The only thing left to do was to explore *up* the tunnel, and see where the stream came from. Maybe it flowed into the tunnel at a place where he could get out. On the other hand, of course, it might actually have its source underground, and not go into the open air at all until it poured out through the close bars of the iron gate. That really seemed rather more likely.

'Still, Miranda, we won't give up hope!' said Barney to the little monkey on his shoulder. 'Come on – up the stream we'll go – but before we do that, what about finishing that ham and opening another tin of fruit?'

After a meal of ham and tinned pears the two of them set off up the stream, instead of down. Barney came to the little passage that led to the shaft down which he had come the night before. He passed that, and went on up the stream, keeping to the little rocky ledge. Once the ledge stopped altogether, and Barney had to leap to where it began again, hoping he wouldn't fall into the water and be soaked through!

He went on for about fifteen minutes, flashing his torch round his feet to make sure of his next step. In places the ledge was slimy and slippery and he had to tread carefully. In other places the roof suddenly dipped down and he knocked his head against it before he realised it.

And then he came to a full stop. He couldn't go any farther. The roof had slanted down to the water, and there was no tunnel left – only a gurgling channel of water, hurrying through, pressing along, washing against the rock that completely hemmed it in. It was almost as if it were in a great pipe.

'Unless I get down into the water and make my way through it, completely submerged, head and all, I can't go any farther,' thought poor Barney in despair. 'And I daren't do that! I don't know how long the channel is before it becomes a tunnel again, with a ledge to walk on, and a roof above my head. I'd have to hold my breath under water for goodness knows how long, and probably I'd drown. As for Miranda, she wouldn't come at all. In any case she'd be swept away at once.'

178

There was nothing for it but to go back the way he had come. He was very disappointed. When he came to the little slanting passage leading from the tunnel to the shaft he turned up it. He would climb up the shaft and get into that tiny room above – he would have one more shot at moving that mysterious stone!

So up the passage he went with Miranda, and climbed the shaft to the top. He clambered out into the little room – but no matter how he tried he could not make anything work that stone out of its place! He didn't know the secret, he didn't even know if the stone *could* be moved from this side. Probably it couldn't. Poor Barney – he really didn't know what to do next!

Chapter Twenty-Six

Miranda Gives The Game Away

Nobody came into the underground tunnel that day.
Barney was there all alone with Miranda. He didn't like
it at all, and wished hundreds of times that he had a
watch. He had no idea whether it was twelve o'clock in
the morning or six o'clock in the evening! Actually it was
then about half-past five in the afternoon. Outside it was
broad daylight and bright sunshine. Down in the cave it
was pitch dark unless Barney had his torch on.

He didn't like to keep it on too long in case the battery
went. He knew how to turn on the big lights that flooded
the cavern, but he was afraid of doing that in case the
men came back unexpectedly and saw them. Then they
would know that an intruder was there and hunt for him.
Barney certainly didn't want to be discovered!

'What I want is to find a way of escape and go and tell
the others all I've found out,' thought Barney. 'Then I
suppose we'd have to go to the police – and what a
surprise they would get!'

He had another meal, and Miranda ate some pineapple
chunks from a tin and was extremely greedy over them.
So was Barney. They both liked them very much. Then
the boy went to stretch himself out on the mattress.

'This is very, very boring, Miranda,' he told the
monkey. 'Gracious, are you *still* eating pineapple. You'll
turn into a chunk if you don't look out! Miranda, what
are we to do? Can't *you* think of something?'

Miranda chattered away, sucking at a bit of pineapple.
She had got used to her strange surroundings now – and

as long as she had Barney, and tinned peaches, pears and pineapple she was quite prepared to stay in the tunnel for a long, long time.

'No books to read – nothing to do,' groaned Barney, punching the pillow to fit his head. It's frightful. There's only one thing to be said for this stay down here, Miranda – and that is I'm not spending any money! I've got precious little left, you know. We'll have to get a job soon, Miranda.

Miranda didn't mind that. She liked 'jobs', especially when it meant being dressed up in fine clothes and having people clap and cheer her in the ring, or at a fair. That was grand!

Barney fell asleep about eight o'clock. He slept for four or five hours and then was awakened by Miranda pulling at his ear and chattering.

He sat up, wondering where he was. He felt about for his torch and put it on. Of course – he was in that cavern, a prisoner who couldn't get out! He gazed round, wishing that he knew whether it was night or morning. It really was odd not to know.

'What's up, Miranda?' he said. 'Stop grabbing my ear, silly!'

But Miranda had heard something that Barney had not. She was warning him. He suddenly realised it, when he heard a heavy sound coming up the tunnel. He sprang to his feet.

The men were at work again. Then it must be the middle of the night – his second night there. They must be lowering stuff into the tunnel – soon some of them would be coming along to work the winches.

Barney knew he must hide. He decided to get behind the crates and spy on the men from there. He could hear their talk too. Taking Miranda on his shoulder he made his way to the side of the cavern where the big crates

181

were stored, both full and empty ones. He found a place inside an empty crate. He could peer through the cracks.

Soon lights appeared down the tunnel and came nearer – the torches of the men walking up the tunnel. Then Barney heard their voices. There were five men this time. One or two were evidently foreigners, and spoke with a strange accent. Barney could barely understand what they said.

He gathered that more crates had arrived that night – dropped by an aeroplane somewhere not far off. Somehow they had been transported to the tunnel – and were now about to be pulled up the stream by means of the wire rope wound up by the powerful winches.

And then Barney realised something he had not guessed before. The crates were not dragged up in the water just as they were – but were apparently put on narrow, solid and very strong little rafts of wood. It was these rafts that the man with the pitchfork guided. The crates were heavy, the current was swift, and the rafts and crates bobbed about as they came up against the stream.

Barney watched breathlessly, peering through the crack in the empty crate. The men were soon hard at work, working the winches, which whined and screeched, shouting to one another, pulling in the boxes and crates and cases as they appeared on their bobbing rafts. There were six of them.

Soon they were piled up with the others. Then one of the men, one of the chiefs, or perhaps a foreman, gave an order. Two men manhandled a crate from the store, and opened it.

It was full of bales of what looked like silk. Barney tried hard to see, but it was difficult. Then another crate was opened and Barney saw revolvers being thrown out in a heap. A third crate was opened, and the dull leaden-looking bars Barney had seen before, were flung out on the floor of the cave.

From another corner a man brought small boxes, and what looked like small canvas bags. The goods were rapidly packed in these. Barney guessed why. They would now be quietly disposed of in small quantities here and there. They were thrown on one of the bobbing rafts and the man with the pitchfork guided the raft down the stream, soon disappearing from sight.

Another raft was loaded and another. Then the men stopped work and had a meal. Barney hoped they wouldn't discover that some of their tins were gone! They didn't. They opened a tin of chicken, a tin of meat and three tins of fruit. They found some bottles and opened those too, drinking from them without bothering about glasses or cups.

They lighted cigarettes and talked. It was difficult to hear what they said, and Barney could only catch a word now and again. They talked about horses and cars and food and the cinema, as far as he could tell.

Miranda watching from Barney's shoulder, saw one of the men toss an empty peach tin away. To Barney's horror she leapt from his shoulder, squeezed out of the crate and bounded over to the tin. She picked it up, chattering with pleasure because there was still some juice in it.

The man turned and saw her. His mouth fell open in amazement. He rubbed his eyes and looked again. Miranda was now licking out the tin.

'Hey, Jo,' called the man. 'Look here!'

Jo turned – and he too gaped in astonishment at the sight of Miranda. He got up at once.

'Look, you fellows – a monkey! Now where in the name of goodness did it come from?'

All the men gathered round Miranda. She looked up

at them impudently. One of the men stroked her gently. In a trice Miranda was on his shoulder, pulling his hair.

The men began to laugh. They gathered round the little monkey, teasing her, petting her, and even opened another tin for her.

'How did she get here?' said Jo, in the greatest wonder. 'We've never seen her before. Where did she come from? Surely she hasn't been here all the time.'

'Course she hasn't. Don't be a fool, Jo,' said a big man with a scar right down his face. 'What I want to know is – did she come with anyone?'

Now it was Jo's turn to laugh. 'That's a funny joke, that is! How would anyone get in here? There's only one way in and that's ours – and no one but us knows it.'

'Well, how did the monkey get here then?' demanded the man with the scar.

'Oh – monkeys squeeze in anywhere,' said Jo. 'Artful little things, they are. Look at this one, eating a bit of peach just like you might – holding it in its hand and all!'

Barney watched Miranda angry and afraid. Little idiot! She might give the whole game away now – betray the fact that he was there, in hiding.

She sat there, eating the peach, gradually getting very full indeed. In fact, she was now so full that she felt she could not eat the fine half peach that one of the men gave her as soon as she had finished the piece in her hand.

She suddenly thought of Barney. She would give him the peach. He liked peaches too! So she leapt away from the crowd of admiring men and went straight to the crate in which poor Barney was hiding! She disappeared inside, chattering.

'Is that her hiding place?' said Jo, and went to peep in at her, flashing his torch. Then he gave a tremendous shout.

'HEY, LOOK HERE!'

The men came running up. They saw Barney crouching in the empty crate – with Miranda trying to push the peach in his mouth!

The men pulled him out roughly. 'What are you doing here? How did you get here, into this tunnel? Go on, you tell us everything or we'll make you very sorry for yourself!'

Barney looked round at the angry, glowering men. Now he was done for – silly little Miranda, her greed had made her give him away to the men. Jo shook him hard and Barney almost fell over.

'You tell us how you got in,' said Jo, between his teeth. 'Go on – quick!'

'All right,' said Barney. 'I'll show you. Let me go – I've not done any harm. I was only exploring a bit. Come on – I'll show you where I got in.'

Chapter Twenty-Seven

Miranda Does Her Best

Barney led the men up the tunnel, and then up the little passage to the shaft-hole. 'I came down there,' he said.

'Well – we know all about that old shaft,' said the man with the scar. 'It leads up to a little stone room and that's all.'

'Yes – but there's a movable stone in the wall there, that gives on to the old cellars of Rockingdown Manor,' said Barney. 'I moved the stone by accident when I was in the cellars, and got through the gap. But the stone closed up again and I couldn't get back. So I came down the shaft and into the tunnel. I hid there. That's all.'

'Anyone know anything about this movable stone?' said the man with a scar, sharply, looking round at the men. They shook their heads.

'I'll go up with you,' said the man, and he climbed up the shaft. Jo pushed Barney up behind him and then followed. 'Go on up – you show him this wonderful stone!'

Barney showed the man the stone that moved. He looked it over carefully and then swung his torch all over the wall. He called to Jo to come up.

'Jo – see that stone? It's worked by a lever somewhere. Look for a little groove in the wall and a staple or something jutting out, almost unnoticeable. Destroy the mechanism. I'm not having anyone else find this secret way in!'

'So that's the explanation of this mysterious room,' said Jo, elbowing Barney aside. 'It must have been secretly built when the old house was first put up, two or three centuries ago – with a secret way in. What a nice quiet way of disposing of your enemies!'

'Very,' said the man with a scar, in a dry voice that Barney didn't like at all. 'Now get down the shaft, boy – and we'll decide how to dispose of *you*. Good heavens is that monkey still on your shoulder?'

Back in the cavern the man questioned Barney carefully. When he heard that the boy was more or less a tramp, going from fair to fair and circus to circus, and had slept in the old house because he needed shelter, his face cleared a little.

'I see. Then you heard these noises, I suppose, and came down to explore – and found the secret of the moving stone. Well – you seem a likely enough lad – the kind we can train in our way of business – bit of smuggling now and again. Like to join us?'

'No,' said Barney.

That was quite the wrong thing to say. The man was taken aback. He scowled at Barney and then gave him a sharp box on the ears.

'Right! If that's the way you feel about it, you can keep out. But you won't like it. You'll be kept here till we can get you out, and then you'll be taken abroad in an aeroplane, and got rid of somewhere in a foreign land. We'll sell you to somebody who'll be glad of your help!'

'Anyway he can work for us now,' said Jo. 'There's always plenty to do. The only difference will be that he works for nothing because he's a fool, instead of working for good pay.'

Barney felt his heart go cold. How long would these men keep him here, working underground for them? He felt sure they would not allow him to go up into the daylight with them. He would always be left behind here, in the dark, with the sound of the stream for company.

'How long are you going to keep me here?' he asked, as boldly as he could.

'Maybe four weeks – maybe four months – it might even be four years,' said the man with the scar, enjoying frightening the boy. 'Depends how long our job goes on. You'll soon get quite fond of this place won't you!'

Barney didn't think he would at all. He said nothing more. He was afraid of these rough-looking, scowling men, afraid they would beat him or ill-use him. He wasn't going to learn their illegal business – but he could quite well see that he would have to turn to and do a lot of the dirty work for them, or else have a very bad time indeed. They would make as much use of him as they could.

Certainly the men made him keep hard at work that night! He had to help to guide the rafts up the stream, he had to help to take the crates and boxes to the side where they were stored, and he was given the job of undoing those that were to be sorted and repacked at once. He said nothing but did what he was told, though as slowly as he could.

His brain was working hard. How was he to escape? There must be some way. If only he could get a message through to the others! They must be very worried about him by now. They would have gone down to the cellars to look for him – and found his rug and cushion – but nothing else to show where he had gone! They couldn't tell Miss Pepper – and they certainly wouldn't tell Mr King.

Barney had been surprised that Mr King had not appeared underground with the men that night. Perhaps he directed operations from above ground. Well, if he came, Barney meant to tell him what he thought of him, even if it meant a beating! What a fraud, what a hypocrite, what a humbug! Barney spend quite a lot of time thinking bad things of Mr King. Little did he know what different ideas the other children had of him now!

The men worked for several hours, and then went. They left Barney underground, of course. 'We'll be back tomorrow night,' said Jo. 'And you'll have to work hard again, so sleep for the day!'

'I don't know if it's day or night down here,' said Barney, sullenly. 'It's always pitch-dark.'

He spent a very miserable day indeed down in the darkness, switching on the big lamps at times to give him a change, though the men had forbidden him to do this. But he was not going to spend every hour in darkness. His torch was getting a little dim. He must save it.

He slept all the afternoon, though he did not know it was that time of day. He awoke about five o'clock and had a meal with Miranda. He had quite forgiven the little monkey for giving him away. He was very glad she was with him, to amuse him with her ridiculous ways and to keep him company.

He felt very wide awake when he awoke, and wondered if it was night or morning. Perhaps it was morning as he felt so lively. He would have been surprised to know that it was getting on for the evening!

He began to think of some way out of his difficulties. There simply *must* be some way. He looked at Miranda. She had found a pencil belonging to one of the men and was scribbling on a piece of paper taken from an empty packing case. She showed her scribbles to Barney, evidently thinking she had been very clever.

Barney pretended to read it. 'Please rescue us – we are in an underground tunnel.' Very clever, Miranda! Very clever indeed – and beautiful writing.'

He was just handing back the paper to her when a thought suddenly struck him. Miranda was used to taking notes or articles to people. Could she – could she possibly

189

take a message from him to the others? She was a very
tiny monkey – if she knew she was to go on a message,
wouldn't she be able to find *somewhere* to get out from
this tunnel, somewhere to squeeze through? She was so
very small.

Barney had taught Miranda the trick of taking notes in
the way that all good trainers teach their animals – by
coaxing and reward. Many a time he had petted her and
fondled her, and said someone's name over and over
again, so that she would know where to take the note to
– and when she had found that person and delivered the
note, she had always been rewarded well by the one who
received it.

Would she be able to find Snubby and take a note to
him? Would she be able to squeeze out *somewhere*? It
was worth trying even if nothing came of it.

Barney had a note-book in his pocket. He took it out
and borrowed the pencil Miranda was using.

He began to write. He told briefly what had happened
to him and where he was. 'How you can rescue me I don't
know,' he wrote. 'I don't even know how you're to find
the place in the roof where the men enter, dropping down
on a rope. All I can say is it must be some place where
there is a dip in the ground – some spot where the tunnel
is very near the surface. Do what you can.'

When he had finished the note he folded it two or three
times, took some thin string from his pocket, and tied it
up carefully. Then he felt about for Miranda's collar which
was buried in her thick neck-fur, and he tied the note
firmly to it.

'Snubby,' he said to the little monkey, fondling her.
'Take it to Snubby. You know Snubby, don't you?
Snubby, my friend who likes you so much. Take it to
Snubby, to Snubby. Go find Snubby, Miranda. Snubby!'

Miranda listened, patting Barney's hands with her little

brown paws. She knew quite well what he meant. She was to take the letter that Barney had put round her neck to his friend Snubby – the nice boy with the dog.

She leapt off Barney's shoulder and bounded over the rocky floor to the tunnel. Barney watched her. Where was she going? Did she know a way out? He couldn't believe that she did because she had not been away from him for even a minute!

Miranda went up the tunnel, not down. Barney was surprised. There is no way out there, Miranda! But in about twenty minutes she was back again, the note still round her neck. She had been up the shaft and into the little room at the top, remembering that that was the way they had come in – but of course there was no way out for her there, so after scrambling round for a while she had come back.

Barney petted her again. 'Go on, find Snubby,' he commanded. 'You can find a way out if you try. Find Snubby, Miranda. It's very, very important!'

Miranda went off once more – and this time she didn't come back. Barney wondered about her. Had she found a way out? If so, where was it? He was quite sure that if there was some hole or cranny through which she could squeeze she would certainly find it.

Miranda had remembered the other place she had been to with Barney – the iron gate. She had sensed the daylight on the other side, and now she remembered it. Snubby would be somewhere out in that daylight. She must find him.

She arrived at the barrier. More daylight came through now, because Fred had torn away so much of the overhanging greenery, and had pulled at the ivy that clung so thickly to the bars. Miranda climbed lightly up the gate.

The bars were set very close indeed, too close even for Miranda to squeeze through. She tried her hardest. She

191

almost got stuck in one place, and in her fright tore herself free so roughly that she made her leg bleed.

She sat down to lick it, chattering comfortably to herself. Then, feeling tired with her efforts she curled up in a corner and fell asleep. She slept for two or three hours and then awoke. She stretched herself and then felt the note round her neck. Ah – she must take it to Snubby. Barney had said so.

She looked consideringly at the barrier. She felt a little afraid of it since it had hurt her leg. She chattered rudely at the gate, and then leapt on to it once more. She made a really good examination of it, from top to bottom, seeking for a way of escape.

And, at the bottom, she found a place where a bar had broken away at the surface of the water. Miranda got soaked as she squeezed through it. It was a tight fit, but she managed it! Now she was on the other side of the gate, in the dusk of evening. Snubby! She must go and find Snubby. But which way was she to go?

Chapter Twenty-Eight

A Thrilling Night

The three children went to bed feeling down in the dumps that night. Even Mr King had confessed that he didn't know which way to turn. Barney really did seem to have vanished into thin air, and there appeared to be no more steps they could take either to find him or to clear up the mystery.

'I don't want to go to bed,' said Diana. 'I know I shan't go to sleep.'

'Oh, yes you will,' said Mr King firmly. 'Off you go. It's ten o'clock already. Good gracious me, what would Miss Pepper say if she knew how late I have kept you up!'

They all went off, grumbling. Loony raced ahead of them. He never seemed to mind going to bed. He tore into Mr King's room, found his bedroom slippers, which were fleece-lined, and lightheartedly tossed them down the stairs. He then growled at all the rugs, dragged them into a heap where Mr King would be sure to fall over them, and left them there. Then he shot up the stairs as if a tiger were after him, landing on Snubby's bed in one last mad leap.

'Loony dog,' said Snubby, who was taking off his socks. 'Loony! Mad! Potty! Crazy!'

'Woof,' said Loony happily, and flung himself on Snubby to lick every bit of him that he could.

Diana did fall asleep quickly, though she had felt certain she wouldn't. So did Roger. Snubby lay awake a little time and then slid off into a peculiar dream about Barney and Miranda.

He was awakened some time later by Loony. Snubby sat up in bed and felt for his torch. Blow, where was it? The moon shone into the room through the trees, and gave a dim light, so he tried to see by that.

Loony was at the window, growling fiercely. He was on the window-seat just inside the window, and kept making darts at something outside, snapping and snarling.

'What's up, Loony?' said Snubby in surprise. He wondered if a burglar was trying to break into his bedroom. No – of course not – no burglar would face a growling dog like that!

Then something leapt right in through the window, sprang on to the top of a picture, and then up to the top of the window-curtain with a flying leap.

'Miranda! Oh, Miranda! It's *you*!' cried Snubby, recognising the tiny creature as she leapt across a ray of moonlight. 'Where's Barney?' Loony was now barking the place down, very angry to think that Miranda should dare to leap in at his master's window at night, when he, Loony, was on guard! Snubby threw a book at him. 'Shut up, idiot! You'll wake the whole household. Shut *up*, I say!'

Loony subsided at last, and sprang on to the bed jealously. Miranda was now on the bar of the bed at the back. Snubby got out of bed and switched on the light, just as Diana and Roger, awakened by the noise, switched on theirs. Roger appeared sleepily at the door.

'Whatever's the matter with Loony? Has he gone mad or something?'

'No – look, Miranda's back!' cried Snubby, and at her name the little creature sprang to his shoulder, cuddling into his neck. Snubby put up his hand to pet her, and at once felt the note tied to her collar.

'I say – what's this? A note! I bet it's from Barney!' he cried. He took off the note and undid the string round it. He opened it out. Roger came to read it with him, and Diana too, eager to join in the excitement.

'*Well*!' said Snubby, when they had all finished reading it. 'Fancy all this happening to Barney. Gosh – what a pity nobody can get that stone down in the cellars to move now. Fancy to think Barney's down underground where the river is. Would you believe it!'

'We'll have to rescue him somehow,' said Diana at once. 'I say – won't Mr King be thrilled to hear of this!'

'Better go and tell him,' said Roger, and all three went racing down the stairs, bursting into Mr King's room after a very quick knock. He was asleep.

But he woke up completely as soon as he read Barney's note. 'My word! This is news! So that's where the goods go to – where Barney is now. In some cavern underground, reached by way of the stream in the tunnel. But how can we find where that hole in the roof is, the one the men use to drop the goods down? I see it all now . . . the only missing link is the bit where the hole in the roof is. We've got to find that, and all is clear!'

'Can we do something about it tonight?' asked Snubby, excited

'I can – but you're not going to,' said Mr King firmly, to the bitter disappointment of all three children. He got out of bed and went down to the telephone. Fred and Jimmy and two other men were told to come along to Rockingdown Cottage. 'Things are moving!' said Mr King.

He shooed the children away and dressed. He was ready by the time the other men came. The children said goodbye so meekly that Mr King ought to have guessed they had something up their sleeves – but he didn't.

Under their dressing-gowns the children were fully

dressed! They meant to follow Mr King and the four men, and to see 'the fun' as Snubby put it.

Before he went off with his men, Mr King took a long look at a map he had. He put his finger on a certain spot. 'We know that the hole in the roof of the river-tunnel is in some place where the ground dips considerably,' he said. 'That means a hollow somewhere – and there's only one place where there is a hollow on Rockingdown Hill, and that's where the farmhouse is built that you went to the other day, Jimmy.'

'Right,' said Jimmy. 'That's it! The job is worked from there. Old Daws doesn't know anything about it, of course – he's too old – it's all done under his nose and he doesn't suspect a thing! I reckon it's that son-in-law of his who's in with the gang. He's a nasty piece of work.'

'Well – we're going there now,' said Mr King. 'We'll be quite a surprise-party! We might even catch them red-handed. But if they're not there we've got to find that hole in the tunnel roof and do a little dropping-in ourselves. Well, children – we'll see you in the morning!'

They said goodbye to the three children and strode off into the night. 'We needn't hurry,' said Roger to Snubby, seeing him begin energetically to strip off his dressing-gown. 'We know where they're going. We mustn't follow too close behind in case they spot us and send us back. We'll go in about five minutes' time.'

So they waited, very impatiently, for about five minutes, and then, with Loony at their heels, they set off. Miranda had gone again, though nobody saw her. They looked for her and came to the conclusion that she must have gone back to Barney.

They knew the way to the farm well now, and picked the best route they could. Once they got to the little backwater that led to the pond in the farmyard they knew they were getting very near. They crept alongside the water and came to the pond.

'Look – do look – that must be Mr King and his men – seeking everywhere with torches,' said Snubby in a whisper. 'They haven't waked anybody at the farm yet. Funny the dogs aren't barking.'

'Let's hide somewhere safe,' said Roger. 'Look – here's an old barn. We'll go in there and hide in some straw.'

They went into the old barn. A great heap of manure was in one corner. A pile of straw was in another. The children slipped into the straw and pulled it over them. They could wait there till things boiled up a bit – then they would creep out and see what was happening. The moonlight slanted into the barn and filled the place with light and with black shadows. It was all very exciting indeed.

Loony was as quiet as a mouse. Snubby's hand was on his collar. 'I simply can't think why the farm dogs don't bark,' began Snubby in a whisper. 'What's happened to them?'

'Don't know – either somebody's keeping them quiet, for some reason, or they're not here,' said Roger, also puzzled.

His first idea was right. The farm dogs were being kept quiet by someone who had spotted Mr King and his men – someone who wanted others to escape before the dogs barked, when he would have to come out into the open, and answer Mr King's awkward questions!

Suddenly the barn door was pushed slowly and softly open. Roger saw it and clutched Snubby and Diana, whispering into their ears. 'Look – someone's coming in. Keep Loony quiet.'

A man came in, silently, and slunk over to the manure heap. Another followed and another – a whole line of them. Who were they? Where had they come from? The

197

children had no idea. Loony stiffened and the fur on his neck rose up, but he made no sound.

Roger regretted bitterly that he had come into the barn with the others to hide. There might be a fight in here, when Mr King and his men came seeking with their torches – and Diana might get hurt.

He peered out of the straw. The men had pitchforks and were moving the manure heap rapidly. Then one knelt down and loosened something in the floor. He took out what looked like boards. Then he swung himself down and disappeared. All the men followed him save one. He stood there alone, panting as he pitchforked the manure back into place.

The children watched silently, their hearts beating fast. The hole in the roof of the tunnel! Why, it was here, in the floor of the barn – just a little way away from them. The men had gone down into the tunnel – the river must flow directly under this old barn. It probably fed the pond and the backwater in some way, as well as going on and on down to the iron gate.

The man who was left threw down his pitchfork on the manure and crept to the door. He went out and disappeared . A minute or two later the dogs of the farm began to yelp madly, and a voice called out sharply.

'Who's there! Come out and show yourselves. What are you doing on my farm at night?'

Then Mr King's voice answered sternly, and there was quite a meeting in the middle of the farmyard. The old farmer did not appear. He was sound asleep. It was the son-in-law who did all the talking.

'What nonsense! I know nothing about smuggled goods – nothing about entrances to underground rivers. You must be mad. Haven't the police anything better to do than look for things that aren't there and never have been? I tell you, you can go all over the place from top to bottom and you'll find nothing suspicious at all!'

Roger suddenly flung aside the straw in which he was hiding and ran to the door. Mr King might be wild with him for coming here, when he had forbidden him – but he had to say what he knew. He shouted at the top of his voice.

'Mr King! Mr King! We know where the hole is. It's in here, in the barn. And a lot of men have just escaped down it, waiting for you to go – then they'll come out again.'

There was an astonished silence. 'Well – you little pest! You've come after all – and the others too, I suppose,' said Mr King. He strode over to the barn with his men.

Roger pointed to the heap of manure. 'It's under there. You'd never have guessed. Fork it aside and you'll see! Gosh – isn't this EXCITING!'

Chapter Twenty-Nine

The End of it All

Barney was in the cavern when Miranda came back without the note. He petted her, very pleased. He gave her a big piece of pineapple from a tin as a reward. Now the others knew where he was – they would think of a way to rescue him.

And then things began to happen very quickly indeed. The men arrived in a hurry, queerly silent. They didn't work the winches. They brought no rafts with cases on them. They clustered together in the cavern, their faces anxious. They seemed to have forgotten all about Barney.

He didn't like the look of them. Supposing they had been driven underground because Roger had got on to the police, and they had got wind of it? They might guess that Barney had had something to do with it, and might turn on him. He decided it would be a very, very good thing to hide.

But where? Not in the empty crates – they would think of that at once. He would climb up the rocky wall of the cavern at the back and find a ledge to lie on. Barney silently crept away right to the back of the vast cavern and made his way up the wall, carefully feeling for jutting-out bits to hold on to with his hands and feet, climbing up bit by bit.

He found a very narrow ledge, so narrow that he almost rolled off it if he took a deep breath. But it was hidden from down below. He lay there with Miranda, listening.

And now came other voices, shouting and calling commands. Barney could hear Mr King's loudest of all, and was astonished. *Mr King*! Had he come down to be with the other men too then? Barney had no idea that the coach had nothing to do with the men. He was most amazed to hear all that Mr King shouted.

'You may as well give in! We're armed, and we know all about you. Either you surrender now, or we seal up the hole in the roof and leave you to starve.'

'We won't surrender,' Barney heard Jo say to the others. 'We've got plenty of food here. We shan't starve.'

'And how long will that last us?' said the man with the scar. 'A week at the most. Don't be a fool, Jo. We're caught here like rats in a trap. Why did we ever come down? If we had thought for one moment we'd have known that we had done for ourselves as soon as we came down here!'

They talked again, heatedly, urgently, some for surrender, some for staying down. Mr King shouted again.

'I'll give you five minutes. Stay down if you like, whilst we get hold of your chief up here – yes we know all about him – and he'll talk all right to save his own skin. He's talked before, you know. We'll come and collect you when you want to be collected. A little starvation diet won't do you any harm.'

'I'm giving up,' said the man with the scar. 'It won't do us any good to try and shoot it out, or to refuse to surrender. You all know we're caught. We've had a good run for our money. Well, I'm off to surrender. Anyone coming with me?.'

'What about that boy? said Jo suddenly. 'Can't we do a bit of bargaining over him? Can't we say we'll keep him down here with us and starve him to death?'

'I'd forgotten about him!' said the man with a scar. 'Where is he? Find him.'

But they couldn't find him. They didn't see him lying

201

precariously on a high ledge at the back, trying not to breathe.

'Well,' came Mr King's stentorian voice, 'your time is up. We're getting out – and the hole will be sealed up. A man will be on guard in the barn. Knock three times on the boards over the hole if you want to surrender.'

'Then the men got panic-stricken. They surged towards the tunnel, forgetting Barney.

'We'll give in! ' shouted Jo. 'You're on top, and we know it all right. We're coming.'

'One at a time, round the corner of the tunnel,' came the directions. 'Hands up as you come, or we fire.'

So, one at a time, round the corner of the tunnel went the men, holding their hands as high as they could, stumbling over the rocky ledge. And one by one they were hauled up the hole, and had handcuffs neatly clicked on their wrists as soon as they were in the barn. Jimmy and Fred greeted one or two of them by name.

'Well, if it isn't Jo! You just can't stay out of trouble, can you, Jo? And here's Frisky again, large as life and twice as natural – to think you're in this racket too! And who would have thought of meeting *you* here, Scarface?'

The last man was out. Mr King spoke sharply to him. 'Where's the boy who had the monkey? If you've harmed him things will go hard with you.'

'I don't know where he is,' said the man sullenly. 'He's not there. We looked for him.'

Roger could keep quiet no longer. He went to the hole and peered down it. 'Barney! BARNEY! Miranda! Come along, we're here. Everything's safe.'

Barney was already coming along the tunnel. He had watched the last man go, and reckoned it was safe for him to appear again. He heard Roger's yell and yelled back.

'I'm coming! I'm coming!.'

He was hauled up. The three children and Loony fell on him and almost suffocated him. They were overjoyed to see him.

'We got your note! Miranda brought it!'

'The hole in the roof was under a manure heap – in this old barn!.'

'Are you all right? Are you hungry?'

The handcuffed men eyed the children in amazement. Where had they sprung from in the middle of the night? How very extraordinary. The chief, who had sent the men down into the hole, and covered up the boards with manure, looked sullen and downcast. He was the old farmer's son-in-law, and under cover of getting in men to help on the farm, and to do repair work, he had brought in these villains, persuading them to help him in his illegal doings.

'And now,' said Mr King, looking quite sternly at the four children, 'it's really time you behaved like children and got yourselves to bed. Barney, I'm glad to see you safe – but you've had a very narrow escape, I think. As for you others, how you dared to follow me after I'd said you were not to come amazes me – and if you hadn't unexpectedly been of the very greatest help, I should have a lot more to say about disobedience. As things are I shall probably not say anything.'

He grinned suddenly, and the children grinned too. Good old Mr King! 'I suppose we can't stay any longer then?' said Roger.

'Not one moment,' said Mr King. 'And *this* time I expect complete obedience to my orders. Get back home and get into bed. I'll see you in the morning. I've got to stay here and see this little lot safely put away for the night!'

Barney, Roger, Diana, Snubby, with Miranda and Loony, took a last look at the sullen men, and then stumbled back home, Snubby yawning loudly, and setting everyone else off too. Then he sneezed.

'Oh dear – don't say you've caught cold,' said Diana in alarm. Snubby's colds were awful, and he sniffled dreadfully.

'No – just pepper up my nose,' yawned Snubby. 'Oh my – what will Miss Pepper say – and Roundy – when they hear what we've been up to!'

They all got into bed eventually. Barney was given one of the spare-room beds and cuddled down into it with Miranda, marvelling at its softness.

In the morning they could hardly believe all the happenings of the night before. Barney was thrilled to wake up and find himself in the cottage instead of in the dark cavern. There was such a tremendous chattering upstairs that Mrs Round came up to see what was the matter as soon as she arrived.

She listened, open-mouthed. She couldn't say anything at all except, 'Well, I never – you young limbs! Well, I never!'

When Mr King arrived in time for breakfast she regarded him with the greatest of awe. She cooked him a very, very special breakfast of ham and eggs. She never once took her eyes off him, even backing out of the room so that she could look at him till the last moment.

'What in the world have you told Mrs Round?' said Mr King, half-irritated. He looked tired but pleased. He tucked into his breakfast eagerly.

The children finished their own breakfast, which was not quite so special as Mr King's, and waited patiently for him to push away his plate and light his cigarette. Ah – there he was at last, puffing away.

'Well – it's all tied up nicely,' he said. 'Very, very nicely. Tanner, the son-in-law of the old farmer, and incidentally a very bad lot, has spilt the beans – in other words has told us everything. It has saved us quite a bit of trouble. I'm afraid, however, he'll get into a spot of trouble himself when he's out of prison, because the others won't easily forget how he betrayed them!'

'Serve him right,' said Snubby, who hated disloyalty.

'It was a very pretty little plot,' said Mr King, puffing at his cigarette. 'All kinds of goods were flown here from different countries – the aeroplane touched down in that field you know of – threw out the goods and made off again. The cases were manhandled to the stream, and put on the little rafts Barney has probably told you about. They were pulled up-stream by two men rowing the little unnamed boat that presumably belonged to the farmer's boy.'

'In the dark, I suppose?' said Roger.

'Oh, yes – always at night,' said Mr King. 'They were then manhandled again to the barn and dropped down the hole into the water – the rafts were dropped first, of course, and it wasn't very difficult to arrange the cases safely on the rafts, tie them to the wire rope, and then wind them up to the cavern by means of the winches. Once there, the cases were perfectly safe and could be unpacked, and the goods sorted and repacked in small packets and bags, ready for sale secretly.'

'They must have made a lot of money,' said Roger.

'They did,' said Mr King. 'They made just a few mistakes, though. They hired an electric launch which came slinking up the river to collect all these small packages and parcels, and they didn't pay the owner what they owed him – so he talked a bit – and his talk came round to us. That's what really made us suspect there was something going on, on a rather big scale.'

'What other mistakes did they make?' asked Roger

'Well – they didn't realise that thuds and bangs underground are often magnified when a building stands overhead,' said Mr King. 'Though even if they did realise it they would probably think that as the house was empty, nobody would hear them. But the *biggest* mistake of all was that they didn't realise there were four tiresome children, to say nothing of a monkey and a dog, who were going to suspect their poor old tutor, and snoop round him and his doings, and fall headlong into the mystery themselves! Aha – that was a very big mistake indeed!'

They all laughed, and Loony tugged madly at Mr King's shoelaces. 'No good, Loony,' said Mr King. 'They're special ones, made of leather, quite unchewable.'

'What *will* Miss Pepper say?' said Diana. 'She's coming back today!'

Once she had recovered from her amazement, Miss Pepper said rather a lot. She rounded on Mr King for deceiving her regarding his ability to coach. 'All those wonderful testimonials!' she said. 'I'm shocked, Mr King.'

'Don't be,' said Mr King. 'These kids have learnt a lot since I've been here. As for the testimonials, they were all true – I did do some coaching before I took up my present job. Cheer up, Miss Pepper – at least you weren't here when all this blew up.'

'I *should* have been,' said Miss Pepper. 'It is scandalous that all this should happen when I was away.'

'Yes. We ought to have waited till you came back,' said Mr King, and that made everyone laugh.

'Well, I'm glad it's all cleared up happily,' said Miss Pepper. 'What a tale! What will their parents say.'

'You don't need to bother about that,' said Mr King. 'I'm going to see them when they come back, and tell them everything myself. I can assure you that they will not blame you for anything, Miss Pepper.'

'I can't stay on at the cottage after all this,' said Miss Pepper. 'Not that I meant to, anyhow – because I'm taking my sister away to the sea, and I mean to take the children too. It will be *so* much nicer for them – bathing, sailing, fishing – much more to do than there is here.'

This was fine news. The children were thrilled. 'What about Barney? Can he come too?' Snubby asked.

'Well, there isn't really room, but I dare say we can squeeze him in,' said Miss Pepper. 'He certainly seems one of us now.'

But Barney shook his head. 'No, thank you,' he said. 'I've got a job. I'm joining a fair tomorrow – it's on its way through Rockingdown Village today. I met someone I knew who told me about it when I went to the village for Mrs Round this morning. It's time Miranda and I earned our living again!'

This was disappointing, very, very disappointing. They would miss Barney terribly. Would they ever see him again? Would he find his father some day? Now they would never know!

But when the children heard that the fair was actually coming to the seaside place where Miss Pepper was taking them, in ten days' time, they cheered up. They would see Barney then!

'And I also must say goodbye,' said Mr King. 'I have my living to earn as well – but not as a coach, I am thankful to say. I must get back to headquarters, and forget this pleasant little interlude with children, and monkeys and dogs!'

'Only one monkey and one dog,' said Snubby.

'And quite enough,' said Mr King, pushing Miranda off his shoulder and Loony off his feet. He stood up. 'I'm saying goodbye now. You were my bitter enemies at first – but I hope we're friends now!'

'Oh, *yes*,' said everyone, and then he was hugged by Diana, and banged on the back by the boys, whilst Loony barked madly.

Barney went down the front path with him, having

said goodbye too. The children watched them go, feeling rather sad that such a wonderful adventure had come to an end.

'All the same, I feel that we'll have more adventures with Barney and Miranda some day,' said Snubby, picking Loony up and squashing him till be squealed. 'I feel it in my bones.'

And I shouldn't be surprised if he's right!

Enid Blyton

MYSTERY

Enid Blyton

THE RILLOBY FAIR
MYSTERY

Chapter One

First Day of the Holidays

''Morning, Mother! 'Morning, Dad!' said Roger, and ruffled his father's hair as he passed him, and dropped a kiss on his mother's curls.

'Don't *do* that, Roger,' said his father impatiently, smoothing his hair down. 'Why are you late for breakfast? And where's Diana?'

'Can't imagine,' said Roger cheerfully, helping himself to an enormous plateful of porridge. 'Asleep, I suppose.'

'Never mind,' said his mother. 'It's only the second day of the holidays. Roger, you can't *possibly* eat all that porridge – with sausages to follow.'

'Oh, jolly good,' said Roger, sitting down in front of his great plateful. 'Any fried onions with them?'

'Not at breakfast-time, Roger. You know we don't have onions then.'

'I can't imagine why not,' said Roger. He began to eat his porridge, craning his neck to read the back of his father's newspaper.

As the newspaper was folded in two, the reading matter was upside down for Roger, and his father glanced at him irritably.

'Roger! What are you screwing your head round like that for? Have you got a stiff neck?'

'No – only just reading that exciting bit in the paper about the dog that . . .'

'Well, don't. You know it's bad manners to read a

5

paper when someone else is reading it,' said his father. 'Don't they teach you manners at school?'

'No. They think we learn them at home,' said Roger cheekily.

Mr Lynton glared over the top of his newspaper. 'Well, then, perhaps I'd better teach you a few these holidays,' he began. And just at that moment Diana burst into the room, beaming.

'Hallo, Mother! 'Morning, Dad! I say, isn't this a heavenly day – all daffodils and primroses and sunshine! Gosh, I do love the Easter hols.'

'Get your porridge, dear,' said her mother. 'Roger, you haven't taken *all* the cream surely?'

'No, there's a spot left,' said Roger. 'Anyway, it won't hurt Diana to have plain milk. She's too fat.'

'I'm *not!* Am I, Mother?' said Diana indignantly. Her father gave an exasperated click.

'Sit down, Diana. Eat your porridge. If you *must* be late, be late quietly. Breakfast is at eight o'clock – and it's now half-past!'

Mr Lynton gathered up his newspaper, put it beside his wife's place, and went out of the room.

'What's the matter with Dad this morning?' asked Diana, pulling up one of her stockings. 'Blow this stocking. It keeps coming down. Why is Dad so mouldy, Mother?'

'Don't talk like that, Diana,' said Mrs Lynton. 'There's nothing wrong with your father except that he does like you two to be punctual for meals – and also he's heard that his Uncle Robert is coming to stay. You know the dear old fellow bores your father terribly.'

'Oh my goodness – is Great-uncle Robert *really* coming?' said Roger. 'Whatever for? And where are you

6

going to put him? Snubby's coming tomorrow, isn't he – and he'll have the only guest-room.'

'Well, he can't now – he'll have to sleep in your room,' said his mother. 'I'll have a bed put up there. I'm sorry, Roger – but it's the only thing to do. Uncle Robert must have the guest-room.'

'Oh gosh – Snubby sleeping with me – and playing his fool tricks all the time,' groaned Roger. 'I shan't mind having Loony in the room – but Snubby's awful.'

'I'd very much rather you didn't have Loony sleeping in the bedroom with you,' said Mrs Lynton. 'He's a very nice spaniel, I know, although he's completely mad – but I do *not* like dogs in bedrooms.'

'Mother! You say that every single time Snubby and Loony come to stay,' said Diana. 'And you know quite well that if you turned Loony out into the kennel Snubby would go too, and sleep with him there at night.'

'Yes, I know,' said Mrs Lynton with a sigh. 'I don't know which is worse – Snubby or Loony.'

Snubby was a cousin of the two children, and owned a black cocker spaniel called Loony, short for Lunatic. Snubby's parents were dead; so he spent his holidays staying with various relations. Mrs Lynton was sorry for him and fond of him, and he came more often to her house than to anyone else's.

'He's coming tomorrow, isn't he?' asked Diana. 'I'll order a big bone for Loony today when I go by the butcher's. Dear old Loony. I wonder if he's still mad on brushes. Mother, last summer hols he took every single brush he could find. He put some of them down a rabbit-hole. We found quite a collection there one day.'

Mrs Lynton hurriedly made up her mind that she would warn the household to keep all brushes out of Looney's reach. Oh dear – what with Snubby and Loony and Uncle

7

Robert, it looked as if things would be much too hectic for the next few weeks.

'I wonder what Snubby will say to Great-uncle Robert,' said Diana with a giggle, helping herself to sausages. 'Oh, Mother – I just can't see them together, somehow. Uncle Robert's so haw-hawish and pompous – and Snubby's so mad and idiotic.'

'You'll just have to keep Snubby and Loony out of your uncle's way, that's all,' said her mother, getting up from the table. 'Well, I'm sorry I can't wait for you two any more. I see you've finished up the toast and have begun on the loaf of bread. When you've finished that perhaps you'd like to call it a meal! I cannot imagine how you can put all that away.'

'Easy,' said Roger, and grinned at his mother as she went out of the room. She smiled back. It was nice to have the children at home again, but it did take a little time to get used to their enormous appetites, careless ways and constant sparring.

Silence fell when Mrs Lynton had gone out of the room. The two munched away hard, gazing out of the window. Daffodils danced at the edges of the lawn, and wallflowers shook the scent from their velvet petals. Sunshine flooded the garden and the two children felt happy and excited. The weeks stretched before them – no lessons, no rules – only day after day of sunshine and holidays, enormous meals, ice-creams – and Loony, the dog, to take for walks.

'Heavenly,' said Diana, coming out of her daydream. Roger knew what she had been thinking, and he agreed.

'Yes. Super,' he said. 'I wonder how Loony will get on with Sardine.'

Sardine was their big black cat, so-called, because of her great fondness of the tinned fish called sardine. The grocer was always astonished at the amount of tinned sardines Mrs Lynton bought – fancy a family eating as many sardines as that! But it was Sardine the cat who ate it all, and waxed fat and sleek on it.

'I should think Loony will give Sardine a frightful time,' said Roger, scraping out the marmalade dish.

'I shouldn't be surprised if Sardine doesn't hold her own quite well,' said Diana. 'Let me have a scrape of that marmalade, Roger. Don't be a pig.'

'I wish Great-uncle Robert wasn't coming,' said Roger, handing over the marmalade pot. 'I wonder why he's coming. He doesn't usually come in our hols. It's the last thing you'd think he'd want to do, considering he thinks all children are perfect pests.'

'Diana! Haven't you two finished *yet?*' called Mrs Lynton from upstairs. 'Come along. I want you to help me with Snubby's bed. I'm putting the play-room divan into Roger's room. Roger, come and give me a hand with it.'

'Never a moment's peace!' said Roger with a grin at Diana. 'Come on. Let's give a hand.'

They tore upstairs, falling over Sardine as they went. The big black cat fled up in front of them, tail in air, green eyes gleaming wickedly.

'Sardine! Do you *still* lie on the stairs, you wicked cat?' shouted Roger. 'You be careful tomorrow, or Loony will get you if you don't look out!'

'Loony'll get you if you don't look out. Loony'll get you if you don't look out!' chanted Diana, and skipped into Roger's room to help her mother. Sardine was sitting on the window-sill there, her long tail waving from side to side.

'What have you two been doing to make Sardine so cross?' asked her mother.

'Well, I like *that!* She was lying doggo on the stairs waiting to trip us up!' said Diana indignantly.

'Lying catto, you mean!' said Roger with a chortle.

'Oh, Roger – you sound like Snubby when you say things like that!' said his mother. 'Diana, make Roger's bed whilst he and I bring in the divan.'

They were busy that day, preparing for Great-uncle Robert and Snubby – what an odd pair! Great-uncle Robert was so old and polite and pompous, correct in every way – and Snubby was so very much the opposite, cheeky, idiotic and unexpected in all he did. Mrs Lynton had quite a few qualms when she thought of them in the house together.

As for Loony, he would probably drive the old man mad. All the same Loony was a darling, and Mrs Lynton, like everyone else, had fallen under his spell. Dear, silky-coated, melting-eyed Loony. There was probably only one person in the household who would regard Loony with bitter dislike – and that was Sardine.

At last the two rooms were done. The guest-room looked nice and bright and clean. Flowers arranged by Diana stood on the dressing-table, bright yellow daffodils matched by the yellow towels hanging by the basin.

Roger's room looked different, now that it had the extra divan in. It wasn't very big anyhow, and looked very crowded now, with the divan and an extra chair. Mrs Lynton also added an old rug in one corner for Loony to sleep on.

'Oh, Mother! What's the good of that?' said Roger. 'You know where Loony always sleeps – on Snubby's feet.'

His mother sighed. It looked as if these holidays were going to be just a little bit *too* exciting. She was quite right – they were!

10

Chapter Two

Snubby Enjoys Himself

Snubby was pleased to be going to his cousins' home for the holidays. He liked Mrs Lynton, their mother, and he quite liked Mr Lynton, though he was secretly afraid of his sudden tempers. It would be good to see Diana and Roger again.

His luggage had gone in advance. He only had a small bag with him – and Loony, of course. He was now waiting for the train, a snub-nosed, red-haired, freckled boy of twelve. He whistled tunelessly as he waited, and Loony pricked up his ears as he always did when his beloved master made a noise of any sort.

The train came in with such a roar and rumble that Loony was startled. He jerked away in alarm, and rushed into the waiting-room, where he cowered under a seat.

Snubby followed, indignantly. 'What do you think you're doing, idiot, rushing away like that! Anyone would think you'd never seen a train before. Come here!'

The train gave a piercing whistle, and Loony cowered back still farther. Snubby had a job to get him to move.

'Look here – the train will be gone before we've caught it if you don't look out!' shouted Snubby, exasperated. 'Come OUT, I tell you. What's come over you?'

He dragged poor Loony out at last, lumped him into his arms and staggered to the train. The porter was already slamming the doors.

'Hey you – get in quickly!' yelled the man. 'Train's just going!'

Poor Snubby had no chance to choose his carriage carefully as he usually did. He liked a completely empty one, so that he could occupy each corner in turn, and look out of any window he liked. There was no time to look into even one carriage now. He wrenched open a door, threw Loony in, and fell in himself, landing on hands and knees. The porter slammed the door, and the train moved off.

Loony retired under the seat. Snubby glared at him. 'Idiotic dog! You nearly made us miss the train!'

He got up and dusted himself down. He looked round the carriage. Only one other person was there, thank goodness.

The one other person stared at Snubby in annoyed surprise. He was an old man with a head of silvery-white hair, a real mane. His eyes were a faded blue and he had a small pointed beard, also very white.

'My boy,' he said, 'it is most inadvisable to leave so little time for catching a train.'

'I've been waiting for twenty minutes,' said Snubby indignantly. 'Here, Loony, come on out. You'll get filthy under there.'

Loony appeared, his tail well between his legs. The old man looked at him with dislike.

'Dogs!' he said. 'I think they should travel in the guard's van. They always smell. And they scratch themselves in such an objectionable manner.'

'Of course dogs smell,' said Snubby, sitting down opposite the old man. 'It's a nice smell, a doggy smell. So is a horsy smell. And I like cow's smell too. And as for . . .'

'I don't think I want to discuss smells,' said the old man. 'I do *not* like the smell of dogs, and I do *not* like the way they scratch themselves.'

'Loony never scratches,' said Snubby, at once. 'A dog

12

only scratches when he's got heaps of fleas. I keep Loony jolly clean. Brush him every single day, and . . .'

Loony put himself into a peculiar position and began to scratch himself very hard indeed, making a thumping noise against the floor of the carriage.

Snubby pushed him crossly with the toe of his shoe. 'Shut up, idiot. Didn't you hear what I just said?'

Loony looked up politely, and then began to scratch himself again. The old man looked disgusted. 'Do you mind taking him to the other end of the carriage?' he said. 'Bearing in mind your remark about dogs only scratching themselves when they have a large number of fleas, I don't feel too happy about having him in quite such close proximity.'

'What's that mean?' asked Snubby obstinately, not moving. 'I tell you, he hasn't got fleas, he's never . . .'

'I don't think I want to discuss fleas,' said the old man stiffly. 'Well, if you won't move your dog, I must move myself. But I must say that children nowadays are not remarkable for their good manners.'

Snubby hastily removed Loony to the other end of the carriage, feeling rather ashamed of himself. The spaniel tried to climb up the seat, but the old man looked so very disapproving that Snubby changed his mind about letting him.

Loony fortunately went to sleep. Snubby undid his case and took out a paper-covered book. He settled down to read. The old man looked to see what Snubby was reading. The book had a most lurid cover and an extraordinary title. It was called *SPIES! SPIES! SPIES!*

Snubby curled himself up, lost to the world. The old man was astonished to see such a peculiar title.

'What is your book about?' he asked at last.

13

Snubby thought that was a silly question, considering that the book's title was plainly to be seen.

'It's about spies,' he said. 'Stealing old maps and plans and things like that.'

The old man gazed at Snubby and then made a curious remark. 'Spies! I never thought of that! It might have been spies.'

Snubby looked up, astonished. 'Funny old fellow!' he thought. 'What's he talking about now?'

'It's strange you should be reading a book about old documents being stolen,' said the old man. 'Because I've just left a place where there's been a theft of that kind. Terrible, terrible!'

Snubby stared at him. 'What exactly was stolen?' he asked.

'The letters of Lord Macaulay, of maps of the county of Lincolnshire, and the correspondence between Lady Eleanor Ritchie and her sister,' said the old man, shaking his head solemnly. 'And the old recipes of the Dowager Lady Lucy, and . . .'

This was all Greek to Snubby. He began to think the old man was pulling his leg. All right, he could do some of that too!

'And I suppose the pedigree tables of all the dogs went too, and the letters written by Lord Popoffski,' he said, solemnly and sympathetically.

Now it was the old man's turn to stare. 'Ah – I see you don't believe me,' he said with dignity. 'Well, let me tell you this, young man. The thief got into a locked room without unlocking it. He got into a room with every window fastened and didn't unfasten one. He left no fingerprints, he made no noise.'

Snubby didn't believe a word. He looked disbelievingly at the old man.

'Well,' said the old fellow, 'that's a strange story, isn't it? Too strange for me. I've left the house where it all happened, and I'm not going back there. I don't like thieves who go through locked doors. Do you?'

Snubby put down his book. If there was to be a bit of story-telling, well he would do some too.

'Funny you should tell me this, sir,' he said earnestly. 'I'm running away too. I've unearthed a Plot, sir, a very sinister Plot.'

'Good gracious!' said the old man, alarmed. 'What kind of a plot?'

'Sort of atom-bomb plot, sir,' went on Snubby, enjoying himself. 'They tried to get me, sir – and they very nearly did.'

'Who tried to get you?' asked the old man, amazed.

'Sh!' said Snubby mysteriously, looking all round the compartment as if he thought 'They' were listening. 'It's the Green Hands, sir – surely you've heard of that gang?'

'No. No, I can't say I have,' said the old man. 'Who are they?'

'An international gang, sir,' said Snubby, enjoying himself more and more, and marvelling at his powers of invention. 'They've got the secret of the atom bomb, sir – and I stumbled on it by accident. They captured me and wanted me to work for them.'

'What – a boy like you?' said the old man.

'They can use boys,' said Snubby. 'For experiments and so on, you know. Well, I didn't want to be blown to bits, did I?'

'Good heavens!' said the old fellow. 'This is incredible. You should go to the police.'

'I'm running away,' said Snubby, sinking his voice to a whisper. 'But "They're" after me, sir – the Green Hands.

15

I know they are. They'll track me down. They'll get me in the end.'

'But this is unbelievable!' said the old man, mopping his forehead with a big white silk handkerchief. 'First I stay in a house where thieves go through locked doors and fastened windows – and now I travel with a boy hunted by – by what, did you say – the Green Hands. Do they – do they have green hands?'

'They wear green gloves,' invented Snubby wildly. 'Beware if you ever see anyone wearing green gloves, won't you? Man *or* woman.'

'Yes. Yes, I certainly will,' said the old man. 'My poor boy – have you no parents to look after you?'

'No,' said Snubby, telling the truth for the first time in five minutes. 'I haven't. I'm fleeing to the country to stay with my cousins. I hope the Green Hands don't track me there. I don't want the whole lot of us blown up.'

'Good heavens! Incredible! The things that happen these days!' said the old man. 'Take my advice, my boy, and go to the police.'

The train drew to a stop. Snubby looked out casually, and then leapt to his feet suddenly, startling the old man considerably.

'Golly! This is my station! Here, Loony, wake up! Stir yourself. Good-bye, sir – and I hope you catch your locked-door thief.'

'Good-bye, my boy. We've had a most interesting con-versation – and take my advice, go to . . .'

But his words were lost in the whistling of the engine and the slamming of the door. Snubby was gone and so was Loony. The old man sank back in his seat. Well, well, well – what was the world coming to? To think that even a young boy could be mixed up in such extraordinary plots. Most alarming.

'Nobody's safe these days!' thought the old man gloomily. 'It's all *most* alarming.'

Chapter Three

An Unexpected Meeting

Snubby arrived on the platform very hurriedly, fell over Loony and sat down with a bump. A squeal of laughter greeted him.

'Oh, Snubby!' cried Diana's voice. 'You *always* fall out of a train! Hallo, Loony!'

Loony flung himself on Diana in a mad bound, almost knocking her over. He barked and yelped, pawing her ecstatically. She had to push him off at last.

'No, Loony, no more. Get *down*. Snubby, tell him. He's just as loony as ever, isn't he? I say, Roger's sorry he couldn't come and meet you, but he's gone to the next station to meet Great-uncle Robert. Why you couldn't both come to the same station, I don't know! I suppose Great-uncle thought the next one was nearer to us.'

'Who's Great-uncle?' asked Snubby in surprise. 'I've never heard of him before. Surely he's not coming to stay?'

'Yes, he is. Maddening, isn't it, considering it's our hols,' said Diana as they walked out of the station. 'He's not a bad old thing, only awfully pompous and polite. Mother didn't know till yesterday that he was coming. We've had to put you in Roger's room.'

'Oooh, good,' said Snubby. 'Loony will like that.'

'Does he still take every brush he can find?' asked Diana. 'He was awful last summer hols.'

'Yes, he's still pretty bad about brushes,' said Snubby.

'And mats. And cats too. I say – you've got a cat now, haven't you?'

'Yes. A big black one called Sardine,' said Diana. 'She's almost a year old, so she's still pretty idiotic at times. I don't know how she'll get on with Loony.'

'It'll be a lively household,' said Snubby, pleased. 'Cats and dogs flying all over the place, and us three, and your old Great-great-uncle.'

'Only *one* Great,' said Diana. 'He's Daddy's uncle. Well, there's our house. Loony remembers it, look! He's rushing in at the gate. My word, he'll startle old Sardine – she's basking on the wall!'

Snubby ran after Loony. Loony had already discovered Sardine, and was chasing her madly round the front garden, yelping in excitement. Sardine flew into the house, Loony raced after her, and Snubby tore after them both.

Mrs Lynton was amazed to see Sardine flash past her head and land on top of the bookcase. She was even more amazed to see Loony coming in like a streak of black lightning, followed by a shouting Snubby.

'Oh! It's *you* arriving, Snubby. I might have guessed,' she said. 'There's really not much difference between you and a tornado. How are you, dear?'

'Hallo, Aunt Susan!' said Snubby. 'Come here, Loony. Oh, good – Sardine's gone out of the window now. Gosh, so has Loony.'

He disappeared at top speed, and Mrs Lynton sat down again with a sigh. Peace always vanished when Snubby arrived. There were loud cries from the garden, and finally a scream from Diana.

'Mother! Here's Great-uncle in a taxi with Roger.'

Mrs Lynton got up hurriedly. She wondered what Uncle

19

Robert would say when he found the front garden full of yells and yelps, howls and yowls, and screaming children.

She went into the garden, and hissed at Snubby. 'Catch Loony at once. Take him away. Go and wash your hands or something!'

Snubby gave her a startled glance. How cross she sounded! He gave a piercing whistle and Loony responded at once. He arrived like a cannon-ball at Snubby's heels, and the two disappeared indoors just as Great-uncle Robert opened the front gate. Diana smoothed back her hair and went to welcome him too.

'So nice to be here at last, my dear Susan,' said the old fellow. 'Such a peaceful place – far from thieves, and wars and spies!'

Mrs Lynton felt astonished. 'Oh, we're peaceful enough here, out in the country,' she said. 'Come along up to your room. You will like a wash, I expect.'

'Thank you, my dear, thank you,' said Uncle Robert, and followed his niece up the stairs. She took him to the guest-room and put his bag down for him.

'Very nice room,' said Uncle Robert. 'Very nice view too. Beautiful. Ah – who's this?'

It was Loony. He came nosing into the bedroom, having smelt somebody new. He stood at the door, wagging his black stump of a tail, his long ears drooping like a judge's wig at each side of his head. Uncle Robert looked at him.

'Most peculiar,' he said. 'There was a dog in the train, in my carriage, *exactly* like that!'

'Oh, well – black cockers are very much alike,' said Mrs Lynton. 'Now you wash, Uncle Robert, and then come down to lunch. You must be hungry.'

She went to a cupboard on the landing to put some things away. Snubby was whistling in Roger's room, brushing his wiry hair and making it stand up straighter than ever. He suddenly missed Loony.

'Hey, Loony! Where have you got to?' he said. He went to find him. Ah, there he was, standing in the doorway of the room next but one. He went to get him. Somebody came walking out at the same moment, stepping carefully over Loony, who didn't attempt to move out of the way. He never did if people were stupid enough to walk round or over him.

Snubby stopped in the utmost amazement when he saw Great-uncle Robert. He stared as if he couldn't believe his eyes.

Great-uncle Robert stared too.

'Incredible!' he muttered, taking a step backwards and nearly falling over Loony. 'You again! What are you doing here?'

'I'm staying with my cousins,' said Snubby, horrified to see that the old man in the train had suddenly become Great-uncle Robert. Gosh, this was frightful. That awful story he had told him – about the gang called Green Hands! Suppose he told Aunt Susan about it, what in the world would she say? She wouldn't understand at all. She would be furious!

'So you ran away here,' began Uncle Robert. 'Do your cousins know why?'

'Sh!' said Snubby desperately. 'Don't say a word to anyone. Remember the Green Hands! They'll get you too if you split.'

'Split?' repeated Uncle Robert faintly, not understanding the word.

'Blab. Spill the beans. Give the game away,' said Snubby urgently. 'Don't say a word. Just remember the Green Hands!'

The gong in the hall suddenly sounded for lunch, and both Uncle Robert and Snubby jumped violently.

'Sh!' said Snubby again, and looked all round him as if he were being hunted.

'I'll remember the Green Hands,' said Uncle Robert in a stronger voice. 'But be careful, my boy, do be careful.'

He went downstairs, wiping his broad forehead with his silk handkerchief. He had escaped from one house where thieves made their way through locked doors – only to come to another place where there was a boy hunted by the Green Hands. Where should he go next? Incredible, quite incredible.

Up on the landing, half-hidden by the open cupboard door, was a most astonished Mrs Lynton. She had overheard the extraordinary conversation and couldn't understand a word of it. What was all this talk of Green Hands and all the shushings and warnings she had heard? She was filled with amazement.

'What's Snubby up to now? And how does he know Uncle Robert? And what *is* this talk of Green Hands?' she thought, shutting the cupboard door impatiently. An agonised yowl made her jump. She opened the door hurriedly and Sardine jumped out.

'Silly cat! Why put your tail in the door when you know I'm going to shut it?' said Mrs Lynton. 'You're always doing things like that. There now, I'm sorry I hurt your tail. And just look out for Loony, because I don't want you streaking across the dining-table as soon as you see him!'

Loony was downstairs with the others. He had attached himself to Great-uncle Robert, much to Diana's surprise. He was sniffing round his feet and pawing at his legs in a most friendly manner.

'He's acting just as if he's met you before,' said Diana.

'Er – is he?' said Uncle Robert, not knowing quite what to say. 'Snubby – call him off, will you? I don't particularly want his fleas, you know.'

'How do you know he's got fleas?' asked Roger, surprised. 'Has he, Snubby?'

It looked as if the conversation was now going to be awkward. Snubby pulled Loony away and shoved him firmly under the table.

'Of course he hasn't got fleas,' he said. 'You'd jolly well know if he had. Why, a chap at school had a dog that had about three hun . . .'

Mrs Lynton came in, still looking puzzled. 'What are you talking about?' she asked, sitting down at the head of the table.

Nobody told her. She didn't encourage subjects of that sort at meal-times. Uncle Robert took his place gingerly, looking under the table to see exactly where Loony was.

'What's that noise?' inquired Mrs Lynton, hearing a thump-thump-thump on the floor under the table.

'Oh, just Loony scratching himself,' said Diana.

'Oh dear, Snubby – and I hope you haven't brought Loony here with . . .' began Mrs Lynton.

'No Aunt Susan, I haven't,' said Snubby hurriedly. 'I say – is that chops – and chip potatoes – and ONIONS! Golly, how smashing!'

The subject was safely changed. Mrs Lynton served the meal, still wondering about such curious things as Green Hands. She glanced at Uncle Robert. He seemed such a nice, harmless old fellow. What *did* he mean, whispering about running away and Green Hands up on the landing with Snubby?

It was really most extraordinary!

23

Chapter Four

Great-Uncle Tells His Story

After the meal Snubby escaped into the garden with Roger and Diana, Loony at their heels. They all went into the little summer-house, which faced south and was very warm in the April sun.

'Gosh! It's as hot as summer,' said Roger. 'I'll really have to take off my coat. I say – Great-uncle is rather an old stick, isn't he? We'll have to mind our manners a bit now, or he'll get going on the "good old days when children knew their manners, and were seen and not heard," and all the rest of it.'

'I've got something to tell you,' said Snubby, rather awkwardly. 'About Great-uncle.'

'Go on then – out with it. What have you been doing? Using his hair-lotion for Loony or something?' asked Roger.

'Don't try and be funny,' said Snubby. 'It doesn't suit you. Listen – I came in the train with him, and I got off at the North Station and he went on to South, where you met him. We had quite a lot of – er – conversation.'

The other two looked at him in surprise. 'You did?' said Diana. 'Well – why ever didn't you say so then? Why keep it such a deep, dark secret?'

'Well, you see – it's like this – he told me a silly story about running away from somewhere he'd been staying, because thieves had got through locked doors and stolen papers and things,' said Snubby. 'Lord Somebody's letters and Lady Somebody's recipes – a lot of awful nonsense.

24

And – well – *I* told him a story too. I thought to myself, well, two can play at this game, and I sort of let myself go.'

'Do you mean you went and stuffed him up with some frightful fairy tale?' said Roger. 'Whatever did you tell him?'

Snubby related the story he had told to Great-uncle Robert, ending with his running away from a gang called Green Hands, who always wore green gloves. Diana and Roger listened in astonishment that ended in giggles.

'Gosh, Snubby – you really are the biggest fathead that ever lived!' said Roger at last. 'What in the world did you go and stuff Great-uncle up with that for?'

'Well, how was I to know he was your Great-uncle?' demanded Snubby. 'I didn't know you'd even got one. And I certainly didn't know he was coming to stay with you. I got a shock, I can tell you, when I saw him in the guest-room. I nearly passed out.'

'You'll get another when he tells Dad the rigmarole you told him,' said Roger. 'Dad doesn't like fairy tales of that sort. He doesn't understand that kind of joke.'

'I know,' said Snubby dismally. 'I've warned Great-uncle not to say a word. He really believes it all, you see. I expect he's terrified of the Green Hands Gang now – just as terrified as he is of the thieves that walked through the locked doors at the house where he was staying.'

'Well, he must be a mutt if he believes a word you say,' said Diana. 'Oh dear, Snubby – you always bring trouble with you. Now don't you go frightening the old man with sinister notes, or drawings of green hands or anything.'

'Oooh – that's an idea,' said Snubby, sitting up. 'Oooh, I say – wouldn't he have a fit!'

'Yes, he would – and the first thing he'd do would be to tell Dad, and you'd get a whacking,' said Roger.

25

'That's no go then,' said Snubby, who had quite clear memories of one of Uncle Richard's whackings. 'I don't want to go too far with Uncle Richard.'

'You'd better not,' said Roger. 'He's not in a very good mood so far these hols – because Great-uncle has come to stay, I think – and what with that, and us, and you and Loony, life seems pretty grim to him at the moment.'

'Poor Dad,' said Diana. 'We'd better keep out of his way.'

'It's an idea,' said Snubby, making up his mind not to obtrude himself on his Uncle Richard any more than could be helped. 'I say – I wonder if Great-uncle will tell his thief-story to Uncle and Aunt.'

He did, that very night. They were all sitting in the lounge together, the children playing a game, Mrs Lynton sewing, her husband reading, and Loony having one of his lengthy rolls all over the floor.

Great-uncle filled his pipe and then spoke to Mrs Lynton. 'It's really very kind of you, Susan, to have me here at such short notice,' he said. 'But to tell you the truth I was at my wits' end. I simply *had* to leave the Manor House.'

'Did you, Uncle Robert? Why? Weren't you comfortable?' asked Mrs Lynton.

'Oh yes, quite. Very warm, comfortable house, the Manor House at Chelie,' said Uncle Robert. 'But there were such extraordinary goings-on, you know.'

Mrs Lynton looked rather startled. The children nudged one another and laid down their cards. 'Now it's coming,' whispered Snubby.

Mr Lynton put down the evening paper. 'What extraordinary goings-on?' he asked. 'Surely not much can happen in a house like that, that's more a museum than anything else.'

'It's a place of great treasures,' said Great-uncle reprovingly. 'It belongs to Sir John Huberry, as you know, a man who collects rarities of many kinds – in particular old papers, letters and documents.'

'Er – hasn't he got some of Lord Macaulay's letters?' said Snubby innocently, remembering what Great-uncle had mentioned in the train.

There was a surprised silence, during which Loony could be heard scratching himself vigorously.

'Shut up, Loony,' said Snubby, and poked him with his toe. Loony stopped.

'Well, it's the first time I've ever heard you make an intelligent remark,' said Mr Lynton in surprise. 'I shouldn't have thought you had ever *heard* of Lord Macaulay's name.'

'Er – Snubby is quite right,' said Great-uncle hastily. 'There were some of Macaulay's letters, they were among the stolen articles. Richard, it was the most extraordinary theft. Doors were locked. Windows were fastened tightly. There was no skylight or other way into the room where these papers were kept. And yet one night thieves got in, took the whole lot, and vanished the way they came – through locked doors or fastened windows! What do you think of that?'

'I think it's rather foolish to make a statement like that,' said Mr Lynton. 'Thieves can't get through locked doors unless they have a key.'

'Well, they hadn't a key,' said Great-uncle. 'The keys are kept on Sir John's key-ring in his pocket. There are no duplicates in existence. What is more – the doors showed no fingerprints of any sort.'

'The thieves wore gloves,' said Mrs Lynton.

'*Green* gloves,' said Snubby before he could stop himself.

27

Great-uncle looked extremely startled. Mrs Lynton stared at Snubby, puzzled. First it was Green Hands, now it was Green Gloves. What did he mean?

Mr Lynton took no notice of Snubby's remark. He just put it down to Snubby's usual silliness.

'Well, Uncle Robert,' he said, picking up his paper again, 'all I can say is, if that's what you ran away from – the idea of thieves going through locked doors – it wasn't very sensible of you. You should have stayed to try and find out who stole the papers. Why, if your hosts didn't know you well, they might think it was you, as you ran away.'

'I hardly think so,' said Great-uncle, on his high horse at once. 'No, my dear Richard, that is quite unthinkable. Quite.'

'I expect it was gypsies or tramps,' said Mrs Lynton soothingly.

Great-uncle gave a most unexpected snort. He looked scornfully at Mrs Lynton. 'My dear Susan! *Do* you think a gipsy or a tramp would know what papers were valuable and what were not? This thief knew exactly what to take.'

'Well, I've no doubt the mystery will be solved sooner or later,' said Mr Lynton, opening his paper again. 'I imagine if the thief is as clever as you say, he'll try his hand somewhere else.'

'He's already tried it three times,' said Great-uncle. 'Sir John told me. He thinks it must be the same thieves because each time they apparently passed through locked doors quite easily.'

'Well, I'll believe somebody can go through locked doors when I see them,' said Mr Lynton dryly.

'Great-uncle – do you think the thief will steal papers again somewhere?' asked Diana. 'I'd like to read about it, if he does. Would it be in the papers?'

'Oh yes,' said Great-uncle. 'It's always in the paper. I think I've got a report of the last theft in my bag. You can go and get it, if you like.'

Roger sped upstairs with Loony at his heels. Loony always went upstairs with everybody if he could, and then tried to get in their way going down again, either by getting between their legs, or hurling himself on top of them as they went down. There was a thunderous noise after a minute or two, and then a crash and a yelp.

'Oh dear,' said Mrs Lynton. 'Are you hurt, Roger?'

Roger came limping in, followed by a saddened Loony. 'I've smacked him,' he explained to Snubby. 'He did his cannon-ball act at me and sent me flying down the stairs. He's loonier than ever. I've got the paper. Where's the burglary reported, Great-uncle?'

Great-uncle found the report. It wasn't much more than a few lines. The children read them eagerly.

Then Diana noticed an advertisement nearby and pointed to it.

'Look,' she said. 'There's a notice about a fair held in the same town. I wonder if Barney and Miranda were there.'

'Is this the Barney you told me about – the boy with the monkey that had the adventure with you last summer holidays?' asked his mother. Roger nodded.

'Yes. He's awfully nice, Mother. He leads a peculiar sort of life, you know – going from fair to circus and circus to fair, earning his living with Miranda, his monkey. She's a darling.'

Mrs Lynton looked doubtful. 'Well, I don't like monkeys,' she said. 'But from all you have told me, Barney seems a nice boy, though a strange, roving kind of character.'

'I wonder if he's at the fair advertised here,' said Diana,

looking at the notice again. 'Look, Roger – it gives all the performers – the main ones, anyway – Vosta and his two chimpanzees, Hurly and Burly – what lovely names; Tonnerre and his elephants. Shooting gallery in charge of the famous cracksman, Billy Tell . . .'

'Short for William Tell, I suppose,' grinned Snubby. 'Go on.'

'Hoopla stalls, roundabouts, swing-boats – no, it doesn't say anything about a boy with a monkey,' said Diana, disappointed. 'Though perhaps they wouldn't mention him, really – he wouldn't be one of the chief performers.'

'Anyone got his address?' asked Snubby. Nobody had. Barney was a very bad letter-writer, and the children had not heard from him since Christmas.

'Come on, let's finish our game,' said Roger, losing interest in the paper. 'No, you can't get on my knee, Loony. Go and play with Sardine – a nice little game of Spit-and-Hiss, or Growl-and-Snap. You'll like that!'

Chapter Five

Diana Has An Idea

A day or two went by. Great-uncle tried to settle down and go on writing what he called his 'Memoirs,' which Roger said were another name for 'Nodding over a Pipe.' Snubby had settled in at once, as usual. He was perfectly at home, and Roger's usually neat bedroom now always looked exactly as if a whirlwind had just passed by.

'If Snubby doesn't mess it about, Loony does,' Roger complained. 'I'm tired of keeping my shoes and the bed-room slippers and hair-brushes in a drawer so that Loony can't get them.'

'So am I,' said Diana. 'And I do wish he wouldn't drag all the mats in a heap and leave them on the landing or in the hall for people to fall over. I nearly broke my ankle twice yesterday. As for poor Great-uncle, he's so scared of falling over mats or brushes left about that he walks like a cat on hot bricks – lifting up his feet very gingerly indeed.'

Roger laughed. 'Oh dear – that lunatic dog put half a dozen brushes into the pond this morning, and two of them were Great-uncle's. Snubby told him he supposed Mother was washing the brushes in pond-water because it was good for them – and he believed him!'

'There's Loony now – barking at Sardine, I suppose,' said Diana. She leaned out of the window. 'Loony, Loony! Shut up! Haven't you learnt by now that once Sardine is up on the wall you can't get her off. SHUT UP!'

Her mother's voice came floating up from the garden. 'Diana! Stop yelling out of the window like that. Your Great-uncle is trying to work.'

'That means Loony's woken him up from a doze,' said Diana, pulling her head in. She put it out again. 'Mother! Mother! Shall I do the flowers this morning?'

'Will you *stop* shouting out of the window?' called back her mother, whilst Great-uncle Robert flung down his pipe in exasperation and stood up. He would go for a walk! What with dogs barking, and children yelling, and now his niece yelling too, the house was unbearable. Yes, he would go for a walk!

But at the sight of him appearing in coat and hat with a stick in his hand, Loony flung himself on him in delight. A walk! People with hats and coats on meant only one thing – a WALK! Loony snuffled round Great-uncle's ankles, thrilled, and then rolled over on his back, doing what Snubby called his 'bicycling act,' riding an imaginary bicycle upside down!

'You are *not* coming with me,' said Great-uncle firmly. 'I don't like you. You can only do two things well, and I don't like either of them. You can bark louder than any dog I know, and you can scratch yourself more vigorously.'

But Loony meant to come with him. He kept so close to Great-uncle's ankles all the way to the gate that he almost tripped him up. 'Home!' said Great-uncle sternly. 'HOME.'

'Woof,' said Loony, and sat down expectantly, exactly as if Great-uncle had said 'Bone,' not 'Home.' The old man tried to open the gate quickly and slip out without Loony – but Loony was up to that game. He was out in the road with Great-uncle at once, dancing round him maddeningly.

32

The old man lost his temper. 'Snubby!' he yelled. 'Call this dog of yours. CALL HIM, I say. Do you hear me, boy?'

A woman opposite came over to Great-uncle. 'I'm so sorry,' she said, 'but may I ask you not to shout and not to let your dog bark so much? Your shouting and his barking have kept my baby awake half the morning.'

Great-uncle was really exasperated. He walked off down the road, thumping the pavement with his stick.

'*I* kept her baby awake. What rubbish! And calling Loony *my* dog! I wouldn't own him for a hundred pounds.'

But it certainly looked as if he did, because Loony kept faithfully with him during the whole of the walk, occasionally half-disappearing down a rabbit-hole, but always coming back. Poor Great-uncle.

He bought himself a paper and came back, reading it as he walked. He suddenly stood still and gave an exclamation. Loony sat down beside him and looked at him. What was this old gentleman up to now? Loony hadn't any use for him really, except to snatch a walk with him now and again.

'Look at that!' said Great-uncle. 'Another robbery – same kind of thing – and same way of going about it. Locked doors again! Extraordinary!'

He showed the report of the new theft to Mrs Lynton when he got back. The children crowded round in interest.

'See?' said Great-uncle, pointing to the paragraphs with a beautifully clean and polished nail. 'Another robbery. Rare and valuable papers again. And not a trace of the thieves. Doors locked and windows bolted. And yet the things are gone. There's something strange about all this.'

'Green Hands,' whispered Roger mischievously behind

him. Great-uncle turned sharply, but Roger's face was innocent.

'Can I borrow the paper, please?' asked Diana. 'Thanks awfully.'

She took it to the summer-house and the three of them pored over it. Diana looked rather pleased with herself.

'I've discovered something,' she announced to the others. 'Have you?'

Roger considered. 'No. What?' he asked.

'Well, you know the first paper we saw, the one Great-uncle brought with him and let us read?' said Diana. 'Do you remember the bit about the Fair?'

'Yes. What about it?' said Roger. 'There's nothing about a Fair in this paper.'

'I know. I've looked,' said Diana. 'But did you notice what the first paper said about the Fair – where it was going to next? It said it was going to *Pilbury*. Pilbury. Does that ring a bell?'

'Gosh, yes,' said Roger at once. '*This* theft is at Pilbury. I see what you're getting at. Either the Fair goes to places where there are rare papers to be stolen – or somebody in the Fair makes inquiries at each place they go to, to see if there are any in the neighbourhood worth stealing.'

'That's what I meant,' said Diana. 'Let's find out if the Fair was actually at Pilbury when the papers disappeared, shall we?'

'Yes. Though I must say we're rather jumping to conclusions,' said Roger. 'It's probably sheer coincidence.'

'I bet it is!' said Snubby. 'Just like Diana to think she's spotted something clever!'

Diana gave him a push. 'Get out of the summer-house if you're going to talk like that. Go on! If you're not interested, you needn't be.'

'I *am* interested,' protested Snubby. 'And don't shove

34

me like that. If you want a shoving match you know who'll win. You won't anyway. And all I said was . . .'

'If you say it again, out you go,' said Diana, getting angry. 'I'm tired of you today, Snubby. You've hidden my gloves, I know you have, and you left my bedroom door open so that Loony could take my mats again. And *now* just look at Loony. He's got somebody's brush again. It's Great-uncle's hairbrush this time.'

Snubby ran to get the brush away from Loony, who at once regarded this as a wonderful game and danced away down the garden, flinging the brush up into the air and catching it in his mouth.

Diana turned to Roger. 'Roger, there mayn't be anything in my idea at all. Let's find out first whether the Fair *is* at Pilbury. And then let's try and find out where it's going to next – and see if a theft of rare papers is reported from there too.'

'It's quite an idea, Di,' said Roger. 'We'll bike over this afternoon – it's not more than ten miles away. We'll leave Snubby behind. I'm getting tired of him.'

So they said nothing of their plans to Snubby, but got out their bicycles without his seeing and had a look to see if the tyres were all right. Yes, they were.

They set off after lunch, creeping off whilst Snubby was arguing with their mother about some missing shoes which she was perfectly certain Loony knew something about. They mounted their bicycles and rode gleefully off down the road. 'Sucks to Snubby!' said Roger. 'Won't he be wild? He'll hunt all over the place for us!'

It was a long way to Pilbury, farther than they thought, but they got there at last. They rode all through it but could see no Fair. Diana felt a little dampened.

'We'll ask someone,' said Roger, and he got off his bicycle. He called to a small boy nearby.

35

'Hey, Sonny! Is there a Fair in Pilbury, do you know?'

'There *was!*' called back the boy. 'But it's gone. Went yesterday – to Ricklesham, I heard.'

'Thanks!' said Roger, and beamed at Diana. 'Well, it *was* here – and now it's at Ricklesham. We'll just see if there's a robbery there next. Then we'll KNOW your idea's got something in it. I say – this is rather exciting, isn't it!'

Chapter Six

Snubby Says Something Silly

Snubby was most annoyed with the other two when they came back. 'Where have you been? You beasts, you've been for a bike ride and didn't tell me!'

'Well, you were so jolly unbelieving in the summer-house we thought we'd go off alone,' said Diana. 'Sucks to you, Snubby!'

'Whatever's the matter with Loony?' asked Roger, staring at the spaniel in surprise. 'Why is he looking so dismal? He didn't even come rushing to meet us.'

'He's in trouble,' said Snubby. 'So's Sardine. They chased your mother's ball of wool all round the lounge and didn't have the sense to see it was joined to a jersey she's knitting. They undid the ball for about a mile of wool, rolled it out to the kitchen, and almost into the pond. Aunt Susan's awfully cross. She smacked poor old Loony so hard that he went under the sofa for half an hour, and she tried to smack Sardine but she escaped.'

'Just like a cat!' said Roger. 'Poor old Loony.'

'You go and eat up Sardine's dinner,' said Diana encouragingly to Loony.

'He wouldn't touch sardines if he were starving,' said Snubby. 'Where have you been, you two?'

They told him. 'So you see, the Fair's gone to Rickle-sham now,' said Roger. 'And now we'll just wait and see if any burglary occurs there.'

'I wish we could hear from Barney,' said Diana. 'He

might know some of the people in the Fair. He's been all over the country now in fairs and circuses and shows.'

'I'd like to *see* old Barney again – and dear little Miranda,' said Snubby, who had a very soft spot for the small monkey belonging to Barney. 'Is it any good writing to Barney's last address?'

'We did that,' said Roger. 'No answer came at all. We'll have to wait till he writes to us himself.'

A strange dog ventured into the garden. It went out again at top speed as Loony hurled himself at it, yelping madly. 'He's feeling better now,' said Snubby, looking at Loony. 'His tail's got a wag again.'

Loony disappeared into the house, his little tail wagging. He came out again with the brush from the sitting-room fireplace.

'Look at that!' said Roger, exasperated. 'I'm always carrying brushes about now – putting them back in their places. Loony you're dippy.'

He and Diana went in with the brush. Snubby went off to the summer-house with a book. But Great-uncle was there, smoking his pipe.

'Oh, sorry, sir,' said Snubby, and began hastily to retreat.

'Quite all right, my boy. Come along in,' said Great-uncle. 'There's plenty of room for two. I want to talk to you.'

Snubby never liked to hear that a grown-up wanted to talk to him. It usually meant a ticking-off of some sort. He sat down with a sigh.

'About this gang of yours,' said Great-uncle in his rather pompous voice. 'This – er – Green Hands Gang – wasn't that what you called it? Have you heard anything more about them? Or was it possibly a little make-up of yours?'

Snubby considered. He didn't really want to give up his lovely idea of a Green Hands Gang that wore green gloves. On the other hand, it wouldn't do to work up Great-uncle about it, because he might be foolish enough to say something to Uncle Richard. Then the fat would be in the fire. Uncle Richard wouldn't see that a silly pretend didn't matter. He would call it a lie, and treat it as such. And Snubby wouldn't be let off lightly.

'I think the gang have lost track of me,' said Snubby at last, deciding that would be the safest thing to say. 'I haven't heard a word from them since I've been here,' he added truthfully.

'Really?' said Great-uncle, eyeing Snubby in a way he didn't much like. 'Er – perhaps you think the gang have bigger fish to fry? Other things that are more important than you?'

Snubby blinked. Was Great-uncle getting at him? A sudden thought flashed into his mind and was out in words before he could stop it.

'Yes, I think you're right, sir – and I think you'll hear of their activities next at Ricklesham!'

'Ricklesham!' said Great-uncle, surprised. 'Why Ricklesham?'

Snubby now wished he hadn't spoken so quickly. He fidgeted uncomfortably on the wooden seat.

'Don't know, sir. Just a hunch. You see, if you knew that gang as well as I do, you'd sort of know where they were going to – to – operate next.'

'Bless us all!' said Great-uncle, staring at Snubby. 'I don't know what to make of you. Talking of gangs and how they operate – and looking just a dirty, untidy boy with the most disgusting fingernails I ever saw.'

That was a nasty jab. Snubby took a hurried look at his nails. Everybody was always worrying him about them. Why couldn't they mind their own business? He didn't sneer at their clean nails – why should they sneer at his dirty ones? He got up.

'I'll go and clean my nails, sir,' he said, pleased at having thought of such a good excuse to get away before Great-uncle asked more searching questions about the gang!

'A very good idea,' said Great-uncle. 'And while you're about it, wash behind your ears and see if you can possibly reach the back of your neck.'

Snubby fled. Nasty sarcastic old man! Snubby brushed his nails hard with the nail-brush and thought darkly that it would be rather nice to have a real gang to frighten people like Great-uncle.

Diana called to him from her room. 'Snubby, is that you? Come here a minute.'

He went into Diana's room. She and Roger were sitting on her bed with a map spread out between them.

'What's that?' asked Snubby.

'It's a map with Ricklesham on it,' said Diana. 'We thought we might as well see exactly where it is in case we want to go over to the Fair. It's about six miles off. We'll take you with us next time if you behave yourself.'

'Gosh – look at Snubby's nails! He's cleaned them!' said Roger, astonished. 'You turning over a new leaf, Snubby?'

'Shut up,' said Snubby, feeling quite ashamed of his spotless nails. 'Great-uncle's been on at me about them. I say – I said rather a silly thing to him.'

'Well, that's nothing new,' said Roger. 'What did you say this time?'

'He began asking me in a sneering sort of voice about the Green Hands Gang,' said Snubby. 'And when I said I hadn't heard a word from them, he said in a horrid

scornful voice, "I suppose they've got bigger fish to fry!"
And I said yes – they might be operating next at
Ricklesham.'

There was a moment's silence. Diana and Roger stared
at Snubby in dismay.

'Well! You're a bigger idiot than I thought you were,'
said Roger at last. 'Suppose there *is* a robbery at Ricklesham, what's Great-uncle going to think? That it *is* your
silly Green Hands Gang, and you *are* mixed up in it. And
he'll most certainly split on you and tell Dad.'

'I know,' said poor Snubby, looking very downcast. 'I
thought of all that afterwards.'

'You're crazy,' said Diana. 'Here we are on the track
of something exciting – and you go and blab about it to
Great-uncle, and mix it up with your idiotic fairy tale.'

'Perhaps there won't be a burglary at Ricklesham,' suggested Snubby hopefully. But that didn't find favour with
the others either.

'That's right. Pour cold water on our ideas now,' said
Diana. 'Tell us we're wrong. Make out it's silly to . . .'

'I'm not, Diana, I'm not!' cried poor Snubby, feeling
that whatever he said would be wrong. 'I'll believe anything you tell me, really I will.'

'Shall we let him go with us if we go to Ricklesham, or
not?' said Roger grimly to Diana.

'We'll see,' said Diana. 'Any more fat-headedness on
his part, and we don't tell him a thing.'

Snubby departed to find Loony, feeling very subdued.
He fell over on the stairs, and Roger and Diana heard
him rolling down, yelling.

They grinned. 'That's Sardine again,' said Diana. 'She
always lies in wait for Snubby on the stairs.'

'Do you really think there'll be a burglary, at Ricklesham?' asked Roger, folding up the map.

41

'Well – not really,' said Diana. 'I did feel it was a sort of hunch, you know – but it's a bit far-fetched, actually, isn't it? I don't suppose anything will happen there at all.'

'We'll watch the papers,' said Roger. 'And what a thrill it will be if we see Ricklesham in the news!'

Chapter Seven

Snubby in Difficulties

Three or four days went by. Each morning the three children took the paper after the grown-ups had finished with it, and pored over it.

But Ricklesham was never in the news. It was most disappointing. And then suddenly it was!

Mr Lynton was glancing down the paper one morning, when something caught his eye. He read it quickly and then spoke to Great-uncle Robert.

'Uncle,' he said, 'here's a bit of news for you. Didn't you have something to do with the arranging of some old seventeenth-century documents – I've forgotten what they were – for the Forbes-King Collection?'

'Yes. Yes, I did,' said Great-uncle. 'A very fine collection that was – most interesting old letters. Why, what does it say about them?'

'They've been stolen!' said Mr Lynton, the three children sat up at once in excitement.

'*Stolen!*' echoed Great-uncle. 'No – have they really? Where from?'

'They were on loan to a Mr Curtice-Knowles at Ricklesham House,' said Mr Lynton. Diana gave an exclamation. Roger kicked her under the table. Snubby looked anxiously at Great-uncle.

'Ricklesham House! *Ricklesham*, did you say?' said Great-uncle in a faint voice. 'Good heavens! *Ricklesham!*'

He looked at Snubby. Snubby had said that the Green Hands Gang might operate at Ricklesham next – and lo and behold, what it had done but steal valuable old documents there? Great-uncle did some rapid thinking. Then that meant – yes, it must mean – that the Green Hands Gang that Snubby was afraid of was the same one that was mixed up with the continual theft of precious documents!

'It must have been that very gang that came into Chelie Manor House when I was there, and stole all those papers,' thought Great-uncle Robert. 'Fancy that boy being mixed up with them. Most extraordinary. I'll have to have a long talk with him about all this. Really, the police should be told.'

Snubby wouldn't look at Great-uncle. He was terrified that he would suddenly ask him awkward questions. Fortunately Mrs Lynton plunged into the matter, and asked several questions.

'But, Richard! Do you think that it's the same thieves who went to Chelie Manor House when Uncle Robert was there? Does it say anything about locked doors? Did the thieves go through fastened windows and locked doors again?'

'Yes. Apparently it is just as mysterious a theft as the others,' said her husband. 'There is a small room set apart at Ricklesham House for these old and rare papers, and they are displayed under glass cases. The door to this room was locked, of course. The windows are not only safely fastened, but also barred, so the paper says.'

'And yet the things were stolen!' said Mrs Lynton. 'Well, it certainly sounds very mysterious. The police must be very puzzled.'

Great-uncle took the paper and read the report very carefully. There was no mention of a Green Hands Gang. How on earth did Snubby know that there was going to be a crime committed at Ricklesham? He lifted his head to have another look at Snubby. But Snubby had gone.

He had mentioned to his aunt in a low voice that he didn't want any more breakfast. Could he go, please?

'Don't you feel well, dear?' began Mrs Lynton, but seeing that Snubby's cheeks were the same fiery red as usual, she felt there was nothing serious wrong. So she nodded, and Snubby slipped away, thankful that Great-uncle was buried in the paper.

There was an excited meeting in the summer-house that morning. Snubby, Diana and Roger rushed there as soon as their jobs were done. Loony rushed too, sensing the excitement.

'Roger – Great-uncle kept on and on looking at me at breakfast-time,' said Snubby, as soon as they were safely in the summer-house. 'I know he's going to ask me awkward questions. I don't want to meet him at all. Say you don't know where I am, if he asks you.'

'Well, we can't tell a lie, if we *do* know where you are,' said Diana. 'But we'll do our best not to give you away. It serves you right for talking too much. Now, of course, Great-uncle will believe in your silly Green Hands Gang all over again, because of this upset at Ricklesham.'

'I know,' groaned Snubby. 'Loony, go and sit outside on guard. *On guard*, do you hear? And you jolly well know what that means. Bark if you see anyone coming!'

Loony thumped his little tail on the ground, as he sat himself down in the sunshine. He knew what 'On guard' meant all right. Of course he did. He barked loudly at once, and Snubby, in a great flurry, squeezed himself under the seat in the summer-house, while Diana and Roger sat just above, their legs hiding him.

But it was only Sardine arriving. She had seen Loony and wanted to have a game. So she came walking up the path, waving her tail in the air as usual, black and sleek and purring.

Loony knew now that her purr meant 'Pax! Don't chase me!' just as she knew when he wagged his tail, it meant the same.

Still, he had to bark, as he was on guard, and Sardine paused in surprise. She sat down a good way from Loony and began to wash herself. Loony could never imagine why cats washed themselves so much. They were always doing it.

'It's all right, Snubby – it's only Sardine,' said Diana, peering out of the summer-house. 'Shut up, Loony. You're on guard for people, not cats! Shush!'

Loony stopped barking. Sardine strolled right up to him, purring very loudly. He wagged his stump of a tail. Sardine lay down, stretched herself out on the path and patted his nose with her paw. Loony gave the tiniest bark. It meant 'Sorry, I can't play now, but I'm on guard.'

So Sardine went to sleep, leaving a crack of one eye open, just in case. Loony also settled down, shutting both his eyes, but listened with his long, droopy ears.

Snubby came out from under the seat, draped with cobwebs and powdered with dust. 'That idiot of a Loony,' he grumbled. 'Look at me – I'm in a frightful mess!'

'I can't see that you look much worse than usual,' said Diana, looking at him. 'Come on, sit down again. We really have got something to discuss.'

They talked and talked about the affair. They had all read the bit in the paper now. They knew that once again valuable letters had been stolen, and that once again the thief had apparently passed through locked doors and barred windows.

And, more important still, they knew that once again the Fair had been in the same district as the burglary.

That couldn't be sheer coincidence – it couldn't be chance. The Fair – or somebody *in* the Fair – must be connected with these strange thefts. And that somebody must be clever enough to know about rare documents, where they were, and how to get them.

'The two things don't seem to go together, somehow,' said Roger thoughtfully. 'I mean – you don't associate show people with a knowledge of that kind of thing. You have to be a person like – well, like Uncle Robert – to know about historical documents. you have to have a lot of specialised learning.'

'You mean, you have to be an antiquarian,' said Diana, showing off a little. 'That's what people of that kind are called. Uncle Robert told me.'

'Gosh – I always thought an anti – anti-whatever-you-said, was somebody who was against keeping aquariums,' said Snubby, surprised.

Roger laughed, 'You would! Anyway, it's not anti-aquarium, idiot, it's antiquarian.'

'Sounds just the same to me,' said Snubby. 'I say – are we going to Ricklesham? Do say we are!'

Roger looked at Diana, and they both nodded solemnly.

'Yes, said Roger. We'll go to the Fair, and we'll snoop round and see if we can find out anyone there who's an antiquarian. Then we might be on the track!'

'That's an awfully good idea,' said Snubby. 'We can put the police on to him at once.'

'It won't be as easy as that!' said Diana scornfully. 'We . . .'

Loony set up a tremendous barking again. Snubby dived beneath the wooden seat once more, and Roger and Diana sat close to hide him.

47

'It's Great-uncle this time all right,' said Roger. 'Keep still, Snubby. We'll do our best for you.'

Great-uncle came to the entrance of the summer-house. He looked in.

'Ah,' he said. 'I thought I should find you here. I want to talk to Snubby.'

'We'll tell him, Great-uncle,' said Roger politely.

'Your mother said he was here,' said Great-uncle.

'Did she?' said Diana. 'Is she busy, Great-uncle? Does she want me yet?'

('That was a quick change of subject!' thought Snubby admiringly from behind her legs.)

'No. She didn't say she wanted any of you,' said Great-uncle. 'Do you know where Snubby is?'

'He's not far off,' said Roger truthfully. 'Loony's never very far from him, you know.'

Loony wagged his tail at his name. He was most astonished to see Snubby under the seat, and would have liked to go to him, but every time he went near either Roger or Diana, they pushed him off with a determined foot.

'Do you think he'd hear me if I called him?' asked Great-uncle. 'I really do want to speak to him. It's important.'

'You could try shouting,' said Diana.

Great-uncle shouted, 'Snubby! SNUBBY! I want you! SNUBBY!'

There was no answer, of course, except that Loony barked, and Sardine fled up to the wall.

'Do you think he heard me?' said Great-uncle.

'Er – if he's near enough, he would certainly hear you,' said Roger cautiously. 'Never mind, Great-uncle. I'll tell him you want him next time I speak to him.'

Great-uncle called again, feeling somehow certain that

48

Snubby was not very far away, otherwise why was Loony there?

'SNUBBY! I WANT YOU!'

'Great-uncle! That woman with her baby in the house opposite is looking out of the window,' said Diana. 'I hope her baby isn't asleep.'

'Bless us all! I forgot the baby,' said Great-uncle. 'The mother will be after me again. Well, you tell Snubby I've been looking for him, will you?'

He went off down the path, and Roger and Diana heaved sighs of relief. 'You can come out now, Snubby,' said Roger. 'He's gone.'

Snubby came out, dirtier than ever. 'You did jolly well,' he said admiringly. 'Never told a lie at all, and didn't give me away either. Thanks awfully.'

'I don't know how you're going to manage to avoid Great-uncle all day long,' said Diana. 'It'll be difficult!'

'It won't,' said Snubby, beaming. 'Let's bike over to Ricklesham for the day – take our lunch and everything.'

'Right! That's a fine idea,' said Roger. 'I'll go and ask Mother now. Come on, Di. Stay here, Snubby, and we'll fetch you when we're ready. So long!'

Chapter Eight

Off To The Fair

Mrs Lynton thought it would be a very good idea for the three to go off for a picnic. It would be a change to have a nice quiet house for once. Uncle Robert would like it too.

'Where's Snubby?' she said. 'Your Great-uncle has been calling all over the place for him. Has he got into trouble with him?'

'I don't think so,' said Roger. 'Mother, I suppose we couldn't have hard-boiled eggs, could we, and tomato sandwiches? And I suppose there aren't any jam tarts left over from yesterday, are there?'

'You're doing quite a lot of supposing,' said his mother. 'Suppose you go and ask Cook what she's got? She happens to be pleased with you because you took the trouble to fetch the fish for her yesterday, so I've no doubt she will look favourably on all your supposing.'

Cook did. She willingly did them hard-boiled eggs, put salt and pepper into a screw of paper, made tomato and lettuce sandwiches by the dozen, added plain bread and butter for the eggs, nine jam tarts and enormous slices of ginger cake.

'Oooh I say! Can you really spare us some of that?' said Roger. 'You only made it yesterday. It's chockful of bits of ginger and some chopped cherries. It's a heavenly cake.'

Great-uncle appeared in the doorway. 'Oh! I thought I heard you here. Have you seen Snubby?'

Roger turned to Cook. 'Have *you* seen Snubby?' he asked innocently.

Cook shook her head. 'Hasn't been near the kitchen this morning,' she said. 'And *that's* unusual. I never did see a boy that came snooping round for titbits so often. No, nor a dog either.'

'It's funny I can't find him,' said Great-uncle irritably. 'He's always about when he's not wanted, and never here when he is. Now I've got someone coming to see me in a few minutes.'

He went. Diana winked at Roger. 'Did you hear that? He's got someone coming to see him – so we'll just be able to slip off nicely with Snubby. Let's get some bottles of ginger beer to take with us and we'll be ready.'

In five minutes' time they were ready. The lunch was packed into two neat parcels. Roger and Diana carried the food and drink to the bicycle shed. 'I'll just pop round to the study and see if Great-uncle's got his visitor yet,' said Roger. He came back immediately.

'Yes, he has. Come on, get the bikes. I'll wheel Snubbys'. Hurry!'

They hurried. They put the lunch into the baskets, and strapped a big oblong box on to Snubby's back mudguard. They put a small rug inside. That was for Loony if he got tired of running beside them. He was very good at sitting in the box and going along like that.

They wheeled the bikes to the summer-house. Loony ran to meet them in delight, barking madly. Bikes meant a long, long run! No time for rabbit-holes alas – but still a lovely long run.

Snubby peered out. He could hear them ringing their bicycle bells to tell him he was safe.

'Got everything? Oh *good*!' he said. 'Where's Great-uncle?'

'He's seeing somebody,' said Diana. 'We've got the lunch basket and some ginger beer. We've strapped on Loony's carrier too. Let's go while the going's good.'

So they went. They cycled down the path and round by the window. Great-uncle saw them, and stared after Snubby in exasperation.

'There he is! I thought he'd turn up just when I couldn't see him!'

Loony ran along by Snubby's bicycle, his red tongue hanging out, feeling very happy indeed. He knew the children would not go too fast for him. If he got tired Snubby would be the first to notice and stop. Then he would be lifted into the carrier box, and be taken along like a lord in a carriage. How Loony looked down his long black nose at other dogs then!

'We'll picnic at the Fair or near it,' said Roger. 'We shall have plenty of time to look at everyone then, if we're sitting down in the Fair field.'

'Got any money?' said Snubby, jingling his in his pocket. 'I like a Fair. I shall go on the roundabout and on the swings and have a go at hoopla. I threw a ring over a super torch last time.'

'I've got plenty of holiday money left,' said Roger. 'So has Diana. More than I have. We'll be all right.'

'We'll buy some ice-creams too,' said Diana. 'You'll have to remember not to take Loony on the roundabout, Snubby. He was awfully sick last time.'

'Yes. He wasted a perfectly good dinner,' said Snubby. 'Didn't you, Loony? Are we going too fast?'

Loony was too out of breath to answer with a bark. He didn't look tired. He loped along on his silky black legs, his long ears flap-flapping as he went.

They stopped and put him into the carrier-box after about three miles. That was as much as he could do at a run. He sat in the box panting, his tongue hanging out looking as long as his ears!

'Now, hold tight, Loony,' said Snubby, getting on again. 'Here we go!'

Loony kept his balance perfectly, and enjoyed his ride enormously. Snubby didn't enjoy it quite so much because Loony was rather heavy! Still, it was better than leaving him behind.

They came to Ricklesham at last. They had a look at the house from which the valuable papers had been stolen. There was a policeman on guard at the gate. That impressed the three children very much. They got off their bicycles and looked at the big gateway.

'No one allowed in without a pass,' said the policeman. 'Not even a dog!'

The children grinned. 'Do they know who the thief was yet?' asked Roger.

'Not a clue,' said the policeman. 'You on the job too?'

The children laughed and rode off. 'He little knew we *were* on the job, more or less!' said Diana, 'Now let's ask where the Fair is.'

They asked a woman. 'Over the Longlands Field the other side of the wood,' she said, pointing.

They thanked her and rode off, Loony in the carrier again because of the traffic. They skirted the wood and came to open country. At the edge of it, in a big field, was the Fair.

'Here we are!' said Roger, coming to a standstill, and leaning against the fence on his bicycle. 'Looks pretty good to me. Quite a big Fair.'

There were round and oblong tents with flags flying. There were caravans of all colours and shapes round the field. There were horses grazing nearby, and at the far end, tied to a tree, were two enormous elephants.

The roundabout was not going. It stood there, gay but silent, set all round with wooden animals and birds, lions, tigers, giraffes, swans, cats, dogs, bears and what looked like a chimpanzee. Swingboats were there too, but no one was using them.

'It's dinner-time, I expect,' said Roger, looking at his watch. 'Yes. It's a quarter to one. I expect everything will be going strong this afternoon.'

'There's a shooting range over there,' said Snubby. 'I'll have a shot afterwards. I was pretty good last time I shot at a Fair.'

'Well, tell me when you're going to shoot and I'll get a mile away,' said Diana. 'I say – what a big Fair this is – heaps of stalls and tents and things. And there's nobody that looks in the least like an anti . . .'

'Shut up,' said Roger. 'Hedges and fences have ears as much as walls. Come on – let's go through the gate and ask if we can picnic in the field. We'll say we're going to spend money at the Fair afterwards.'

They went though the gate, and a shock-headed boy shouted to them. 'Hey, you – you're not allowed in till two o'clock.'

'We're coming to the Fair all afternoon, called back Roger. 'We only want to have our picnic here now. Do you mind?'

'Okay,' shouted the boy. He was a strange-looking fellow, with his shock of yellow hair, ears that stuck out at each side of his head, and very wide grin. He was small too, smaller than Snubby, and yet he looked about fifteen.

'Wonder what *he* does in the Fair,' said Roger getting the lunch packet out of his bicycle basket. Di, you've got the drinks. Loony's biscuits are in *your* basket, Snubby. Better keep him by us, or he'll be eaten up by that pack of mongrels over there.'

Loony had no intention of wandering away if there was any lunch going. Nor did he like the look of the lean, hungry-looking dogs that were sitting down at a distance, watching. He growled at them just to tell them who he was.

It was a lovely picnic. The hard-boiled eggs went down well, and so did the sandwiches. Loony got one or two, but not many, because the children were so terribly hungry. He got no jam tart or cake, but managed to beg two pieces of bread and butter from Diana.

'What's the time? Is it two o'clock yet?' said Snubby. 'I can see some people wandering along up to the gate. I expect the roundabout will start going soon.'

The Fair people were on the move too. Some shutters were being taken down from the stalls. A man went over to the swing-boats and idly swung one. The shock-headed boy went to the shooting range and handled a few guns, whistling shrilly.

An elephant trumpeted and made Loony jump. People came out of caravans, and hastened to various tents. The Fair was opening!

The children cleared up the litter. Even Snubby was good about that. Never a scrap of paper was left lying about the grass when they had finished any picnic. Loony snuffled about the crumbs.

'Look – what's that coming along?' said Diana suddenly. 'Golly – it's a *monkey*, isn't it – all dressed up. Oh, how sweet. She's coming over here to us. She's rather like Miranda, isn't she?'

The little creature came right up to them and took a flying leap to Snubby's shoulder. She whispered excitedly in his ear, and pulled his hair. The others watched intently.

'Roger – Roger, it *is* Miranda, I know it is!' cried Diana

suddenly. And when she heard her name the tiny creature bounded up on to Diana's shoulder and put her little paw down the girl's neck – just as Miranda always used to do!

'Well, if Miranda's here, Barney is too!' cried Snubby. 'Come on – let's look for him. Fancy that – *Barney*!'

Chapter Nine

Good Old Barney Again!

They passed the shooting-range, where the shock-headed boy was still polishing the guns and whistling.

'Is there a boy in the Fair called Barney?' asked Roger.

'Yep. That monkey's his,' said the boy, with his wide grin. 'Lovaduck! Fancy Miranda going to you like that – fussing you up good and proper, isn't she?'

'Barney *is* here!' said Diana joyfully, and the three smiled at one another. 'What a bit of luck – and what a surprise too!'

Loony was jumping up, trying to reach Miranda. He knew her all right! She suddenly dropped down on his back, and rode him like a horse, as she used to do. But he knew how to deal with that! He promptly rolled over and off she went.

She bounded chattering on to Snubby's shoulder. She was dressed in a tiny red skirt and a little blue coat with silver buttons down it. She looked too amusing for words.

'Dear little Miranda!' said Roger, patting the tiny monkey paw. 'You saw us first, didn't you – you recognised us all right and came along straightaway!'

'You'll find Barney up by the Hoopla Stall!' called the shock-headed boy. 'He runs it.'

They hurried to the stall he was pointing at. A boy stood there with his back to them, arranging the goods neatly on the round stall, so that people might throw hoops at them, and try to ring a prize.

'That's Barney!' cried Diana. As he heard his name the

boy swung round – and sure enough, it *was* Barney – Barney with his corn-coloured hair, his brown-as-a-berry face, his strange blue eyes set so far apart – and his wide, engaging grin.

'Well, *here's* a go!' he cried in amazement. 'You kids – all three of you. Hiya, Roger, Diana! Hiya, Snubby and Loony. Still the same old mad dog, I see!'

Loony, of course, recognised Barney immediately and had hurled himself at him in his usual lunatic way, barking and whining, licking and nuzzling, doing all he could to tell Barney how pleased he was to see his friend once more.

Miranda leapt to Barney's shoulder, chattering excitedly.

'Miranda found us first,' said Diana. 'She came over the field to us. We didn't recognise her at first because she's wearing clothes now and she didn't before. Oh, isn't she sweet, Barney?'

'It's grand to see you, *grand*,' said Barney, his blue eyes brilliant with pleasure. 'I've been thinking of you a lot – wanting to see you all again. What are you doing here? You didn't know I was here, did you?'

'No, of course not,' said Roger. 'We came over for a certain reason – we'll tell you about it some time when we're alone – and we never really hoped to see *you*, of course!'

'You might have told us you were so near us, Barney,' said Diana reproachfully. 'We only live a few miles away, you know.'

'Is that so?' said Barney, surprised. His geography was not at all good. He never had much idea where he was, as he wandered round. 'Well, to think of that! I'm not much good at writing letters, anyway. Still, you're here. You on holiday or something?'

58

'Yes. We're home for the Easter hols,' said Snubby. 'We've got about three more weeks, Barney. How long are you going to be here?'

'We're here a week,' said Barney. 'Excuse for a bit – I've got to get this show going. I'm in charge of the hoopla, you know. It's not my own stall, of course. I run it for the owner. You watch Miranda, and see what she does! She's a scream!'

He handed out some rings and received the money in return. The customer stood by the bar that separated her from the stall, and took aim with a wooden ring.

'Got your eye on the alarm clock, Miss?' called Barney. 'Now then, steady does it!'

The ring bounced on the stall, touched the clock and lay still, half on the clock, half off. The woman tried again and yet again, using her last ring.

'Hard luck, Miss,' said Barney sympathetically. 'You nearly did it. Miranda, get busy!'

And Miranda got busy! She leapt to the stall, gathered up the rings deftly in her tiny paws, and handed them back to Barney. The children laughed in delight.

'Oh, Barney! Isn't she clever!'

'You watch her now,' said Barney, as more people came up to the stall. 'Go on, Miranda, do your job.'

Miranda looked at him inquiringly. She made a little chattering noise and picked up a dozen or two of the wooden hoopla rings. She slipped them over her left arm. She held out her paw for the pennies the people presented, and gave each one three rings!

The customers were amused and delighted. They called their children to watch Miranda, and soon there was a great crowd round the hoopla stand.

'She really is wonderful,' said Diana. 'Barney, you must

do awfully well at this stall with Miranda to attract attention like this.'

'We do,' said Barney. 'I've made more money at the stall then anyone else ever has. I don't get the money, of course. I give it to Tonnerre, who owns the Fair, and takes it about.'

'Tonnerre! What a strange name!' said Diana. 'Is he French?'

'Yes, he is,' said Barney, looking surprised. 'How do you know?'

'Well, "tonnerre" is French for thunder,' explained Diana.

'Is it really?' said Barney. 'Well, I never knew he had such a good name. It suits him fine!'

'Why?' asked Snubby, watching Miranda giving out rings again, and taking the money to give to Barney.

'Well, he's got a thunderous voice, and he's enormous, and he stamps about all the time,' said Barney. 'He's got a fearful temper, and he's an old miser – under-pays everyone and kicks them out if they don't do well enough for him. There he is, over there, look – the elephants are his.'

The children looked where Barney pointed. They saw the two elephants having their ropes undone from the tree, in order to take children for rides. The man with them was a giant-like fellow, with legs like tree-trunks, enormous feet, and great shoulders. He was shouting at the patient elephants, and his voice carried right over the field.

'It sounds as if somebody's turned the wireless on as full as can be!' said Roger with a grin. 'What a voice! Tonnerre is a good name for him. He looks as black as thunder too.'

'He always does,' said Barney. 'He's not a pleasant

60

fellow to work with. There are about twenty people who go with the Fair wherever it goes – the rest of them join it here and there, leave it, others come in their place, and so it goes on. I've been with it about four months – we've been all over the place.'

'I don't like the sound of Mister Thunder,' said Diana. 'Is there a Mrs Lightning, by any chance?'

Barney laughed his uproarious laugh, that made everyone want to laugh with him.

'No. He's not married. If anyone could be called Mrs Lightning, it's old Ma over there – by the caravan, see? My word, her tongue's sharp as a knife. If she flashes out at anyone, they just shrivel up. Even Tonnerre goes off hurriedly if she begins to scold him!'

Ma was a peculiar-looking old woman. She looked more like a witch than anything else, as she stood stirring something in a big iron pot over the fire just outside the caravan. She had a shock of perfectly white hair, brown monkey eyes, and a chin and nose that almost met. She stood over her pot, muttering.

'I'm sure she's making a spell of some kind!' said Diana with a giggle.

'There's plenty of us show-folk that think the same,' said Barney. I don't. But lots do. They're scared stiff of Old Ma. There's only one person can do anything with her, and that's Young 'Un. He's the kid in charge of the shooting-range, see – over there!'

'Oh – the shock-headed boy,' said Snubby. 'Yes, we've seen him. He's a bit like a hobgoblin, with ears sticking right out of his head – a nice hobgoblin, though. He's got hair just like Ma's, only a different colour, of course – it sticks up straight like hers.'

'She's his grandma,' said Barney. 'He gets round the

61

old lady all right. But nobody else does. Don't you go near her – she'll fly at you like a cat!'

'Could we see the chimpanzees?' asked Diana. 'We saw them advertised in a paper. They were called Hurly and Burly.'

'Oh yes – they belong to Mr Vosta,' said Barney. 'You'll like him. Full of fun, and will do anything for you – too much sometimes. Can't say no to anyone! He's been with the Fair for years, and slaves for Tonnerre day and night. I can't understand it myself. *I* shan't stay with this Fair for long being kicked around by that bad-tempered Tonnerre!'

The Fair sounded a fascinating place, with its loud-voiced Tonnerre, its sharp-tongued Old Ma, the shock-headed Young 'Un, Vosta and his chimpanzees – and Barney and Miranda, of course. The three children stood by the hoopla stall and looked round the Fair eagerly, wondering which of all these people would be the most likely to be the thief who could get through locked doors and fastened windows.

They hadn't told Barney about that yet. There hadn't been a chance, with customers coming and going. It would be best not to say anything till they were quite alone with him.

'You go on round the Fair and have a look-see for yourselves,' said Barney. 'I *could* leave Miranda here to look after the stall – she's as good at it as I am – but if Tonnerre sees I'm gone he'll yell the place down.'

'Right, we'll come back later. My word, it *was* a fine surprise to see you, Barney! Best surprise we've had these hols!'

Chapter Ten

An Interesting Afternoon

They went round the Fair, looking at everything and trying everything too. They went on the roundabouts and on the swings, they rode on the elephants and they paid to go in and see the wonderful chimpanzees. They didn't miss a thing!

'Make the roundabout go as fast as you can,' Snubby asked the boy in charge of it.

'Hold on tight then, said the boy with a grin. 'What about your dog?'

'No. He's sick if he goes on,' said Snubby. 'He'll sit by you and wait. Sit, Loony, sit!'

He chose the chimpanzees, and the others chose the lions. The wooden animals went up and down as well as round and round. The music began to play, and the roundabout moved off.

The boy kept his word and ran the machinery as fast as it would go. The children had to cling tightly to the animals or they would have been thrown off. Diana began to feel sick. The other three riders began to yell at the boy.

He slowed down and grinned again. 'That all right for you?' he asked Snubby, who was now looking slightly green, and found that he couldn't walk straight. Nor could the others.

'It was wizard,' said Snubby. 'Faster than I've ever been. It was worth the double fare!'

Not only the roundabout had gone fast, but the music

too – and Tonnerre had heard it, of course. His face went purple, and he yelled at the roundabout boy. But the music was so loud that the boy didn't hear the yells. It was only when the roundabout had stopped, and Tonnerre had parked his elephants for a minute, shouting all the while, that the poor boy knew what he was in for!

'You! You, boy! You toad of a boy!' yelled Mr Tonnerre in his thunderous voice. 'What you think you do, eh? You want to make people sick? You want to break my machine? Ar-rr-r-r-r-r-r-r!'

He finished off with a noise so like the growl of a giant dog that Loony was astonished, and leapt to his feet. Biff! Tonnerre boxed the roundabout boy's ear with a resounding slap.

Snubby stepped forward. 'Mr Tonnerre! It was my fault. I paid him double fare to go fast.'

It looked as if Mr Tonnerre was about to box his ears too. Then he turned to the roundabout boy, 'Ah! Aha! Double fare. Where is the money? You think to keep it for yourself! Give me all the money you have got. Queeek, queeek!'

'Queeek, queeek!' apparently meant 'Quick, quick.' Mr Tonnerre had a peculiar accent, English and French mixed up with American and Cockney. He towered over everyone, as elephantine as his two elephants.

He turned to Snubby next. 'You come to ride on my elephants, no, yes? For double fare I make them trit-trot like horses. Yes!'

'No, thanks,' said Snubby. 'I mean – yes, I'd *like* to ride on your elephants, but no trit-trotting, thank you. I don't feel as if I could bear a trotting elephant.'

So they rode on the great elephants, and swayed from side to side in a most alarming manner. Loony refused to get up with Snubby. He retired behind a tree, very much afraid of the enormous creatures that appeared to have tails in front as well as behind.

'Now you go watch Mr Billy Tell,' said Mr Tonnerre in his enormous voice, as he helped them off the elephants. 'He very, very clever man. Crick-crack, his gun goes, and off goes the apple on Young 'Un's head.'

'Billy Tell does the same act as William Tell, who was probably his great-great-great-great-great-uncle,' remarked Roger, as they made their way to a tent marked in enormous red letters, 'BILLY TELL.'

Old Ma shambled over to look after the shooting-range when Young 'Un went to stand inside Billy Tell's tent with an apple perched high on his shock of hair. He grinned as the children came in to watch.

'Hiya!' he said. 'Come to watch my hair being singed?'

Billy Tell was dressed in a redskin suit, and looked rather grand. He would have looked grander if he hadn't been quite so dirty. There was a long wait until enough people had paid to come into the tent.

Billy Tell sat looking bored, with his gun across his knee. Young 'Un cleverly walked about balancing the apple on his head all the time, collecting the entrance money.

The news had got round that it was Snubby who had paid double fare to the roundabout boy to make the roundabout go fast. Young 'Un came up to him grinning.

'Sure you haven't paid double to see Billy shoot off the tips of my ears?' he asked Snubby.

Snubby liked him. 'You bet I have,' he said. 'So look out!'

He hadn't, of course, and Young 'Un knew it. He stood with his back to a steel sheet, the apple on his head. Billy Tell stood up at last and walked to the other end of the tent.

He took aim casually. 'BANG!' The apple was split into a hundred bits and pieces, and Young 'Un wiped some out of his eyes.

He set another on his head. Billy Tell put his head between his legs and took aim from there. 'BANG!' Again the apple split into tiny pieces. Everyone applauded loudly. Loony crouched against Snubby's legs, frightened at the bangs so near to him.

Young 'Un wiped his face again and walked over to the children. 'Good shooting! he said. 'I'm a good shot too – a jolly good one. I shot a weather-cock off a steeple once.'

'Garn!' said Billy Tell's drawling voice. 'You and your tales! Here, take my gun and clean it. And tell Old Ma I'll have sausages for my supper tonight.'

'Yes, Dad,' said Young 'Un, and somehow the children felt surprised. So Billy Tell was his father – and Old Ma was his grandmother. What an interesting family to have!

'Have you got a mother?' asked Snubby.

'Naw! One woman in the family is enough for me to manage!' said Young 'Un, winking towards Old Ma, as she stood at her shooting-range.

'Say, Ma,' he said to her as they came up. 'Billy Tell says please to give him sausages tonight.'

'Sausages!' squealed the old lady. 'What does he think I am? Sausages cost money, you tell him, the varmint, and rabbits and hares don't cost nothing at all if they're shot – and what's his gun for, I'd like to know? Think he's got it just for shooting apples off your turnip head! Where is he? I'll give him sausages, so I will!'

'Well, Ma, that's all he *asked* you to give him – sausages!' yelled Young 'Un cheekily, and put his hands behind his sticking-out ears the better to hear all the rude names Old Ma called him as she went back to her caravan.

Snubby had a turn with a gun, trying his hardest to shoot one of the ping-pong balls that bobbed up and down on the top of the little fountain of water spouting continually at the back of the range. But he couldn't shoot one.

Young 'Un took a quick glance to see if Billy Tell, Old Ma or Tonnerre were anywhere near. Then he took a gun, aimed it – and bang went one ping-pong ball, bang went another, bang went a third! There was no doubt about it, Young 'Un was a very good shot. Snubby quite believed he had once shot a weather-cock down!

'Now you choose a prize,' he said to Snubby. 'Go on – I like you. Choose one of these here prizes.'

'But *I* didn't shoot the balls off the water,' said Snubby in astonishment.

'Don't matter. I did, and nobody's to know that,' said Young 'Un. 'I like you, see – no stuck-up nonsense about you or your dog. Go on, quick – take a prize. What about them there toffees. They're good.'

It took Snubby quite a long time to convince Young 'Un that he thought it wrong to take a prize he hadn't won. Young 'Un gave way at last, but he didn't understand in the least. He didn't seem to know what honesty meant where that kind of thing was concerned.

'It's awfully *nice* of you,' poor Snubby kept saying, 'but it isn't *right*.'

'Aw shucks,' said Young 'Un, and gave in. 'You better go with the others now. They're yelling to you to have a swing. Choose the boat at the end. It's best and you can make it go high.'

What with roundabout riding, elephant riding, shooting, going in swing-boats, and sampling all kinds of other things, the children hadn't much money left by the end of the day! They had bought themselves enormous sticky buns in the bun-tent, and slices of cake, and lemonade, and had carried a good share over to Barney, who was still in charge of the hoopla, and doing very well; partly, of course, because of Miranda's amusing antics.

'When do you get off?' asked Diana. 'We shall have to be going soon. Couldn't you come back to supper with us?'

'I'd like to do that,' said Barney, his eyes shining with delight at the invitation. 'I'll get Young 'Un to take over from me. Old Ma always takes over from him about now. If I give him sixpence, he'll come to my stall. I'm due for an evening off, so Tonnerre can't say anything if I go. Sure your mother won't mind me coming?'

'She won't mind – she wants to meet you,' said Roger. 'We've told her all about you – how we met you last summer and had that adventure at Rockingdown. How can you get to our place? We biked.'

'Oh, I can borrow a bike,' said Barney. 'Miranda can either ride on my shoulder or on the handle-bars, she doesn't mind which.'

'She can ride in the carrier-box with Loony if she likes!' said Snubby. But she didn't like. She preferred to ride in the middle of Barney's handle-bars, her soft monkey-hair streaming backwards in the wind, and her funny little skirt flapping hard.

They left the Fair behind. It was gay and noisy and crowded now. The stall-keepers were shouting, people were laughing, the roundabout was playing its harsh music. Snubby wished he could stay.

'Come on,' said Roger, as he lingered behind. 'We'll be late. And don't forget we've got to tell Barney our secret – we'll have to make time for that!'

Yes – their secret. Barney might be able to help them over that. How surprised he would be when they told him!

Chapter Eleven

Barney Comes to Supper

'I shall have to be careful not to give Great-uncle a chance to nab me and ask me awkward questions,' said Snubby as they rode off.

'It will be easy to get out of that if we've got a guest with us,' said Roger. 'Look where you're going, Snubby, you idiot – you rode over that hole that nearly tipped poor Loony out of his box.'

'Sorry, Loony!' called back Snubby.

Barney had tried to clean himself up a little in order to meet Mrs Lynton. He put on clean flannel trousers, and a clean, or nearly clean, sweater, His shoes were bad, but he could do nothing about those because he had on his only pair! His toes poked out of one, and Roger wondered if he had a pair that would fit Barney; but it looked as if Barney's feet were bigger than his.

They arrived home tired and hungry. Loony leapt thankfully out of the basket and ran straight to the kitchen to beg for a bone. Cook wasn't there. But there was a dish of sardine put down for the cat. Loony went over and sniffed at it. Should he take a bit? He was so hungry. No – it smelt nasty. Let Sardine the cat have it!

Sardine came in and spat at him. He ran at her and she fled out of the kitchen, up the passage and up the stairs. Into Roger's room she went, and leapt up on the chest of drawers.

Somebody else was sitting there! It was Miranda the

monkey, waiting for the boys. Sardine got the shock of her life. She had never seen a monkey before.

She went off like a firework, fizzing and hissing and spitting, her tail three times it's size. Miranda looked at her in horror. Whatever was this explosive animal?

In a fright, Miranda leapt down to the floor, scampered on all fours across the room, out on to the landing, and into Great-uncle Robert's room. He was there, brushing his mane of silver hair. He was startled to see a monkey leap on to his bed. Then came Sardine, and after Sardine came an excited Loony. The three of them rushed round the room twice and then disappeared.

Great-uncle sat down suddenly. What a household! A monkey! Had he seen right? Really, his bedroom was becoming a menagerie. He would have to speak to his niece, Susan, about it. No guest could be expected to put up with hordes of monkeys, cats, and dogs running in circles round his bedroom.

Roger was trying out his shoes on Barney. They were too small. Roger remembered what a lot of shoes Great-uncle had. Surely he could spare a pair. He went along and knocked at the door.

'Who is it now?' asked Great-uncle pettishly, as if he half-expected some more animals.

'It's me, Roger,' said Roger, 'Great-uncle, have you an old pair of shoes you could give me?'

'What's come over this household?' said Great-uncle. 'First my bedroom's full of . . . oh, well, never mind. What on earth do you want a pair of my shoes for? They won't fit you!'

'It's for a friend of mine who's come to supper,' explained Roger.

'Did he come without shoes then?' asked Great-uncle. 'Good heavens, there's that monkey again! If I can find out who's brought a monkey to this house and let it loose, I'll . . . I'll . . . I'll . . .'

Roger departed hurriedly. If Great-uncle knew it was the owner of the monkey who wanted the shoes he wouldn't lend them or give them, that was certain. 'Come on, Miranda you little wretch!' he said to the excited monkey. 'Don't rush all over the place. You'll give my mother a fit if she meets you on the stairs.'

He rummaged in the hall cupboard and found an old pair of tennis shoes belonging to his father. At least Barney's toes wouldn't stick out of those. Barney put them on gratefully.

'Do I look too awful to come to supper with you?' he asked Diana anxiously, when she came to see if the boys were ready.

'No, you're quite all right,' she said, hoping that her mother would think so too – and even more, her father. 'I've told Mother you're here. She is looking forward to meeting you.'

Barney was nervous. He had seldom been in a big house, and he was afraid his manners were bad. But he needn't have worried. He had naturally good manners, and a pleasant voice. When Mrs Lynton saw his strange blue eyes, set so wide, and noticed the anxious expression in them, she gave him an even warmer welcome than she had planned.

'So you're Barney! I've heard all about you. Richard, this is Barney, the boy who went through those hair-raising adventures with our three last summer.'

Mr Lynton looked up. He expected to see a gipsy-looking boy, sly and shrewd. Instead he saw Barney, with his bright, corn-coloured hair brushed back, his honest eyes, and straight, fearless look. He held out his hand.

71

'You're welcome, Barney,' he said. 'Any friend of Roger's is a friend of mine.'

Roger's heart warmed to his father. Good old Dad! He might be hot-tempered and strict and all the rest of it – but he had the right thoughts and feelings every time. Barney blushed with relief and pleasure. What nice parents Roger and Diana had – and how lucky they were!

'Mother – do you *mind* Miranda?' asked Diana anxiously, as she saw her mother's eyes stray in the monkey's direction for the first time. Miranda was sitting demurely on the back of a chair, looking most amusing in her little skirt and coat. Diana had given her a doll's bonnet and she was wearing that too.

'Oh dear!' said her mother, and began to laugh helplessly. 'Richard – do look at that. I don't think I shall mind her, Diana, if she doesn't come too near me. I really *don't* like monkeys, you know.'

'Shall I take her out?' asked Barney at once.

'No, no,' said Mrs Lynton. 'If I can put up willingly with Sardine and Loony, I can surely put up with a harmless little creature like this. But what your Great-uncle will say I cannot imagine.'

Great-uncle was a little late for the meal. Loony had hidden his evening shoes and it took him a long time to find them. When he came down at last, it was to find the family very friendly indeed with Barney and Miranda. It would have been difficult for him to make any trouble about them.

Barney thoroughly enjoyed himself. He loved the well-cooked food, the chatter, the laughter, the spotless mats, the flowers on the table, in fact, everything. Mrs Lynton liked him very much. How could this boy be a circus boy, a boy who wandered about with Fairs, who probably hardly ever had a bath – and yet was nice enough to make a good friend for her son?'

Mr Lynton liked Barney too. 'Have you no parents?' he asked.

'My mother died some time ago,' answered Barney. 'I never knew my father. He doesn't know anything about me, I'm afraid. All I know is that he's an actor, sir – and used to act in Shakespeare's plays. I've been looking for him all over the place, but I haven't found him yet.'

'Do you know the name he plays under?' asked Mr Lynton, thinking that surely any father would like to have a son like this turning up to claim him.

Barney shook his head. 'No, I don't even know what he looks like. I don't know his right name either, sir, because my mother was in the circus, and took her name always, not her married name. I'm afraid I'll never find him.'

'It seems doubtful, I must say,' said Mr Lynton. 'Well, – you seem to have done quite well on your own.'

After supper the four children went out into the garden. It was about half-past eight, and still light. They went into the summer-house and put Loony on guard again.

Miranda came too, of course. She had been on her very best behaviour at supper-time, and sat on Barney's shoulder all the time, accepting pieces of tomato from him, and a few apricot slices from the pudding dish. Now she sat on Snubby's shoulder, and tucked her little paws into his collar to keep them warm. He loved her. Loony was jealous and tried to get up on Snubby's knee.

'Now – what is it you wanted to tell me?' Barney asked, when Loony had been sent outside on guard.

'Well,' said Roger, hardly knowing how to begin. 'It's a peculiar story really – our Great-uncle is mixed up in it too. It's like this . . .'

He told the whole tale, with the others joining in occasionally.

'So you see,' he ended, 'we did just wonder if the Fair has got anything to do with robberies – whether somebody in the Fair knows enough about old papers and documents to steal them when the show goes near a museum, or near any other place where it's known that valuable papers are kept.'

'And we want to find out how the thief can go through locked doors,' said Diana. 'It's a bit like magic. You'd want a spell to do that!'

'Perhaps it's Old Ma!' said Snubby, remembering how witch-like she looked, bent over her iron pot.

Everyone laughed. Barney sat in silence, considering. 'I don't know anyone in the Fair who's interested in old things except Tonnerre,' he said at last. 'Tonnerre collects tiny carved ivory statues – but I've never heard of him collecting old papers. I shouldn't have thought he was educated enough to know whether they were valuable or not – or even where to go for them.'

'And surely *he* couldn't go through locked doors!' said Diana, remembering how enormous Tonnerre was.

'No, he couldn't,' said Barney.

There was a silence. 'Who decides the place where the Fair is to go?' asked Diana suddenly. 'Well – Tonnerre, I suppose, as he owns the Fair,' said Barney, 'Why? Oh – I see what you mean. Somebody knows where rare papers can be got – and that somebody decides to take the Fair there, in order to steal them. Yes – well, as far as I know Tonnerre always decides. He gives the orders anyway.'

'Does anyone else in the Fair collect anything?' asked Snubby, playing with Miranda's tail.

'No – only Burly, one of the chimps!' said Barney with

74

a laugh. 'He collects toy animals – didn't you know? If you'll only give him a toy animal he'll be your slave for life! Odd, isn't it?'

'Very odd,' said Diana, and laughed. 'What does Hurly collect?'

'Sweets! But they don't last long!' said Barney. 'You have to be careful of your pockets with Hurly. If you've got any sweets or chocolates there he'll pick your pockets as quickly as anything.'

'We must really make friends with them,' said Diana. 'We hardly spoke to them today, there was so many things to see. Well, Barney – you can't really help us much, can you, about the probable thief in the Fair – except – that it is more likely to be Tonnerre than anyone else.'

'There's Vosta,' said Barney thoughtfully. 'And there's Billy Tell. Both artful as can be. But somehow I can't see either of them knowing about rare papers. Why, I don't believe Billy Tell can read!'

'Oh well – perhaps it really is just chance that the burglaries occur when the Fair is in the district,' said Diana. 'I wonder where it's going to next.'

'Didn't I tell you? It's coming near *here*,' said Barney. 'About a mile away, I think. On Dolling Hill over at Rilloby.'

'How *smashing*!' said Snubby. 'How absolutely super. We'll see you every single day then – and I'll tell you what – we'll take it in turns to watch old Tonnerre! I BET he's the one. I've a feeling in my bones!'

Chapter Twelve

Plans!

The four children talked for a long while that night in the summer-house. Now that Barney, too, seemed to think that Diana's 'hunch' might have something in it, they were keener than ever to solve the mystery.

Snubby had an unexpectedly good idea. 'I say – I wonder if there's any place at Rilloby or near there that has a museum or rare collections of any kind,' he said.

'Now *that's* a brainwave of yours,' said Diana warmly. 'You don't often have a brainwave – but that really is an idea.'

'Yes. If we find out any place like that near the Fair – or within a mile or two – we could perhaps watch it,' suggested Roger.

'Gosh, yes – watch it and see if Tonnerre came wandering round it to snoop about,' said Snubby.

'We couldn't help seeing him if he did, he's so enormous!' said Diana.

'And if we did see him wandering about we could go to the place at night and see if we could catch him getting in,' went on Snubby excitedly. 'We might learn a thing or two about locked doors and how to get through them then?'

Everyone began suddenly to feel very thrilled. Could they really do all this? Well, perhaps they couldn't – but it would be very exciting to try.

'The thing to do first is to find out whether there is a museum or anything near Rilloby,' said Roger.

'How can we do that?' asked Diana. 'I've never heard of one – and we've lived here for years.'

'It might not be a museum,' said Roger. 'It might be a private collection of some sort – like the one Great-uncle was arranging at Chelie Manor House. Gosh, *I* know how to find out!'

'How?' said everyone.

'Well, ask Great-uncle, of course!' said Roger triumphantly. 'He'd know. I do believe he knows where every single valuable letter, map, plan, chronicle and all the rest of it is in the whole of Great Britain. He really is very learned, you know. These antiquarians are.'

'Anti what?' inquired Barney, who had never heard the word before. Diana explained.

Barney listened solemnly. He always liked to pick up any bit of knowledge that he could.

'Well, now – who's to ask Great-uncle about this?' said Roger.

'Not me, said Snubby promptly. 'He'd think I was getting the information out of him to hand to the Green Hands Gang!'

'Don't be an idiot,' said Diana.

'He *would*,' said Snubby firmly. 'He may be learned and all the rest of it, but he believes anything you tell him. I mean, he swallowed all about the Green Hands Gang and the rest of it absolutely whole! You should have seen his hair stand on end when I told him.'

'Don't exaggerate, said Roger. 'Anyway, we wouldn't dream of *you* asking him anything. You'd only make a mess of it, and say something silly.'

Snubby subsided. Diana considered the question. '*I'll* ask him,' she said. 'I'll take my autograph book to him for his autograph – he'll like that – and then I'll get him talking about collections of signatures or something like that – and from that I'll get to other collections of papers – and I can ask him what I want to know quite casually. He won't suspect a thing.'

'That's well worked out, Di,' said Roger approvingly. 'You do that tomorrow. Snubby had better still keep out of Great-uncle's way, in case he's asking too many awkward questions about how he knew there was to be a robbery at Ricklesham. You really were an idiot over that, Snubby.'

'All right, all right, tell me again,' said Snubby sulkily. 'Always going on at me – and yet *I* thought of the best idea this evening.'

'Yes, it *was* a good idea,' said Roger, 'We'll let it cancel out that mistake of yours! I say, isn't it getting dark!'

'Mother will be after us in a minute, saying it's bed-time,' said Diana.

'Then I'd better go,' said Barney, and he got up. 'This has been a lovely evening for me. Thanks an awful lot. Are you coming to the Fair tomorrow?'

'Of course,' said Diana. 'We'll see you every day till we go back to school, Barney. I'm glad Mother likes you. You can come here often now.'

'Dad likes him too,' said Roger. 'Well, see you tomor-row, Barney. Is Miranda asleep? She's been awfully quiet.'

'Sound asleep,' said Barney. 'She's inside my shirt. Feel her – warm as toast. She works hard at the hoopla stall with me, you know. Loony's been quiet too. I suppose he's tired out with his long run.'

He was! He was stretched out on the step of the sum-mer-house sound asleep too.

'He wouldn't have been much good as a watchdog this evening!' said Roger, poking him with his foot. 'Here, wake up, you sleepy hound! Didn't you know you were on guard?'

'Woof,' said Loony and sat up very suddenly.

'Good-bye, Barney,' said Diana. 'I'm awfully glad we've found you again. Don't forget to keep an eye on Tonnerre.'

'I'll remember,' said Barney with a laugh. 'His caravan stands near to ours. I'll keep an ear open all night now to hear if he creeps out of his van – and I'll watch to see if he puts his light on in the middle of the night.'

'And if he creeps out, follow him,' said Roger.

Barney slipped away to his bicycle. Mrs Lynton's voice could be heard calling the children. It was quite dark now, but the evening was very warm for April.

'I like the smell of those wallflowers,' said Snubby, sniffing hard as they walked down the path. 'Now, if I were a dog I'd go round sniffing at all the nice-smelling flowers – they'd just be the right height for sniffing.'

'Look – there's Great-uncle standing by Mother,' said Diana, clutching Snubby. 'I bet he's waiting to have a few quiet words with you, Snubby.'

'Gosh,' said Snubby, and stopped.

'Go to bed quickly,' said Roger. 'Go in the back way and slip up the stairs. Don't undress. Get into bed at once, so that if Great-uncle comes up to find you, you'll look fast asleep. Quick!'

Snubby slipped round to the back door, ran through the kitchen, much to the astonishment of Cook and Anna, and disappeared upstairs, Loony at his heels. He fell over Sardine on the way, of course, and Loony took the opportunity of getting in a little nip as he passed. Aha! That would teach Sardine to lie in wait on the stairs. An explosive spitting noise followed Loony as he bounded off.

Snubby ran into his bedroom, slipped off his shoes without unlacing them, and flung himself under the sheets. He left out just the top of his shock of red hair.

'Where's Snubby?' said Mrs Lynton, when the others appeared at the door. 'Great-uncle wants a word with him.'

'Oh, dear. I think he's gone to bed,' said Diana.

'*Has* he?' said her mother, astonished to hear that he had gone to bed before he was sent. It was usually quite a job to get Snubby off to bed. 'He must be very tired.'

'Well, we went on a long bike-ride today,' said Roger. 'I'll say goodnight too, Mother. I'm half asleep already. Did you like Barney?'

'Very much,' said his mother. 'Ask him here whenever you like. And – if you can tell him without offending him – say to him that he can have a hot bath whenever he'd like one. I'm sure there are never any hot baths at a Fair.'

'Oh, Mother – you *would* think of that!' said Roger with a laugh. He gave her a hug. 'I'm so glad you liked him. Goodnight and sweet dreams. Goodnight, Great-uncle.'

'Goodnight,' said Great-uncle. 'Er – I'll just come up with you and see if Snubby's asleep. I really do want a word with him.'

He went up with them. Mrs Lynton went too, rather puzzled. Why did Uncle Robert keep wanting to talk to Snubby? What could Snubby have done?

Nothing was to be seen of Snubby but a tuft of red hair, and a small mound under the bed-clothes. Loony was lying on his feet.

'Fast asleep!' said Mrs Lynton. 'Don't disturb him, Uncle Robert. He's tired out. Oh dear – look at Loony on the bed. I don't like to take him off in case I wake Snubby.'

Snubby gave a gentle little snore. 'Idiot!' thought Roger. 'Now he's going to overdo things as usual.'

'Well – I'll talk to him tomorrow,' said Great-uncle, and he and Mrs Lynton went out.

'Snubby, they've gone,' said Roger and pulled the clothes down. But Snubby didn't move. He *was* fast asleep! In all his clothes too.

'What a boy!' said Diana. 'Let him be. He's really tired out. So's Loony – not a flicker in him! Good-night, Roger. We'll have some fun now we've found old Barney again!'

Chapter Thirteen

Diana does her Bit

Most fortunately for Snubby, Great-uncle Robert had one of his bad nights that night, and asked to have his breakfast in bed the next day.

Snubby was full of glee. 'I thought I'd have to get down early to breakfast, gulp a bit of porridge and make that do,' he said, 'so as to be away from the table when Great-uncle came down. But now I shall be able to have a proper breakfast. Goodo!'

'We'll go over to the Fair after dinner today,' said Diana. 'I've got to help Mother do all the flowers and turn out some of my cupboards. We could take tea over to Ricklesham and have it with Barney. We'll take enough for him too.'

'And that will give you a chance to get on to Great-uncle about any museum or private collection,' said Roger. 'Snubby, you'd better spend the morning doing errands for Cook. Then you'll be out of the way.'

'Oh,' said Snubby, who was never very keen on doing errands. 'All right. I'll see if Cook wants anything. She said something about somebody fetching a new roller for the wringer. I'd have to go to Rilloby for that.'

'Well, that would take you out of Great-uncle's way for ages,' said Diana. 'You can go mooching round the toy shops, and have a few ice-creams at the dairy, and forget where you've left your bike, and take ages finding it again, and . . .'

'Don't try and be funny, Diana,' said Snubby, giving

her a push. 'You'll be an old nagger when you grow up if you don't look out. Like Old Ma!'

'I shan't – and don't push me like that,' said Diana, shoving back. 'Why do little boys give people pushes and shoves when they get annoyed?'

'Same reason as big girls do, I expect,' said Snubby, and went off pleased with himself.

He went to the kitchen and asked Cook if there were any errands she wanted done. She stared at him in surprise.

'What's come over you? Want me to make you meringues or something for dinner?'

'Oh no – I mean yes – well, no, I don't ask you for *that* reason,' said Snubby, getting into a muddle. 'What I mean is – meringues didn't enter my head – but if they're in yours and you want to make them for dinner, well, all I can say is, you go ahead!'

'You're after something. *I* know!' said Cook. 'Well, I'll think about the meringues. And seeing you are suddenly so helpful, yes, I'd be glad if you could get the new roller for my wringer. I keep on and on about it but nobody fetches it.'

'*I'll* fetch it, Cookie,' said Snubby. 'Anything else?'

'Well, bless me, you can't be feeling yourself to come and *ask* for jobs,' said Cook. 'Still, I may as well take advantage of it! You can bring back the kippers with you – and seeing that you're going all the way to Rilloby, would you leave a note at my sister's house to say I'll be over on Wednesday? And if you could call at the cobbler's and get me my best shoes, and . . .'

'Here! Wait a minute! I haven't got all day to spare,' said Snubby, suddenly feeling that he was taking on more than he had bargained for.

'I was just about to finish and say I'd be making meringues for your dinner,' said Cook with a twinkle.

'You'd better write all those things down while I get my bike,' said Snubby. 'I'll be back in half a jiffy.'

He came back and took the list from Cook. She had added one or two things. It was a real chance to get everything brought back, with Snubby in such a rare obliging mood!

'I'll just give you a jam tart to munch before you go,' said Cook, and went to the larder. 'Oh, by the way, your Great-uncle was in here a minute ago asking for you.'

Snubby vanished at once, without even waiting for the jam tart. Cook was most surprised.

Great-uncle marched into the lounge, where Mrs Lynton was doing the flowers. 'I'm looking for Snubby,' he said.

Mrs Lynton leaned out of the window and called to Diana, who was picking daffodils for the vases. 'Diana! Where's Snubby? Great-uncle wants him.'

'Oh, Mother – he's just gone to Rilloby on his bike,' said Diana, coming to the window. 'He told me he's fetching the new roller for Cook's wringer, and he's bringing back the kippers, and fetching some mended shoes; and . . .'

Mrs Lynton couldn't believe her ears. '*Snubby* is doing all that – on his own?' she asked disbelievingly. 'What's come over him?'

'Oh, he can be helpful when he likes,' said Diana, and turned away to hide a smile. 'I'm afraid he won't be back for ages, Great-uncle.'

'A nuisance this,' grumbled Great-uncle crossly. 'Slippery as an eel, that boy. Anyone would think he was avoiding me.'

'Oh, no, Uncle Robert,' said Mrs Lynton. 'Of course he's not. Why should he?'

'I shan't be in to lunch, my dear,' said Great-uncle, not bothering to answer her. 'I'm going up to London to see an old friend of mine.'

'Oh, Great-uncle – before you go will you sign my autograph album?' called Diana suddenly. Dear me, she mustn't let him slip off without asking him a few important questions!

'Ask your Great-uncle another time, dear,' said her mother exasperatingly. 'He's off to catch a train.'

'Oh, I'm not going just yet,' said Great-uncle, beaming at Diana. 'I'll sign Diana's album. I've got an old sixteenth-century proverb I once found in an old document that I'll write in for her – and I'll write it exactly as I saw it, in the old printing.'

'Oh, thank you,' said Diana. 'I'll get my album now. I'll bring it into the study, Great-uncle. I expect you'll be in there.'

'I will, my dear, I will,' said Great-uncle. So Diana took her album there, and the old man painstakingly printed in old letters the sixteenth-century proverb he had once found.

'There!' he said. 'Can you read that?'

'When ye thunder-clouds come, think on the Storm-cock bird – he sings,' Diana read with difficulty, for the shape of the letters and the spelling of the words were strange.

'Very nice, isn't it,' said Great-uncle. 'We haven't a saying like that in these modern times.'

'Well, we have, really,' said Diana. 'You know – "When you're up to your neck in hot water, think of the kettle – and sing!"'

'Ah – h'm!' said Great-uncle, surprised. 'I've not heard

85

that. Typical of these times – flippant, my dear, flippant, where the other proverb is beautiful.'

Diana wasn't sure what flippant meant. It somehow reminded her of tiddly-winks. Yes – you *flipped* the counters – so they were probably flippant. She decided not to enter into that question, but to push on with what she wanted to know.

'Great-uncle, you know an awful lot about old things, don't you?' she said.

'Yes, my dear. It's always been my great interest – delving into the past, spreading my net there, and seeing what I can bring up,' said Great-uncle.

'You've brought up some wonderful old things, haven't you?' said Diana.

'Well – *you* probably wouldn't think they were wonderful,' said Great-uncle. 'I'm interested really in old writings, you know – particularly old letters, which give us a vivid picture of the times in which they were written.'

'I suppose you know every collection in the country?' said Diana in an awed voice.

Great-uncle was flattered at Diana's interest. 'No, no,' he said. 'I know the most famous ones, of course – and many of the minor ones – but not all, my dear, no, not all!'

'Are there any interesting collections near here, Great-uncle?' asked Diana, bringing out her important question quite airily. She was pleased with herself! 'Any near Rilloby, for instance?'

'Now let me see,' said Great-uncle, considering. 'Well – there's Marloes Castle, of course – but there's only a very *small* collection there. Lord Marloes was more interested in animals and birds than old documents. He's got a fine collection of those, so I hear – began to stuff them himself as a boy.'

'Are the documents valuable – very valuable?' asked Diana.

'Yes – yes, I suppose they are,' said Great-uncle. 'I know some Americans were after them last year, so Marloes told me. He wouldn't sell, though. They're all family letters and historical documents relating to his own estate – he'd never part with them. He wouldn't part with his stuffed animals either! Now – I wonder – I believe I can get in touch with him in town – would you and the others like to go and see his collection of animals, if I can get you permission?'

'Oh, yes, *please*, Great-uncle,' said Diana, delighted. This was a bit of luck. They could have a good look round the collections, and see the lie of the land – then if there happened to be a burglary there they would be able to picture the rooms and everything.

'Well, I'll telephone Marloes and see if he's back in town,' said Great-uncle. 'I'll take you over to the old castle myself, and you can look at the stuffed animals and I'll have another look at the documents. It'll be quite a day out, won't it, my dear?'

'Oh, *yes*,' said Diana. 'Thanks awfully, Great-uncle. We'd all love to come.'

'Dear, dear, look at the time!' said Great-uncle, getting up in a hurry. 'I shall miss that train.'

He went off, and Diana shut up her album thoughtfully. She considered she had done very well indeed. She had found out where valuable papers were – in Marloes Castle – and it was possible that Great-uncle would take her and the others there – and they would be able to do a good snoop round. Wonderful!

She went out to find Roger. 'Roger! Roger! Where are you? Quick, I've got good news.'

Mrs Lynton heard her calling, and saw her talking excit-

edly to Roger. What could the 'good news' be, she wondered. How surprised she would have been if she had
known!

Chapter Fourteen

At the Fair Again

Snubby arrived home complete with everything Cook had asked for. She beamed at him. 'There are two meringues for each of you,' she told him, 'and there's one over. I'll tell your aunt I made it specially for you. So you can have three.'

'Smashing!' said Snubby, pleased. 'I say, this roller thing was frightfully heavy. I shall think twice before I say I'll fetch one again.'

'Oh, we shan't want one for years,' said Cook. 'Loony, come out of the larder. Bless us all, if I leave that larder door open for so much as half a moment that dog's in there.'

'LOONY!' yelled Snubby, and Loony backed out hurriedly. Oh, the smells in a larder! It was a far, far better place than the biggest, smelliest rabbit-hole.

Roger and Diana went to tell Snubby the news about Marloes Castle. He was excited.

'Gosh! That's a bit of luck. You're clever, Di, to manage all that. How did you wangle it?'

'Easy,' said Diana. 'Great-uncle just gobbled down all I said.'

'I told you he'd swallow anything,' said Snubby. 'Now you can see why he swallowed my Green Hands Gang yarn.'

'Well, if he really does get permission to take us over the collection, and there's a burglary some time, we'll be able to picture how it's done,' said Roger. 'We'll make a plan of the rooms where the collections are – or anyway of the room where the papers are. The thief won't be interested in the stuffed animals.'

They had a very good lunch indeed, and enjoyed Cook's meringues immensely. They wished there were far, far more.

'Can't you go shopping for Cook every single morning?' said Diana to Snubby.

'No, I can't,' said Snubby decidedly. 'If you want meringues again, *you* go shopping for her. I've done my bit. My bike almost broke down with all the weight it had to carry. Poor Loony had to run all the way back. I couldn't possibly carry him as well. Anyway, the carrier-box was full of shoes and things.'

'Are you going to see Barney today?' said Mrs Lynton after lunch. 'If so, take him this shirt, will you? It's one that's too small for your father, and it would do for him nicely.'

'Right, Mother. He'll be pleased,' said Roger. 'We're just off now. Cook's packed us up some tea. It'll be nice for you to have an afternoon without us *or* Great-uncle, won't it!'

They were off at last, and Mrs Lynton sank down thankfully on the sofa with a book. Now for peace!

They arrived at the Fair after it had opened and heard the roundabout music a long way away. Barney was on the lookout for them. He waved cheerily as they came up. Young 'Un waved too, and so did the roundabout boy. Now that it was known that they were Barney's friends they were welcome any time, whether they had money to spend or not.

There was no one at the hoopla stall just then, Hurly and Burly, the two chimpanzees, were giving their show in Vosta's tent and most people had gone to see them.

They were able to tell Barney their news about Marloes Castle.

'Jolly good,' grinned Barney. 'I've got no news, I'm afraid. I've kept an eye on Tonnerre, but he's done nothing suspicious. All I've heard is that we move to Rilloby tomorrow.'

'I saw the notices this morning,' said Snubby. 'There were posters advertising Rilloby Fair all over the place.'

'It'll be easier for you to see me when we're there,' said Barney. 'Nearer for you.'

'Where's Miranda?' asked Snubby, missing the little monkey suddenly.

'Gone to watch Hurly and Burly do their tricks,' said Barney. 'They love her, you know. Hold her and nurse her like a baby – especially Burly, the one that likes toy animals.'

'Could we go and peep in at Hurly and Burly?' asked Diana. 'Have they finished yet?'

'Almost,' said Barney. 'I'll take you over. There's nobody likely to come to the hoopla stall till the chimps' show is over. Look out for Old Ma today. She's in one of her tempers. Even Tonnerre is keeping away from her.'

They kept an eye open for Old Ma, but they didn't see her. They heard her though, muttering loudly in her caravan. Young 'Un saw them as they went by and winked.

'Have to go and give Old Ma a spanking soon,' he grinned. 'Getting above herself, she is!'

Barney took them to Vosta's tent. He nodded to the attendant and let them peep inside. Hurly and Burly were just finishing their performance. Burly was riding a bicycle made specially for him, and Hurly was standing on the handle-bars, turning somersaults as the bicycle went

91

round and round the small ring of grass. He landed neatly back on the handle-bars each time.

'Good, aren't they?' said Barney.

Hurly did one last somersault and landed on Burly's head. Burly leaped off the bicycle. He bowed to the audience and Hurly fell off. Everyone laughed and clapped. Burly ran to Vosta and put his hairy arms round him. Vosta patted the big chimpanzee and gave him an apple.

Hurly got over-excited at the shouting and clapping and began to turn somersaults at a terrific rate round the ring, making peculiar noises. Then he scampered round on all fours.

Something landed on his back. It was Miranda, seeing a chance for a ride! Burly snatched her off Hurly's back and began to nurse her in his arms, making little crooning noises.

'Ladies and gentlemen, the show is now over!' shouted Vosta, seeing that nobody made a move. Nobody wanted to, because the chimpanzees and Miranda were so funny!

But the tent was cleared at last and Vosta came up to the children, carrying Miranda. He was very fond of her too. She was busy pulling his tie undone, chattering without stopping.

'Hallo, folks,' said Vosta. 'What do you think of my chimps?'

'They're champs – absolutely champion,' said Snubby, making one of his frightful jokes.'

'And you're a *chump*, a champion chump,' said Roger, joining in. 'I say, Mr Vosta, how did you teach your chimps to ride a bike?'

'Didn't have to teach them,' said Vosta. 'They saw me riding mine one day, and when I put it down Hurly got on it and rode off straightaway. Then Burly had a go. Like to have tea with us this afternoon?'

'Oh *yes*,' said all three. Diana turned to Barney. 'What about *you*? Can you, Barney?'

'Yes. I'll get Young 'Un to come across again,' said Barney. 'Well, I must be getting back to my stall. Going on the roundabout, Snubby? Don't you get Jimmy to run it too fast again, or you'll get into trouble. I can see old Tonnerre's got his eye on you today.'

Tonnerre was with his elephants, watching the children and Loony. He shouted to them in his enormous voice.

'You come to ride on my fine elephants, yes, no?'

But they didn't ride on the elephants. 'I'd rather go on the roundabout,' said Snubby. 'It's not so sway-about as the elephants. Come on, Loony.'

They spent a pleasant afternoon, and went to every stall. They saw Brilliant the Juggler, they watched the hoopla, with Miranda gathering up the rings so deftly, they went to the skittles and threw balls to knock them down for prizes.

Diana was the only one who managed to knock down three skittles and win a prize. The boy in charge of the skittles waved his hand towards a pile of prizes.

'Take what you like, Miss. Nice to see a girl beat her brothers. Shouldn't have thought it!'

That made Roger and Snubby immediately pay to throw some more balls, of course, just as the boy had meant them to. He winked at Diana.

'Not so good as you yet, see, Miss? Only knocked one skittle down between them. Poor shots, aren't they?'

Diana looked at the pile of prizes. She chose a small toy dog, much to the boys' surprise. Roger teased her about it.

'Baby! Fancy choosing that! Why didn't you take that little blue vase?'

'I've chosen it for a purpose,' said Diana. 'You wait and see!'

'Pity there's nothing for Loony to go in for,' said Snubby. 'I bet he'd win like anything.'

'He'd win a rabbit-hole scratching competition,' said Roger. 'I never did see a dog scratch so fast at a rabbit-hole as he does.'

'Or with so little result!' said Diana. 'What he'd do if he really came upon a rabbit in a hole I can't imagine. Probably back out in a frightful hurry!'

'Woof,' said Loony, knowing they were talking about him. Snubby patted his silky head.

'They're saying horrid things about you,' he said. 'Never mind. You're the best dog ever! A super dog, a real smasher.'

'There's Mr Vosta calling us,' said Diana. 'He says he's going to have tea. Get the things out of the bike-baskets, Roger – we'll share them. And I'll tell Barney to come along now if he can.'

They all went to Vosta's caravan. Inside was a small table spread with a marvellous tea – and sitting at it already were Hurly and Burly, wearing feeders!

'Get up, chaps, and bow!' said Vosta, and the two chimps rose and bowed politely.

'This is going to be fun!' said Diana, and she was right!

Chapter Fifteen

A Nice Afternoon – and a Sudden Ending

It was rather a hilarious tea-party, because Miranda and Loony were there too. Miranda behaved really badly – like a spoilt child. She snatched at this and that, she took things off Burly's plate, and she teased Loony unmercifully.

'Miranda! I'll give you to Tonnerre to deal with if I have any more nonsense!' said Barney sternly.

'Oh, let her do what she wants to,' said Snubby, delighted. 'She's frightfully funny like this. Look – she's picking all the cherries out of the cake now.'

Hurly reached out a hairy paw and smacked Miranda sharply. He liked cherries too! Miranda made little crying noises and Burly reached out his paws and picked her up, cradling her against his red-striped jersey. Hurly at once pulled her tail, which lay across his plate.

Burly then punched Hurly, and Vosta hammered on the table. 'Behave yourselves! Don't you know how to behave when visitors are here?'

The chimpanzees looked ashamed. Hurly took off his sailor hat and hid his face behind it. The children squealed with laughter.

The tea was fine – a peculiar mixture, but very appetising.

'It's the sort of tea I like,' said Snubby, pleased. 'Potted meat and bread and butter, and tinned pineapple and cream, and cherry cake and biscuits, and our own tomato sandwiches and jam tarts.'

'And there's ham here too, if you'd like it,' said Vosta hospitably.

Snubby did. It was amazing what he could put away when he really liked a meal. The others did their best but he outdid them all. Vosta grinned to see him munching away happily. He liked Snubby, and he loved Loony.

Loony lay with his head on Vosta's foot. Snubby felt quite jealous! It wasn't often Loony did that with anyone.

'Vosta's a magician with animals,' said Barney. 'He's better with Tonnerre's elephants than Tonnerre is himself.'

'Ho, Tonnerre! Br-r-r-r-r-r!' said Vosta unexpectedly. 'All those years I have worked for him and still he shouts at me. Br-r-r-r-r!'

Hurly imitated him. 'Br-r-r-r-r-r!' Then he bent down and looked under the table. Loony was near him, his head still on Vosta's foot. Burly made crooning noises to Loony, who lifted his head and looked astonished.

Burly suddenly disappeared below the table, and put his arms round the surprised spaniel. He tried to lift him up. Loony yelped and snapped, but he did not bite. Snubby rescued him.

'It's all right,' said Barney. 'Burly is cracked on monkeys and dogs and cats – he's got a nursemaid idea of himself, I think – wants to nurse them all. Vosta, show us Burly's collection of toy animals.'

Vosta opened a cupboard. Inside were a good number of toy animals – a teddy bear, a tiny monkey, two pink cats, a golliwog, and a few others. Burly made a grab at them.

He set them out on the tea-table, his eyes watchful in case anyone tried to take them from him. But nobody did. They were his toys, precious to him. They watched him arrange them to his liking.

Then Miranda snatched the teddy bear and was off to the top of the caravan with it at once, sitting by the chimney, chattering. Burly leapt up, growling strangely, Vosta forced him back.

'Stop it now. Silly of me to have let him have his toys out with Miranda there. Barney, can you get the bear back before there's trouble?'

Barney went out of the caravan and called sternly to Miranda, who was still hugging the chimney, looking very comical in her little skirt and coat.

Burly made a miserable, howling noise. Diana felt sorry for him. She remembered something she had brought for him and felt in her pocket for the little toy dog she had won for a prize at the skittle match. She held it out to Burly.

He looked at it in surprise. He sat up and reached out a paw for it. He took it very gently and set it down on the table, still keeping hold of it. He stroked it with his other paw and crooned to it. He was a strange chimpanzee!

He forgot about the bear that Miranda had taken. He gave his whole attention to the little toy dog.

'He loves it,' said Vosta. 'That was nice of you, Miss Diana. He's all right now – forgotten about the bear. Good thing too. I thought he was going to turn nasty for a minute.'

Burly took up the toy dog and looked at Vosta, making a deep chattering noise as if he were talking. Vosta understood.

'Yes, it's yours, Burly,' he said. 'Yours. You can put it with your other toys.'

Burly gathered all the toys up and put them back in the cupboard. Barney came in at that moment with the teddy bear. Burly took it, and put that in the cupboard too. He placed the little dog in the very front.

Vosta shut the cupboard and rubbed Burly affectionately on the head. 'Funny fellow, ain't you? Isn't this a nice girl to bring you a present like that?'

Burly understood. He put out a big paw and stroked Diana gently on the arm, making a funny crooning sound as he did so.

'He's thanking you,' said Vosta. 'And now look at poor old Hurly – he feels left out of all this!'

Hurly was stretching out both hands as if to say. 'What about me? I haven't had anything!'

'I've brought him some sweets,' said Snubby, remembering, and felt in his pocket. Roger began to feel in his too. 'I got him some chocolate,' he said.

But neither of the boys found the sweets or chocolate. They were puzzled. 'I've lost the sweets,' said Snubby. 'Blow!'

Barney smiled his wide smile. 'I guess Mr Vosta can find them for you. Watch!'

Vosta spoke sternly to Hurly. 'Hurly! Turn out your pockets. Go on, you heard what I said – your pockets!'

Hurly made a whimpering sound and stood up. He pulled at his pockets. Vosta slipped his hand in, and out came a bag of sweets and a bar of chocolate!

'He's a pick-pocket when there's any sweets around.' said Vosta. 'Can't blame him. He's only a chimp and he doesn't really know right from wrong when it comes to things like honesty. Bad boy, Hurly! Very bad!'

Hurly took off his hat and hid his face behind it again. But he peeped over it, his bright eyes looking at Vosta.

'Give them back to him, Mr Vosta,' said Snubby. 'He's an awful dear. They both are. Gosh, I wish I had a couple of chimps of my own. It's the first thing I shall buy when I'm grown up.'

'It will be fine to see three chimps walking together down the road,' said Vosta solemnly, and laughed to see Snubby's indignant face.

'Hallo – Tonnerre's taken his elephants off somewhere,' said Barney, when the tea-party was over and the little company climbed down the steps of the caravan to the grassy field.

'He's probably taken them to Rilloby,' said Vosta. 'That's where we go tomorrow. He sometimes takes his elephants the day before we leave. They are so slow in their walking.'

Snubby pricked up his ears. If Tonnerre had gone for the evening, it would be a good idea to snoop round his caravan a bit – look in at the window, or at the door – see if there was a safe there that valuable papers could be kept in, perhaps.

He didn't say anything to the others. He wanted to snoop by himself – and anyway three or four people would be noticed at once round a caravan. He waited till Roger and Diana had gone on the roundabout again and then he set off to Tonnerre's big caravan.

Loony went with him, puzzled by the sudden 'hists' and 'pssts' that Snubby suddenly addressed to him. He trotted at his heels obediently. He liked the Fair. It was full of astonishing smells, and amazing animals. He didn't much like the mongrel dogs though, and kept strictly to himself where they were concerned.

Snubby came to Tonnerre's caravan. No one seemed to be about. He looked underneath it. It was hung with all kinds of things below – but then, so were all the other caravans. The underneath of a van was a convenient place to put a lot of things not wanted for a time.

99

He stood on a wheel and peeped in at a window; but the curtain was drawn and he couldn't see inside. He went to the other side of the van. Ah – the curtain was not drawn across there. He could see in quite well.

Snubby took a good, long look. It seemed a fairly ordinary caravan really – a bunk for a bed – a table that folded down – a stove in one corner for heating – a chair and a stool.

But what was that under the bunk? Snubby could see something sticking out a little. It looked like a black box – a good big one.

Would precious papers be kept in there? The more he looked at that box the more he felt certain that it was full of stolen papers!

He decided to go round to the door and see if it had been left unlatched. But it hadn't, of course. It was locked. Snubby bent to peep through the keyhole to see if he could get another view of that big black box.

Three things happened at exactly the same moment! Loony gave a terrific growl. Somebody gave a tremendous yell that almost deafened Snubby – and a hand descended on a very tender part of him with a terrific whack!

Snubby yelled and fell off the caravan steps. Loony yelped too, as the hand dealt him a slap as well. Snubby caught sight of a giant-like figure about to whack him again, and he rolled over quickly, jumped up and fled.

An enormous voice came after him. 'YOU! COME HERE! I'LL TEACH YOU TO PRY! YES!'

It was Tonnerre. He had only taken his elephants for a little walk down the lane and back – and had just caught Snubby nicely.

He tore after Snubby and Loony, shouting. Everyone stared. Roger and Diana saw Snubby shoot past like a bullet out of a gun, with Loony at his heels. After them

100

came Tonnerre, black as thunder, yelling for all he was worth.

'Gosh – we'd better go,' said Roger. 'Come on, Di – slip round to the back of the stall, and we'll get behind the vans and creep down to the gate. What in the world has that idiot of a Snubby done? See you at Rilloby tomorrow, Barney – I *hope*!'

Chapter Sixteen

A Morning at the Castle

Snubby had a bad time from the others that evening. 'Messing things up! Putting Tonnerre against us! Even perhaps putting him on his guard!' raged Roger on the way home. 'What do you want to go snooping round his caravan like that for?'

'It's just the sort of crazy thing that Snubby *would* do,' said Diana. 'Making everyone stare. I don't feel as if I want to go to the Fair any more.'

'Oh, shut up,' said Snubby, angry with the others and angry with himself too. 'Going on and on at me. I tell you I thought Tonnerre had gone off to Rilloby with his elephants. Anyway, I wasn't doing any harm.'

'Harm! You keep *on* doing harm!' said Roger. 'What with your silly Green Hands Gang, and your blabbing about the possibility of a theft at Ricklesham, and now this snooping round Tonnerre's caravan.'

There was a silence as the three rode on down the road. Snubby was really very much upset about it all. 'He went off like a crack of thunder,' he said at last. 'And I got a frightful whack.'

'Not nearly frightful enough,' said Roger at once, and Snubby gave up trying to make peace. Let them be as cross as they liked! He still had old Loony. Loony never raged at him or nagged him or thought badly of him. Never.

Great-uncle Robert was not back from town when they arrived home. Snubby was glad. Now he wouldn't have to go dodging about all evening to avoid him. They had their supper with their mother and father, and then Snubby wandered off alone with Loony. The others still looked annoyed with him.

Great-uncle came back about half-past nine. Snubby, bored, had retired to bed. Roger and Diana were just about to go.

'Had a good day, Uncle Robert?' said Mrs Lynton, taking his coat and scarf from him.

'Yes. Most interesting, my dear, most interesting,' said Uncle Robert. 'And I've got a nice bit of news for the children. Where are they?'

They were in the lounge, clearing up their things. 'Well, my dears,' said Great-uncle, beaming at them. 'I managed to get in touch with Lord Marloes this morning. And he's given me permission to take you to his castle – and see his collection of rare papers and interesting animals. We'll go tomorrow, if you like.'

'Oh, thanks, Great-uncle! That's fine!' said Diana. Roger beamed too. Now they would be able to have a look round before the thief came – if he meant to come!

'I thought you'd be pleased,' said Great-uncle. 'I'm pleased myself. I haven't seen his collection for years. It will refresh my memory nicely.'

Mrs Lynton looked slightly astonished. She went out into the hall with Diana and Roger when they left the room to go up to bed.

'Do you really want to go looking at dull old papers?' she said. 'Because you *will* find them terribly dull, you know – and dear old Uncle Robert can be a bit of a bore when he's explaining them. I know because he often took me with him when I was a girl.'

'It's all right, Mother – we shall love it,' Diana assured

her. 'It's really the stuffed animals we want to see. There's quite a good collection of them there.'

'Oh well – you go if you like,' said her mother. 'It will please your Great-uncle tremendously.'

It certainly did! He set off with them at ten o'clock the next morning in a specially hired car, smiling all over his face. He was so pleased about the little expedition that he quite forgot that for the last two days he had wanted to talk to Snubby about something important!

Loony, alas, was not allowed to come. 'I'm sorry, but no dogs are allowed in the castle,' said Great-uncle, quite determined in no circumstance to take Loony. Loony had only to see Great-uncle to take it into his head to sit down and scratch himself violently – and the old man wasn't going to have him indulging in a prolonged scratch in the car!

They arrived at the castle. It was not really a very large one, more like a big mansion in fact. The big iron gates at the entrance to the drive were opened by the lodge-keeper, who came out of his little lodge nearby.

'Your pass, please sir,' he said, and Great-uncle gave it to him.

'That's all right, sir,' said the man. 'Quite busy this morning, we are! Yours is the third pass I've checked today. Well, we've got a nice little museum up there, sir – and be sure to look at the albino badger, sir. I caught him myself! His lordship was downright pleased with me.'

'We'll look at it, my man,' said Great-uncle, and the car went on up the drive to a large front door. A butler opened it, and the pass was shown once more.

'This way, sir,' said the butler, in a voice as pompous as Great-uncle's. Snubby nudged Diana and she smiled. She knew what Snubby was thinking.

The man took them down a stone-floored hall, and up

a vast flight of marble stairs that swept round in a magnificent curve to the floor above.

They went up to another floor, and the man led the way to a small wing built off from the main part of the house. He unlocked a big wooden door that led into a dark stone passage. Another door stood at the end. He unlocked that too.

It led into a big room that was lined with books from ceiling to floor.

On they went, through the room to the other side, where a small, stout door was let into the wall. This was unlocked by two different keys!

'You keep the place well locked,' said Roger. 'Two locked doors, and now a third one, double-locked! You don't mean burglars to get in!'

'No, sir,' said the butler. 'His lordship prizes his collection greatly. Here you will find the stuffed animals, sir, and beyond, on those shelves, are the papers. Before you leave, sir, I must ask you to wait whilst Mr Johns, the custodian, checks up the collection. We have to do that, sir, otherwise it would be easy for people to put something valuable in their pockets – there are plenty of dishonest people about these days!'

'That's all right,' said Great-uncle. 'Check all you like. It's good to see such care taken of a valuable collection. There have been so many thefts lately.'

'Yes, sir,' said the butler and locked them into the room!

'We're locked in!' said Diana, half-alarmed.

'That's quite usual,' said Great-uncle. 'It's just a sensible precaution. We have to ring that bell when we are ready to go. Hallo – there's somebody else here.'

There were two people – one an old, old man who was so bent that it was quite impossible to see his face. The other was a younger man with a beard and very bushy eyebrows indeed. He had a moustache, and was altogether a most hairy-looking person.

'He's even got hairs growing out of his ears!' whispered Snubby to Diana. 'Like eyebrows!'

'Sh! He'll hear you,' said Diana crossly. Snubby's whispers were always much too loud.

The two men were examining the various papers set out and labelled on the shelves. The bearded man glanced round at the newcomers and then lost interest in them. He turned the pages of a manuscript carefully over and over, as the children wandered round.

'Di! You go and listen to Great-uncle Robert and we'll have a look round,' whispered Roger. 'I'll make a rough plan of the room – just in case, you know!'

Diana went with Great-uncle and began to ask him questions. The old man began a lengthy explanation of this manuscript and that one. Diana was very bored. She hardly understood a word. She looked round for the boys. They were walking all round, looking here and there. They were not really very thrilled with the stuffed animals, which were a poor, mangy-looking lot, some with the moth in their furry coats.

The white badger was there, looking extremely dirty. There were two foxes with a litter of cubs, all stuffed and standing together, looking very unnatural. There was a pole-cat with one eye. The other had apparently dropped out at some time and had not been put back. There were two squirrels, red ones, outside what was supposed to be their nest. The very moth-eaten head of a young squirrel peeped over the edge of the dusty nest.

'I don't think much of these,' said Snubby, disgusted. 'They must be animals Lord Marloes stuffed when he was

106

a boy, and was so proud of them that he couldn't bear to part with them. They're horrible.'

'What's that fellow doing?' whispered Roger suddenly to Snubby, nudging him. Snubby looked at the man with the beard. He was laying something down on one of the manuscripts, moving it up and down the page.

'It's only a magnifying-glass, idiot,' said Snubby. 'You've seen Great-uncle using one on his old papers. Don't be so suspicious!'

Roger looked a bit crestfallen. He turned to look at the bent old man. How could anyone be so bent! It must be dreadful. Even when he walked from shelf to shelf he was so bent that he was forced to look down at the floor all the time.

Roger was glad when the two men rang the bell and went. The custodian, a wrinkled old man, came in, shut the door, and went rapidly through the papers on the shelves to make sure they were all there. He didn't even glance at the animals!

'I expect he hopes somebody *will* steal them some day, the horrible moth-eaten things,' said Snubby, as the two men went out with the custodian. The door was once more double-locked.

'Now I'm going to make a sketch of the room,' said Roger. 'Just in case!'

'Put in the other two locked doors leading to the room,' said Snubby, watching Roger beginning to draw. 'Oh, you're doing it awfully well. What are those – windows?'

'Yes. They're well and truly fastened. Did you notice?' said Roger. 'And they've got bars outside too. Nobody could get in there.'

He looked up to see if there was a skylight, but there wasn't. He sketched in where the shelves were put and put dots for the stuffed animals on the floor. He marked where the chairs were, a desk, the fireplace, and a small table on which stood some kind of plant.

It really was quite a good drawing. Roger felt rather pleased. Snubby admired it whole-heartedly.

They glanced at poor Diana. She was looking rather pale, having been standing beside Great-uncle for about an hour, listening wearily to a lecture she didn't understand and didn't like.

'Poor old Di!' said Roger under his breath to Snubby. 'She looks fed up. Shall we go and take her place?'

'No,' said Snubby firmly, 'You can if you want to. I'm not going to. I should be sick.'

'Well, go and be sick,' said Roger. 'Great-uncle would take us all out then. You couldn't be sick in here.'

Snubby caught sight of something on the broad mantelpiece. It was a clock. The hands pointed to half-past eleven. Snubby tiptoed over to it, opened the front of the clock and turned the hands till they said half-past twelve. Roger gave a snort of laughter, which he hurriedly turned into a sneeze.

Snubby went up to Great-uncle Robert. 'Er – Great-uncle – I just hate to interrupt you – but do you think it's time to go? The clock on the mantelpiece says half-past twelve.'

'Bless us all! How the time flies!' said Great-uncle in amazement, and rang the bell for the custodian. 'Incredible! Quite incredible!'

108

Chapter Seventeen

The Fair Moves to Rilloby

They went home in the car, Roger longing to show Diana his really excellent drawing. Great-uncle rambled on, unable to stop. The children listened, bored, wishing they were home.

'Thanks awfully, Great-uncle,' said Roger politely. 'We've had a wizard morning.'

'A *what* morning?' asked Great-uncle, puzzled.

'Wizard. Smashing. Super,' explained Snubby. 'Thanks a lot.'

'I'm very glad, very glad,' beamed Great-uncle, thinking what nice interesting children they were all of a sudden. He really must take them to some other collection some time. 'Now you'd better go and get tidy for dinner,' he said. 'Dear me – I hope your mother won't think I've brought you back too late.'

Considering that it was only ten to twelve, and not ten to one, as Great-uncle thought, Mrs Lynton thought they were back very early, not late. As for Great-uncle, he was simply amazed to find what a long time there was before the dinner-gong went! He couldn't understand it at all.

Roger showed his map to Diana. 'Now,' he said, 'if there's a burglary we shall have a map of the whole place. It may be very, very useful.'

Loony was so pleased to see them again that he had one of his mad fits, rushing up and down the stairs at top speed, in and out of all the bedrooms, sending mats flying this way and that. Sardine was scared out of her life and fled to the top of the grandfather clock, where she sat swinging her tail like a pendulum till Loony's madness had exhausted itself.

Great-uncle locked himself into his bedroom when he realised that Loony was having a mad fit. That dog! If he wasn't barking, he was scratching, and if he wasn't scratching, he was going mad. Th only really satisfactory dogs were stuffed ones, Great-uncle thought. At least they didn't scratch!

The children didn't go to see Barney that day, partly because Mr Lynton was at home and told them all to come out into the garden and help him with some trees he was chopping down; and partly because they knew the Fair was moving to Rilloby, and they thought that Barney might be too busy to want them that day.

Snubby had a third reason. He was still smarting from the enormous whack Tonnerre had given him, and he thought it would be wise to allow him to forget what had happened. He meant to give Tonnerre a very wide berth in future!

Barney turned up himself that evening with Miranda on his shoulder. He waited in the garden till he saw Roger. Then he whistled his low clear whistle.

Roger turned. 'That you, Barney?' he called. 'Oh, good! Had any supper? We've had ours, but we can easily ask Cook for something for you.'

'I wouldn't mind a bit of cake,' said Barney, who had had very little to eat that day in the move to Rilloby.

'Come to the back door. We'll ask Cook for something,' said Roger. They appeared at the back door and Cook gave a shriek to see Miranda.

'Land sakes! Is it a monkey? Don't you dare to let it come into my kitchen. Whatever next!'

110

However, she calmed down enough to cut poor hungry Barney some sandwiches and gave him a big chunk of treacle tart. He held up a sandwich to Miranda and she delicately took out a bit of tomato from the middle and ate it.

'A monkey now! What next!' said Cook.

'You come to Rilloby Fair and you'll see a couple of chimpanzees,' said Roger. 'You should see them ride their bicycles.'

'Now that I *don't* believe,' said Cook. 'All right, I'll come and if I see two chimpanzees riding bicycles, well, I'll eat my best Sunday hat.'

'You look out – you'll have to go to church in your *second* best hat now – you'll have eaten your best one,' grinned Roger.

Barney hadn't any news except that they had moved the Fair successfully to Dolling Hill at Rilloby, and that Tonnerre seemed to have recovered his temper and had spent a happy afternoon spring-cleaning his two elephants.

'Spring-cleaning them! What do you mean?' said Diana, who had joined them with Snubby.

'Oh, he gets a step-ladder, and a can of oil, and a brush – and he oils the creases in their skins and rubs them all over,' said Barney, eating the sandwiches very fast indeed. 'He loves that job. It's put him into quite a good temper.'

'He gave me an awful whack,' said Snubby. 'I can hardly sit down.'

'Serves you right,' said Diana. 'If you always got what you always deserve, you'd always never be able to sit down.'

'I don't like that remark,' said Snubby, having worked it out bit by bit. But by that time Roger was showing

111

Barney his map of the room in the castle and nobody took any notice of him.

'How are Hurly and Burly?' asked Diana. 'Do they get upset with a move?'

'Not a bit,' said Barney, giving Miranda a tiny piece of treacle tart. 'Oh, you little nuisance – you've dropped it down my neck!'

'What – the treacle?' said Diana sympathetically. 'How awful.'

That reminded Roger of something. 'Would you like a bath?' he asked Barney. 'Mother says you can have one any time.'

Barney hesitated. 'Well – I'd awfully like one now if she really means it. I'm filthy with all the moving today. I just can't seem to get clean in cold water, and that's all I get.'

So Barney was escorted to the bathroom, where he stared at the great, cream-coloured bath, quite overcome. Diana brought him a thick, cream-coloured towel, a very big one.

'What's this?' he asked, thinking it was a bed-quilt or something. He was astonished when she told him it was only a towel. His towel was usually a very dirty rag of a handkerchief. How he enjoyed that hot bath! Miranda sat on the cold tap and looked on in amazement. What *could* Barney be doing in water that smoked? She put one small foot down into it and curled it up with a squeal.

'Did it bite you?' asked Barney, soaping himself all over, and replacing the soap in its dish. Miranda took it up and smelt it. She nibbled it and flung the soap into the water in disgust. She spat out the bit she had nibbled.

'Miranda, that's not nice behaviour in a bathroom like this,' said Barney. 'Now where's the soap gone?'

He hunted in the water for it and then lay peacefully in the warmth. Loony scratched at the door.'

'Sorry. The bathroom's engaged, Loony,' murmured Barney, half asleep. Then he heard the voices of the others outside in the garden and he sat up, reaching for the wonderful towel.

It was a lovely night, and the children walked back to the Fair with Barney in the moonlight. Miranda couldn't understand Barney's sweet-scented smell. It didn't seem like Barney! She sat on Snubby's shoulder all the way, hoping Barney's nice Barney-smell would come back to him.

As they came to the gate of the field where the Fair was being held, someone came out. It was Tonnerre, all by himself. Snubby recognised him at once and hid quickly in the hedge. The others walked boldly on.

'Evening, sir,' said Barney politely. Tonnerre peered at him.

'Oh, it's you. Give an eye to my elephants, will you, when you get in? Young 'Un's with them now, but they're restless – they don't like a move.'

'Yes, sir,' said Barney. 'Will you be long, sir?'

'No. Just one hour,' said Tonnerre. 'Going down the road and back.'

Roger pulled Barney to him. 'Where's he *really* going? You go on into the field. I'll follow him and see where he's going. You never know!'

Barney nodded and went through the gate. Snubby detached himself from the hedge. He had heard Roger's whisper.

'I say – are we really going to follow Tonnerre?' he asked excitedly. 'Loony would be awfully good at following his track if we lost it.'

'He won't follow it because he's jolly well not coming,'

said Roger. 'Nor are you. You take Di home. I'll do the tracking! Go on now, Snubby. I must get after him, or I'll lose him.'

He left the other two and ran down the lane. Where was Tonnerre going? Was he really only going down the road and back?

He came to a fork and saw Tonnerre's figure in the distance, enormous in the moonlight.

'Oho!' said Roger to himself. 'He's taken the turning to Marloes Castle. Now what do you think of *that*?'

Chapter Eighteen

Snubby Enjoys Himself

Tonnerre strode on down the road, right in the very middle of it, his shadow black behind him. Roger followed. Marloes Castle was, by the signpost, half a mile away – not very far from Rilloby Fair! Roger kept close to the hedge, not wanting Tonnerre to see him.

He felt excited. What was Tonnerre going to do? Surely he wasn't going to commit any kind of robbery at that time of night? It was early, surely, for thieves!

'If I see him shin up over the wall, or do any other funny business, I shall call the police somehow or other,' thought Roger. 'I'd better notice if there's any house on the way that has telephone wires running to it – because I could go and ask to use their telephone. Gosh, this is exciting!'

He thought of the room in the little separate wing of the castle – protected by two locked doors and a third one double-locked. Windows fastened and barred. Well, well, if Tonnerre could go through all those, leaving them still locked and fastened, he was a very clever man indeed!

Tonnerre walked on and on. Roger kept well back in the shadows at the side of the lane. Tonnerre did not turn to see if anyone was following him. He simply walked straight on.

Marloes Castle loomed up in the distance. It had a high wall all round it. Its windows gleamed in the moonlight. Roger tried to see the barred window of the room where the stuffed animals and valuable old papers were kept.

He spotted it at last. How on earth could a great fellow like Tonnerre climb up a sheer, straight wall, and get through barred windows?

Tonnerre did nothing of the sort, of course. He came to the big iron gates, and there he stopped for the first time. He peered through at Marloes Castle, his great arms holding on to the gates as he looked this way and that.

Roger held his breath. What was going to happen now?

It was all very disappointing. Nothing happened at all. Tonnerre simply went on walking round the walls of the grounds, went all the way round, followed by Roger, and finally arrived at the iron gates again, and went back by the way he had come!

'Well!' thought Roger, 'what a long walk I've had for nothing! All the same, perhaps Tonnerre was looking to see how he could get in some other night. Making his plans. Yes, that's it, I expect. He means to come back some other night and get in. But *how* does he mean to do it? It beats me!'

Roger saw Tonnerre safely back to the Fair field, and then went home. Mrs Lynton was cross with him for being so late. 'The others have been in for a long time,' she said, 'and have gone up to bed. Do you know it's ten o'clock? I'm surprised at you, Roger. I suppose you've been with Barney – but do remember that although I like him very much, I shall not allow you to keep the hours he does.'

'Sorry, Mother,' said Roger, and said no more. He couldn't possibly explain about Tonnerre.

The others were very disappointed when they heard that all that Tonnerre had done was to peer through the gates of the castle and walk round the walls.

'Still, I think you're right when you say he was looking

round and laying his plans,' said Diana. 'Good night! We'll talk about it again tomorrow.'

They all went to the Fair again the next day, after it had opened. They saw Cook there, having an afternoon off. Snubby went over to her.

'Got your best Sunday hat out, ready to eat?' he said. 'You'll see the two chimps riding their bicycles this afternoon. Come on – I'll buy your ticket. I've never seen anybody eat their hat, and I'd just love to see you gobble yours.'

'Go on with you now,' said Cook. She went with all of them into the tent where Hurly and Burly gave their performances. Vosta nodded to them, and gave Cook a front seat. She was very pleased.

Her eyes nearly fell out of her head when she saw Hurly and Burly doing their tricks, and when they rode the bicycle round and round the grass ring, Burly on the pedals first, with Hurly on the bars, and then the other way about, she exclaimed in wonder.

'Well, I never did! Well, I never did in all my life! Well, who would have thought of that now! Well, of all the extraordinary things!'

Snubby grinned. 'You'll have to eat your words as well as your hat. When can I come and see you at your meal, Cook? And do you eat your hat with a knife and fork, or just chew it?'

'Get away with your nonsense now,' said Cook in a daze, watching the chimpanzees going head-over-heels without stopping. 'It fair makes me dizzy watching them do that.'

'Yes, but what about your Sunday hat?' persisted Snubby. 'You can't go back on your word, you know.'

Cook began to feel uncomfortable. 'Go on now, you know a hat can't be eaten,' she said. 'You let me off, you

117

little pest, and I'll make you some more meringues. Oh, my goodness, what are the creatures doing now? Tell this one to go away – I don't like its hairy face!'

Hurly had come up to Snubby, grinning all over his funny face. He patted Snubby, and then, as Cook appeared to be Snubby's friend, he patted her too. She rose from her chair and fled out of the tent, scared and trembling.

'Well, there now, I never did in my life!' she kept saying to herself. 'I never did!'

Snubby wondered what it was she never did. He followed her and reminded her of her bargain.

'Remember – either you eat your hat or I eat your meringues!'

'You're a caution, you are,' said Cook. 'You keep away from me now. I want to enjoy myself. You and your hats and meringues!'

Snubby kept carefully out of Tonnerre's sight. He kept as far from his caravan as possible too. He didn't want another whack! He saw the others by the hoopla stall and went to have a word with them. 'Cook's not going to eat her best Sunday hat – she'll make us some meringues instead.'

'Good work!' said Roger. 'Hallo – here comes Old Ma. Wonder what she wants.'

Old Ma came up to the hoopla stall. Her bright-bird-like eyes darted all round. She spoke to Barney.

'You seen Young 'Un anywhere, Barney? I want him to come and watch my pot for me. I got to do some washing and I can't do both.'

'He's gone to help with the elephants,' said Barney. 'There's such a lot of people here today that Mr Tonnerre can't cope with everyone that wants rides. There he is, look. Billy Tell's got the shooting-range.'

'Never anyone to help Old Ma,' muttered the old woman, and turned to go.

'I'll come along and stir up your pot,' said Snubby, thinking it might be interesting to talk to the old woman.

'You! The only thing you'll ever stir up is trouble!' said Old Ma, and went off into a cackle of laughter. 'All right – you come along then – and you can get me some water from the stream. I've not got enough.'

Snubby found that he had taken on more than he bargained for. He had to fetch various pails of water from the stream first of all, then he had to fetch more wood for the fire, and then stand and stir the big iron pot with a long iron spoon whose handle got hotter and hotter.

'What's in here?' asked Snubby, peering into the bubbling liquid.

'Ah, don't you ask no questions and you won't get no lies,' answered the old woman, now busy washing clothes in a tub. Snubby grinned. By the smell it seemed as if rabbit, hare, a chicken or two and possibly a duck were all in the big pot. Snubby felt that he wouldn't at all mind having a plateful of the delicious-smelling concoction.

Ma began to talk as she washed. Snubby listened, fascinated. She talked about Bill Tell and Vosta and many others he didn't know – Presto the conjurer, Sticky Stanley the clown, Mr Volla and his bear, Madame Petronella and her parrots – people in other circuses and fairs, people she had known and had never forgotten. Out came the names in a never-ending stream, all with some story attached to them.

'What about Mr Tonnerre?' ventured Snubby. 'Have you known him long?'

'Long! Too long! Ah, that man's temper. It doesn't bear thinking about,' said Old Ma, rinsing a peculiar-looking garment in her tub. 'Always he had a temper,

119

always he was shouting, always he was big – but what a wonderful acrobat! Ah, to see him on the tight-rope – why, he could dance better on that than most men on a dance floor.'

Snubby was amazed. Tonnerre an acrobat! How very extraordinary. He didn't look a bit like one. He was so big and heavy – and yet, when Snubby thought of it, he walked very lightly and softly when he wanted to – as he must have walked when he caught Snubby snooping round his caravan!

Snubby remembered how easily and lightly he leapt up to the necks of his elephants when he wanted to, too. Yes – he must have been a fine acrobat.

'Does he do any – er – acrobating – now?' asked Snubby.

'Who? Tonnerre?' Old Ma gave a squeal of laughter. 'That fat old man! He is nothing but an elephant now – but still he can walk the tight rope, and he can leap his own height from the ground. But the strongest thing about Tonnerre now is his temper. He is afraid of nothing, that one – nothing but one thing.'

'And that's you, isn't it, Old Ma?' said Snubby with a grin. 'I say, how long have I got to stir this stuff? The smell is so super that I can't stand it much longer unless I keep licking the spoon.'

Old Ma cackled again. She liked Snubby and his cheek. 'You stay and have dinner with Old Ma,' she said. 'Just you and that dog of yours. What's his name now? Snubby, isn't it? And yours is Loony. Well, well – whoever named *you* was a clever one!'

'Here, Ma – you've got it all wrong,' protested Snubby, leaping out of the way as Old Ma emptied her tub of soapy water much too near him.

'Mind out, Loony,' she said to him, and both dog and

120

boy minded out. 'Now you set yourself down and wait a minute – and I'll give you the best meal you've ever tasted in your life. Old Ma knows how to cook, she does!'

Chapter Nineteen

More Doings of Snubby

The others were quite jealous when they saw Old Ma ladling out an enormous plateful from her iron pot and presenting it to Snubby.

'Look at that now,' said Barney in amazement and envy. 'Never seen Old Ma so generous before. How does Snubby do it? Getting supper from Old Ma and meringues out of your cook, and . . .'

'Just pure cheek,' said Roger. 'Gosh, look, Old Ma's putting a plate down for Loony too. How wild all those mongrels look, sitting in a ring there, watching!'

Snubby came over to the others at last, looking very satisfied with himself and his supper. Loony looked more than satisfied. He looked extremely fat and developed a fit of hiccups at once.

'Stop it,' said Snubby severely. 'Hiccups mean you've been over-eating. Don't give yourself away like that, Loony!'

Loony did another hiccup and looked surprised. Sneezes and hiccups always surprised him. They were so sudden and seemed to belong to him in some mysterious way that he couldn't understand. He sat down and began to nod, feeling full and comfortable.

Snubby suddenly got the hiccups too, and retired to get over them, annoyed at the laughter and remarks of the others. He decided to buy some sweets for Hurly and Burly. He could see Vosta walking them round the field, holding them by their paws, one on each side of him.

They loved a walk like that, when there were plenty of people to see.

Vosta brought them over to the hoopla stall. Miranda chattered to the two chimpanzees, showing them the row of wooden rings she had pushed up her left arm ready to hand out to customers. Hurly held out a hand for some.

'No, you don't,' said Barney swiftly.

'Why not?' asked Roger.

'Well, he rings everything in sight,' said Barney. 'Never misses. And then he makes such a clamour for the things he's ringed. He's as cute as can be.'

'Oh, do let's see him!' begged Diana. Snubby came up and joined in too. He had a pocketful of cheap sweets for the chimpanzees, and some better ones for himself and the others.

'Go on – let him throw,' said Snubby. 'I'll pay for the rings for him.'

'I'll let him have them for nothing,' said Barney. 'But don't you let him grab the things he rings like he did last time, Mr Vosta. He smashed one of my clocks.'

Hurly threw a ring. It fell exactly over a small doll. He chattered excitedly. Everyone clapped him. He threw another, and that slid beautifully over a little green vase. The third one fell round a packet of cigarettes without touching it. It really was good throwing.

Miranda deftly gathered up the rings and slipped them back on her arm. She held out her hand to Hurly for the penny he should have given her for them.

'It's all right. He's not paying,' said Barney. 'And he's not having the things he ringed either. Take your great paws away, Hurly!'

Hurly was longing to get the things he had ringed. Snubby felt quite sorry for him. It did seem a shame to throw so well and not have any reward. He remembered the sweets he had bought.

He put his hand into his pocket to get the ones he had bought for them – and they were not there, of course!

'Hurly! You've pinched the sweets I bought for you!' he cried, and pulled the chimpanzee's hairy arm. Hurly at once put it round him and hugged him affectionately.

'No. You're a wicked pick-pocket,' said Snubby severely. 'Mr Vosta, I bought some sweets for them both, and they're gone!'

'Hurly. Turn out your pockets!' said Mr Vosta sternly. Hurly whimpered and pulled at one of his pockets. Out came a bag of sweets!

'Bad boy! Naughty boy!' said Vosta, smacking him hard. 'No more rings for you! No more sweets either!'

'Keep the sweets and give them to Hurly and Burly later on,' said Snubby. 'I bought them for them. I say, can't you let Burly throw rings too?'

'Yes. But he goes wild after a bit and throws them at everybody,' said Vosta. 'So we don't encourage him to begin. Come along, Hurly and Burly. We'll go and see Mr Tonnerre and say goodnight to him and his elephants.'

The chimpanzees loved the two elephants and went willingly to see them. Snubby roared to see one of the elephants put his trunk round Burly and lift him right to the top of his great head. There sat Burly, swinging himself to and fro, chattering excitedly.

'I wish I belonged to a fair,' said Snubby enviously. 'Gosh wouldn't I like to have a couple of chimps like that – I'd have a string of monkeys too – and some elephants – and I wouldn't mind a bear or two.'

'I think we ought to be going home to supper,' said Roger, looking at his watch. 'I suppose you can't come too, Barney, tonight?'

'I'd love to,' said Barney, 'but there's no one to take over my stall, and as you can see, we're pretty busy tonight. Young 'Un can't take it – he's still with the elephants.'

'Bad luck. Come on, Snubby – we shan't get any supper if we don't go now,' said Roger.

'I can't face supper tonight,' said Snubby dolefully. 'Not after Old Ma's helping out of her pot. I just can't face it. I say, Barney – *could* I take over the hoopla stall for you – and you go and have supper with the others?'

'What will Tonnerre say?' said Barney doubtfully. 'I daren't go and ask him. He'll probably run you out of the field if he sees you at the stall.'

'I'll go and ask Old Ma,' said Snubby suddenly. 'Tonnerre's afraid of her. If she says I can, I will.'

He went off to where she was hanging out clothes on a line she had put up from caravan to caravan. 'Ma,' he began, 'I'm afraid of asking Mr Tonnerre – so can I ask you instead? Barney wants to go off for a bit. May I take over his stall? I'll do it properly.'

''Course you can, Loony,' said Old Ma, with a twinkle. 'You and your dog Snubby can surely look after a stall for an hour or two. I'll manage Tonnerre if he starts shouting around.'

'What's she call you Loony for?' asked Roger, who had followed him. 'All right – you needn't tell me. I can guess, it's quite a good idea on her part!'

Snubby scowled. Then he cheered up. He was to have the hoopla stall to himself – that was fine! He'd make a terrific lot of money and show Barney what he could do!

'Shall I leave Miranda to help you?' asked Barney.

'No thanks. I can manage with Loony,' said Snubby. 'Go on, all of you. Leave me to it. I shall do fine.'

They went off and left him, all feeling very hungry.

125

Snubby must indeed have eaten a magnificent meal not to be able to manage two suppers!

Snubby had a good time with the stall. He really let himself go. He tried out the loudest voice he possessed and it really was a pretty good one.

'Walk-up, walk-up, WALK-UP! Walk-up, walk-up, WALK-UP!' he bellowed. 'Finest stall in the Fair. Clocks, cigs, chocs, bowls, spoons, brooches, pins, ring anything you like! Try your skill, try your SKILL! Mothers, come and beat the fathers, sisters, come and beat your brothers, choose what you like and ring it. Walk-up, walk-up, WALK-UP!'

People listened in amusement, surprised to see such a small boy in charge of the stall. Snubby was only twelve, and with his snub nose, red hair and masses of freckles, to say nothing of his cheeky grin, he made people smile whenever they looked at him.

They drifted over to the hoopla stall and soon he was doing a brisk business. Loony was very useful. He kept watch for any rings that fell to the ground and picked them up at once.

'You're as good as Miranda,' Snubby told him, and Loony wagged his stump of a tail, pleased.

Tonnerre soon spotted that it was not Barney in charge of the stall, and he wandered over to see what was up. When he saw Snubby, his face took on its look of black thunder. Snubby saw him and was petrified.

But Old Ma was there at once. 'You let him be!' she cried shrilly. 'He's doing fine! You lay a finger on him, Tonnerre, and I'll tell you some of the things you did when you were a lad. Yes, and I put you across my knee many a time, and you yelled like . . .'

But Tonnerre was gone. He was no match for Old Ma's tongue and he knew it. Anyway, the boy was doing well

126

and taking money. There was no need to interfere. Plenty of time later on to take it out of that snooping little rogue if he wanted to.

Snubby stayed there till Barney came back. The others weren't with him. 'Your aunt says you're to go straight back,' he told Snubby. 'I don't think I ought to have left you here, really. She didn't seem very pleased. Thanks a lot. I *say* – did you take all that money?'

'Yes. It was easy,' boasted Snubby. 'And you should have seen Tonnerre turn green when he came up and saw me raking in all that money – more than he's taken all night with his elephants, I bet. He just faded away, and didn't say a word to me. I just looked him in the eye, and . . .'

'Go on – you didn't do anything of the sort,' said Barney, who knew Snubby's little ways very well indeed, by now. 'But anyway, thanks very much. I enjoyed my supper and going to your home again.'

Snubby remembered the sweets he had bought for himself and the others. He felt hungry and thought he would like a few. He could give some to Barney too. He put his hand into his pocket – and gosh, the sweets weren't there! Blow – that tiresome Hurly must have taken them at the same time as he had taken the other bag. Snubby felt annoyed. Really, Hurly might have been content with just *one* bag! He wasn't only dishonest, he was greedy too!

'I'm just going over to Vosta's caravan to see if Hurly's got some more sweets of mine,' said Snubby. 'I'll be back.'

He went over to the van. It was in darkness except for a very small oil-lamp burning on a shelf with a safety-ledge. Snubby knocked.

A chattering noise greeted him, and he heard the creaking of bunks. Hurly and Burly slept in the same van as

Vosta. He would never be separated from them, even at night.

'Are you there, Mr Vosta?' asked Snubby. But Vosta was not there. Only the chimps were there, curled up in their blankets on the small bunks they had. Hurly came to the door and opened it. Both Chimpanzees could do ordinary things like that.

'Hurly! Did you take my sweets?' said Snubby severely. 'Turn out your pockets!'

But Hurly had no clothes on! He always had to undress at night, and he stood there dressed only in his hairy coat. Loony sniffed at his legs. With a bound Burly was beside them, trying to lift Loony up in his arms.

'Oh, Burly, don't – Loony doesn't like it,' said Snubby, trying to rescue poor Loony. 'Get back to bed. Go on. Do you HEAR me?'

To Snubby's surprise, the chimpanzees obeyed him. They got back under their blankets, making a few peculiar noises to one another. Snubby saw their clothes on the floor nearby. He saw that there was a bulge in one of the pockets, and he slipped his hand into it. He pulled out his paper bag of sweets.

'Bad Hurly!' he scolded. 'Go to sleep, both of you. I shan't buy you sweets again if you behave like this. Goodnight, you couple of scamps!'

Chapter Twenty

A Most Exciting Find

Snubby went over to Barney again, but Barney didn't want any sweets. He had had such a fine supper, he said!

'Do go home,' he begged Snubby. 'Your aunt will be so annoyed. She'll never ask me to supper again. Do go, Snubby.'

Snubby went. Very fortunately for him, his aunt was telephoning to somebody, so he simply crept behind her, gave her a kiss and rushed upstairs before she could turn and scold him.

'You're frightfully late, Snubby,' said Roger's sleepy voice. 'I say, Mother wasn't at all pleased at us leaving you there with the hoopla stall.'

Snubby yawned. He suddenly found that he was really very tired. He said a few words to Roger, and fell into bed after a very short wash and a rub-over of his teeth.

It was the next morning that he discovered something that excited the three of them so tremendously that they could hardly do their morning tasks!

Snubby overslept. He rushed down late to breakfast, got a scolding from his uncle, and decided that he had better go straight upstairs and make his bed as soon after breakfast as possible, to get out of any further scolding from his aunt.

He stripped his bed. Under the pillow was the bag of sweets he had rescued from Hurly's pocket the night before.

He picked them up, wishing that toffees didn't ooze out and make everything sticky.

Stuck to the bag was a bit of torn paper. Snubby pulled it away without thinking.

There was something written on it, but first he didn't even bother to read it. Then a word caught his eye.

'Castle.'

That rang a bell in Snubby's mind immediately, of course, and he smoothed out the dirty, sticky bit of paper at once. Part of two words were there, and the whole of one.

This is what Snubby read:

He stared in excitement. He gave such a whistle of surprise that Roger came over and looked at the paper too.

'What's this?' he said. 'Where did you get it? Why the excitement?'

'Roger! Hurly stole a bag of sweets last night – and I went to get it out of his pocket in his van – and stuck to the bag was this torn bit of paper. It must have been part of a note,' said Snubby, his face red with excitement. 'See what it says?'

Roger looked at it a lot more carefully. He took it from Snubby, and his face went red too.

'Gosh, yes – 'oes' – that's the end of Marloes, I suppose. "Marloes Castle. Midnight." That last word must surely be part of 'midnight.' I say, Snubby – we're on to something now!'

The two stared at one another, thrilled. Loony whined and scraped at Snubby's leg. What was up?

'Let's tell Di,' said Snubby, and they called her. She was as excited as they were.

'Let's work it out,' said Roger. 'How did this bit of paper get into Hurly's pocket with the sweets to begin with?'

'Well, you know what Hurly is – he picks up anything he sees on the ground,' said Snubby. 'Or he takes things out of people's pockets. He may have got this from anywhere! Somebody must have torn it up, that's plain – and probably thrown it away on the field. This is just one of the bits.'

'Who handed the note out – and who *got* the note?' wondered Diana. 'Or did a messenger come and give it to somebody in the Fair? Or did it come by post to somebody, who read it, noted what it said, and tore it up? We can't tell.'

'The only thing we do know is that *somebody* got the note – and *somebody* is going to Marloes Castle at midnight – and we can jolly well guess why!' said Snubby. 'I say – isn't this thrilling – absolutely super.'

'Smashing,' agreed Roger. 'I wonder who *got* the note. Do you suppose the one who got it is to meet the one who sent it?'

'There's only one way of finding out,' said Snubby, his eyes shining, and his voice solemn. 'Only *one* way. We'll have to go there at midnight ourselves and watch.'

There was a silence. 'I say – what a thrill!' said Roger. 'But – we don't know what night. The note only says

131

"Midnight" – it doesn't say Monday, Tuesday, Wednesday – though the whole note must have, of course.'

'Well, we'll go *every* night then!' said Snubby.

There was another silence. 'Anyone know how long the Fair's going to be at Rilloby?' said Diana at last.

'Barney says till Wednesday,' said Snubby. 'And today is Thursday. Five more nights till they go – and on one of them we know there's a robbery going to take place.'

'Had we better tell the police, do you think?' asked Diana. The boys looked at her scornfully.

'What! When we're nicely on the track now! Don't be a spoil-sport!' said Roger. 'Besides – what exactly can we tell the police? About Diana's hunch – our suspicion of Tonnerre – and this torn note? They'd laugh at us.'

''Course they would,' said Snubby, who couldn't bear the thought of handing over this mystery to anyone else. 'Just like a girl to think of the police.'

'All right, all right. *I* don't want to,' said Diana. 'But I don't see how we can go on watching Marloes Castle for five nights running. We'll be so sleepy we won't be able to do a thing the next day.'

'Di – the note says *midnight*,' said Roger, exasperated. 'That means the robbery will be done then – and we can go home and go to sleep.'

'Pooh – as if we'd any of us go to sleep after seeing a robbery done,' said Diana. 'All right, I'm not really making difficulties. I'm just seeing what's the best thing to do.'

It really was a most exciting thing to discuss. Mrs Lynton couldn't imagine what was the matter with the children that morning – no beds made, no jobs done, even Loony not brushed!

'What mischief are you planning, I should like to know,'

132

she said. 'Diana, the *beds*! If they are not made in the next twenty minutes I shall be REALLY CROSS.'

Of course, Barney had to be told. They streaked over to Rilloby Fair as soon as ever they could, and got him into a corner where nobody could possibly hear them, or see the torn bit of paper they handed him.

Barney was amazed. 'Well, think of that!' he said. 'Diana was right. There *is* somebody in this Fair who's got something to do with the robberies.'

'We saw Tonnerre going off to the castle the other night,' said Diana. 'But the thing is – I can't picture him doing any acrobatics – climbing up walls and so on. He's so big.'

Snubby remembered what Old Ma had told him. 'He *was* a very fine acrobat,' he told the others. 'And Old Ma says he can still walk tight-ropes and do things like that although he's so enormous.'

'How do you suppose he goes through locked doors?' asked Diana.

'Perhaps he has skeleton keys, or whatever you call them,' said Snubby. 'Or perhaps he can wiggle the locks with a wire like some burglars can. Or perhaps . . .'

'It's all perhaps, perhaps,' said Diana impatiently. 'If only we could find out something solid – it's impossible to think of Tonnerre doing the robbery – and yet he went off to the castle the other night – and we know he's the one who decides where the Fair's to go – and it *always* seems to go to a place where there is some valuable collection of papers.'

'It's a good old mystery,' said Snubby. 'And we're going to solve it. We've only got to hide somewhere in the grounds of the castle some time before midnight and watch who comes, and what he does. Easy!'

'Oh, *very* easy!' said Diana mockingly. 'And how do

you suppose you're going to get into the grounds – can *you* walk through a locked gate – or through a high wall?'

'It's easy enough to get into the grounds,' said Barney. 'There are spikes at the top of the wall. We can chuck up a rope-ladder, let it catch on the spikes, and climb up.'

'Well, I'm not sitting on any spikes, thank you,' said Diana promptly.

'Diana's not very helpful, is she?' said Snubby, getting annoyed with her. 'Let's leave her out of it.'

'No,' said Barney. 'She's in it all right. Of course she doesn't want to sit on spikes. Nobody does. But we'll just take half a dozen sacks, fold them, and pop them over the spikes. We can climb over easily enough then.'

'And hide somewhere where we can watch the windows of that wing,' said Snubby. 'Gosh – we'll go tonight, won't we? All of us! What an adventure!'

'Yes – tonight,' said Barney. 'We'll meet at eleven o'clock, near the gate. And for goodness' sake, keep quiet – just in case somebody else is hiding there too.'

Chapter Twenty-one

Midnight at the castle

Snubby could hardly contain himself all day. He whistled and sang and was altogether so noisy and restless that Great-uncle Robert nearly went mad. Wherever he was he could hear Snubby making a noise. What was the matter with that boy?

The evening came at last. To Mrs Lynton's surprise, Snubby didn't seem to be hungry for his dinner. Nor Diana. Roger ate stolidly as usual. He wasn't so excitable as the other two.

'Do you feel quite well, Snubby?' asked Mrs Lynton anxiously when he refused a second helping. 'And you too, Diana?'

'I'm all right,' said Snubby, and Mrs Lynton, looking at his bright red cheeks and shining eyes, had no more doubts of his health.

'I suppose you've been stuffing yourself up with sweets and ice-creams again,' she said. 'Well, I shall think *twice* about getting you a nice supper if you do that.'

They all went to bed at the usual time but they didn't undress. Roger fell asleep and had to be awakened at half-past ten.

'Are Mother and Dad in bed yet?' whispered Roger.

'Yes. They went early, thank goodness. There isn't a light anywhere except in Great-uncle's room,' said Diana. 'He's reading in bed, I expect.'

They crept downstairs, warning each other to look out for Sardine. But Sardine was away on business of her own that night. Loony crept down with them, his tail-stump wagging. What was up?

They went into the moonlit garden, and out of the gate. Then they made off across the fields to Marloes Castle. There was a short-cut to it which didn't take very long.

They came to the big iron gates, and then disappeared into the hedge on the other side. Diana gave a sudden little scream.

'Shut up, idiot!' said Roger fiercely in a low tone. Diana pulled away from him, shaking.

'There's somebody there already!' she whispered. 'Oh, Roger!'

So there was. But it was only Barney and Miranda, who had got there first, and happened to choose just the bit of hedge that Diana had pushed herself into! Barney came out grinning.

'Sorry I scared you, Diana. You scared me too. You were all so quiet I didn't hear you. I got an awful fright when you pushed against me in the hedge.'

'Have you seen anything or anyone?' asked Roger.

'Not a thing,' said Barney. 'Come on. We'll choose a place to get over the wall. I've got a rough rope-ladder and a few thick sacks. Carry the sacks, Roger and Snubby, and I'll take the rope.'

With Miranda on his shoulder, and Loony at his heels, Barney led the way, keeping to the shadows of the hedge. They came at last to a place where the wall curved round, and the spikes did not seem to be quite so thick.

'This'll do,' said Barney in a low voice. 'Snubby, will Loony growl if he hears anyone, and warn us?'

'Yes, of course,' said Snubby. 'Loony, do you hear? You're on guard. On guard!'

'Woof,' said Loony, understanding at once, and he sat down, ears, eyes and nose all on guard together.

136

The four of them got busy. Barney deftly threw the rope-ladder up to the spikes. The first time it slithered back again. The second time the spikes held one of the rungs. Barney pulled. It was quite tight. Up he went like a cat, his feet treading the wooden rungs lightly. 'Chuck up the sacks,' he whispered down. Roger and Snubby threw them up one by one.

Barney put them in a neat pile over a dozen or so of the sharp, pointed spikes. Then, sitting on the sacks, he pulled at the rope-ladder till he had got a lot of loose slack up – enough to let half the ladder down the other side into the grounds!

'That's jolly clever!' thought Roger admiringly. 'A ladder up to the top – and a ladder down the other side – and a pile of sacks in the middle to protect him against the spikes! I should never have thought of all that.'

'Come on up,' whispered Barney.

Diana went up first. Barney helped her over and she sat on the sacks beside him. He then helped her down the other side. Then came Roger. Then Snubby, hauling up Loony with great difficulty, helped by Barney.

'No good leaving him outside the wall,' gasped Snubby. 'He'd bark the place down. Gosh, Loony, you're an awful lump. Whoa there – you're falling! I say, he's gone down the other side at top speed. He'll break his legs!'

There was a thud and a yelp. Diana called up softly. 'It's all right. He's not hurt. He's like Sardine, always falls on his feet!'

Barney pulled up the ladder so that no one could climb up it from the road. The place he had chosen to climb over the wall was in deep shadow, and nobody could see the pile of sacks on the spikes from the road, Barney slipped down and joined the others.

'Where shall we hide?' whispered Roger, excited.

137

Barney stood a moment or two to get his bearings. 'There are the barred windows up there,' he whispered. 'Let's make our way to that clump of trees. We can watch the windows easily from there.'

They crept from tree to tree and shrub to shrub until they were under the clump that Barney had decided on. From there they could easily see the barred windows. Now, if any thief were going to enter from outside, they couldn't possibly help seeing him!

They found a dry place under a bush and huddled together, parting the branches to keep a good lookout on the windows. From somewhere not far off a church clock began to strike. It chimed first – and then deep clanging sounds came through the moonlight night.

'One, two, three,' counted Snubby under his breath. 'It's going to strike twelve. It's midnight! We must watch out. Lie down, Loony. Not a whimper from you! On guard, old fellow. On guard!'

There wasn't a sound anywhere. Then a nightingale began to sing. But it didn't sing for long – just tried out its notes and stopped. Not for a week or two would it sing all night long.

Not even an owl hooted. The children watched the moon move slowly along the sky, and waited patiently. Loony listened with both his ears. Diana always thought he would be able to hear much better if his ear-holes were not covered up by such long, drooping ears. But, drooping ears or not, he still heard twice as well as they did.

The church clock chimed the quarter and then the half-hour. Snubby yawned. Diana felt cold. Miranda cuddled inside Barney's shirt and went to sleep.

The clock chimed the three-quarters. Still there was no sound. There was not even a tiny breeze blowing that night, and no mouse or rat or rabbit was to be seen or heard.

'I say – I don't think the thief's coming tonight,' whispered Barney. 'It's long past midnight. This can't be the night. We'd better go.'

Nobody minded! They were cold and tired. The excitement had fizzled out and they all thought longingly of nice warm beds. Loony gave a sigh of relief when he felt them on the move once more.

'Come on, then,' said Diana thankfully. 'We've had enough for tonight. We'll try again tomorrow.'

They made their way to the wall, still keeping well in the shadows, just in case anyone was about.

Over the wall they went and down the other side. Barney sat on the sacks beside the rope, unhitched it from the spikes, and threw it down to Roger.

'Have to leave the sacks here and hope no one notices them,' he said, taking a flying leap to the ground. He landed on hands and knees and rolled over, quite unhurt. He sat up.

'Don't you think the sacks will be noticed by anyone coming down the lane?' asked Diana anxiously.

'No. This bit of the wall is well hidden by trees, and unless anyone is actually walking just below, looking up, I don't think they'd be noticed,' said Barney. 'We'll stuff the rope-ladder under this bush. Save us carrying it to and fro.'

They were silent and disappointed as they went off down the lane. They said goodnight at the fork, and Barney went one way and they another, taking the short-cut across the fields.

'Better luck next time,' said Roger to Diana rather gloomily, when he said goodnight. 'Gosh, I'm sleepy.'

They all overslept the next morning, of course, and Mr

Lynton told them wrathfully that they would have to go to bed an hour earlier that night.

But alas, when the evening came, Barney, Roger and Diana were all feeling ill! Diana and the two boys had gone over to see Barney at Rilloby Fair, and Roger had bought some sausage sandwiches. Snubby refused them, and bought himself some tomato sandwiches, of which he was very fond.

As he was the only one who didn't feel very sick that night, everyone felt that the sausage sandwiches must be to blame! Barney put Young 'Un in charge of the hoopla stall and staggered off to the caravan he shared with somebody else, feeling very ill. Roger and Diana got home somehow, and promptly collapsed in the hall, groaning.

Snubby rushed to tell Mrs Lynton. 'It's the sausage sandwiches,' he explained. 'There must have been something wrong with them. They feel awfully sick.'

They were, poor things. Mrs Lynton got them into bed and dosed them well. Snubby looked in on them and was quite shocked to see them looking so green.

'Oh, I say – what about tonight?' he asked in a loud whisper. 'Will you be able to go and watch?'

Roger groaned. 'Of course not. I don't feel as if I shall ever be able to get up again.'

Diana didn't even answer when he asked her. She felt really ill. Snubby tiptoed out with a most surprised Loony, and fell over Sardine on the stairs.

'Oh, Snubby – *don't* do that,' said Mrs Lynton crossly, looking out of the lounge door. 'Can't you possibly be quiet when people are feeling ill?'

'Well, I like *that*!' said Snubby indignantly. 'How did I know Sardine was lying in wait for me? It's Sardine you want to nag at, not me.'

'Now, Snubby, don't you talk to me like that,' began Mrs Lynton, advancing on him. But Snubby fled.

What about tonight? *Some*body ought to watch, surely? All right – Snubby would watch all alone!

Chapter Twenty-two

A Night Out For Snubby

Snubby went to bed very early, for two reasons. One was that Mrs Lynton was worried about the other two, and was inclined to be very cross with Snubby. He thought it best to get out of her way. The other was that he had quite made up his mind to go and watch in the castlegrounds by himself that night, and he wanted to get a little sleep before he went.

So he popped off to bed immediately after supper and took an alarm clock with him, set for a quarter-past eleven. He put it under his pillow, wrapped in a scarf so that it would be heard only by him. He hoped Roger wouldn't hear it.

Roger was sound asleep, exhausted by his bouts of sickness. Snubby didn't undress. He just got into bed and shut his eyes. Immediately he was asleep, and slept peacefully till the alarm went off. Loony, who was on his bed, leapt up in fright, barking.

'Shut up, you silly, crazy idiot!' said Snubby fiercely, and Loony shut up. Snubby lay and listened for a moment, after he had shut off the alarm. Had anyone heard?

Apparently not. Roger muttered something in his sleep, but that was all. Nobody else seemed to be stirring. Good! Snubby got cautiously out of bed, and felt for his clothes, remembered with agreeable surprise that he was fully dressed, and got his coat out of the cupboard. He had been cold the night before, and Snubby didn't like feeling cold!

'Come on, Loony – and if you fall over Sardine on the stairs I'll drown you,' Snubby threatened. They got downstairs safely, and were soon running over the fields, Loony surprised but pleased at this second unusual excursion.

They came to the castle walls as the church clock struck the three-quarters. 'A quarter to midnight,' thought Snubby, feeling feverishly about in the bush for the rope-ladder. 'Blow it – where's the ladder? Is this the right bush?'

It wasn't. Loony knew the right bush and dragged out the ladder for Snubby. Then followed an agonised five minutes with Snubby trying to throw the ladder up to the spikes.

It wasn't as easy as it had looked when Barney did it. Snubby grew extremely hot and agitated.

'Go up and stick, you beast of a ladder!' he muttered. And miraculously, the ladder did stick on a spike or two, and held.

Up went Snubby joyfully, pleased to find that the ladder was fairly close to the pile of sacks that Barney had left on the spikes. He lifted them off and pulled them to the rope-ladder. Soon he was sitting on them, the spikes beneath him blunted by the sacking. He hauled up the ladder in the way that Barney had done, and soon half was on one side of the wall and half on the other. Snubby felt really proud of himself.

As he climbed down the other side, into the grounds, the church clock struck midnight. 'Dong, dong, dong,' it began. A whine reached Snubby, and he stopped short.

'Blow! I've forgotten Loony. I don't see how I'm going

143

to get him up without help. He'll have to stay on the other side. I'll put him on guard.'

He climbed up to the top again, and whispered to Loony. 'It's all right, old fellow. I shan't be long. You're on guard, see? On guard.'

Loony settled down with a whimper. All right, he would be on guard – but he thought it was very mean of Snubby to go off without him.

Snubby crept over to the clump of trees where he and the others had stood the night before. It was a moonlit night again – but with much more cloud about. There were periods of brilliant light and then periods of darkness when the moon went behind clouds. Snubby settled down under a bush and waited.

He felt extremely pleased with himself. He had been the only one sensible enough not to take the sausage sandwiches. He had actually got over the wall by himself – and he didn't feel a scrap scared. Not a scrap. He hadn't even got Loony with him and he felt as brave as a lion. Yes, Snubby felt very pleased with himself indeed, ready for anything that might happen.

The moon went in. Everywhere became dark – and in the darkness Snubby thought he heard a little noise. He didn't know if it was near him or not. He listened, and thought he heard another small noise. No, it wasn't near him – it was over by the castle, he thought. He waited impatiently for the moon to come out again.

When it came out Snubby got a terrific shock. A black shadow seemed to be climbing up the side of the castle walls! Up it went, and up, lithe and confident. Snubby strained his eyes. Who was it? It was too far away to see. Was it Tonnerre? No, surely it wasn't nearly big enough for him – but the moonlight played tricks with your eyes.

It looked as if the black figure was climbing up a pipe,

leaping on to window-sills, climbing up again – now scrambling up ivy. This was the thief all right. No doubt about that!

But how was he going to get through the barred windows? Snubby held his breath to see. The bars were so close together. Oh, *blow* the moon – it had gone behind a cloud again.

When it came sailing out once more there was no sign of the climbing figure. It had vanished. Snubby suddenly began to feel very scared indeed. His hair gradually rose up from his head with a horrid prickly sensation. Shivers went down his spine. He longed for Loony.

His eyes began to play tricks with him. Was that a figure standing at the bottom of the castle walls, far below the barred windows? Or was it a shadow? Was that a figure half-way up the walls? No, no, that was the outline of a small window. Was that a figure up on the roof by the chimney? No, no, of course not, it was a shadow, just the shadow of the chimney. And was that a . . . ?

Snubby groaned and shut his eyes. He was scared stiff. Why had he come? Why had he thought he was so brave? He daren't look anywhere because he thought he saw sinister figures creeping, climbing, running. Oh, Loony, Loony, if only you weren't on the other side of the wall!

There was a noise near him. Somebody was panting not far off. Snubby turned quite cold with fear. He stayed absolutely still, hoping that whoever or whatever it was would go away.

But it didn't. It came nearer and nearer. There was the crack of twigs, the rustle of dead leaves under the bushes. Snubby nearly died of fright.

And then, worse than ever, something stuck itself into his back and snuffled there. Snubby was absolutely petrified. WHAT was it?

145

A tiny whimper came to him, and Snubby felt so relieved that he could have wept. It was LOONY!

He got the spaniel's head in his hands and let the delighted Loony lick his face till it was wet all over. 'Loony!' he whispered. 'It's really *you*! How did you get here? You couldn't climb that ladder! Oh, Loony, I was never so glad to see you in all my life!'

Loony was simply delighted at his welcome. Having been left on guard, he had been afraid that Snubby would be very angry to see him. But it was all right. Snubby was pleased, very, very pleased. It didn't matter that Loony had left the place he had to guard, had found a convenient hole by the wall, and had enlarged it to go underneath it with terrific squeezings and struggling.

Everything was all right. He had found his master, and what a welcome he had got!

Snubby recovered completely from his fright. He sat with his arm round Loony and squeezed him, telling him in whispers what he had seen. Then he stiffened again as Loony growled softly, his hackles rising at the back of his neck.

'What is it? What's the matter? Is it the thief coming back?' whispered Snubby. But it was quite impossible to see anything because the moon was now behind a very big cloud indeed. Loony went on growling softly. Snubby didn't dare to move. He thought he heard noises from the direction of the castle and longed for the moon to come out again.

It came out for a fleeting instant and Snubby thought he saw a black figure descending the walls again, but he couldn't be sure. Anyway he was sure of one thing – he wasn't going to move from his hiding-place for a very long while! He didn't want to bump up against that terrifying robber.

He cuddled up to Loony, and put his head on the dog's warm, silky-coated body. Loony licked him lovingly.

Most surprisingly, Snubby went to sleep. When he awoke he couldn't at first think where he was. Then, with a twinge of fright, he remembered. Good gracious – how long had he been asleep? He waited till the church clock struck again, and found with relief that he hadn't slept for more than half an hour. How could he have gone to sleep like that? Anyway it should be safe to go home again now. Surely the thief would have gone long since. My word, what a tale he had to tell the others!

Feeling a good deal braver with Loony at his heels, Snubby pushed his way cautiously out of the bush. The moon came out and lighted up the castle brilliantly. Nothing was to be seen of any climbing, creeping figure. With a sigh of relief, Snubby made his way to the wall.

Somehow he missed his way and wandered too far to the left, towards the iron gates. And then he got a really dreadful shock!

He came through a little copse of trees and found himself looking into a small dell – and from the dell many pairs of gleaming eyes looked up at him! He could see small shadowy bodies behind – but it was the eyes that frightened him. The moon sent its beams into the little dell and picked out the glassy, staring eyes that seemed to watch Snubby warily.

Loony growled and then barked, his hackles rising again. He backed away and began to whimper. Then Snubby knew that poor Loony too was scared, and he turned and fled. How he ran, stumbling through bushes and shrubs, tearing his coat, scratching his legs, away, away from those gleaming eyes that waited for him in the dell.

How he found the ladder he never knew. He climbed

147

up it, pulled it up behind him, loosened it from the spikes and sent it down to the ground. He left the sacks and flung himself to the ground. He wasn't as clever as Barney at this kind of thing, and fell far too heavily, twisting one ankle and bruising and grazing his knees badly.

Loony ran to find his hole. He squeezed through with difficulty and raced up to Snubby. Snubby was trembling, almost in tears. He flung his arms round Loony's neck.

'Keep with me, Loony. Let's go home. There's something strange about and I don't like it. Keep near me.'

Loony had every intention of doing so. He wasn't feeling too happy himself. He kept as close to Snubby's feet as he could, almost tripping him up at times. The two of them took the short-cut across the fields and got home at last.

Roger was sound asleep. So was Diana. Snubby longed to wake them up and tell them everything, but he hadn't the heart to. They had both been so very, very sick.

But he woke them up early in the morning and told them! He shook Roger and woke up Diana. He made Roger go into Diana's room, and then he told them both.

'I had an adventure last night,' he said. 'You'll never believe it. Listen!'

Chapter Twenty-three

It's All In The Papers!

Roger and Diana still felt a little weak from their upset
of the day before. They were not too pleased at being
awakened so early. But they soon pricked up their ears
when they heard Snubby's story.

He exaggerated, of course, which was a pity. He related
how he had gone to the wall and got over it, how he had
waited without Loony, and how he had suddenly seen the
black figure climbing up the wall.

'Up and up,' said Snubby, 'jumping from window-sill
to window-sill, climbing up the ivy, using pipes – gosh,
you should have seen him. Talk about an acrobat!'

'Was it Tonnerre?' asked Roger excitedly.

'Might have been,' said Snubby. 'I was too far away to
see. And there was a figure at the foot of the walls too –
and one on the roof – and . . .'

By the time Snubby had finished it sounded as if the
castle grounds had been swarming with thieves!

'I saw something else too,' went on Snubby. 'Both of
us saw them, Loony too. And Loony was really scared.'

'I bet you were too,' said Diana.

'I was as brave as could be!' said Snubby most untruth-
fully, having completely forgotten his terror. 'Do listen.
Well, we came to a little kind of dell – and there lying in
wait for us were all kinds of things with gleaming eyes!'

'And I suppose you did what any sensible person would
have done – you took to your heels and fled?' said Roger.

'Well – I didn't stay long,' admitted Snubby 'Nor would you.'

'You bet I wouldn't!' said Roger. 'What did they do? Snarl? Growl? Call out?'

'Oh – a kind of mixture of all the lot,' said Snubby, exaggerating wildly again. 'And one or two took a step forward as if they were going for Loony and me.'

Diana and Roger couldn't help being impressed by all this. 'Could you take us to see this field?' asked Roger.

'In the daytime, not at night,' said Snubby promptly. 'We'll go this morning.'

But they didn't. When Snubby got down to breakfast, late as usual, but forgiven because he offered to take up breakfast trays to Roger and Diana, he found everyone exclaiming over the morning paper.

'What's up?' asked Snubby, and suddenly he knew. Of course – the robbery! It would be in the paper!

So it was – with big headlines.

STRANGE ROBBERY LAST NIGHT
AT MARLOES CASTLE
STUFFED ANIMALS TAKEN AND LEFT IN
GROUNDS
IS THIEF A MADMAN?
HOW DID HE GET IN THROUGH FASTENED
WINDOWS AND LOCKED DOORS?

Snubby looked over the shoulders of the grown-ups and read the report. There it all was. Somebody had mysteriously got into the locked room and had taken – dear me, how strange – taken all the smaller animals, but apparently nothing else!

Snubby felt himself blushing. Gosh – those gleaming eyes – they must have been the eyes of the stuffed animals that the thief had put together in that little dell. Why had he said anything about the creatures making noises – and moving towards him? Oh, gosh, the others would rag him like anything!

Snubby ate his breakfast very soberly. He didn't say a word about what he knew. He would let the grown-ups discuss it, and wondered what to say to Roger and Diana upstairs. He was very puzzled. Why had the thief stolen worthless animals? Why hadn't he taken the valuable papers there? It didn't make sense. Was the thief really a madman? Then he must be a different thief from the one that so sensibly took rare papers!

And anyway how did even a madman get into that room? Snubby had seen him climbing the wall – but according to the papers the windows were still fastened and the bars unbroken.

Great-uncle Robert suddenly gave a loud exclamation and made everyone jump.

'Listen to this. It's in the stop-press news. They've found a clue to the thief.'

'What?' Mr and Mrs Lynton and Snubby chorussed.

Great-uncle Robert lowered the paper and spoke in a very peculiar kind of voice.

'The clue they've found, out in the grounds, is – a *green glove!*'

He stared hard at Snubby. Snubby went pale. Gosh – how extraordinary. Why ever had he made up that fool story of the Green Hands Gang that wore green gloves. It was going to haunt him for the rest of his life.

'I think,' said Great-uncle ominously, 'I think it must be the Green Hands Gang. What do *you* think, Snubby?'

Mr and Mrs Lynton stared at Great-uncle and Snubby in bewilderment. Snubby swallowed down his last bit of toast, nearly choked, and got up.

'I – er – I don't know anything about a Green Hands Gang,' he said. 'Nothing at all. Aunt Susan, I'll go and get Roger's tray and Diana's.'

Mr Lynton turned to Great-uncle when Snubby had gone. 'What *is* all this?' he said. 'It sounds like a film plot or something – Green Hands Gang! Absurd!'

'The time has come for me to tell you what I know,' said Great-uncle solemnly. 'It isn't much. I dismissed it, the last few days, as Snubby's silly make-up – but now that a green glove has been found, things look different.'

Whereupon he told them the fairy tale that Snubby had told him in the train, about the gang that had its hold on Snubby because of his stumbling on their plot, his running away, and how he had told Great-uncle that the gang, called the Green Hands Gang because they wore green gloves, would be operating at Ricklesham – stealing valuable papers.

'And bless us all, so they did,' said Uncle Robert. 'And here's a theft again – and a green glove is dropped!'

'Snubby's been pulling your leg, Uncle Robert,' said Mrs Lynton soothingly. 'I'll speak to him about this.'

'Yes – but the *green glove*!' said Uncle Robert. 'The boy couldn't have made that up. There actually *is* a clue of a green glove.'

'Coincidence – sheer chance,' said Mr Lynton impatiently. 'Snubby doesn't know a thing. He wants a good whacking and I'll see he gets it.'

'No, no – don't do that,' said Uncle Robert in alarm. 'I really do think Snubby knows something. Give him a chance, Richard. I wouldn't have given him away if I'd known you would whip him.'

'Oh, it's been coming to him for some long time,' said Mr Lynton, gathering up his letters. 'You can tell him from me that he's going to get a whacking – unless, of course, he really *does* know something and can produce a member of this wonderful gang who actually *does* wear green gloves. Pah!'

Out he went. Great-uncle Robert sighed. He was getting mixed up in a lot of things. Dear, dear – to think Marloes Castle was burgled – and not one of those precious papers taken – only the stuffed animals. Extraordinary!

Snubby tiptoed into the room where only Great-uncle was left there.

'What did you tell them?' he demanded. 'Uncle Richard's furious. I can tell by the way he went out.'

'My boy, I told them what you had told me – and they not only disbelieved your whole tale – in *spite* of the green gloves,' said Great-uncle solemnly, 'but your uncle, I very much regret to say, is going to give you a beating – unless you can – er – produce one of the green glove thieves.'

'You shouldn't have given me away,' said poor Snubby, feeling very sorry for himself indeed. 'Didn't I twist my ankle last night, and bruise and cut my knees – look – and now I'm to have a whacking. It isn't fair. Especially as I know more than anyone else about the burglary!'

'Do you?' said Great-uncle, startled. 'Or is that just another of your tales?' he asked more cautiously. 'Tell me.'

'I'm not telling you or anybody else a single thing,' declared Snubby, almost in tears. 'Sneaking and blabbing like that! Getting me a whacking. It's not fair. I wish there *was* a Green Hands Gang – I'd jolly well set them on to everyone in this house, and be glad to!'

He went out and slammed the door. Great-uncle was upset and worried. He also felt extremely muddled. Dear, dear, Snubby was a most unreliable and really extraordinary boy!

Chapter Twenty-four

The Police Arrive

Suddenly quite a lot of things began to happen. The first one was the arrival of the police!

'I say – there's Inspector Williams coming up the front path – and somebody in plain clothes with him – a detective, I should think!' called Roger in excitement.

'Why should they come here?' said Diana. Snubby began to shake at the knees. Had Great-uncle said anything to the police about the Green Hands Gang? Surely not!

Poor Snubby crept into the boxroom and shut the door. He was absolutely certain that the police had come to question him about his idiotic Green Hands story.

'I'll never make up a tale again, never,' vowed poor Snubby. 'This one has followed me and followed me – and however much I say I made it up, no one will believe me now that a green glove has been found.'

The Inspector asked for Great-uncle Robert. He and his colleague were shown into the study.

'Mr Robert Lynton?' asked the Inspector. 'I've come in connection with this peculiar Marloes Castle case, sir. Lord Marloes asked us to come and have a word with you. He is thinking of placing all his papers somewhere in safety now that a thief has actually been able to get into the room where he keeps them. Funny business that, sir – taking the animals and leaving the papers. Must be mad, I should think.'

'Very strange indeed,' agreed Great-uncle. 'Er – does

Lord Marloes want me to do anything about the papers for him?'

'Yes, sir. He wondered if you would go up to the castle and advise the custodian how to pack them, and in what order they should be packed, and so on,' said the Inspector.

'I'd be pleased to,' said Great-uncle.

'There's another thing,' said the Inspector. 'When you went there with the children the other day, sir, did you notice two other men there?'

'Yes, I did,' said Great-uncle. 'Why?'

'Well, sir, anyone visiting the Marloes Collection has to have a pass on which is written his name and address,' said the Inspector. He gave Great-uncle three passes. 'That's yours, sir, with the names of the three children on. That's another visitor's, a Professor Cummings, a very, very bent old fellow. And here's another – name of Alfred James Smith, address given 38 Thurlow Crescent, Leeds. Well, we've checked yours, of course, and Professor Cummings' – addresses given, correct. But in the case of this third one, sir . . .'

'It's false, I suppose?' said Great-uncle, getting excited. 'But why? And what's the connection between a man with a false name and address coming to look at the papers, and another man, presumably mad, coming to steal the stuffed animals. It doesn't make sense.'

'You're right, it doesn't,' agreed the Inspector, and the plain-clothes man nodded his head. 'But it may be there *is* a connection, and we want to find out all we can about this fellow with the false name and address. Can you give us an exact description, sir?'

'Well, no, I can't. I hardly noticed him,' said Great-uncle. 'But why not ask the three children? They're as

155

sharp as needles, all of them. They'll give you a full description.'

'Good idea. Can you get them for us, sir?' said the Inspector. Great-uncle rose and went out. He called loudly.

'Roger! The police want to have a word with you three. Come down, will you?'

Roger felt excited. What was up? He went to fetch Diana. 'Where's Snubby? Snubby! I say, SNUBBY! Where are you? The police want to talk to you.'

Snubby's heart went cold inside him. He clutched at the trunk he was sitting on. Now what would happen to him?

'SNUBBY! Where *are* you?' yelled Roger. He opened the boxroom door. 'Gosh, what do you think you're doing in here, all alone with Loony? Didn't you hear me calling you? Come on down. The police want a word with us.'

Snubby rose and with shaking knees went down the stairs. Roger and Diana skipped down, thrilled.

'Good morning, youngsters,' said the Inspector with a very nice smile. 'I want a word with you. Now did any of you notice the two men who were in the room with you at Marloes Castle, when you went to see the animals and the papers?'

Snubby's heart lightened a little. Perhaps the police hadn't come for him after all.

Roger nodded. 'Yes, I remember them quite well. One was very old and bent – he bent so far forward that we couldn't see his face.'

'And the other one was so hairy you couldn't see *his* face either!' said Diana.

The plain-clothes man, who had been writing in a little notebook, looked up at this description.

'How hairy was he?' he asked.

'Well,' said Diana, 'he had very thick hair on his head, thick shaggy eyebrows, a thick moustache and a beard. You couldn't tell what he was really like at all, because he was all hair!'

'Was he big?' asked the detective.

'Yes,' said Diana, 'a heavy sort of man. Why, do you know him?'

The detective was turning back some pages of his note-book. 'Your description happens to fit men who were known to visit two collections of rare documents, some of which were stolen recently,' he said. 'It fits exactly, in fact.'

The children digested this in silence.

'Then do you think that's the man that stole the other papers – and stole the animals from Marloes Castle too?' asked Roger at last. 'Why should he take those moth-eaten animals?'

'Ask me another!' said the detective. 'Now – would you know this hairy man again if you saw him?'

'Yes – if he was still hairy,' said Roger. 'But I should think most of the hair was false!'

'You're probably right,' said the Inspector. 'Er – did you see the man's hands, by any chance?'

The children frowned, trying to remember. 'I saw him using a magnifying glass, sliding it up and down the pages,' said Roger. 'And as far as I can remember he had quite ordinary hands – I didn't notice that they were very hairy, now I come to think of it – and perhaps they should have been as he was such a hairy man. Great-uncle Robert's got an awful lot of hair – and his hands are hairy on the back – look.'

Everyone gazed at Great-uncle's hairy hands. He looked rather uncomfortable, and put them in his pockets as soon as he could.

'Would you say that the hairy man could wear this glove?' said the Inspector, producing a green glove from his pocket.

The children gazed at the glove. Loony went over to it and sniffed it excitedly. He pawed at it and whined.

'Why – he knows who wore that glove!' said Snubby, astonished. 'That's the way he always acts if you show him anything that smells of a person he knows.'

'Aha – now we're *getting* somewhere!' said the detective, sitting up suddenly. 'You sure your dog knows the owner of that glove? Quite sure? Then that narrows things down considerably. The owner of the glove must be somebody you children know.'

'Gosh!' said Roger, his thoughts flying to Tonnerre at once. He looked closely at the glove. It was a small one, made of the very softest, finest leather imaginable. No – he didn't think it would fit Tonnerre. As far as he remembered, Tonnerre had very large hands – or had he? Perhaps he hadn't – perhaps Roger only thought that because Tonnerre was enormous and therefore it seemed right for him to have large hands.

Snubby took the glove and looked at it. Loony stood on his hind legs, still sniffing and whining. If only he could speak – what name would he say?

'Who wears this glove, Loony?' asked Snubby.

'Woof!' said Loony at once. The detective took the glove from Snubby and tossed it to the Inspector. He didn't want Loony to nibble their biggest clue.

'You haven't answered my question,' said the Inspector, pocketing the glove. 'I asked you if you thought the hairy man could have worn a glove as small as this.'

The children thought hard.

'Yes, he might,' said Roger.

'I don't remember,' said Diana.

'He couldn't possibly,' said Snubby.

'Hmm – very helpful!' said the Inspector with a laugh. 'Well thanks, children. That's all I want to ask you. Keep your eyes open for the hairy man, will you? It's just possible he might tell us a few interesting things if we can find him.'

Snubby escaped thankfully, throwing a grateful glance at Great-uncle Robert.

Loony tore after the children. Roger stopped to pat him. 'So you know who the owner of the green glove is, do you?' he said. 'Who wore that glove so as not to leave fingerprints, Loony? And where's the other glove of the pair? Can't you find it? Can't you tell us anything?'

'Woof-woof!' said Loony joyfully, enjoying this earnest conversation, and leaping round Roger excitedly.

'It's funny about that hairy man, isn't it?' said Diana. 'What was he doing there that day, if he was the thief? Looking to see if there were any papers worth stealing – or what?'

'Goodness knows,' said Roger. 'It's all a muddle – the hairy man – the green glove – the stolen animals – and Loony knowing who it is! It's really very, very peculiar.'

Chapter Twenty-five

Quite a Lot of Talk!

Roger and Diana felt quite themselves again, and suggested going over to see Barney to see if he had got over his sick attack too. They had a tremendous lot to tell him!

'Yes, you go and see him,' said Mrs Lynton. 'A walk on this sunny morning will do you good after that nasty attack you had yesterday. Be careful what you buy at the Fair, *please*. You'd be wise not to buy any food there at all, after your horrid experience.'

They went off together, Loony wild with delight at the thought of a walk. He capered ahead, putting his head down every hole they came to, sniffing for rabbits.

Barney was quite all right again. He had felt very sick and ill all night, but had at last gone to sleep and slept soundly till ten o'clock that morning. Now he was up and about, whistling, giving his hoopla stall a really good clean down.

'It's Saturday,' he explained. 'We always get most people that day, so I like to have everything looking spick and span. Hey, Miranda, leave Loony alone. If you pull his long ears, he'll pull your long tail!'

But that's just what Loony couldn't do because Miranda aggravatingly went and sat up on top of the round roof of the stall, swinging her tail well out of poor Loony's reach!

'Barney – have you seen the paper?' said Roger urgently.

'No,' said Barney, surprised. 'What's up? Gosh – you

don't mean to say there's been a robbery – at the castle! Blow! We've missed it. We were ill and didn't go to watch.'

'Sh!' said Diana warningly. 'We've *heaps* to tell you, Barney. Can you come into some safe place for half an hour where no one can hear us?'

'Let me finish cleaning my stall and I'll come,' said Barney, looking thrilled. 'I'll be another ten minutes. Go and talk to the chimps. They seem rather down in the mouth this morning.'

So they were. They sat together, their arms twined round one another, looking very mournful. 'Have they had sausage sandwiches too?' asked Snubby of Vosta. But Vosta seemed cross and answered him shortly.

'Don't be silly. I'd never give them that kind of food. They're all right. Tonnerre's been at them, that's all. They can't bear his shouting.'

'Nor can I,' said Roger, putting his hand to his ears. He could hear Tonnerre yelling loudly. Somebody else was getting into trouble too. It was Young 'Un. He came along howling, holding one side of his head.

'Whacked me for nothing,' he wailed, and showed the children his red and swollen ear. 'Said I'd kept some of his elephant-ride money for myself. I didn't. But I will next time.'

'No, you mustn't,' said Diana, shocked.

'Why not?' asked poor Young 'Un. 'Look, he's boxed my ears for something I didn't do. All right, I'll go and do it then, to earn my punishment. I'll be straight with him then.'

'Straight with him and crooked with yourself,' said Roger. 'Don't do anything wrong, Young 'Un. You'll be sorry.'

Young 'Un didn't think so. He'd get even with Tonnerre, see if he wouldn't. He went off muttering.

The children left the bad-tempered Vosta, and his mournful chimps with their arms still round one another, and went to see if Barney was ready. He was.

They went off to the caravan Barney shared with another boy. 'We'll be all right here, if we talk quietly,' said Barney. 'Now – what's in the paper? What's happened?'

They had bought a paper on the way and they showed it to Barney. His face was a study as he read about the curious robbery.

'Stuffed animals! Are they valuable?' he asked.

'Not these,' said Roger. 'They're the ones we saw ourselves, up in the castle – moth-eaten, badly-stuffed things.'

'And *I* saw them in the castle grounds last night, where the thief had put them – and where the police found them this morning,' put in Snubby. Barney's eyes nearly fell out of his head.

'*What?*' he said. 'Did you go last night? All by yourself, to watch? My, but you're a brave one!'

Snubby swelled with pride at this. He told his story to Barney, who listened with intense interest.

'Barney – do you know anyone who wears green gloves – small ones?' asked Diana eagerly. 'Especially an acrobatic man – one who could climb up steep walls and jump from sill to sill and all that?'

'Does Tonnerre wear green gloves ever?' asked Snubby in a whisper.

'Never seen him wear any gloves at all. Never seen anyone in the Fair wear gloves,' said Barney. 'Why, they'd laugh at it!'

162

'Is there anyone in the Fair who's an acrobat and has small hands?' asked Diana. 'Anyone at all?'

Barney thought hard. 'There's Vosta,' he said at last. 'He's a fine acrobat, you know, though training chimps is his job here. And he's got small hands, almost like a woman's.'

Vosta! Could it be Vosta?

'Did the figure you saw climbing up the wall look anything like Vosta?' Roger asked Snubby. Snubby considered.

'Well – it's difficult to say, because I really couldn't see him clearly. All I know is he seemed absolutely certain and confident in all his movements,' said Snubby. 'As if he was quite used to such amazing climbing and leaping.'

'It can't be Vosta,' said Barney. 'He wouldn't be such an idiot as to steal the wrong things. The one who steals the papers and things must either know them himself or be told in great detail which to take. Vosta wouldn't be such an idiot. Something went wrong last night.'

Roger got out his map – the map he had made of the room in the castle.

'We mustn't forget that once again the thief apparently got in through fastened and locked windows,' he said. 'The paper says he didn't go through the locked doors because there's a burglar alarm set there, which rings if a door is opened at night. And the alarm didn't ring, so the doors weren't opened.'

They looked at the map, poring over it. It was obvious that the thief meant to get in through the windows, as he climbed the outside walls. But how did he unfasten windows that were locked on the inside? And how in the world did he squeeze through the narrow bars?

'Give it up!' said Roger. 'Unless by any chance he was Santa Claus and came down the chimney! Now that's an idea – would the thief be Santa Claus, do you suppose? Snubby, did it look like Santa climbing up the walls?'

'Don't be daft,' said Snubby. 'All the same – I *did* think I saw a figure up on the roof, by the chimney.'

'You saw figures everywhere, according to you,' said Diana disbelievingly. 'The trouble with you, Snubby, is that we never know how much you are exaggerating.'

'You don't suppose the thief could come down the chimney, do you?' asked Roger suddenly. 'Joking apart, I mean. Look, I've marked where the fireplace is in this map. There was only one chimney up on the roof of that wing, because I expect all the fireplaces in the wing are under one another, in each room, and one chimney serves for all.'

'These old houses have very wide chimneys,' said Diana. 'Big enough for a man to come down them quite easily, I should think.'

'That fireplace didn't look awfully big, though,' said Snubby, remembering. '*I* could have got down, perhaps – but I'm pretty certain that a fellow as big as Tonnerre couldn't.'

'Then we'll have to rule the chimney out too,' said Roger. 'It's strange, you know. It's impossible for anyone to have gone through the burglar-alarm doors – it's impossible for anyone to have unfastened the windows from outside – and we're agreed that the chimney and fireplace are too small for anyone to get down those. All these impossibilities – and yet *somebody* found it possible to enter that room, and take from it a dozen or so stuffed animals!'

'He couldn't have taken them all at once,' said Snubby. 'There were too many. He must have made a good many journeys. I suppose he did all his climbing up and down whilst I popped off to sleep for half an hour.'

'Well! You didn't tell us that before!' said Diana.

'I didn't think about it,' said Snubby.

Footsteps came up the caravan steps at that moment and the door was flung open. Tonnerre stood there, black as thunder.

'So! This is where you idle with your fine friends, Barney!' he roared. 'Reading the newspapers, too, when you should be doing your work!'

He snatched the paper from Barney and tore it across. Snubby began to tremble. He really was scared of Tonnerre.

'Get back to your work,' he roared to Barney. 'And you! You clear out of my field!' he shouted at the others. 'Not this boy, though. Aha, it is the little snooper again. I will take him to my caravan and teach him a few things. Come, my little snooper.'

Poor Snubby was hauled off before the others could do anything. Roger and Barney ran off after the angry Tonnerre, but they might as well have been dogs barking at a bull for all the notice he took of them. He really was in a towering rage!

Barney ran to Old Ma. 'Old Ma – can you go after Mr Tonnerre and make him let Snubby go? He hasn't done anything.'

But even Old Ma was afraid of Tonnerre that day. 'A black-hearted man he is,' she said, staring after him as he dragged poor Snubby to his van. 'I can't do nothing with him in one of his black moods.'

But Loony wasn't afraid of anyone if they were hurting his beloved Snubby. He flew at Tonnerre, snapping and growling. He snapped at his ankles all the way up the steps of Tonnerre's caravan, he tore his trousers as he went in, and he bit his leg so hard, at last, that Tonnerre dropped Snubby with a yell and turned on the dog.

165

Loony shot out of his way under the bunk-beds. Snubby took his chance and leapt down the caravan steps, taking them all in one bound. Tonnerre leapt after him, also taking the steps in one bound.

Loony was scrabbling under the bunk. He came out with something in his mouth, and shot down the steps with it. He dropped it on the ground and went after Tonnerre again at top speed.

Diana, standing nearby, quite petrified by all this, looked to see what Loony had dropped. She stared in the greatest amazement.

It was a green glove – partner to the one that the police had shown the children that morning!

Chapter Twenty-six

The Second Green Glove

Diana picked up the glove at once. She stuffed it into the pocket of her dress. She didn't know why she did that – she just felt that it was important that she should.

Snubby was now outside the field gate. Loony was worrying Tonnerre's ankles, and the giant-like man was kicking out at him, shouting. All the people in the Fair ground were watching, most of them silent.

Barney sidled up to Roger. 'Take Diana and go. Go through the gate at the opposite end of the field. Snubby's all right now – he'll race home. Don't come back here. I shall leave this Fair today. Tonnerre's got his knife into me, and I won't work for him any more. I'll come to your home and tell you what's happened as soon as I can. Go quickly now.'

'Will you be all right, Barney?' asked Diana anxiously, as Roger pulled her away to the gate Barney had pointed to.

Barney nodded. 'I know how to look after myself. Tonnerre's had some bad luck – something's gone wrong with him. He's always like this then – a dangerous fellow. Did you notice his hands? Enormous! *He* couldn't have worn that green glove!'

Diana had no time to tell him about the other glove. She was being dragged out of the gate at top speed by Roger. They set off to skirt the field, and join poor Snubby.

They found him sitting on a fence by the roadside,

Loony licking his ankles. He looked rather pale, and gave them a watery grin.

'Hallo,' he said. 'So you escaped all right. Gosh – I'm scared stiff of Tonnerre. I shall dream about him all night.'

'Come on home, quick. I've got something to show you,' said Diana.

They went home together, Loony at their heels, occasionally looking back to see if Tonnerre was by any chance stalking them. But he wasn't, of course. He was probably giving poor Barney a bad time now!

Diana could hardly contain herself. She was bursting to produce the glove! 'Come into the summer-house quickly,' she said. 'Come on!'

They all went in and sat down. Sardine strolled in to join them. Loony wagged his tail, feeling so pleased with himself for biting Tonnerre that he couldn't even find it in him to chase Sardine.

Diana put her hand in her pocket and took out the green glove. The boys stared at it.

'Where did you get it?' asked Roger. 'Did the police leave it somewhere?'

'No – it's not the glove they brought. It's the other glove!' said Diana. 'What *do* you think of that?'

Roger snatched it up with a loud exclamation. 'Good gracious! Where *did* you get it?'

'*I* didn't get it,' said Diana. 'Loony did. When Tonnerre took Snubby into his caravan, Loony followed, snapping and snarling. And when he came out he had this green glove in his mouth! He must have picked it up from the floor of the van.'

Both boys stared at the glove, and Roger fingered it and turned it over in his hands. 'What exactly does that mean then!' he said. 'As far as I can see, it means that

168

although Tonnerre himself can't wear these, he lends them to someone who does – in other words, he lends them to the thief!'

'That's right,' said Snubby. He bent down and held the glove to Loony's nose. The spaniel at once whined and sniffed excitedly.

'See? He knows the owner of *this* glove too – it's the same owner as the glove he sniffed this morning. It's somebody at the Fair,' said Snubby.

'It's Vosta then,' said Roger. 'I noticed he had quite small hands this morning.'

Diana slipped the glove on to her own hand. It fitted her perfectly. She laughed. She put on a mysterious, sinister voice.

'I belong to the Green Hands Gang,' she said in a deep, hollow voice. 'See my green glove!'

Great-uncle Robert was coming up to the summer-house with a book when he suddenly heard these words spoken in a very peculiar voice indeed. He stopped, alarmed.

Who was that speaking? What an extraordinary voice! And good gracious, was that a green-gloved hand appearing out of the door of the summer-house?

It was. Diana was now doing a weird dance in the little house, and waving her green-gloved hand about.

Great-uncle Robert was very surprised indeed. He suddenly walked determinedly up to the summer-house and looked in, expecting to see something extraordinary.

All he saw was the three children and Loony, very startled by his sudden appearance. Diana put her green-gloved hand behind her back at once.

'What *is* the meaning of this?' Great-uncle asked irritably. 'Diana, where did you get that glove. Tell me at once.'

169

There was silence. Diana glanced desperately at the boys.

'Well?' said Great-uncle in quite a nasty voice. 'Are you going to tell me – or would you rather I called your parents? Diana, I am quite sure you children know something that *we* ought to know – that maybe even the police ought to know.'

'We'd better tell him,' said Roger to the others. 'Anyway, I think it's got a bit beyond us now we've found this glove. All right, Great-uncle, we'll tell you all we know – and really, it's quite a lot.'

'But first you'll have to believe that Snubby's tale of the Green Hands Gang was all a lot of nonsense,' said Diana. 'Or else you'll get muddled. It's just chance that a pair of green gloves has come into this.'

'Will you please begin to tell me all you know,' said Great-uncle impatiently, and sat himself down on the wooden seat in the summer-house.

Roger began the tale. Diana and Snubby added bits to it that he forgot. It was a long tale and an extraordinary one, especially the bit where Snubby had come across the gleaming-eyed creatures in the dell the night before. Great-uncle grunted.

'Hmm. An alarming experience. I hope it taught you a lesson! Tut-tut! What a story! And now what about this glove? It seems to me that this fellow Tonnerre had better be handed over to the police for questioning.'

Snubby thought that was an awfully good idea. Aha! He'd get a bit of his own back on Tonnerre then! Yes, Snubby certainly thought that was a very good idea.

'Give me the glove,' said Great-uncle importantly. 'And understand this – the matter is out of your hands *entirely* now – you've nothing to do with it, and you must

170

keep your noses out of it, or you'll get into trouble. This is for grown-ups to solve, not children.'

But alas, not even Great-uncle, or Mr and Mrs Lynton, or even the police seemed to be able to solve the mystery of Rilloby Fair and the thefts at the castle.

Mr Tonnerre said he didn't know anything at all about the green glove. Somebody must have put it into his caravan. He had never, never seen it before. Why should he have a green glove so small? See his enormous hands! It would fit his thumb and no more.

'Did you lend them to the thief to wear, in order that he might leave no fingerprints?' asked the Inspector patiently for the twentieth time. But Tonnerre shook his great head impatiently.

'What have I to do with thieves who steal stuffed animals? I, who have live ones of my own. I tell you, I know nothing, of this pest of a green glove. NOTHING AT ALL'.

And so the police had to let him go, because they certainly could not prove that he had lent the gloves to anyone, or that he even knew the thief. He went back to his van grumbling loudly, and everyone kept well out of his way.

Then the police called on Vosta. What did *he* know about the gloves? Were they his? Had he ever worn them? Could he climb walls? Would he please put them on?

He did so – and certainly they seemed rather small for him, although his hands were not very large for a man.

The two chimpanzees watched the policemen when they went to Vosta's tent to interview him. They still seemed rather subdued, especially Burly, and sat quietly with their arms round one another's necks.

They were interested to see the gloves. They got up and peered at them and patted them.

'Anything new interests them,' said Vosta, pushing the chimps away. 'Go and sit down, you two. Look out for your handkerchief, sir, if you've got one in your pocket. They'll be after it, especially Hurly, who's a real pickpocket.'

It was impossible to get anything helpful out of Vosta at all.

He just said he didn't know, he didn't know whose the gloves were, he didn't know who the thief was, he didn't know anything.

The Inspector put the gloves into his pocket impatiently. He felt that both Tonnerre and Vosta *did* know something – but he was up against a blank wall. He could ask no more questions, go no further.

He went off with the detective. Vosta made a grimace after them. He watched them go all the way across the field.

He didn't see Hurly show Burly something. He didn't see Burly hold out his paw for it. He didn't see the chimps tuck their find under the blankets in their bunk.

Hurly had picked the Inspector's pocket as he turned to go. He had got the pair of green gloves – and now they were well hidden under the blankets!

The gloves excited Burly. He wanted to put them on. He must wait till Vosta wasn't there, because Vosta would take them away.

Chapter Twenty-seven

Sunday – and Monday

The next day came. It was Sunday. It seemed very peaceful and quiet after all the excitement of the day before.

Barney turned up in the morning with Miranda. He saw Roger at the window and waved. Roger opened the window and shouted to him. 'The others are in the summer-house. I'm just coming.'

Barney went to the summer-house, and found Diana and Snubby there with Loony. Loony gave Barney and Miranda a tremendous welcome.

'I say!' said Barney, looking at Diana in awe. 'You going to a party or something? You're all dressed up. And Snubby looks awfully *clean*.'

'No, we're not going to a party,' said Diana, surprised. 'It's Sunday, and we've just been to church, that's all. Don't you ever go?'

'No. But I'd like to,' said Barney. He wanted to do everything these friends of his did, if he could. 'Hallo, Roger!'

Roger walked in, also looking very clean and spruce. 'Hallo, Barney,' he said. 'Have you left the Fair?'

'No. Tonnerre won't let me go till the Fair leaves Rilloby,' said Barney. 'But he's better now. Not nearly so fierce. I really think the visit of the police gave him a fright. I came to see if you'd got any more news. Solved the mystery yet?'

'No. I don't think it ever *will* be solved,' said Roger. 'It's just a list of impossible things – things that can't

173

happen and yet did – with a pair of green gloves complicating everything still more.'

'Listen,' said Barney. 'I shan't be able to see you tomorrow. Vosta's having the day off, goodness knows why – and I'm to see to the chimps. Young 'Un is taking the hoopla stall. You mustn't come to the Fair again, of course. You'd be like a red rag to a bull if Tonnerre caught sight of you.'

'Well, can't you spend the day with us today?' said Diana at once. 'The Fair doesn't open on Sundays. Wouldn't you like to be with us?'

'Well, yes, of course I would,' said Barney, his blue eyes shining. 'I love your home. But would your mother mind? And what about your father? He's home today, isn't he?'

'They won't mind if we keep out of their way,' said Diana. 'They do like us to be quiet on Sundays, of course. But we can always talk and read.'

'You lend me another book of Shakespeare's,' said Barney. 'I'll be quiet enough then!'

The others laughed. It always amused them to see Barney labouring through a play of Shakespeare – determined to understand it, so that if ever he did come across his unknown father who had once acted in so many of Shakespeare's plays, he would at least have *something* in common with him.

'I'll lend you *Hamlet*,' said Roger. 'You'll like that. There's a super ghost in it.'

Mrs Lynton was very willing for Barney to spend the day. Great-uncle Robert was not too pleased to see yet another child, complete with monkey, added to the riotous trio.

'How I'm ever going to get my Memoirs written, I don't

know,' he complained to Mrs Lynton. 'Children and dogs and cats and monkeys everywhere I go!'

'You go and have your little nap in the study and I'll send the children outside on this wonderful day,' said Mrs Lynton.

'I said "my Memoirs", not a nap,' said Great-uncle with dignity, and retired to the study. He carefully put out paper, fountain pen and notes on the table, headed a page 'Chapter Five,' and then promptly settled down in an armchair and went to sleep.

'Now don't you dare to disturb your Great-uncle,' Mrs Lynton warned the children. 'Don't let Miranda leap in at the window on to him – and don't let Loony bark – and see that Sardine doesn't get into the study and jump up on Great-uncle's knee.'

'Right, Mother,' said Roger. 'And I'll tell that loud-voice thrush to pipe down, and shoo all the bees out of the garden, and as for that earwig I saw stamping about this morning, I'll . . .'

'Now, now, Roger!' said his mother, smiling. 'Don't be ridiculous. Go along to the summer-house and don't let me hear a sound from any of you!'

Sunday was very peaceful. Barney enjoyed it more than anyone. It was heaven to him to be in a family, in a home, to belong, even for only one day, to a little company of people who liked him and accepted him as one of themselves.

'They can't understand what it's like not to have any people of your own, not to have a home you can always go to – no, not even Snubby understands, although he's got no parents. He belongs here. I don't belong anywhere,' thought Barney soberly. 'Perhaps if I ever find my father, I shall have a home with him, and belong there.'

The children talked a lot about the green gloves. Tonnerre, Vosta, the castle and the rest. They went over and over everything again and again. What a mystery!

'The Mystery of Rilloby Fair!' said Diana. 'It would be exciting if we could solve it.'

Barney went back to the Fair reluctantly that evening. Miranda had enjoyed her day as much as he had. 'Goodbye,' he said. 'I'll see you on Tuesday – if I can get over here. The Fair leaves on Wednesday, you know, and I certainly shan't go with it. I don't want to work for Tonnerre.'

'What will you do then, Barney?' asked Diana.

'Oh, I'll get another job somewhere,' said Barney. 'But I'll keep in touch with you. I'll send you a card telling you where I am always. And perhaps I shall be able to get a job somewhere near here when the summer holidays come.'

He went off. The children all went to bed, feeling tired. 'Though I can't imagine why,' said Snubby. 'We simply haven't done a thing today – not even taken poor old Loony for a walk.'

'Woof,' said Loony hopefully. But there was no walk that night!

The next day Great-uncle announced that he was going to Marloes Castle to arrange to pack up the valuable papers there, in order that they might be locked away in safety.

'I shall go about three o'clock,' he said. 'And seeing that Diana here has such an interest in old documents, I'd be glad to take her with me. She would be a help, I'm sure.'

Diana was horrified. What, spend ages listening to dry information about centuries-old papers that she couldn't even read – all alone with Great-uncle! She gazed round at Roger and Snubby in despair.

They looked back. Poor old Diana! How awful! Then a thought came into Roger's mind. It would be rather interesting to go to that room again – and have a good look round. He might find a clue the police had missed. Anyway, it would be fun to see if there was any single place where the thief could have come in.

'It's just conceivable there might be a secret passage somewhere,' thought Roger. 'I never thought of that!'

He pictured himself tapping round the wall of the room. He could have a look at the fireplace too, and see if it really was big enough for, say, Tonnerre.

'Great-uncle, I should like to come too,' he said politely.

'So should I,' said Snubby. 'I'd awfully like to have a look round the grounds, Great-uncle. Do you think Lord Marloes would mind?'

'Dear me – so you would all like to keep me company this afternoon?' beamed Great-uncle, pleased at finding himself so popular all of a sudden. 'Very well. I will certainly take you. I see no harm in your looking round the grounds, Snubby, if you behave yourself.'

He said nothing about Loony and neither did Snubby. But when Snubby heard that Great-uncle was going in a car he knew there was no hope for Loony.

'I'd like a walk, Great-uncle,' he said, 'so if it's all right with you I'll walk across the fields and join you at the gates.'

'Certainly, my boy, certainly,' said Great-uncle. 'Anything you like! We'll have a grand time together!'

'We shall have to be back in good time for supper,' said Snubby suddenly. 'There'll be meringues.'

'How do you know?' asked Diana.

'Cook told me. She wouldn't eat her Sunday hat yesterday, though I begged and begged her to – so we're eating meringues to-night instead.'

Mrs Lynton looked astonished. 'What's all this about Cook's Sunday hat? Oh, Snubby, you haven't been upsetting Cook finding fault with her Sunday hat, surely?'

'Aunt Susan! She's got a *marvellous* Sunday hat,' said Snubby indignantly. 'It's got three roses, a wreath of violets, and five carnations in it. It's wizard. I can quite well understand why she doesn't want to eat it.'

'There *are* times when I think you are not quite sane, Snubby,' said Mrs Lynton. 'I don't know *what* your masters at school think of you.'

'Oh, they think the same as you,' Snubby assured her cheerfully. 'I don't mind. It's all the same to me.'

That afternoon the car came for Great-uncle, and he and Diana and Roger got into it. Snubby had already gone off with Loony. He was to meet them at the gates.

'Now for a nice happy afternoon,' said Great-uncle, pleased. 'Nothing I like better than browsing among old, rare papers, breathing in the air of past centuries. What a peaceful place that old room is.'

It wasn't going to be. It was going to be just about the most exciting place in Rilloby that afternoon. But Great-uncle didn't know that!

Chapter Twenty-eight

Things Begin to Happen

Snubby met them at the castle gates with Loony. Great-uncle eyed the spaniel with annoyance.

'I didn't say you could bring that dog!'

'You didn't say I wasn't to,' pointed out Snubby in a reasonable voice. 'Stop scratching, Loony. You do seem to have a bad effect on Loony, Great-uncle. It seems as if he's *got* to scratch whenever he sees you.'

'You can't bring him into the castle,' said Great-uncle determined not to enter into a conversation about scratching again. 'You'll have to stay out here in the grounds.'

Snubby didn't mind. He meant to explore the grounds thoroughly, and see if he could find any clues. He also meant to go and find the dell again, where the stuffed animals had been, and enjoy remembering that terrifying episode. He wondered if the sacks were still up on the wall. And what about the rope-ladder? Was it still under the bush?

'I expect it's there still – and the sacks too,' he thought. 'The police said nothing about those. Gosh, they're not very bright. I'd have spotted those at once if I'd been one of the police on the job.'

Great-uncle presented his pass. He and Diana and Roger were taken into the castle, whilst Snubby wandered off into the grounds with an excited Loony, who foresaw all kinds of rabbit adventures for himself that afternoon.

Roger was impatient to be inside the room with the double-locked door. The butler unlocked one door – then the second one – and finally the third one, with its two keys. They then were in the old room, with its shelves of yellowed papers.

Roger and Diana glanced round with interest. Half the stuffed animals were gone, of course. The police had not brought them back. They were probably still somewhere in the police station, staring at the policemen with their lifeless, glassy eyes.

'All the big animals are left,' said Roger. 'I suppose the thief couldn't manage them. The squirrels are gone – and the fox-cubs, but not the foxes – and the pole-cat – and the albino badger. He wasn't very big either.'

'Diana – we'll just go carefully through all the papers before we pack them,' said Great-uncle, longing to explain pages upon pages to poor Diana. 'Now this one . . .'

Diana cast a look of misery at Roger and went to listen. Roger began to look round. He examined the windows. Nobody could *possibly* undo those fastenings from outside! And only the very smallest, thinnest person could squeeze through the bars.

He went to the double-locked door and examined that. No thief could come in that way without keys – and if he had the keys, the burglar alarm would ring as soon as the door was opened. No – that way was impossible too.

He went to the fireplace. It was an old-fashioned open grate. As the fire was never used, there were no fire-irons at all, but only an old fire-screen made of wrought-iron.

Roger bent down and tried to look up the chimney. It looked decidedly narrow. 'I *might* be able to squeeze up,' thought Roger. 'But I doubt it – and it would be frightfully uncomfortable. I dare say it widens out a bit above though.'

He looked at the fireplace itself. It was full of bits and

pieces that had fallen down the chimney. 'Of course, they *might* have been dislodged by somebody getting down, but on the other hand, bits and pieces always *do* fall down chimneys,' thought Roger, feeling rather like a detective.

He went to the window and looked out. He saw something that filled him with extreme amazement! He stared intently. Then a shout came to his ears.

'I say! Look at this!' cried Roger suddenly, making Diana and Great-uncle jump violently. 'What's going on down there?'

He might well ask. Snubby, down in the grounds, was also feeling extremely astonished. He had been wandering round with Loony and had come to the little dell where he had seen the stuffed animals, when he heard a sound nearby.

He had turned – and looking down at him from out of the bushes was a hairy, grinning face with shining eyes! Snubby got a frightful shock. He thought it was one of the stuffed animals come to life!

'Gosh – what is it?' he said, and took a step backwards. Loony gave a delighted bark and rushed into the bushes where the hairy face was. Snubby was amazed. Loony should have barked or growled! Instead of that he had yelped in delight and gone off with the Face!

Then Snubby heard yells and recognised Barney's voice. 'Come here, you pest, you! Do you hear! Where have you gone?'

'It's *Barney!* What's *he* doing here?' said Snubby, full of surprise. 'Loony, where have you gone? Hey, Barney, where are you?'

Barney's voice came back, surprised. 'That you, Snubby? What are *you* doing here? I say, have you seen Burly? He's gone completely mad, so look out.'

'*Burly!*' said Snubby, more amazed than ever. 'What's

he here for? Gosh, yes, I've seen him. At least, I saw his grinning face. He's gone now, and taken Loony with him.'

He made his way towards Barney's voice. Barney was on the road side of the wall. He called again.

'I'm going to see if our rope-ladder is still under the bush, and the sacks on the wall, if the police haven't found them! I'm coming over. I simply must find Burly. He's gone crackers.'

He found the rope-ladder under the bush and soon had it up on the wall. He climbed it quickly and sat on the sacks. He looked all round to see if he could spot Burly.

'What happened to make Burly so mad?' asked Snubby. 'Why did he come all the way here?'

'Don't ask *me!*' said Barney. 'I was in Vosta's caravan with both chimps when bless me if Hurly didn't pull out a pair of green gloves from under the blankets of his bunk.'

'What – the ones we saw?' said Snubby.

'I don't know. The police had those – but I wouldn't put it past Hurly to sneak them out of the Inspector's pocket,' said Barney. 'I bet that's what he did! Anyway, Burly snatched them and put them on – and they fitted him marvellously. Like a glove, in fact! He kept stroking them and muttering to himself, and then he rapped at the cupboard where his toy animals are kept.'

He stopped for breath, still keeping a look-out for Burly from the top of the wall.

'Well, I hadn't the key to his toy cupboard. Vosta's got that,' said Barney. 'So he couldn't have his little toy animals to play with. Then he just seemed to go mad! He banged himself with his arms, and yowled like anything. And then he was out of the window like a streak, haring over the Fair field!'

'Gosh!' said Snubby, enthralled with this story. 'Go on!'

'Well, I followed him, of course,' said Barney. 'And he came straight here. I couldn't catch him up. He was up and over the wall as easy as anything – *he* didn't need a ladder. Well, I suppose he's somewhere in the grounds. What's made him come here?'

Before Snubby could answer a deep voice spoke from the other side of the wall. 'I'm afraid I shall have to hold you for questioning concerning this here ladder,' said the voice. Barney almost fell off the wall.

'Golly – it's a bobby,' he said. 'Where were you?'

'I've been hiding behind that tree ever since we found this here ladder hidden, and the sacks on top of the wall,' said the policeman. 'We reckoned whoever put them there might use them again, if we didn't let on we'd found them. And seemingly we were right. You come down, and let me take you to the police station for questioning.'

'No,' said Barney, and scrambled down the other side as fast as he could. 'I must find Burly,' he said to the petrified Snubby. 'And Miranda too. She scampered after him over the wall, and left me standing on the other side! Come on – take no notice of the bobby. We can easily shake him off!'

He dragged poor Snubby into the bushes, whilst the annoyed policeman began to climb slowly and painfully up the rope-ladder. 'Take me to the place you saw Burly in just now,' said Barney. 'He may still be near here.'

Snubby took him to the dell – and sure enough, there was Burly, with Miranda and Loony! Burly was behaving in a peculiar fashion. His head held in his hands, he was rocking to and fro, making a little whimpering noise.

Miranda was stroking him, and Loony was licking him. It was plain that the chimpanzee was very unhappy.

He looked extremely peculiar in his red shorts, red-striped jersey – and *green gloves!* What was the matter with him? Why was he behaving like that?

Burly suddenly sprang up. He gave a loud howl and bounded away. Loony ran after him and Miranda ran too, whimpering. Both the animals knew that something was wrong with Burly.

Burly ran through the trees to the castle walls. Barney gave a shout. 'Hey, Burly, come back! Come to old Barney!'

That was the shout that Roger had heard up in the old room on the second floor. He looked out and saw Burly tearing over to the castle, with his green gloves on, and behind him came Loony and Miranda, followed at some distance by Barney and Snubby – and behind them, good gracious, a policeman!

No wonder Roger could hardly believe his eyes. But what was to come was even more unbelievable.

Burly came to the walls of the castle. He leapt to a window-sill. He leapt to the gutter-pipe and shinned up it rapidly and easily. He leapt to another window-sill, and up another pipe. Then he climbed confidently up the thick ivy nearby, right to the roof.

'Look at that,' said Snubby, awed. 'What a climb. It was *Burly* I saw the other night! I'm sure it was!'

Burly was now on the roof. He ran to the one and only chimney and peered down it. He leapt into it and disappeared.

Down in the room below three startled people stared at one another. Great-uncle, Roger and Diana had tried in vain to see what was happening outside. They had lost sight of Burly when he had begun to climb up the walls – and then had caught a quick glimpse of him again as he leapt on to their window-sill and off. What in the world was he doing?

They heard a noise in the chimney. Roger ran to it. Two hairy legs appeared, and then Burly swung himself down into the fireplace, blinking. He had managed it easily.

He stood there, looking at three amazed people. Diana spoke to him. 'Burly! What are you doing?'

Ah! That was the kind girl who had given him a toy dog. Burly was no longer frightened to see people staring at him. He came out into the room, looking very strange in his extraordinary dress.

Great-uncle shrank back. He had never seen Burly before. To him the chimpanzee looked fierce and savage. He was horrified to see Diana go up and take the green-gloved paw. Suppose the creature bit her?

But Burly didn't bite. He stroked Diana's arm, and then he looked round the room. He sniffed the air. He ran to the shelves where the yellowed parchments were.

The three watched him, amazed. What was he doing now? Burly smelt each pile. He stopped at one and took out a paper. He sniffed at another lot, and took another piece of parchment. Great-uncle watched him, gaping.

Roger touched Diana's arm. 'The solution of the mystery!' he said. 'I see it all now. How *could* we have been so blind?'

Chapter Twenty-nine

Burly is Very Clever

All three watched the chimpanzee as he sniffed through the papers and took one here and one there. He seemed quite certain which to take. There was no hesitation at all.

'How does he know which to choose?' said Great-uncle Robert, puzzled. 'He's taking one or two of the most valuable – I can see that. But how does he know?'

'He sniffs before he pulls a paper out of its pile,' said Diana. 'Look, each time, he sniffs first.'

'Well! Of course! *I* know how he knows which papers to take!' exclaimed Roger suddenly. 'Diana – do you remember that hairy man – how we watched him sliding his magnifying-glass up and down some of the papers?'

'Yes, I remember,' said Diana.

'Well, he must have had something on the base of the magnifying-glass that was rubbed off on the papers,' said Roger excitedly. 'And the stuff would leave a smell – and when the chimp was sent to take certain papers he knew which to take because of the smell. See him sniffing at them all now!'

'Remarkable. Most remarkable,' said Great-uncle, who looked rather dazed. 'I suppose he's trained to do that. Chimpanzees must be extremely clever.'

'Oh, they *are*,' said Roger, watching Burly take yet another paper. 'But that's an old circus trick, Great-uncle, to smear papers with something that smells, so that an animal will instinctively choose those. Who trained *you*, Burly?'

Burly looked up at his name and gabbled something. His green-gloved hands worked quickly through the parchments.

'No fingerprints, you see – not even a chimp's prints left behind!' said Roger. 'I wonder what made him come along here this afternoon to do the job he should really have done the other night?'

'Perhaps he saw the gloves – and they reminded him,' suggested Diana. 'Oh – what's he going to do now?'

Burly had caught sight of the stuffed animals. He dropped all his papers on the floor and whimpered. He ran across to the few animals left and lifted up a fox. Great-uncle quietly gathered up the papers, opened a drawer in the nearby table, and put them inside. He meant to have them examined to see exactly what gave them the smell that Burly recognised so easily.

The chimpanzee sat down on the floor and nursed the stuffed fox. Diana nudged Roger.

'I'm sure I know what happened the other night,' she whispered. 'He came for the papers with no other idea in his head but to do the sort of job he's often done before, and he must suddenly have seen the stuffed animals staring at him in the moonlight! You know how mad he is on toy animals – he must have thought these stuffed ones were extra big toy ones – possibly put there for *him!*'

'Yes – and he took them into the grounds, one after the other – just the little ones that he could manage easily,' went on Roger. 'Poor Burly. He stood them all in the dell, and for some reason left them there. But he didn't take any of the papers. He was so wrapped up in the animals.'

'And I expect that's why the chimps were so miserable

the next day when we saw them,' said Diana. 'Somebody had scolded Burly hard – and he was upset, so Hurly was upset too. Do you remember how they sat with their arms round one another, looking thoroughly miserable?'

'Who had scolded them?' wondered Roger. 'Vosta, do you suppose?'

'Maybe. And probably Tonnerre too, because Vosta said he had, you remember?' said Diana. 'Somehow or other Tonnerre's in this mystery, Roger. I'm sure he is!'

Burly put down the fox and picked up a stuffed dog, very moth-eaten indeed. He nursed that too. Then he got up and looked at the fireplace, evidently considering whether or not he could get up the chimney with such a large animal.

There suddenly came the sound of doors being unlocked. Voices were heard. Burly looked alarmed. He ran to Diana and crouched down beside her, chattering. She patted him gently on the head. 'Don't be afraid, Burly. I won't let anyone hurt you!'

The door of the room was unlocked with its two separate keys. It opened. In poured Barney, Snubby, Miranda, Loony, the policeman, the custodian and the butler!

'Is Burly here? He went down the chimney!' cried Snubby.

'Yes – there he is!' cried Barney and ran to the chimpanzee, who took his hand trustingly. He loved Barney. Miranda leapt on to the chimpanzee's shoulder, chattering. He looked happier at once.

The policeman looked absolutely bewildered. What with cheeky boys, a spaniel and a monkey, and now a chimpanzee he didn't really know what to do. He looked with relief at Great-uncle, glad to see a responsible-looking grown-up.

'Perhaps you can help me, sir?' he said. 'What's all this here about?'

'Constable – we have found the one who stole the stuffed animals,' said Great-uncle solemnly. 'Before our very eyes this afternoon he stole more valuable papers.'

'Then I shall arrest him,' said the constable at once, importantly. 'Which of them is it, sir?'

'It's the chimpanzee,' said Great-uncle. 'Be careful how you arrest him!'

Snubby gave a chortle at the sight of the policeman's alarmed face. Loony sat down and began to scratch himself violently. Burly put down the stuffed dog he was hugging and took Miranda into his arms instead, nursing her and crooning.

'Hrrrm, I find that beast rather pathetic,' said Great-uncle unexpectedly. 'Can't blame him for anything he's done, Constable. Whoever trained him is responsible. That's the fellow you want – the trainer.'

Heavy footsteps came down the little passage to the door, and in came the Inspector. The policeman had telephoned for him as soon as he had got into the castle, and he had jumped into his car and come along at once.

'Well,' he said, looking round at the big company in amazement. 'You're a mixed lot, I must say. My word – *the green gloves*! Look who's wearing them – well, well, well!'

He stared at Burly as if he couldn't believe his eyes. The chimpanzee stared back. He remembered the Inspector. This was the man out of whose pocket Hurly had taken the green gloves. He took them off suddenly and flung them on the floor.

The constable began to talk to the Inspector, trying to tell him what had happened, but Barney interrupted. 'I can tell you all that happened, sir,' he said. 'I can see it all now! I understand why the sight of the gloves sent Burly here again. I understand why . . .'

'Speak when you're spoken to,' said the Inspector. He turned to Great-uncle. 'Mr Lynton, sir, perhaps *you* would say a few words first. I'm all at sea.'

Somehow or other, first by this person and then by that, he was told every single thing. He listened, astonished and almost disbelieving. He was shown the fireplace where Burly had come down. He was shown the pile of papers that Burly had so carefully chosen after sniffing at them. He sniffed at them too.

'I can smell something myself,' he said, sniffing again. 'Yes – a very clever trick. The chimp had no other way of telling which were the valuable papers and which weren't, except by smell. There's somebody remarkably clever behind all this. Who is it?'

Everyone took a turn at sniffing at the papers. Certainly they had a faint, elusive smell, quite distinguishable.

'So that's how the other thefts were planned,' said the Inspector thoughtfully. 'Someone examined the collections first, and smeared the papers he wanted with something to make them smell. He must also have examined how the chimp could get in and out – a skylight sometimes, a chimney another time, a small window a third time, or maybe a ventilator – somewhere impossible for a grown man to get through. But the chimp could always manage to climb and wriggle through a tiny entrance – he's small and supple and a born acrobat.'

'A most remarkable and successful plan,' put in Great-uncle. 'If we could only lay our hands on the hairy man who was here the other day smearing the papers with something on the base of his large magnifying-glass – you'd have the ring-leader, Inspector.'

'Yes,' said Barney. 'But there must be two or three go-betweens, Inspector. Vosta must be one. He'd have to take Burly to whatever place had been chosen, and point out the way to go up the walls. And there must be another go-between too – the one who warns Vosta what to do – the one who received the note we found a bit of the other day – that said "Marloes Castle. Midnight." Who received that note?'

'Quite a lot of loose ends to tie up!' said the Inspector. 'Well, we'll see if we can tie up a few today. We'll take this chimp back to the Fair, and find out where Vosta is – he may be back by this time.'

The custodian and the butler, neither of whom had said a single word, so completely amazed and bewildered were they, let the little company out of the castle. The Inspector took the pile of papers with him that Burly had so carefully chosen. Burly went down the stairs holding Barney's hand, chattering away to him.

Two cars stood outside – the Inspector's and the one that Great-uncle had hired. 'Room for everyone,' said the Inspector genially. 'Hop in. We'll all go to the Fair. Take the chimp, the monkey and the dog into the other car, if you don't mind. Now – are we all set? To the Fair then!'

Chapter Thirty

The Mystery is Solved

Vosta was back in his tent, puzzled to find Burly gone, when they all arrived in the field. He looked frightened when he saw the Inspector. Burly ran to him and flung his arms round him.

'What have you been up to?' said Vosta to Burly. 'And where have *you* been?' he said to Barney. 'I told you not to leave the chimps.'

'Illia Juan Vosta, I have some questions to ask you, and I must warn you that anything you say may be taken down and used in evidence against you,' said the Inspector sternly. The constable took out a black notebook and licked his pencil, preparing to write.

Vosta looked extremely alarmed. 'I haven't done anything,' he stammered.

'You have trained this chimpanzee to steal, and to break into various buildings,' went on the Inspector in a cold, calm voice. 'We know that various papers are smeared with a substance that the chimpanzee can smell, and these are the papers he takes. We know further that . . .'

'I didn't have anything to do with that,' cried out Vosta, turning very pale. 'I've always said it was a mug's game, using the chimp. I've never had anything to do with it.'

'Except that you lent your chimpanzee, which you yourself had trained to steal, and you took him each time to the place where the theft was to be committed,' said the Inspector in a voice that sent a shiver down Snubby's back. 'Didn't you, Vosta?'

'They're not my chimps,' muttered Vosta. 'And I never trained them to steal. They were trained before I had them.'

'Whose were they before you had them?' rapped out the Inspector.

Vosta looked terrified. 'They were Tonnerre's,' he said in a low voice. 'He trained them. He trained Hurly to pick pockets, and he trained Burly to do all kinds of other stealing tricks. Burly's clever. You can teach him anything.'

'Why did you take on the chimpanzees from Tonnerre?' asked the Inspector.

'I was an acrobat,' said Vosta, still in a low voice. 'And I hurt my back. So Tonnerre offered me the chimps if I'd keep on with him in the Fair – and do one or two things he wanted.'

'I see. And one of the things he wanted was that you should take Burly to whatever building he told you, and see that he got in somehow and sniffed out the papers he had marked,' said the Inspector.

'*He* never marked them,' said Vosta. 'He didn't know a thing about old papers. I used to take them from Burly and give them to Tonnerre – and he passed them on to someone else. I don't know who – but it was the fellow who did the marking of the papers. This fellow used to tell Tonnerre where to take the Fair – we never knew where we were going.'

'Quite. I imagine he chose whatever place he had marked down for his next theft,' said the Inspector. 'And now just tell me the name of the man at the top of all this.'

'I tell you, I don't know,' said Vosta obstinately. 'Why don't you ask Tonnerre? Why pick on me? I'm only the cat's-paw, I am.'

193

'It's the hairy man,' said Snubby, butting in. 'We do know that – do you know a very hairy man, Vosta?'

'I'm not answering any questions from *you*,' snarled Vosta. 'If you kids hadn't come here, snooping and prying . . .'

'That's enough, Vosta,' said the Inspector. 'Constable, stay here with him. I'm going across to this fellow Tonnerre. He, too, is only a cat's-paw, it seems, but a bigger one than Vosta. Still, maybe he'll lead us to the real villain.'

Barney led him to Tonnerre's caravan. The Fair folk, who had stood around in silence, watching Vosta being interviewed, moved back. Old Ma called out:

'Tonnerre's got a visitor. He's in a black mood. You've got to watch out, Mister!'

The Inspector did not deign to reply. He rapped imperiously on the door of Tonnerre's caravan.

'Get out!' yelled Tonnerre's voice. 'Didn't I say I wasn't to be disturbed?'

'Open up,' came the Inspector's stern voice. The door was flung open and Tonnerre stood there frowning blackly. He shut the door behind him and came down the steps.

'Say what you've got to say and go,' he growled.

'Who's your visitor, Tonnerre?' asked the Inspector mildly. 'Let's have a look at him.'

'He's a gentleman, see? I'm not going to have him dragged into any funny business,' said Tonnerre angrily. 'He's a friend of mine, with nothing to do with you at all. Anyway, what's brought you here again, wasting my time and interfering?'

'Let's have a look at your visitor, Tonnerre,' repeated the Inspector. 'What are you hiding him away for?'

Snubby was so full of excitement and anticipation that

194

he could hardly contain himself. His enemy has met his match! The Inspector wouldn't take no for an answer. Who *was* the visitor?

'I bet it's the hairy man, I bet it is,' said Snubby to himself. 'He's come to get the papers and he's wild with Tonnerre because the chimp didn't get them.'

Tonnerre made no move to open the door – but it suddenly opened behind him and somebody came out on to the top step.

'What is all this disturbance?' said a cultural voice. 'Tonnerre, have I come at an awkward moment? I will go.'

He stepped down, but the Inspector placed himself in front of him. 'Your name, sir?' he asked.

The four children gazed at the man in disappointment. He was not the hairy man. He was quite clean-shaven. He had smooth black hair tinged with grey, no moustache, no shaggy eyebrows, no beard.

'My name is Thomas Colville,' said the man. 'My business with Mr Tonnerre is private – he and I are old friends. I am sorry to see he seems to be in trouble. My business with him can wait.'

'You didn't happen to come and see him about some papers you wanted him to get for you, did you?' said the Inspector stolidly.

'I don't know what you are talking about, my good fellow,' said the man, and pushed by the Inspector impatiently.

Snubby stared at him. No, he certainly wasn't a bit like the hairy man – though he was about the same size and build.

Snubby walked a few steps beside the man, staring at him, much to his annoyance. Then Snubby suddenly gave such a yell that Loony barked wildly and ran to him.

'I say – he *is* the man we saw looking at the papers – the hairy man. He is! I couldn't help noticing the tremendous tufts of hair he had growing out of his ears – and look, he's got them – just the same. It's him!'

Things happened all at once then. The man began to run. The constable, watching from Vosta's tent, saw him, and ran to cut him off. Young 'Un ran out and tripped him up neatly. Tonnerre went mad and tried to hit the Inspector. Loony bit him and then everyone closed in, yelling and shrieking with excitement, so that the poor Inspector didn't know *what* was going on for a few minutes.

'You take your sister and brother home,' he said urgently to Roger. He thought that Snubby was Roger's brother. 'Go on – we may be going to have a rough time here. Telephone the police station and tell them to send up men quickly.'

Roger fled with Diana, Snubby and Loony. He was sorry to go at such a time, but he knew he had to take Diana into safety in case things began to get too rough.

Outside the gate stood two cars – one was the police car, with Great-uncle Robert waiting patiently inside, rather alarmed at the excitement going on in the Fair field. The other was the taxi he had hired, complete with its driver.

'Oh, good!' said Roger, stopping. 'I'd forgotten the cars – and Great-uncle. I say, Great-uncle, things are boiling up terrifically – everything's really smashing – and we've got to telephone the police station for more men. Can we bag the taxi and drive there?'

'Bless us all!' said poor Great-uncle in alarm, and clambered out of the police car as quickly as he could. He got into the taxi and in a quavering voice told the man to drive to the police station.

Great-uncle wouldn't let the car stop at the police station more than half a minute, just time enough for Roger to give his message.

'I must get home,' the old man kept saying. 'This isn't good for my heart. Dear, dear – little did I think I'd get mixed up with a lot of criminals and madmen and chimpanzees when I came to stay with your mother. I must go. I must leave. I can't stay a night longer!'

'But Great-uncle – it's been absolutely *wizard*,' protested Snubby. 'I mean – if you want a first-class mystery, well, you couldn't have a better one than the one to do with Rilloby Fair.'

But Great-uncle didn't want any mysteries or adventures. 'I just want to pack my things and go,' he said. 'That man Tonnerre's a dreadful fellow – I was glad I was safely in the car when I saw him come down the caravan steps as black as – as – '

'Thunder,' said Diana.

'He looked as if he might be the chief of some horrible gang,' shuddered poor Great-uncle.

'The Green Hands Gang,' said Snubby, with a chortle.

Chapter Thirty-one

All's Well!

Great-uncle was as good as his word. As soon as he got in, he found Mrs Lynton, announced his intention of leaving that very night, and went up to pack his bag.

Mrs Lynton was amazed. She looked at the excited children.

'What's the matter with him? What *have* you been doing?'

'Nothing!' said Roger indignantly. 'Oh, Mother, do listen – we've got the most exciting news.'

'Well, here's your father – tell him too,' said his mother. 'And do come in to your supper. You're so dreadfully late, and Cook's made you some meringues for your pudding.'

'Gosh – do you know we've never had any tea?' said Snubby in an injured voice. 'Would you believe it? No wonder I feel jolly hungry.'

'So many things have been happening that it's difficult to know where to begin our story,' said Roger to his mother.

'Go and wash before you begin,' said his mother, suddenly noticing how dirty they all looked. 'Your news can wait. It can't be as important and exciting as all that.'

But it was, of course – and when the three children were at last sitting down to eat an enormous meal, the two grown-ups gaped in astonishment when told the extraordinary tale.

'You should have seen the chimp going top speed up the wall!' said Snubby, waving his fork.

'You should have seen him coming down the chimney!' said Roger, getting out of the way of Snubby's fork.

'You should have seen him sniffing at the papers to see which to take!' said Diana.

It was a very disturbed evening. Great-uncle condescended to have some dinner, when he had packed his bag, and he too added his quota to the tale. The Inspector arrived to make his report. Lord Marloes telephoned to Great-uncle to ask for details of the latest excitement at the castle, and asked him to be his guest in town. Great-uncle then telephoned for a taxi.

'I'm really *very* sorry you've had such an upsetting stay,' said Mrs Lynton. 'Certainly you seemed to be as much in the thick of things as anyone else, Uncle Robert. Say good-bye, children!'

The three stood at the gate and shouted good-bye. The last that Great-uncle saw of them was Snubby holding Loony in his arms, making him wave his paw violently.

'That dog!' said Great-uncle, sinking back into the taxi. 'Well, thank goodness he can't sit down and scratch himself in front of me any more!'

And then Barney arrived. He whistled outside the window, standing half-hidden in the darkness.

'There's Barney!' said Snubby, almost falling from his chair in his anxiety to get to the window.

'Ask him in,' said Mrs Lynton. 'We might as well hear his tale too. I never did know such a set of children for getting into all kinds of trouble!'

'Come in, Barney!' yelled Snubby, and Loony raced out of the room into the garden, barking madly. Barney came in looking rather pale and worried.

Miranda was on his shoulder as usual, and she chattered

199

merrily when she saw the friends she knew. She leapt off Barney's shoulder on to Snubby's.

'Don't let her come too near me,' said Mrs Lynton in alarm. 'I do like her – but I really can't bear monkeys.'

'I'll stick her under my shirt,' said Snubby. 'She's cold.'

Miranda disappeared from view for a while. Loony went and sniffed at Snubby's shirt. He felt a little jealous to think Miranda was so close to his beloved master.

'What happened when we left, Barney?' asked Roger. 'Did everything blow up?'

'Pretty well,' said Barney. 'Tonnerre's been taken off, and so has Vosta. I hear they're not coming back, so I don't know if that means they've gone to prison.'

'They haven't taken Hurly and Burly to prison, have they?' asked Snubby in alarm.

'Of course not,' said Barney. 'Billy Tell's taking care of them. I offered to, but the show-folk say they don't want me there any more. They say I put the police on to Tonnerre and Vosta.'

'But you didn't!' cried all three children indignantly. 'You didn't!'

'Well, they think I did,' said Barney. 'So I've been chucked out. And Miranda too. The Fair's breaking up tomorrow, and everyone's going here, there and everywhere. But nobody wants me to go with them.'

'What – was even Young 'Un horrid – and Old Ma?' asked Snubby, amazed.

'Young 'Un's all right – but he's got to do what the others do,' said Barney. 'Show-folk don't like the police – and if they think somebody's split on them they chuck them out.'

'It's not fair,' said Diana, almost in tears. 'It wasn't your fault that Tonnerre and Vosta and the hairy man got caught. So they should be too.'

'What happened to the hairy man?' asked Roger. 'Was he taken off too?'

'Yes. He's the big man behind all these planned thefts,' said Barney. 'He paid Tonnerre to arrange with Vosta for the chimp to steal the papers. He always went beforehand and marked the papers he wanted. Well, I'm glad Tonnerre's gone. He was a black-hearted fellow.'

'That's what Old Ma said,' put in Roger. 'Well, Barney, what are you going to do? Where are you going to sleep tonight?'

'It's a fine night,' said Barney. 'I'm sleeping in a barn not far off. The farmer said I could.'

'Oh no you're not,' said Mrs Lynton suddenly, entering into the conversation.

Barney looked at her in surprise. The children stared too. They had forgotten that she was in the room, sewing.

'Great-uncle's left tonight,' said Mrs Lynton. 'So we've got a guest-room again. If Diana likes to give me a hand, I'll have the bed made up for Barney. He can stay with you till you have to go back to school – and by that time perhaps we shall have found a job for him.'

Barney was quite overcome. 'It's very good of you,' he began, but he couldn't finish because Snubby swept by him and almost knocked him over. He flung his arms round his aunt's neck and hugged her like a bear.

'Aunt Susan! I was *willing* you to say that! I was! I was! I kept saying to myself, "Say Barney can stay!" and you said it.'

'Oh, don't be so ridiculous, dear,' said his aunt, 'and stop strangling me. It was nothing to do with your "willing" me – I made up my mind to ask Barney as soon as I saw your Great-uncle off in the car.'

Barney's face shone. 'Why – I'll be here about two

weeks,' he said. 'Two whole weeks. But – what about Miranda? You don't like monkeys, Mrs Lynton.'

'Oh, I can put up with Miranda so long as she doesn't leap on to my shoulder,' said Mrs Lynton bravely. 'I dare say I shall get used to monkeys if she comes to stay. After all, I've got used to Loony, and I really didn't think I'd *ever* do that!'

'Woof!' said Loony, hearing his name mentioned. He hadn't stopped watching the lump inside Snubby's shirt, which meant that Miranda was still curled up there.

'It will be *lovely*,' said Diana, thinking of the two weeks ahead. 'There'll be us four – and Miranda – and Loony . . .'

'And Sardine,' said Roger, seeing the big black cat coming softly in, eyeing Loony in a way that meant she was just about to spring on him. 'Yes – we'll have a super time.'

'And a *peaceful* time, I hope,' said Mrs Lynton, getting up to go and make Barney's bed. 'It's all been *much* too exciting for me!'

'Oh, Mother – I *loved* the Rilloby Fair Mystery!' said Roger. 'Every minute of it. I'd like it all over again.'

'No – another one would be better still,' said Snubby, tickling Miranda under his shirt. 'I'd like another mystery, as wizard as this – and we'll have one too! Won't we, Loony?'

'Woof,' said Loony, and jumped up to sniff at Miranda. She put out a tiny paw and pulled his ear.

'Well, as long as you four and Miranda and Loony are together, you're sure to get into plenty of trouble!' said Mrs Lynton. 'But spare me a mystery for a little while, will you? I haven't got over this one yet!'

'Right,' promised Snubby generously. 'We'll give you a bit of a rest, Aunt Susan – and then whoosh, we'll be heading into another mystery – the biggest one that ever was!'

Enid Blyton

MYSTERY

Enid Blyton

THE RAGAMUFFIN
MYSTERY

Chapter One

Off In The Caravan

'This is going to be just about the most exciting holiday we've ever had!' said Roger, carrying a suitcase and bag down to the front door. 'Diana, bring that pile of books, will you, before we forget them?'

Diana picked them up and ran down the stairs after Roger. At the front door stood a caravan. Diana stood and gloated over it for the twentieth time.

'Fancy Dad buying a *caravan*!' she said. 'And oh, what a pity he can't come with us, after all!'

'Yes – after all our plans!' said Roger. 'Still, it's a jolly good thing Mummy didn't back out, when she heard Dad had to go off to America – I was awfully afraid she would! My heart went into my boots, I can tell you.'

'Same here,' said Diana, stacking the books neatly on a shelf in the caravan. 'Have we got our bird-book – we'll see plenty of birds on our travels, and that's my holiday task – writing an essay on "Birds I have seen".'

'Well, don't forget to take the field-glasses then,' said Roger. 'They're hanging in the hall. I say – what did you think about Mummy asking Miss Pepper to come with us, now that Daddy can't manage?'

Miss Pepper was an old friend of their mother's. The children were fond of her – but Roger felt rather doubtful about having her on a caravan holiday with them. 'You see – she's all right in a *house*,' he said to Diana. 'But in a small caravan, with hardly any room – won't she get fussed? We shall be so much on top of one another.'

'Oh well – Mummy must have someone to take turns

at driving the car that pulls the caravan,' said Diana.'And she'll be company for Mummy, too. She's quite good fun – if only she won't keep making us be tidy, and wash our hands and knees a dozen times a day, and . . .'

'What are you two gossiping about?' said their mother, hurrying out to the caravan with some more things, 'If we're going to start off at eleven, we'd better hurry! We've got to pick Miss Pepper up at two o'clock, you know – and that means going over thirty miles an hour if we don't start punctually. Too fast for a car with a caravan!'

'I wish Daddy was coming,' groaned Diana, helping her mother to pack in more luggage. 'Miss Pepper's all right – but Daddy's such fun on a holiday.'

'Yes – it's a pity,' said her mother. 'But at least we haven't got to put up with Snubby this time!'

'Gosh yes – Snubby with us in a small caravan – and Loony too – would be just about the limit!' said Roger. 'Who's he staying with these hols?'

Snubby was their cousin, a ginger-haired, freckled, snub-nosed twelve-year-old boy. He had no father or mother, and so spent his holiday with one or other of his aunts and uncles. Snubby by himself was bad enough, but with his quite mad dog, Loony, a beautiful black spaniel, - he was enough to drive even the most patient aunt and uncle out of their minds.

'He's staying with Auntie Pat, I think,' said Diana. 'Isn't he, Mummy? I bet he's driving her crazy. Last time he stayed with her, Loony got a passion for goloshes, and he took every single one from the hall cupboard and hid them in the rhododendron bushes . . .'

'And the gardener couldn't believe his eyes when he saw them, and he called Snubby, and Snubby asked him why he had sown golosh seed under the rhododendrons!' said Roger, with a sudden snort of laughter.

'Good old Snubby! He *is* a pest, but honestly you can't help laughing at him half the time,' said Diana. 'I bet he wishes he was coming on this caravan holiday with us.'

'Well, thank goodness he's not,' said their Mother. 'Pack those rugs in the corner there, Diana. I really think that's about all. Now I'll go in and see that we've got absolutely everything – and if we have we'd better start.'

She hurried indoors. Diana looked round the neat little caravan, wondering how long it would be before it was anything but neat! She and her Mother and Miss Pepper were to sleep in it at night, and Roger was to sleep in the back of the car. What fun to travel round the countryside, going where they liked – not knowing what county they would sleep in at night – waking up when they liked. Yes – this was going to be something *like* a holiday!'

'There's just one thing I do *wish*,' said Diana to Roger, as they went indoors to say goodbye to their cook and daily woman. 'I wish and wish that old Barney was coming with us.'

'Gosh – so do I!' said Roger. 'And Miranda his monkey too. Dear little Miranda. We haven't seen her for ages.'

'Well, Barney's been travelling about with his father,' said Diana. 'I wonder if he often thinks how he travelled about before – you know, when he was a child and didn't know who his father was, and went about with the people of circuses and fairs. He did plenty of travelling then!'

'And now he's found his father – and a real family of his own – and he's no longer a poor circus boy, all alone in the world,' said Roger. 'And Miranda isn't a lonely little monkey, going everywhere with him, often hungry and cold – but a spoilt little pet, loved by every single one of Barney's family! And thank goodness, Barney hasn't changed a bit.'

'No – he's still the same kind, strong Barney,' said Diana. 'I do hope we see him these hols. Mummy!

7

Mummy, where are you? We really ought to start, you know.'

'Just coming!' called their mother, hurrying downstairs. 'I remembered I must find the sunburn lotion, in case we all get too burnt for words, in this hot weather. Go and say goodbye, dears – and then we'll start.'

Diana and Roger said goodbye to their cheery old cook, and she pressed a bag into their hands. 'Just a few of my special sugar biscuits to keep you going till dinner-time,' she said. 'Have a good time! And see and look after your mother; she's tired after all the packing up.'

At last they were in the car, and it moved slowly towards the front gate, pulling the caravan behind it. Fortunately the gates were wide and the posts were not even scraped. Away they went down the lane, the caravan running smoothly behind them, rocking just a little now and again when they went over a rut. Soon they were out on the main road – the holiday had begun!

They stopped for a picnic lunch on the way, and then drove on towards Miss Pepper's. 'We shall be late,' said Roger, 'but it doesn't matter, Mummy – Miss Pepper would be *most* surprised if we were punctual!'

'I dare say – but she's sure to be quite ready ten minutes beforehand,' said his mother. 'And I shall feel just as I used to when she looked after me in my teens – very very guilty!'

Miss Pepper was waiting for them on her doorstep, her suitcases beside her. She looked as tall and thin as ever, but her eyes twinkled as usual behind their glasses, and she smiled warmly.

'Well, here you all are, bless you!' she said. 'And wonder of wonders not more than fifteen minutes late! Had your dinner?'

'Yes, Miss Pepper,' said everyone, and Roger leapt out to take her luggage. He stowed it away in the caravan.

'What a fine caravan!' said Miss Pepper approvingly. 'Well, well – I never thought I'd ever sleep in a caravan – and here I am, quite looking forward to it!'

'I'll drive on for some way,' said the children's mother. 'Then you can take a short turn at driving if you will. We thought we'd make for that lovely little lake at Yesterley. The children can bathe then. Isn't it a mercy it's such glorious weather?'

'It certainly is,' said Miss Pepper, settling herself in the front seat. 'Dear me – it seems strange not to have Snubby with us. He's always come with the children when I've been with them before.'

'He's staying with Auntie Pat – and I expect he's driving her mad,' said Diana. 'All the same, I wish his dog Loony was with us – darling Loony – I do love him.'

'H'm,' said Miss Pepper, doubtfullly. 'I'm fond of him too – but I don't think I should be fond of him long if he went for a caravan holiday with us. He's not a very *restful* dog.'

It was very pleasant driving along that sunny day, with three weeks stretching before them, lazy, lovely weeks, full of picnics, bathes, ice-creams – and perhaps sleeping out in the open air instead of in the caravan? Roger made up his mind to suggest it that very first night – not for his mother or Miss Pepper, just for himself and Diana.

The car purred on and on – where would they stop for the night? Nobody knew and nobody cared. The caravan rolled on behind them, and every now and again Roger looked back to make sure it was still safely there.

'We're going to have fun!' he said to Diana. 'For three whole weeks – nothing but fun!'

Chapter Two

Very Unexpected!

For five days Roger and Diana had a truly wonderful time. For two nights they stayed by the lovely blue lake at Yesterley, and picnicked and bathed. Miss Pepper surprised them all by producing a bathing suit, and bathing too – and what was more she was a very fine swimmer indeed!

'Goodness!' said Diana, lying panting on the white sand that edged the lake. 'Goodness! I had a swimming race with Miss Pepper – and she beat me. And look, she's still swimming, and I've had to come out and rest.'

'She's jolly good,' said Roger. 'So's Mummy, actually. I wish I could float as long as she can – she just goes on and on – and yet it's not salt water! She must waggle her hands about, or something.'

'This is the kind of holiday I like,' said Diana. 'Wasn't it fun last night, sleeping out on the heather? Did you hear that owl hooting just by us? It nearly made me jump out of my skin.'

'Didn't hear a thing,' said Roger. 'I just shut my eyes – and never knew anything till you shook me awake this morning. How long are Mummy and Miss Pepper staying in the water? I'm hungry.'

They were all hungry those first five days, even Miss Pepper, who became quite ashamed of the enormous appetite she suddenly discovered.

'I do wish you wouldn't look so surprised, you two, when I take a third helping,' she said. 'You make me feel greedy – and really, it's only just that I'm very hungry.'

'Aha! *Snubby* would like to hear you say that!' said Roger. 'You always used to tell him he wasn't *really* hungry when he wanted a third helping – but just Plain Greedy!'

'Dear Snubby!' said Miss Pepper. 'I do wonder how he is getting on these holidays. Let me see now – your Auntie Pat hasn't any children, has she – so Snubby won't have anyone to play with. I'm afraid he may make himself a bit of a nuisance.'

'More than a *bit*,' said Diana. 'He can behave like a lunatic when he's bored. He thinks of the most awful things to do. Don't you remember how he thought he'd sweep our chimney one day, when it smoked a little, and then . . .'

'Don't *talk* of it,' said her mother, with a groan. 'I can't bear even to remember that day. I know your father nearly went mad, and chased Snubby round and round the garden with the chimney brush.'

'And fell over Loony,' said Diana.

'Yes. Funny the way Loony *always* gets under the feet of anyone who's angry with Snubby,' said Roger. 'Remarkably clever dog, Loony.'

Each night the four of them sat in the caravan and listened to the news on their portable radio. They hadn't seen a single newspaper since they had set off on their holiday, but as Miss Pepper said, it didn't do to cut themselves off *completely* from everything.

'Someone might have landed on the moon – or started a war – or had an earthquake,' said Miss Pepper. 'We had better listen in just once a day.'

On the fifth night, they were as usual sitting in the caravan, listening to the evening news on the little radio. The children listened with only half an ear, until the announcer came to the weather. that was *really* important! Was the weather *still* going to be warm and sunny?

11

The news came to an end. It had been very dull – a new strike – a long speech by somebody important – a new kind of aeroplane tested – and then there came a message that made them all sit up at once.

Miss Pepper was just about to turn off the radio, when the voice spoke urgently.

'Here is a message, please, for Mrs Lynton, who with her children, is on a caravan tour. Will she please telephone Hillsley 68251 at once, as her sister is dangerously ill? I will repeat that. Here is a message for . . .'

No one spoke for a few seconds, or even moved, as the message was repeated. Then Diana whispered. 'Mummy – it's us they are trying to reach! You're Mrs Lynton – and oh Mummy, does it mean . . .'

'It means that something's happened to your mother's sister – your Aunt Pat,' said Miss Pepper, getting up at once. 'Don't worry too much, my dear – we'll drive straight off to a telephone box, and find out what's wrong.'

'Oh dear – what *can* have happened?' said Mrs Lynton, looking very pale. 'I'll have to go back – I'll have to go to Pat. Oh, I feel quite dazed.'

The children felt dazed too. What a dreadful thing to happen in the middle of a lovely holiday! Poor Auntie Pat – what *could* have happened – 'Dangerously ill' – that sounded very frightening.

'You two children stay here in the caravan,' said Miss Pepper briskly, taking charge as usual. 'I'll drive your mother to the nearest village and we'll telephone. We'll get back here as soon as possible. Cheer up, Diana – don't look so upset, dear. It may not be as bad as it sounds.'

In two minutes Miss Pepper was driving the car down the lane, the children's mother sitting silently beside her. Roger and Diana went outside the caravan, and sat down in the heather. It was a very light night, and, although they could not see to read, they could just see each other's faces. Diana was crying.

Roger gave her a quick hug. 'It mayn't be so bad,' he said. 'I expect Mummy will have to go back, though. We'll have to as well, I suppose.'

'But how can we?' wept Diana. 'Cook's away now, and the house is shut up. There'd be nobody there.'

'I'd forgotten that. And what about old Snubby?' said Roger. 'He can't stay at Auntie Pat's if she's ill – or gone to hospital. What's to happen to *him*?'

'And to us too,' said Diana. 'Mummy will certainly stay to look after Aunt Pat. She's so fond of her. Oh what an *awful* thing to happen in the middle of such a lovely holiday!'

It seemed a very long time before their mother came back with Miss Pepper. The children heard the car coming in the darkness and stood up at once. They ran to it as soon as their mother got out.

'But it wasn't their mother! It was Miss Pepper – and it wasn't their car either, it was a taxi!

'Oh – what's happened? Where's Mummy?' cried Diana.

'Gone off in the car to see to your auntie,' said Miss Pepper, paying the taxi-driver. 'She's had a fall and hurt her head, and the doctors thought she might die. But they've just given your mother a better report of her, and have asked her to get back as soon as she can, as your aunt keeps calling for her.'

'Oh! Poor Mummy!' said Diana, thinking of her mother driving fast through the night, all alone, worrying about her sister. 'Oh, Miss Pepper – do you think Auntie Pat will be all right?'

'From the doctor's latest report, I should think she *will*,' said Miss Pepper, comfortingly. 'So don't fret too

13

much. It's silly to cross bridges before you come to them. Mummy sent you her love, and she says she'll give us the latest news in the morning, if I go into the village to telephone. It's not very far.'

'Will Mummy come back here, and go on with our holiday?' asked Roger.

'No. No, I think I can say that quite definitely,' said Miss Pepper. 'I'm pretty sure she will want to stay with your Aunt Pat till she's really on the mend. We had no time to decide exactly what to do – but I'm afraid you'll have to put up with *me* for a bit, my dears! I promised your mother I'd be with you till she can have you home again.'

'But – what are our plans now, then?' asked Roger feeling rather dazed. 'We've this caravan – but no car – and our house is shut up. Will we leave the caravan here and go and stay with *you*, Miss Pepper?'

'I really do *not* know, Roger dear,' said Miss Pepper. 'Shall we leave everything till tomorrow? Things like this do happen, you know – and then we often find out how strong – or weak – we are! Your mother now, was full of courage as soon as she got over the shock; she was ready to face up to anything!'

'What about poor Snubby?' said Diana. 'He's staying with Auntie Pat. Oh, Miss Pepper – Auntie Pat didn't fall over Loony, did she?'

'No – she slipped off a ladder,' said Miss Pepper. 'Now – I'm going to open a bottle of orangeade, and find those chocolate biscuits and macaroons we had over from lunch – and we're going to have a nice little supper.'

The two children felt glad to have Miss Pepper with them. She was cheerful and brisk, and even made one or two little jokes. Roger felt more cheerful too, after his supper, but Diana was still scared and upset.

'Roger, would you like to sleep in your mother's bunk

14

tonight in the caravan with Diana and me?' Miss Pepper asked. 'I expect Diana would like you in here with us to-night.'

'Yes. Yes. I'd like to sleep here instead of in the open,' said Roger, and Diana nodded, pleased. Now if she was awake in the night and felt scared and sad, she could talk to Roger. Brothers were good to have when things went wrong!

Soon the caravan was in darkness, while three people tried to get to sleep. What news would the morning bring? Good – or bad? And what was going to happen to their holiday?

Chapter Three

Good Old Barney

Next morning Miss Pepper was up bright and early, and woke the two children. 'Wake up!' she said. 'We'll have breakfast and then I'll pop down to the village and telephone your mother. Did you sleep well?'

'Yes, I did,' said Diana, rather surprised, for she had felt sure that she wouldn't sleep at all. Roger had slept well too, and both of them felt more ready to face up to whatever news they would hear.

Miss Pepper made the tea, and Diana cut the bread. Soon they were eating cold ham, and drinking the hot tea. 'Though really, why we don't have orangeade this hot morning, instead of this scalding tea, I can't think!' said Diana.

Immediately after breakfast Miss Pepper set off briskly to the village. She was back in half an hour and the children, who were anxiously looking out for her, ran to meet her, most relieved to see a smile on her face.

'Better news,' said Miss Pepper at once. 'Your mother arrived safely, and your aunt was so glad to see her – and she has taken a turn for the better already.

'Good, good, good!' said Diana, thankfully.

'Apparently she fell from the top of a ladder when she was tying up some ramblers on the wall,' said Miss Pepper. 'And she hit her head on the stone path. Nothing to do with Loony at all! She's in hospital, and your mother is with her. And I'm afraid your mother will have to stay away for quite a while, because there is no one to look after your uncle – so your mother says she'll spend part of her time seeing to your uncle and the other part with your aunt.'

'Oh. Then what's to happen to *us*?' said Diana at once.

'Well, I suppose I'll have to try and hire a car and take the caravan back to my own home,' said Miss Pepper. 'You'll have to come with me, I'm afraid, as your own house is shut up. I'm sorry, dears – very very sorry. This is a horrid end to what was going to be one of your very best holidays. But I honestly don't see what else we can do.'

'I don't either,' said Roger gloomily. 'And I think it's jolly good of you to take all this trouble for us, Miss Pepper. I'm sure you don't want us in your little house! Oh dear – isn't this all horrid!'

'Diana can come with me to find out about a car,' said Miss Pepper as they cleared up the caravan and made up the bunks. 'And Roger can stay here with the caravan. That be all right, Roger?'

'Of course,' said Roger, still gloomy, and watched Miss Pepper go off to the village again, Diana by her side. What a mess up of a glorious holiday! Miss Pepper was good and kind – but the thought of living for two or three weeks in her tidy little house filled Roger with dread.

'We'll be too bored for words!' he thought and then reproached himself for being unkind. Whatever would they have done without Miss Pepper just now! 'We *might* have gone to stay with old Barney, if he hadn't been touring about the country with his father,' his thoughts ran on. 'Oh well – we'll just have to make the best of things, I suppose.'

Miss Pepper and Diana came back in an hour's time, looking depressed.

'We can't get a car anywhere in the village,' said Miss Pepper. 'So we telephoned the nearest town, and somebody is going to try there for us. I do hope we shan't

17

have to take some old crock that will break down halfway home! I'm not really very good at driving cars I don't know.'

Their caravan was set on a heathery hill, just off the road, not far from a farmhouse. The farmer had given them permission to stay on the hill – and, about three o'clock that afternoon, the three saw him coming up to their caravan.

'Oh dear – I hope he's not going to turn us off!' said Miss Pepper in a fright.

The farmer came slowly up to where they were all sitting outside the caravan, his dog at his heels.

'Good afternoon, Ma'am.' he said, in his pleasant country voice. 'There be a message come for you, sent to my farmhouse by the post office. Telegram it be.'

He held out the orange telegram and Miss Pepper took it, suddenly frightened. She tore it open and read it. Then she looked round at the two waiting children, puzzled.

'Listen,' she said, 'it says "Wait till you see us tonight, Barney".'

'Wait till you see us tonight!' echoed Diana, and her face suddenly lighted up. 'Oh, Miss Pepper! Barney and his father must have heard about Auntie Pat's accident, and how Mummy had to go to her, leaving us here! And they're coming here tonight! Oh, how WONDERFUL!'

'They must have heard the message on the radio last night, when we did!' said Roger. 'And they rang the Hillsley telephone number and found out what was happening. Miss PEPPER! Everything will be all right now! Barney's father will arrange about a car and everything. Oh, thank goodness!'

Diana gave a long sigh of relief, and her heart suddenly lightened. Barney was coming – and his nice father. Now things would soon be settled for them. Perhaps they could go and stay with Barney?

18

'Thank you,' said Miss Pepper to the farmer, and he nodded, and left, his dog still at his heels.

'*Wait till you see us tonight!*' said Diana, quoting the telegram again. 'That must mean that they are driving straight to us, wherever they are – and must be rather far away, or they would arrive before tonight. Good old Barney! Now we can just sit back and not worry.'

'You two had better go down to the river and have a bathe,' said Miss Pepper. 'It's so hot today. I won't come with you, because someone had better stay with the caravan. Go along now, and have a good swim. It will do you good.'

So off went Roger and Diana, feeling considerably happier because of Barney's telegram. How good it was to have friends – how very very good!

'We shall see dear little Miranda too,' said Diana happily. 'The best thing about animals is that they don't seem to change, as human beings do! Miranda must have looked the same ever since she was a year old!'

They had a long bathe, and then lay in the warm heather to dry. They were hungry when they got back to the caravan. 'Any news of Barney yet? Or another telegram?' asked Roger. Miss Pepper shook her head.

'No – but Barney said *"tonight"* in his telegram, you know. We shall have to wait in patience. I'm sure they must be down in Cornwall, or up in the north of Scotland or in the Welsh mountains – somewhere quite far away from here, anyway.'

'I'm not going to bed till they come,' said Roger firmly.

'I can't really expect you to!' said Miss Pepper. 'But I hope it's before twelve o'clock!'

The evening drew on, and the sun began to sink low down in the west. At every far off sound of a car going by on a distant road, the three of them stiffened and

19

listened – but car after car purred by in the distance and not one stopped, or came in their direction.

Then at last, just as it was getting really dark, the sound of a car jolting over the rough road next to the old farmhouse came to their ears. 'That *must* be Barney!' said Diana in excitement. They listened anxiously.

The car stopped – and then, a few minutes later they heard it starting up again in the silence of the evening. It was coming over the rough track that led to them!

'It's Barney! It must be!' cried Roger, leaping up. 'The villagers must have sent them to the farm, and the farmer has told them where we are. Barney! BARNEY! BARNEY!'

An answering shout came to their ears. 'Hey! We're coming! The track's rough, though!'

Soon a big car came to a stop beside the caravan, and a tall figure leapt out; Roger and Diana ran to meet it – and to greet dear old Barney, with little Miranda the monkey on his shoulder, chattering excitedly.

'Hallo, hallo!' cried Barney, and hugged both Diana and Roger. 'Sorry to be so long coming – we were right away in Scotland! Heard the news on the radio last night, of course, and telephoned to your mother at Hillsley. How are you?'

'Oh, BARNEY, it's so lovely to have you,' said Diana. 'We simply didn't know WHAT to do when Mummy had to go off and leave us. Is that your father getting out of the car now?'

'Yes. We can leave everything to him,' said Barney, very happy to be with his friends again. 'Every single thing! He's got a marvellous plan. Hallo, Miss Pepper! Isn't this a surprise?'

'It certainly is,' said Miss Pepper. 'Ah, here's your father! Good evening – it *is* good of you to come to us like this!'

'We'll soon fix up some plans,' said Barney's father

shaking hands. 'Sorry about this trouble. Let's go into that fine caravan of yours and talk.'

And in they all went, Miranda the monkey too, chattering loudly, leaping from one shoulder to another and making Roger and Diana laugh in glee. Good old Barney – dear little Miranda – it really was wonderful to see them again!

Chapter Four

A Wonderful Idea

It seemed quite a crowd in the little caravan. Miss Pepper
lighted the safety-lamp, and they all looked at one
another, blinking. Barney's brilliant blue eyes shone as
he looked round at everyone. He was as brown as a berry,
as usual, and his grin just as wide as ever!

His father spoke to Miss Pepper. 'We rang up again
tonight to see how Mrs Lynton's sister was, and she is
just a little better – and will certainly recover well now –
but it will take time.'

'Thank goodness it's better news,' said Miss Pepper. 'It
was such a terrible shock last night. I am so glad to see
you, Mr Martin – I really was worried about what to do
for the best.'

'Well, don't worry any more,' said Mr Martin. 'What
I propose is that I should hitch my car on to your caravan
and . . .'

'And take us home?' said Roger. But our house is shut
up, Mr Martin!'

'Yes, I know that,' said Barney's father. 'And I know
too that it must be a great disappointment to you, to have
your three weeks' holiday broken up – so I think that if
you all joined Barney – or let him join you, which ever
way you like to put it – that would solve your difficulties.'

'You mean – we could have your car to drive the caravan about?' asked Miss Pepper. 'Oh dear – if you mean
me to drive it, Mr Martin, I'm afraid I couldn't. It's so
big, and . . .'

'No, no – I didn't mean that,' said Mr Martin. 'I'll

22

explain. Barney and I are on a week's holiday – and it is almost up, because I have to get back. What I propose is that I hitch up to your caravan, and we go off tomorrow and find some really nice place for you all to stay in – somewhere near a little inn, perhaps, so that you and Diana can sleep indoors there, and the two boys can sleep in the caravan, and . . .'

'Oh! What a WONDERFUL idea!' said Diana, her eyes shining. 'Some place by the sea, perhaps?'

'We'll see,' said Mr Martin, smiling at her excited face. 'If we can find a good spot tomorrow, I'll leave you all there, with the caravan, and drive back home. Miss Pepper will keep an eye on you, I know! When the time comes for you to leave, I'll drive up and fetch the caravan. What do you think of that?'

'Oh – too good to be true!' said Roger. 'I honestly thought we'd have to go home and look after ourselves in an empty house! It's awfully good of you, sir – and of course, solves all our problems – except one!'

'And what problem's that?' asked Mr Martin.

'Well – about Snubby,' said Roger.

'What's going to happen to him?'

'Can't he come with us?' said Diana, eagerly. 'There's room in the caravan for three – or he could sleep in whatever inn or hotel Miss Pepper and I go to.'

'Dear me – I'd forgotten about Snubby!' said Mr Martin. 'Of course he can come too. He was staying with the aunt who's ill, wasn't he, poor fellow. We'll telephone your mother and tell her to send him up to us, when we've decided where you're going to stay.'

Diana heaved a great sigh. 'I was so worried about everything,' she said. 'And now all the troubles are smoothed out. Thank you very much, Mr Martin. And to think we'll have Barney and Miranda with us too!

23

Miranda, do you hear that? You're coming on holiday with us now!'

Miranda heard her name, and chattered in delight. She leapt to Diana's shoulder and pulled her hair gently, pretending to whisper into her ear.

'You dear, funny little thing,' said Diana, fondling her. 'Fancy having you with us too – what a treat!'

'Can I offer you some cocoa – or some orangeade?' asked Miss Pepper. 'I'm afraid there's nothing very exciting to give you for supper.'

'Oh, I nearly forgot!' said Barney, getting up. 'We've got a whole lot of stuff in the car. We didn't stop to have meals at hotels today, we just bought bread and ham and fruit and tomatoes, and ate them as we drove along. We so badly wanted to get here as soon as possible. I'll go and bring some of it in.'

'How lovely!' said Diana. 'I don't know why, but I suddenly feel frightfully hungry.'

'It's because your worries are gone, dear!' said Miss Pepper. 'I feel a bit hungry myself too! It is truly good of you, Mr Martin, to come to our aid like this.'

'Ah well – you've been kind to Barney many a time,' said Mr Martin. 'Hey, what's that monkey doing?'

'Oh – she's got my sponge!' said Diana, with a delighted giggle. 'Miranda, give it to me! Oh look, she's washing her face with it, just as she's seen me do at times. Miranda, that's *my* sponge!'

'Now she's put it into her mouth!' said Miss Pepper. 'Oh, the naughty little thing! Surely she's not thinking of eating it, Diana!'

Barney deftly removed the sponge, and scolded the little monkey, who at once covered her face with her arms, and sat in a corner giving little moans.

'Don't pretend like that!' said Barney, going out of the

24

caravan. 'You're not a bit sorry. I'll be back in half a jiffy, everyone. See Miranda doesn't get your soap, Di!'

Barney was soon back with paper bags and tins. Then they all settled down to a first-rate supper of ham, tomatoes, cheese, ripe plums and orangeade.

'What are you going to do tonight – about sleeping, I mean,' said Miss Pepper to Mr Martin. 'It's such a lovely night, I expect the children will sleep out of doors again, on the heather, with a rug around them. But you won't want to do that, Mr Martin.'

'No. I'd rather go to the little inn in the village,' said Barney's father. 'Barney can stay here with you, of course. I'd like to telephone Mrs Lynton tonight and tell her we'll have Snubby as soon as we can. Tomorrow we'll decide where we'll go – and then I'll let Mrs Lynton know where to send Snubby. Well – I'll say goodnight, I think. I can see Diana yawning her head off!'

'Good night, sir,' said Roger, 'and thanks most awfully. See you tomorrow!' Everyone went to the car to see Mr Martin off, and soon he was jolting slowly over the little track that led back to the farmhouse.

'And now it's bed for all of us,' said Miss Pepper briskly. 'My word, I feel different now – everything straightened out so well! I just wish your mother hadn't had her holiday spoilt, though she won't mind so long as your aunt is on the mend!'

The two boys went out to find a thick patch of heather. 'We'll wash in the stream tomorrow morning,' yawned Roger, settling down on a rug. 'Here – there's enough rug for you and Miranda, Barney.'

Miranda cuddled up into Barney's neck, chattering in his ear. He was sleepy and didn't answer, and she tweaked his hair.

'Now look here, Miranda,' said Barney, undoing her

tiny fingers from his hair, 'I will *not* have you pulling my hair when I want to go to sleep. Settle down!'

And Miranda settled down meekly, her small brown face hidden in his neck. Barney patted her and smiled. What a funny little thing she was!

Miss Pepper and Diana slept in the caravan with the door wide open for air. Miss Pepper sighed with relief as she closed her eyes. Things were turning out better then she had hoped!

In the morning quite early, Mr Martin was back again in the car, complete with new-laid eggs, new-made bread, butter and fresh milk from the farm. 'And very nice too!' said Miss Pepper approvingly. 'Miranda – leave that egg alone!'

'I've been looking at a map,' said Mr Martin, after breakfast, and spread a large one out on the heathery ground, where they had all sat having breakfast in the warm sun. 'The thing we have to decide is where to go! Any ideas, anyone?'

'Somewhere by the sea,' said Roger at once. 'If this hot weather goes on, we'll want to bathe.'

'Not in a big town,' said Miss Pepper. 'Somewhere small and countrified.'

'Somewhere where I can watch birds,' said Diana. 'I've got a holiday essay to write on "Birds I have seen".'

'Oh, don't start talking about that essay again!' said Roger. 'I bet you don't watch for a single bird the whole time!'

Diana glared at him, and Miss Pepper hurriedly interrupted. 'There are birds everywhere, Diana – we really don't need to look for any *special* bird-haunt. Barney, what kind of place would *you* like?'

'Well – I hate modern holiday spots, where there are crowds of people,' said Barney. 'I'd rather go to some quiet old place – where we can laze about in old clothes,

26

do exactly what we like, and not have to bother with anyone else at all.'

'I think we are all pretty well agreed then,' said Miss Pepper. 'But where shall we find a place like that in the middle of summer? Most places by the sea are so crowded now.'

'We'll go somewhere on this hilly Welsh coast, I think,' said Mr Martin, tracing a route with his finger. 'It's lovely country round there. I vote we start off straightaway, and cruise along by the sea – and we'll stop as soon as we find the place we want. Come along – let's pack up and go at once!'

Chapter Five

A Halt For Ice-Creams

Before long they were all on their way. Mr Martin's car was a big one, and there was plenty of room for them all. The caravan swayed along behind, and Mr Martin had to keep remembering that his car was pulling it, and try not to swing round corners too fast!

They drove until lunchtime, and then had a picnic by the roadside, in a little wood. They looked at the map again. 'Soon be by the sea,' said Mr Martin, following the map with his fingers. 'Then we'll look out for a likely spot for you. We'll drive straight through all the big seaside towns, and dawdle along the coast looking for what we want.'

'This is fun!' said Diana. 'Oh, Miranda – you'll be sick! Barney, that's the fourth plum she's taken.'

Barney took away the plum, and Miranda flew into a rage. She leapt onto his head, pulling one of his ears till he shouted. Then she was sorry and tried to creep down his neck, under his shirt.

'Really, you can't help laughing at the naughty little thing!' said Miss Pepper. 'What shall we do when Snubby arrives with that mad spaniel Loony, I don't know! There'll be no peace for anybody!'

'Well, I must say I'm as pleased we haven't that pair in the car with us yet,' said Mr Martin, rolling up the map. 'A mad dog, an idiotic boy, and a naughty monkey would certainly be too much for any driver!'

They drove off again. They came to a big seaside town packed with trippers, noisy and full of litter. 'Straight through here,' said Mr Martin firmly. 'And the next one too. After that we come to a lonely part of the coast, and we'll keep our eyes open.'

Through that town they went, and then right through the next, without stopping. Ah – now they were leaving behind the crowded part of the coast, and coming to deserted bays, lonely sweeps of sand, tiny villages, fishing hamlets. Hills rose up from the coast, and the car had to take a roundabout route, going slowly because of the caravan behind it.

'This looks more like what we want,' said Diana, looking out of the car window at the sea on one side and hills on the other. 'Mr Martin – do you think we could stop for an ice-cream sometime? I'm simply too hot for words, even with all the windows open!'

'Good idea!' said Mr Martin, and he stopped at the next village – a tiny place that ran down to the sea. But there was no shop that sold ice-cream! 'You go on to Penrhyndendraith,' said the woman they asked. 'That's got a fine ice-cream shop there. And if the young ones want a bathe, you tell them to go to Merlin's Cove – there's the finest bathing there in the kingdom.'

'That sounds fine,' said Roger, and they once more drove on. Round the coast they went, with the sea splashing on one side, and the mountains on the other – for now the hills had grown higher, and some of them towered up into the sky.

'Grand country!' said Mr Martin. 'Now – where is this Penny-denny-draith place. Ah – that looks like it – see, built on the slope of the hill.'

They came to Penrhyndendraith. It was a truly picturesque place, a fishing village, with a dozen or so old cottages built along the seafront and others straggling up the slope of the hill behind.

Above the cottages on the hill rose a strange old place

with curious turrets and towers. It was set right against a cliff-like hill, so that the back of it had no windows at all. Some of it was falling to pieces, and it looked in places as if only the ivy held it together!

A signboard was set over the great old doorway, but it was too far away for the children to read what was on it. Diana was more interested in finding the ice-cream shop than in looking at the half-ruined building on the hill. She jogged Mr Martin's arm gently. 'Look – would that be where the ice-cream shop is?' she asked, and pointed to the crooked row of cottages.

Mr Martin stopped the car near them. 'Well, as I can see only one that looks like a shop, that must be it!' he said. 'Yes – see what it says over the door. "Myfanwy Jones, General Dealer".'

'And look – it says "Ice-Cream"!' said Roger. 'In the corner of the window, see? Come on – let's get out of the car.'

So out they jumped and went to the little shop. What a curious place it was! Inside it was very dark, and there was little space to stand, because of the hundreds of things that the shop sold! The goods were piled on the floor, they hung from the walls, they swung from the ceiling!

'It must sell simply everything in the world!' said Diana in astonishment. 'Eatables, drinkables, china, pots and pans, fishing-nets, Miss Pepper, it's like a shop out of an old fairy-tale!'

'And here's the witch!' whispered Roger, and got a frown from Miss Pepper, as an old woman waddled behind the small counter. Her face was a mass of wrinkles, and her snowy white hair was tucked away under a little cap of black net. But old though she looked, her eyes were startlingly bright and piercing.

She spoke to them in Welsh, which they didn't understand. Diana pointed to a card that said "Ice-Cream" and the old lady nodded, and smiled suddenly.

'Two? Three? Four?' she said in English.

'Oooh – twenty!' said Roger at once, and everyone laughed, the old woman too.

'How big are your ice-creams?' asked Diana. The old woman took a scoop and scooped some from an ice-box – a good large helping, which she slapped between wafers.

'Ah – I think two each will be enough for the children,' said Miss Pepper, 'and one each for the grown-ups. What about Miranda, Barney?'

'Oh, one for her,' said Barney. 'She'll probably put most of it on the top of her head, because she's so hot!'

'There is a big seat outside,' said the old lady, nodding her head, as the children took the ice-creams, and they took the hint and went to sit on the hard old wooden bench.

'Not much taste – but VERY creamy and deliciously cold,' said Barney. 'Miranda, please go and sit on the ground. I DO NOT like you to dribble ice-cream all down my neck. Nor do I like it held against my ear. SIT ON THE GROUND!'

The little monkey leapt down to the ground, chattering, holding her ice-cream tightly in her paw. The old lady who was very interested in Miranda, came out to watch her.

'Very good little monkey,' she said, in her lilting Welsh voice. 'You come far?'

'Quite a long way,' said Barney.

'You go far?' said the old lady.

'We don't know. We are looking for somewhere quiet to stay,' said Barney. 'Somewhere near here, perhaps. It is such a lovely country. We don't want a big place, with big hotels – but perhaps a quiet old inn, and . . .'

'Ah, then you go up there, see?' said the old lady, and pointed up to the strange, half-ruined place they had seen on the hills. 'Quiet, very quiet – and the food is, it is so good, so good. And here, it is beautiful, with the sea so blue, and the sand so white, and . . .'

'But – is that old place occupied then?' said Mr Martin, astonished. 'I thought it was just an empty ruin.'

'No, no – my son, he keeps it,' said the old lady proudly. 'It is an inn, sir, you understand? And what food! Big men come here, sir, important men – they say how good the food, how good!'

Nobody could believe that important people would stay at the half-ruined place. The old woman saw that they did not believe her, and she grasped Mr Martin's arm.

'I speak the truth,' she said. 'To my son's inn come Sir Richard Ballinor, and Professor Hallinan, and . . .'

Mr Martin knew those names; 'One is a famous botonist, and the other is a well-known ornithologist – a man who studies birds,' he told the astonished children. He turned to the old lady.

'There are many flowers here, then?' he said. 'And rare birds?'

'Yes, many, many – up in the hills – and round the coves and on the cliffs,' said the old lady, nodding her head. 'Big men come to study them, I tell you, sir. My son, he knows them all. His cooking pleases them, sir, it is good, very good. You go to stay there too, sir? He has not many people now, it is a good time. Very good cooking, sir.'

'Well – we might as well go up and see the old place,' said Mr Martin, taking out some money to pay for the ice-creams. 'Thanks very much, Mrs Jones. We enjoyed your ice-creams. Is there a road up to the old inn?'

'It is very rough, sir. You must go slowly,' said the old woman, smiling delightedly at the thought that they were really going to see her son's place. 'Cooking very good sir, very very good.'

They all went off to their car. 'She's got good cooking on the brain,' said Roger. 'I wonder what the old place is like? It *might* be fun to stay there – there's all we want here, really – fine bathing . . .'

'Wonderful walks, I should think,' said Barney, who loved walking. 'And a jolly fine view.'

'Fishing,' said Roger, watching a small fishing-boat on the bay, its sails filling out with the wind.

'No trippers,' said Miss Pepper.

'And birds for me!' said Diana happily.

'You and your birds!' said Roger scornfully, and Diana immediately gave him a punch.

'Well – up to the inn we go!' said Mr Martin, as they started off slowly up the steep track, leaving the caravan behind for the time being. 'And what shall we find there, I wonder?'

Chapter Six

Penrhyndendraith Inn

The car crawled up the steep hill, on the zig-zagging track. The higher they went, the more magnificent the views became.

Diana gasped when she looked down the hill and saw the wonderful bay, and the great stretch of heaving sea beyond.

'Oh, *look*!' she said. 'How lucky the people are who live in that old inn, Miss Pepper, and look out on that view every day. And see – the view across the hills is glorious too – are those mountains beyond?'

'Yes. And beautiful ones too!' said Miss Pepper. 'Did you ever see such a blaze of heather – why, the hills look on fire with it! My goodness me – I can't help hoping that it will be possible for us to stay in the inn. I've never seen such views in my life!'

At last they reached the old inn. It really looked rather like a half-ruined castle! The great sign above the open door gave its name.

PENRHYNDENDRAITH INN

'Goodness knows how it's pronounced,' said Diana. 'I say – isn't it dark inside! What do we do? Ring the bell?'

'Yes, if there is one – but there isn't,' said Roger, looking all round. 'No knocker either. What do we do? Yell?'

'IS ANYONE HERE?' shouted Barney obligingly, and they all jumped at his enormous yell. A small boy with an untidy shock of hair came running round a corner, followed by a great grey goose. He shouted out something to them in Welsh, and then disappeared into the open doorway, followed by the waddling goose.

'Well – I *imagine* that he and the goose have gone to find the owner of the inn,' said Miss Pepper. 'Ah – here comes someone!'

A lively little woman came hurrying up the hallway to the door, followed by the small boy, the goose still tagging along behind.

'Good afternoon,' said Mr Martin politely. 'Er – Mrs Jones down in the village told us of this inn, and . . .'

The plump little woman smiled all over her face, and rattled out an answer at top speed.

'Oh yes, sir, yes, sir, that would be my mother-in-law, sir, she knows this place well, and a good inn it is, no doubt about that, sir, we get important people here, sir, you should just peep into our visiting books, oh, the fine manes that are there, and my husband, Llewellyn, he is the best cook in the world, sir, he went to London to learn his cooking, sir, in one of the big hotels, very good cooking, oh very . . .'

'Er – what I wanted to ask,' put in Mr Martin, afraid the the lively woman would never stop, 'what I wanted to know was . . .'

'Oh yes, sir, you ask me anything,' said the woman, smiling and nodding. 'Come in, sir, won't you, and see what a wonderful place this is, and oh, the cooking, sir, well can you smell what's baking now, sir? That's my husband, sir, he's always cooking, he's . . .'

This sounded exactly as if her husband was being baked, and Diana gave a sudden giggle. They followed the woman into the great dark entrance, the boy and the goose behind them. Talking all the time, she showed them an enormous, rather delapidated dining-room, and then took them up some stone stairs, uncarpeted, to the bedrooms.

'The beds are comfortable, sir, the view is fine, just you look, sir, did you ever see anything like it?'

Certainly the view was wonderful, and everyone gasped to see it. 'And we don't charge a great deal, sir,' rattled on the little woman. 'You come to us, sir, if you want to stay in these parts, I tell you the cooking is fine, sir, very good cooking!'

Miranda the monkey, stopped the flow of talk quite suddenly, by flinging herself on the grey goose's back. The goose was simply amazed, and began to cackle so loudly that it made everyone jump. The small boy ran to take the monkey off its back, and Miranda promptly jumped on to his shoulder. He screamed in fright and Miranda leapt back to Barney.

'Sorry about that,' said Barney to the surprised woman. 'It was just that Miranda wanted to see what sort of creature the goose was. I don't believe she's seen one before. Er – is the goose *safe*?'

The great bird was advancing on him, its enormous wings flapping, cackling at the top of its voice.

'Take Waddle away,' said the woman crossly to the small boy. 'He must not come indoors. Always I am telling you that.' She turned to the others, but before she could begin one of her long speeches again, Mr Martin spoke firmly to her.

'This is my son, and these other children are his friends. This lady, Miss Pepper, is with them, but I go back home today. Another boy, and a dog, will come soon. Can you let them have meals here – and a bed for Miss Pepper and Diana? The others would sleep in a caravan we have.'

'Oh, sir, it would be an honour, it would be a pleasure to have them!' cried the talkative little woman. 'My name is Mrs Jones, sir, Mrs Llywellyn Jones, and certainly we will look after them all, they shall have the best food, sir, they shall go fishing with our men, they shall have picnics – and very good cooking, sir, and . . .'

'Well, thank you,' said Mr Martin, and turned to Miss Pepper. 'Would you like to stay here, Miss Pepper? I can see already that the children approve!'

'Yes, Mr Martin. I think this is just what we're looking for,' said Miss Pepper. 'The views and the walks will be enough for me – and as for the children, if they can fish and bathe and explore, that's all *they'll* want! Yes – I'd like to stay here.'

'Good, good, good!' cried Diana, and gave Miss Pepper such a sudden hug that she gasped. 'And Snubby will love it too, I know he will. When will he come, Mr Martin?'

'I'll telephone your mother as soon as I can, and arrange for him to come tomorrow, it possible,' said Mr Martin. 'He can come by train to the nearest big town, and then get a taxi to bring him here. And let's hope Loony gets on all right with that goose – what's his name – Waddle!'

'Well – what with Loony the spaniel, Miranda the monkey and Waddle the goose, we may have rather a hectic time,' said Miss Pepper, with a laugh. 'But I've coped with Snubby and Loony before, so I've no doubt I can manage!'

'You go now? You go back home?' said Mrs Jones anxiously to Mr Martin. 'You will not stay to have supper here, and taste the very good cooking?'

'No. I think not,' said Mr Martin. 'I'll go down and pick up the caravan and bring it up here, now that I know the others will be staying. Perhaps I could just have a cup of tea before I leave?'

'You shall, sir, yes, you shall have tea and good, buttery scones!' said Mrs Jones, and fled down the stairs as if she could smell the scones burning in the oven!

'Whew – what a non-stop talker!' said Roger. 'We're going to have some very one-sided conversations, I can see!'

'I don't mind. I like her,' said Diana. 'She goes on and on like a babbling steam, but she's quite interesting. Oh, I *am* glad we're going to stay here. Sniff the air, Miss Pepper – isn't it clean and – and – mountainy? I wonder what Snubby will say – I'm sure he'll love it.'

'Roger – you and Barney come down and help me with the caravan,' said Mr Martin. 'It may be a bit awkward getting it round those zig-zaggy corners – you'd better walk behind and yell to me if I'm not giving it enough room to swing round.'

'Right, sir,' said the two boys, and went down to the car with Mr Martin. They hopped in and went off to fetch the caravan, Miranda jigging excitedly on Barney's shoulder. Miss Pepper and Diana took the opportunity of peeping into the other bedrooms. 'They really look a bit like cells, with their stone walls and stone floors,' said Diana. 'Let's choose one with the best views, Miss Pepper.'

So they chose one with two windows, one window looking out over the sea, and the other into the mountains that rose one behind the other for miles. There were two small beds there, and the stone walls were partly draped with thick old curtains. A great chest stood against one wall, and Miss Pepper looked at it with interest.

'That must be pretty old,' she said. 'Our few belongings will be quite lost in there. And look at the ancient fireplace, Diana – you could almost put one of the beds in there!'

Diana went to the fireplace, and put her head up the chimney. 'I can see the sky!' she called. 'It's a most *enormous* chimney!'

A voice spoke to them from the door. It was Mrs Jones,

nodding and smiling. 'I will show you a better room,' she said. 'This is not so comfortable as the others.'

'But we *love* the view here,' said Miss Pepper, smiling. 'And it really looks very comfortable!'

'No. It is not the best room. Come, I will show it to you.'

And she took Miss Pepper's arm, and led her to another room, a little larger and better furnished. The view, however, was not nearly so beautiful.

'No. I'd rather have the other room,' said Miss Pepper firmly. 'Because of the view, you know.'

Mrs Jones looked suddenly sulky. 'I do not like you to have that room,' she said. 'It is not the best room. I will give you this one.'

But Miss Pepper was used to having her own way, and shook her head with a polite smile. 'No. I have chosen the other room. Now we will go down and see if Mr Martin has the luggage!'

And down they went to the great entrance, where Mr Martin and the boys were already waiting with the car and the caravan, having put the bags and suitcases down on the battered stone steps.

'What about my cup of tea?' said Mr Martin to Mrs Jones, smiling. 'And then we'll just fix up terms, and I'll go!'

'Your tea – your beautiful scones!' cried Mrs Jones and rushed off down the dark passageway, presumably to the kitchen. 'Wait just one minute, sir, just one minute. The cooking here is . . .'

'Very good!' finished everyone at once, and Mr Martin chuckled. 'What a woman! I should think she probably talks all night long in her sleep, wouldn't you?'

39

Chapter Seven

'Cooking Good! Very Good Cooking!'

When Mr Martin had gone, all the three children waving to him madly, and Miranda waving too, Roger put his hand over his tummy.

'Whew! What a tea Mrs Jones gave us! I never tasted such marvellous scones in my life! I had six!'

'Cooking good – very good cooking!' quoted Diana. 'Even Miranda had two scones. What's the time – just gone half past five, not too bad. What shall we do?'

'A little unpacking, please,' said Miss Pepper promptly. 'And a little arranging. I see that your father has put the caravan round the side of the inn, Barney, on that level piece. Is it safe there? There's such a slope down this hill.'

'I'd better put heavy stones under the wheels,' said Barney. 'In case that small boy thinks up anything funny! He looks a bit of a monkey to me. Come and help me, Roger.'

While the boys went to drag big stones to the wheels, Miss Pepper and Diana went upstairs to their room. They expected to find their luggage in the room with two windows that they had chosen, but it wasn't!

'Well! Don't tell me that Mrs Jones has put it in the Best Room that she kept trying to force on us!' said Miss Pepper crossly. 'Go and look, Diana.'

Diana went off to the Best Room, and came back at once. 'Yes, it's there! What a nerve, really. She *knew* we said this one!'

'Well, we'll just go and get the suitcases and bring them

40

here,' said Miss Pepper, deciding that Mrs Jones must be kept firmly in her place, and do what her guests asked. So in half a minute the suitcases were in the room they had chosen, and were being unpacked. There were great drawers in the chest, and the clothes were hurriedly arranged inside.

In the middle of it there came a knock at their door. 'Come in!' called Miss Pepper, in the briskest voice.

In came a tall man with thick, untidy hair, wearing glasses and a surly look. 'Good evening,' he said, 'I am Mr Jones, the innkeeper. You have the wrong room. Please come this way to our Best Room.'

'I've already chosen this one,' said Miss Pepper. 'It's quite empty and I prefer the view. You have no guest staying in it, I know.'

'Madam, you will not like this room,' said Mr Jones, looking even surlier.

'Please don't be so mysterious,' said Miss Pepper, deciding that however well Mr Jones cooked, she was not going to like him. 'Why shouldn't I like this room?'

'There are sometimes noises in the night,' said Mr Jones solemnly.

'Oooh, how thrilling! What *kind* of noises?' asked Diana. 'Howls – yells – moans – or what?'

'You laugh,' said Mr Jones angrily. 'But you will not laugh in the dark of night, when the noises come.'

'Well, we'll see what they are like,' said Miss Pepper, slamming a drawer of the chest shut. 'Then we'll know whether to laugh or not. If you're trying to tell me the room's haunted or something, you're wasting you time. I don't believe in things like that.'

Without another word Mr Jones walked out of the room. Miss Pepper looked at Diana. 'Well – if I wasn't such an obstinate woman, I'd move out into the other room!' she said. 'This is obviously a guest room, and I

41

see no real reason why we shouldn't have it if we want it. Even the beds are made up and are all ready to sleep in!'

Soon all their clothes were stowed away and they went down to see how the boys were getting on. Miss Pepper peeped into the caravan and was astonished and pleased to see everything put away so tidily.

As she stood there talking to the boys, the great grey goose came round the corner, cackling loudly. Behind it came the small, untidy boy, whistling.

He went right up to the caravan and had a good look inside. The goose looked in too, and made as if to climb in.

'Oh no, you don't!' said Roger, and gave it a small push. 'Geese not allowed in here!'

The goose hissed and flapped its wings. The boy put his arms round its neck, and it quietened down. He stared solemnly up at Roger with great dark eyes.

'What's your name?' said Diana, amused.

'Dafydd,' said the boy.

'Oh – David,' said Diana. 'Come and look inside the caravan. Haven't you ever seen one before?'

Dafydd didn't understand what she was saying, but took her hand and went inside the van. He fingered everything with his dirty little hands, and finally took up a small comb from a hair-brush and slipped it into his pocket.

'No, no, Dafydd!' said Barney. 'That's *my* comb, old son! Put it back!'

But Dafydd shook his head, and picked up a tube of tooth-paste. He examined it with interest. Then he suddenly felt something touching his pocket and looked down. It was Miranda, slipping a paw in, and taking out the comb! She was not going to allow anyone to steal Barney's belongings!

She leapt on to Barney's shoulder, chattering angrily,

and began to comb his thick hair. Dafydd stared at her, frowning, rather scared. He said something in Welsh, something rather rude, and shook his little fist at Miranda, who immediately danced about on Barney's shoulder, saying plenty of rude things back to him in monkey-chatter.

'Cackle-cackle,' said the goose outside, and flapped its wings impatiently. Miranda felt sure that it, too, was saying something rude, and she leapt straight off Barney's shoulder down to the floor, and then, with another flying leap she was on the goose's back, clinging to its neck, chattering loudly.

The goose was so astonished that it fled at once, hissing like a dozen snakes, with Miranda riding it. Barney roared with laughter, and Dafydd at once battered him with his small fists, angry that anyone should make fun of his goose.

'Now, now,' said Barney, holding Dafydd's small fists in one of his hands. 'That's enough! The monkey won't hurt your Waddle. You go after him, and I'll call back the monkey. And listen – you're NOT to come inside our caravan if we're not here. Do you understand?'

Dafydd shouted something that nobody could under-stand, kicked Barney on the ankles, wrenched his hands away, and was out of the caravan like a streak of lightn-ing, yelling for Waddle.

'Well – what do you think of *that*?' said Barney to the others. 'I vote we keep our caravan locked when we're out anywhere. What a little rascal!'

'His mother ought to keep him in order,' said Miss Pepper. 'A few good slaps would do him a world of good. Taking that comb right under our noses! We'd better keep our room locked too, Diana, when we're out. Ah, here comes Miranda, looking pleased with herself!'

Miranda did feel pleased with herself. She had put that flappy goose in its place! She had ridden on its back all the way to the cowshed a little way up the hill, the goose cackling at the top of its voice.

'You'd better behave yourself, Miranda,' said Diana, 'or Dafydd will be after you! Him and his precious goose! What a pair!'

'Well, the goose will have to mind its p's and q's when Snubby comes with Loony,' said Barney. 'I can't see either of them putting up with Dafydd and Waddle for long, if they *don't* behave themselves.'

'You two boys will be quite comfortable in the caravan at nights,' said Miss Pepper. 'The bunks are very good. Diana and I have got the room we wanted – the one with the heavenly view – though Mr Jones tried to scare us out of it with tales of noises in the night!'

'Oh, have you seen him?' said Barney. 'He's not what you might call very merry and bright, is he? Roger and I thought he must have some secret sorrow, he looked so glum! But he's no right to try and scare you with tales of noises at night, Miss Pepper.

'Oh, he and his wife are proud of their Best Room, as they call it,' said Miss Pepper. 'He just hoped that a silly fib about noises would make us change rooms, that's all. I don't expect he has even *noticed* what wonderful views our room has!'

'Well, I don't mind noises, or pet geese or light-fingered small boys, so long as we get Good Cooking, Very Good Cooking! said Diana. 'We shall see what supper's like.'

Well, supper was Wonderful! Miss Pepper stared in amazement at the beautifully cooked meal. It began with chicken soup, went on to a fine joint of beef with mounds of roast potatoes, garden peas and the first runner beans, and finished with an ice-cream pudding set round with dainty biscuits of all kinds!

'I *say*! This is the best meal I've had since Daddy took us out to a big hotel in London!' said Roger. '*Look* at

44

this ice-cream pudding – there's enough for a dozen people. Are we supposed to eat it all, Miss Pepper?'

'Well, supposed to or not, I've no doubt you will!' said Miss Pepper, and they did! Miranda had the last little biscuit off the dish, and sat nibbling it on Barney's shoulder as Mrs Jones came in, beaming, to clear away.

'You like your supper?' she enquired, and laughed to hear the loud chorus that answered her.

'Cooking good, VERY good cooking!'

Chapter Eight

'Hallo, Snubby!'

They were all sleepy after their wonderful supper, and were yawning widely when Mrs, Jones trotted in with the silver tray on which coffee cups were set.

'Dear me!' said Miss Pepper, surprised to see the gleaming silver and the steaming coffee. 'Who would have thought that a little country inn like this would do everything so well! No wonder "Big People," sometimes come here, as Mrs Jones boasted! Coffee, anyone?'

'Anything to keep me awake!' said Barney, with a most tremendous yawn. 'Miranda, that sugar is NOT for you. Smack her paw, Diana, please. She's as bad as that monkey of a Dafydd.'

Far away, somewhere in the depths of the great dark hall, a bell shrilled. 'The telephone!' said Miss Pepper. 'I hope that's to say you aunt is getting on well, Diana.'

Mrs Jones appeared. 'Someone for you, Miss Pepper, please,' she said, and out went Miss Pepper, hoping for good news. She was soon back.

'That was your uncle,' she said to Roger and Diana. 'Barney's father got held up, and found he couldn't get back to your aunt's home tonight – so he telephoned your uncle, and told him to send Snubby off to us by train early tomorrow. Snubby is absolutely too thrilled for words, he said, and Loony promptly went mad!'

Everyone laughed. Roger rubbed his hands together. 'Good old Snubby! Funny we should be so pleased to have such a pest with us, but things always seem to happen

46

when Snubby and Loony are around. What time will he arrive?'

'Probably by the half-past twelve train, at Dilcarmock, five miles from here,' said Miss Pepper. 'It's not a bad train. I'll telephone to order a taxi to meet him and bring him here. Your aunt is going on well, so your uncle sounded quite happy.'

'He'll feel even happier tomorrow when he's got rid of Snubby,' said Roger. 'Last time he stayed there Snubby kept pretending to be a Christy minstrel with a banjo and made banjo noises all day long. Uncle and Aunt nearly went crazy!'

Miss Pepper groaned, remembering the holiday at Rubadub when Snubby had fancied himself at playing all kinds of instruments, not only banjoes. 'I only hope he doesn't take it into his head to be a Christy minstrel here,' she said. 'Anyone want any more coffee?'

Nobody did. One by one they yawned again, and Miss Pepper laughed. 'Let's all go to bed,' she said. 'It's getting on for nine o'clock and we've had a very long day. Off to the caravan, boys – and sleep well! See you at breakfast time. It's at half-past eight, so if anyone wants an early morning bathe, there'll be plenty of time.'

'Right. I'm half asleep already,' said Roger, getting up. He gave Miss Pepper a sudden hug that surprised her. 'I think you're a brick to stay on with us like this after our caravan holiday broke up!' he said. 'I hope to goodness you don't hear any unpleasant noises in the night!'

'Well, we'll lean out of one of our windows and yell if we do!' said Miss Pepper, pleased at the sudden hug.

'This will be your last peaceful night, boys,' said Diana, with a grin. 'Tomorrow you'll have Snubby in the caravan with you, and mad-dog Loony!'

The boys left, and Miss Pepper and Diana went upstairs, meeting Mrs Jones on the way. 'A truly wonderful supper, Mrs Jones,' said Miss Pepper. 'Your husband is surely a trained chef?'

'Oh, yes indeed,' said Mrs Jones proudly. 'It was in London Town that he was trained, Miss Pepper, at a big, important hotel. We were so happy there. I was chambermaid, and he was second chef. I wanted to stay – but no, Mr Jones he wanted to come back here, where he was born. His cooking is good, very good!'

Miss Pepper nodded, said goodnight and went on up the stairs, half wondering whether she would find their things removed from their room-with-a-view to the Best Room. But no – their cases were still in the room they had chosen. Good! Miss Pepper was also pleased to see that there was a key in the door.

'Now we can lock our room when we leave it,' she said to Diana, 'and can be sure that that monkey of a Dafydd won't come in with his cackling goose and pocket whatever takes his fancy!'

She and Diana were soon in bed and fast asleep. Were there any Noises in the Night? There might well have been, even if only the wind in the chimney, but neither of them would have heard a thunderstorm that night! The beds were comfortable, the room was airy, and they slept so soundly that they only awoke when Mrs Jones came knocking at their door with cans of hot water.

Breakfast was as good as supper had been. Cold ham, boiled eggs, hot toast, homemade marmalade, creamy butter, and scalding hot coffee . . . Miss Pepper looked at the table with much approval.

'Snubby will like this place,' said Roger, taking his second boiled egg. 'Have you phoned about a taxi for him yet, Miss Pepper?'

'No, there's time enough after breakfast,' said Miss Pepper. 'Did you and Barney bathe? I should imagine you did by your appetites!'

'Well, we didn't!' said Roger, with a grin. 'We slept like logs – and I don't think we'd have wakened when we did if that young Dafydd hadn't come peering in at the caravan window and wakened up Miranda. She leapt out of the window and chased Waddle the goose all over the place, and what with Dafydd's yells and the goose's cackles, we woke up with an awful jump! Why doesn't someone smack Dafydd hard?'

'Someone's going to, if he doesn't look out,' said Barney grimly, rubbing his hands together.

Miss Pepper went to phone for a taxi for Snubby. 'I've ordered one to call here at 11.30,' she said. 'I thought you three would like to go in it to meet Snubby. It's the only one in the village, apparently, so it's probably a poor old crock.'

'Right,' said Barney, pleased at the idea of meeting Snubby at the station. 'We'll have time to go down for a bathe, then. Are you all coming? Merlin's Cove is sup-posed to be the best bathing place, apparently.'

Mrs Jones agreed that it was indeed the best place, when she came in to clear away the breakfast. Dafydd and Waddle also came in with her, and Waddle immediately pecked at a piece of toast left on one of the plates. Mrs Jones didn't say a word of reproof – but Miranda did! She snatched the toast out of the goose's beak, and then pulled her tail feathers hard, chattering angrily all the time.

Dafydd aimed a blow at the monkey, and Barney was immediately beside him, holding his hands tightly.

'No! Do you want to be bitten? Miranda has very sharp teeth. I will show you them. Come here, Miranda.'

Dafydd stared at the monkey's sharp teeth, and turned away, gabbling in Welsh.

'He says your monkey must not hurt his goose,' said Mrs Jones, clearing away. 'Dafydd, go away. You are not to come in here now that we have visitors. Take Waddle with you.'

Dafydd went out sulkily, Waddle following behind. 'Waddle was just a little gosling when Dafydd had him,' said Mrs Jones. 'He broke his leg, and Dafydd mended it – he put a stick, like so – and tied it well. And Waddle's leg mended, and now he will not leave Dafydd, and what a trouble the two are, I give you my word, and what is the use of my scolding him, he hears only what he wants to hear, he does only what he . . .'

It looked as if Mrs Jones was launched on one of her never-ending speeches, and Miss Pepper interrupted her firmly.

'We would rather that Dafydd and Waddle did not come into the dining-room or into our bedroom,' she said.

'But how can I stop them?' argued Mrs Jones, deftly folding up the tablecloth. 'They go where they please, they . . .'

'Not when *we're* here! said Miss Pepper. 'Er – have you ever tried a good smack, Mrs Jones.'

'A smack! A smack is no good with that one!' said Mrs Jones. 'Even if you could get near him with a smack! Like an eel he is, like a slippery eel, and as for Waddle, he is as bad, the way he walks where he wants to walk, and cackles when he wants to cackle, and . . .'

But there was no one to listen to her! The room was empty, the boys had slipped out to bathe, Diana had gone too, and Miss Pepper had hurried quietly out of the room! Mrs Jones went on talking for a long time before she saw she was alone – and even then she didn't stop, but talked away to herself as she carried out the tray to the kitchen.

The boys couldn't find their bathing things, and there was a great to-do at once. 'Miss Pepper! MISS PEPPER! Ask Di if she's got our things with her, will you?' shouted

Barney, as he saw Miss Pepper at her bedroom window. 'Ours aren't in the caravan, that's certain.'

Diana hunted hurriedly in the drawers where she had put her clothes, and a last found the boys' bathing things. She threw them out of the window, and one pair caught on a rambler growing up the wall.

'Ass!' shouted Roger. 'Now I'll have to get a ladder. Why can't girls throw properly!'

'Oh dear – if you don't hurry up, the taxi will be here,' said Miss Pepper, looking at her watch. She called down to the boys. 'I don't think you'd better bathe, after all – you'll miss Snubby's train if you do!'

And then, what a surprise! A piercing, very well-known voice came to their startled ears – surely, surely, it couldn't be SNUBBY'S?

'HALLO, EVERYBODY! HERE I AM!'

And someone came up the slope to the inn – someone very dirty indeed, with straw sticking out of him at every corner and a black dog careering at his heels.

'Snubby! We were just going to meet you!' yelled Roger. 'How did you get here? Your train isn't even due in yet! How AWFUL you look! What in the world have you been doing?'

Chapter Nine

Hot Bath For Snubby!

Snubby marched up to the astonished Roger and Barney, grinning all over his freckled, snub-nosed face. His ginger hair was very wind-blown indeed!

Diana and Miss Pepper ran downstairs most amazed. How like Snubby to arrive so unexpectedly!

'Have I given you a surprise?' he said. 'I thought I should!'

'Snubby – how did you get here so soon? And why are you so *filthy*?' said Miss Pepper. 'Hallo, Loony – good gracious, *you're* all covered in straw too!'

'Well, Uncle got me a ticket for an awful slow train,' said Snubby, rubbing his dirty face with an even dirtier handkerchief. 'And I heard there was a very early one, so I decided to catch that. You see, Uncle was getting pretty fed up with me, really. I arrived at Dilcarmock ages ago, and I got a lift in a cart that was loaded with straw and stuff for Penrhyndendraith, or whatever this place is called. Gosh, it crawled, though, and the straw was frightfully prickly.'

'Snubby, you look too awful for words,' said Diana. 'Honestly, I've never *seen* such a tramp!'

'Well, I did think you'd all be more pleased to see me,' said Snubby, sounding hurt. 'I tell you, I couldn't stay with Uncle any longer. He just glowered at me till I amost changed into a worm. Darling Miranda, are *you* pleased to see me?'

The little monkey leapt on to his shoulder and put her

tiny paws down his neck, chattering softly. Yes – she was very pleased to see Snubby – and Loony too!

Loony was tearing all round the place, sniffing into every corner. He had given everyone a really good lick, and was now interested in all the new smells. And then, quite suddenly, he saw a most fearsome creature coming towards him, hissing like a dozen snakes!

It was Waddle, of course. Waddle, who detested dogs and cats – and monkeys! Waddle considered that the inn belonged to him and to no one else, and woe betide any strange creature who dared to sniff around his domain!

Loony took one look at Waddle and backed away hurriedly. What in the world was this creature? Bird? Animal? Snake? Its head and neck and voice seemed to be those of a snake – but it had wings! Loony let out a terrified yelp and ran to Snubby.

'Don't be an ass, Loony – it's only a *goose!*' said Snubby – and then promptly ran for shelter himself as Waddle, cackling, hissing and flapping, descended upon him and Loony too!

But little Miranda was not going to have her friends scattered like this, and entered into the battle with delight! She flung herself on Waddle's back and clasped her neck as she had done once before, chattering at the top of her voice.

Then it was Waddle's turn to run, and off went the goose into the house, waddling more quickly than ever a goose waddled before, cackling as if the house was on fire! Miranda clung to her tightly, and the goose could not shake her off.

Loony recovered his courage and raced after them, barking madly. Mr Jones, coming to see what the noise was about, met the goose and Miranda with Loony immediately behind them, and was promptly bowled over.

53

He sat down very suddenly indeed, knocked over by the heavy goose, and then trodden on by the surprised Loony.

Miss Pepper put her hands over her face, and groaned. WHY did things like this always happen when Snubby was around? He had only to appear, and the whole world seemed at once to go crazy. And now there was Mr Jones, tall and thin and dour, getting up from the stone hall floor, rubbing himself angrily.

'Oh, Mr Jones – I hope you're not hurt,' said Miss Pepper, hurrying to him. 'The goose frightened the dog, and then the monkey frightened the goose, and the dog ran after them both, and, and . . .'

'And the cow jumped over the moon,' said Snubby with a hoot of laughter. Mr Jones took one look at him and raised his voice.

'Get out of here, you dirty little tramp! Go where you belong, into the gutter! Don't dare to come up to this inn, where decent folk stay!'

There was a surprised silence, while everyone stared first at Mr Jones, and then at Snubby. Snubby glanced down at his dirty clothes apologetically, and then looked beseechingly at Miss Pepper.

'Er – this is a cousin of Diana and Roger Lynton,' said Miss Pepper. 'The one whom Mr Martin arranged to come and stay, you remember. He's had a long – and – er – a very dirty journey. He needs a – a wash.'

Mr Jones glared at them all, and limped back down the hall without a word. Miss Pepper took hold of Snubby.

'You're going to have a hot bath,' she said. 'And I'm going to scrub you from head to foot – you – you dirty little tramp! *Really*, Snubby, I *cannot* imagine how anyone can get as filthy as you look.'

'Where's that goose gone?' said Snubby, pretending not to hear. 'I can't stop old Loony from going for him if he appears again.'

'Don't worry about Loony – he'll retire into the darkest corner he can find, if he sees Waddle,' said Miss Pepper, keeping a firm hold on Snubby and propelled him towards the hall door. 'Thank goodness the creature has disappeared and Miranda's recovered herself. I do wish you'd caught the proper train, Snubby, and not caused all this sensation! We don't want to be turned out of this place. The cooking is so . . .'

'Very very good!' finished Barney, with a grin. He put his arm round Snubby's shoulder. 'Cheer up! Where's your luggage? Get out a bathing suit and come and bathe with us – you'll soon be clean then.'

'No,' said Miss Pepper at once. 'I don't see why he should make the sea absolutely black! Is that all the luggage you've got, Snubby – that small case there? My goodness – you can't have much in it.'

'Well, I thought Roger could lend me what I've forgotten,' said Snubby amiably, going indoors with Miss Pepper. 'Gosh, I feel a bit tired now. Come on, Loony. Is there anything to *eat*, Miss Pepper? I do feel awfully empty. I say, what a place this is! I thought it was a ruin, till the van-man told me it was the inn I'd asked him to drop me at. I say, I do hope I'm going to sleep in the caravan with the others, I . . .'

'Snubby! *Stop* talking for a minute,' said Miss Pepper quite fiercely. 'I want to ask for some hot water for you. Stay here while I go to the kitchen. Don't dare to move from there, because if Mr Jones sees you again he might quite well pick you up and throw you into the sea – and I wouldn't blame him either!'

'I say – you *are* peppery this morning, Miss Pepper darling!' said Snubby, surprised. 'And I'd so looked forward to seeing you again, too. I never . . .'

But Miss Pepper was gone, walking quickly down the dark hallway to the equally dark kitchen, which was huge and rather forbidding. Mrs Jones was there, doing some washing-up in an enormous sink.

'Oh, Mrs Jones – do you think I might have a very large can of hot water?' asked Miss Pepper. 'The children's cousin has arrived and he's really *very* dirty.'

'I will get it at once for you, certainly I will,' said Mrs Jones, reaching for an enormous jug. 'I will bring it up to the bathroom, Miss. In two minutes it will be there.'

Miss Pepper, thankful that Mrs Jones did not chatter on and on as she usually did, went to collect Snubby, determined that he should not escape her.

'You dirty little ragamuffin!' she said as she saw him patiently waiting for her on exactly the same spot where she had left him, Loony sitting beside him. 'You look as if you've just been sweeping a chimney! I never did know anyone who could . . .'

'Get dirty wherever he goes and whatever he does,' finished Snubby with a grin. 'I wonder how many times you've said that to each of us, Miss Pepper! Where's the hot water?'

It wasn't long before Snubby was clean and shining all over, even to the backs of his ears. It wasn't any good protesting that he could wash himself, Miss Pepper was determined to get him really clean. Loony sat beside the bath, watching in alarm, half afraid that it might be his turn next!

'Now dry yourself, and I'll go and find something for you to eat,' said Miss Pepper. '*Look* at the bath-water – what a disgrace! It will take you quite a bit of time to clean the bath!'

Snubby sighed. He thought it was very hard that no matter what he did, he got into trouble. He rubbed himself dry and talked to the listening Loony.

'She called me a *ragamuffin*! What do you think of that, Loony? Except that it sounds a bit like something to eat,

56

it's a horrid name to give to anyone. *Ragamuffin!* Now what am I supposed to put on? Those clean clothes, I suppose – my own vest, Roger's old shorts – and this looks like Barney's shirt, it's so big! Loony, you don't know how lucky you are to be born a dog, and be able to wear the same old fur coat all your life. Like to try this vest on, old thing?'

Loony retreated to the door at once, and scratched at it, whining, suddenly afraid that it might enter Snubby's head to pop *him* into the bath.

'I'm not ready yet, old chap,' said Snubby, looking down into the bath, where the dirty water had already left a black line all round the sides. 'I say, Loony – come and look at this! I've got to clean this bath, and it will take me *ages!*'

Loony put his paws up on the side of the bath and looked down at the water, wagging his tail. He didn't mind looking, so long as he wasn't going to be bathed in it. He couldn't imagine why *anyone* ever had baths. Snubby suddenly sniffed, and bent down over Loony. 'You know, you smell pretty awful,' he said. 'I've a good mind to pop you in too, and . . .'

But very fortunately for the scared Loony, Miss Pepper's voice suddenly sounded outside the door.

'Snubby! What in the world are you doing? Aren't you dressed *yet*? I hope you've cleaned the bath. There is a piece of meat-pie, and some bread and cheese downstairs, if you hurry!'

Snubby hurried at once. He let out the bath water, and hurriedly tried to remove the black line round the bath with the flannel Miss Pepper had given him, finished dressing, and grinned at Loony as he opened the bathroom door. 'Loony – I have a feeling we'll enjoy being here. We're going to have quite an exciting time!'

57

Well, Snubby, you're right. But perhaps it will be rather *too* exciting!

Chapter Ten

Snubby Gets Into Trouble

Snubby thoroughly enjoyed his first day at Penrhynden-draith, and so did the others. They went bathing that lovely morning, and found Merlin's Cove. It was a truly lovely place.

The sands were almost white there, and as smooth as silk to walk on. When the tide was up it swept right into all the caves that made up Merlin's Cove. These ran either a little way or a long way into the high rocky cliff, and two were labelled 'DANGEROUS.'

'Ha – let's see why they are dangerous,' said Snubby, peering into one, and was at once firmly taken by the arm by Barney.

'Any fatheadedness on your part, and you go straight back to another of your uncles and aunts,' he said. 'Do you want rocks falling on your head – or to lose your way forever in a maze of cliff tunnels? Aren't you ever going to grow up, Snubby?'

Loony ran a little way into the dark, low cave, and then turned his head as if to say, 'Come on, Snubby!' but Snubby yelled to him at once.

'Come back, ass! Aren't you *ever* going to grow up?'

They explored some of the other caves, and found most of them shallow, going back only a little way. They bathed twice, and lay in the sun. Miranda hated the water and wouldn't go near it, though Barney at last persuaded her to paddle, and held her paw like a child.

Loony splashed past her, and, once out of his depth

and swimming, turned his head as if to say 'Monkeys are poor creatures! *They* can only paddle!'

'It looks as if we're going to have a pretty good time here,' said Roger, lying on the sand, leaning on his elbow. 'Look – are those fishing-boats coming in? Aren't they lovely?'

They were! They all had brown sails of different shades, and come smoothly in on the wind, the tide taking them to the little jetty not far off. The children scrambled up to go and see the catch. Miranda waited till Loony had come out of the water, and was vigorously shaking himself, and then leapt straight on to his back, clinging there with all her might, jigging up and down as if wanting a ride.

This was an old trick of Miranda's, and one that Loony didn't approve of at all! He set off at top speed hoping the little monkey would be bumped off, but she clung on for dear life, winding her tail round his tummy.

'Loony, roll over on the sand, you idiot!' shouted Snubby, 'Have you forgotten how to get her off!'

Loony promptly rolled over, and Miranda had to leap off, scampering to Barney quickly before Loony could catch her. The children laughed, and ran over to the jetty. They watched the great catch of fish being emptied. There were some large crabs among the catch, and Miranda was most interested in them as they began to walk off sideways.

She tapped one, and almost had her paw caught by one of its big claws! After that she and Loony kept well away from the crawling crabs.

They were all very hungry by dinner time, and went back through the little straggling village and up the slope of the hill to the old inn. They passed the ice-cream shop, and Snubby at once wanted to go in and buy ice-creams when he heard how the others had sampled them the day before.

'No, you'll spoil your dinner,' said Barney. 'Do come on. I feel quite hollow inside with hunger.'

Miss Pepper had had a peaceful morning, except for twenty minutes when Mrs Jones saw her wandering round the old garden of the inn, and came out to talk non-stop. Miss Pepper made up her mind that she would rather go down to the beach with the children than risk being found by Mrs Jones again!

It really was a very pleasant first day, marred only by an accident to Snubby's clothes – or rather to the shirt and the shorts which belonged to Barney and Roger.

Barney suddenly saw that his nice shirt, which had been almost new, was torn right down the back. He felt very cross.

'What on earth have you done to ruin my shirt like that?' he demanded. 'It's my newest one – I hadn't even worn it myself! I didn't mind lending it to you till you had your own clothes sent on – but I do think you might have been more careful with it! And gosh – look at Roger's shorts! Have you sat down in a patch of oil or something? You *are* in a filthy mess!'

Snubby tried to screw himself round to see the shorts. 'I wondered what that horrible smell was that seemed to follow me around,' he said. 'Well, I never! When *could* I have sat in oil? I'm awfully sorry, Roger – and sorry about your shirt too, Barney.'

'Well, I don't know what you're going to do tomorrow for clothes,' said Roger. 'Borrow a skirt of Diana's, I suppose! I'm certainly not going to lend you any more things.'

Miss Pepper was also very annoyed, and stared in horror as Snubby presented himself to her and asked her advice about the oil.

'To think I scrubbed you from head to toe this morning – and you look exactly like a ragamuffin again!' she said. 'Well, you'll have to stay in bed tomorrow while I wash your own dirty clothes, the ones you took off this morning.'

'Oh *no*!' said Snubby in horror. 'Stay in *bed*? I couldn't!'

But Miss Pepper was quite firm about that and the next day Snubby found himself compelled to have his breakfast in the caravan, sitting in his bunk. He was very angry indeed, and Loony simply *couldn't* understand what all the fuss was about.

'I simply daren't borrow anything else of Barney's or Roger's,' groaned Snubby to a sympathetic Loony. 'And as I've only got his old vest to wear, or my pyjamas, I don't see *how* I can go out of the caravan till Miss Pepper cleans up those torn dirty things of mine.'

He lay and thought angry thoughts for a time, and then an idea came into his head. 'That ice-cream shop!' he said. 'I believe it sells second-hand clothes. I'm sure I saw some hanging up. Loony, what about us slipping out and buying some before the others come back? I'm NOT going to lie here all day! I'll turn my pyjama trousers up to my knees so that they are more like shorts – and keep this vest on.'

And, very soon, a rather peculiar figure slipped out of the caravan, and ran down to the little village. Snubby grinned as he looked down at himself, and wondered if the old lady in the shop would notice his peculiar attire.

Old Mrs Jones, her snow-white hair tucked under the black net cap, didn't seem at all surprised to see a small boy in vest and turned-up pyjama-legs.

'You'll be one of the children up at the inn?' she said in her sing-song voice, with a twinkle in her eye. 'Is it an ice-cream you are wanting to buy?'

'Well, yes – among other things,' said Snubby, giving her the grin that always made old ladies love him. 'Look – I've got into trouble over my clothes, and I want to buy some more. Have you got any that would fit me – second-hand ones, I mean?'

'Well, now, there's that pair of long trousers,' said old Mrs Jones, pointing to a most dilapidated pair, hanging on a hook, 'Clean they are, though dirty they look, for I washed them myself. And there's this jersey, red and yellow, gay it is, and not badly worn.'

'Long trousers would be fine,' said Snubby, pleased, and put them on over his pyjama legs. 'Hey, Loony, how do I look?'

Loony barked sharply and wagged his tail. 'He says I look about sixteen, instead of twelve,' said Snubby with a grin. 'Now for the jersey – my word, I've gone gay, haven't I! Is it clean, because if it isn't, Miss Pepper will rip it off me at once?'

'It is clean,' said Mrs Jones. 'And you shall have a cap too – a good one. See the big peak!'

Snubby put it on and fancied himself very much in it. 'Thanks awfully,' he said, 'How much do I owe you?'

'That will be two shillings for the cap, four shillings for the trousers, and three shillings for the jersey – nine shillings – and an ice-cream thrown in for nothing,' said Mrs Jones, laughing at Snubby's peculiar appearance.

'Oh, I say – that's jolly kind of you,' said Snubby, and paid up at once. He took the ice-cream wafer, gratefully.

'It is my son who has the inn where you are staying,' said Mrs Jones. 'So good he is at cooking! He went to London to learn. Ah, to think that a poor boy like my Llewellyn, with never two pairs of trousers to his name, should have gone to London and learnt to cook! And now that inn is his! Always, all his life, he has said to me, "Ah, if only that inn was mine!" How I laughed! "I have five pounds on my old stocking," I said, "and that has taken me eighteen years to save – and you want to own that inn"!'

'Gosh – how did he get it, then?' asked Snubby, licking the last of the ice-cream.

'He made friends in London,' said the old lady proudly. 'Important friends. And they lent him the money to buy the inn he so much wanted. How happy my Llewellyn is now!'

Snubby thought of the cross-looking, dour man he had seen the night before. 'Goodness – he doesn't *look* very happy!' he said. 'I say! I must go! Miss Pepper will be sending out a search party for me or something. Good-bye and many thanks!'

And away he rushed, really a very peculiar figure indeed. What in the world would the others say!

Chapter Eleven

A Very Strange Happening

Snubby had a few moments of doubt as he walked up the steep slope to the inn. 'If they jeer at me I shall run away!' he said to Loony, who wagged his tail sympathetically.

The first person he met was the boy Dafydd, with his faithful goose. Dafydd gave a loud shriek when he saw him and tore off with Waddle behind him – though whether the shriek was because Snubby looked so peculiar, or because he was scared of Loony was not clear! Snubby stared after him, frowning. If that was the effect he was going to have, things were not going to be easy!

Roger, Diana and Barney came out of the inn at that moment. They had been looking everywhere for Snubby, having missed him from the caravan. They looked at him, not recognising him in the least, and wondered why Loony was following this peculiar-looking lad.

Snubby had pulled the big peaked cap down over his face, and he grinned when he saw that the others did not recognise him. He swaggered up to them, hands in pocket, and pretended to speak in Welsh, in a peculiar-sounding hoarse voice.

'Collq-inna-dooly-hector-sonkin-poppyll?' he said, his cap still pulled down over his face.

'What on earth is this fellow saying?' asked Roger, astonished. 'And why is Loony with him?'

Diana gave a sudden shriek, and pulled at Snubby's cap. 'It's Snubby! SNUBBY! Where have you been? Where did you get those *awful* clothes?'

'They're not awful. They're fine – *and* clean,' said

Snubby, turning himself round and round so that they could admire him. 'I bought them at the ice-cream shop – second-hand.'

'Snubby! How *could* you buy clothes like that – you don't know *who's* worn them before!' said Roger.

'What does that matter? I tell you, they're *clean*!' roared Snubby. 'Oh gracious goodness – here comes Miss Pepper!'

What the others had said was nothing to what Miss Pepper said! She insisted that he should go straight back to the caravan and take off 'those TERRIBLE clothes, ESPECIALLY that cap,' and wait till she came with clean ones.

'I'm not going to,' said Snubby obstinately. 'Fancy expecting me to waste a lovely morning like this in that caravan, when I've gone and got myself clothes to wear. It's no *good*, Miss Pepper, I'm going to wear these clothes till my others are clean – and if you all think I'm not fit company for you, all right, Loony and I will keep away from you! Come on, Loony – they're looking at us as if we were a couple of bad smells!'

And with that Snubby marched quickly off down the hill, his peaked cap at a very cheeky angle indeed. Diana called crossly after him. 'Well – you *do* smell in those clothes! You smell dreadful!'

Snubby took no notice at all, and soon disappeared round a bend. Miss Pepper suddenly began to laugh.

'Oh dear!' she said. 'What a *sight* he looks – and yet I really do believe he's quite proud of those awful clothes. I only hope to goodness he won't want to go on wearing them when his own are ready. Well – what are you three going to do today?'

'Bathe – have a walk, perhaps fish if we can get a boat,' said Barney. 'It's a pity Snubby's behaving like this. Why didn't he think of putting on his bathing things – it's warm enough for him to wear them all day on the beach. I'll take them down with me, shall I – in case he does join us, and then I can tell him to wear them, and stay with us.'

So, when the others went down to the beach, they took Snubby's bathing things with them. But there was no sign of him, or of Loony either!

Snubby was angry and hurt. Fancy calling him a bad smell! He caught sight of himself in the glass window of the ice-cream shop as he went by, and stopped. H'm! He did look a bit odd, perhaps. Pity the trousers were so big and sloppy – and the jersey certainly *was* a bit loud. But the cap was fine!

'I suppose we look a bit ragamuffinish again, Loony,' he said sorrowfully. 'Now – what shall we do? I know – we'll find a nice quiet place, and read that code-letter from old Bruce. I'll tell you what he says.'

Loony wagged his tail. He knew who Bruce was – a very close school friend of Snubby's, a rascal almost as bad as Snubby, the bane of their form-master. The two of them had invented a most involved secret code, using both figures and letters. It took Snubby about two hours to write a letter in their secret code – and even longer to decipher any he got from Bruce! Still, it made them both feel very important indeed, and they enjoyed that.

'We'll go somewhere out of sight of the others,' said Snubby to Loony. 'Look – what about going down to that broken bit of cliff over there – see? We could hide among the fallen rocks nicely, and see what old Bruce has got to say in his letter.'

So down they went together and were soon ensconced among the warm rocks, the sea not very far away. Snubby took out Bruce's letter. It was on a squared piece of paper, neatly torn out of his maths book.

Snubby looked at it and gave a small groan. 'It's rather

a long one,' he said to Loony, gazing at the mass of neat little figures, interspersed with letters. 'It'll take us ages to decode. Still, it's all good practice, Loony. You never know when you might have to use a code. Now – let's see – 12 – 6 – J – 567 – P – gosh, what does P stand for now? I wish I had my code-book with me. Hallo – who's this?'

A man was coming over the rocks towards them. He was short and wore a black beard, and dark sunglasses. Snubby glanced up at him, expecting him to pass by. But he didn't.

He came towards Snubby, and stood beside him. 'Give that to me!' he said in an angry voice.

Snubby was extremely startled. He hastily stuffed his precious code-letter in to his pocket. 'What's up?' he said. 'What do you want?'

'That letter!' said the man savagely. 'How dare you open and read it?'

'Well, why shouldn't I? It was sent to me, not to you,' said Snubby, beginning to feel that the man must be crazy. 'Don't be daft!'

'You know you had to meet me here and give me that letter,' said the man, his voice shaking with rage. 'And I find you have opened it and are trying to decipher it! How dare you! I shall see that your uncle beats you well!'

'What on EARTH are you talking about?' said Snubby, absolutely at sea. 'This is NOT your letter. It's mine, and I'm certainly not going to give it to you. It's in a very secret code that my friend and I know.'

'Your friend? Your *friend* knows the code – and you too? You lie!' said the man. 'You are a foolish boy who hopes to make me give you money for handing over my letter.'

'Oh, don't be an ass,' said Snubby, getting up. 'If this is a joke, it's pretty silly. I'm going!'

But to his enormous surprise the man threw him roughly back on the rocks, dug his hand into Snubby's pocket and tore out the letter. He slapped Snubby hard across the face and turned to go. But this was too much for Loony! He began to growl angrily.

What! This man dared to knock Snubby over and slap him! With a very fierce snarl indeed Loony flung himself on the surprised man, who shook him off with great force. He picked up a piece of rock and flung it at Loony, who only just dodged it in time.

'Loony! Come here! He'll kill you!' shouted Snubby. 'He's absolutely mad. Let him go.'

Reluctantly Loony sat down and watched the bearded man clamber up the cliff and on to the roadway. The little spaniel growled angrily till he was out of sight, sad that he could not chase him. He turned to Snubby and whimpered, pawing him as if to say, 'Are you hurt, master? Is everything all right?'

'I'm not hurt, only angry,' said Snubby, 'and jolly puzzled too. Why did he come here to me? Did he think I was someone else? And what on earth was he gassing about – a letter in code, he said – and took my letter from old Bruce! I suppose he saw it was in code. Look here, Loony, there's something peculiar about this. let's go and find the others.'

And off they went along the beach. They soon saw the others sitting on the sands, sunning themselves after a bathe. Snubby went up to them and sat down,

'Got something to tell you all,' he said in a low mysterious voice. 'Listen!'

At once they sat up, grinning at Snubby's peculiar appearance, but eager to hear him. He began to relate what had happened.

They all listened, most astonished. Barney whistled. 'You're not making this up by any chance, are you?'

he said, for Snubby had at times invented some curious stories.

'No! No, of course I'm not,' said Snubby indignantly. 'It's true, every word of it – and here's the bruise I got on my elbow when that fellow flung me down on the rocks.'

He showed them quite a massive bruise. Barney looked at it and frowned.

'Either that fellow was quite mad – or there's something extraordinary going on,' he said. 'Why did he mistake you for someone else, though? You must have looked like the person he was to meet – a real tramp, if you don't mind my saying so, Snubby. A proper ragamuffin! The kind of person who *might* be a go-between, if something dirty was going on.'

'I'll take these things off at once then,' said Snubby hastily. 'Got my bathing things? I'll just pop behind that rock. A go-between! Phew – just wait till I see the real one, if ever I do!' He went behind a rock and hastily flung off his awful clothes, putting on a pair of bathing trunks. And then, *just* as he joined the others, someone passed them, dressed in clothes very like Snubby's – long dirty-looking trousers, a bright woollen jersey, a peaked cap – and behind him ran a small black dog!

'There you are!' whispered Barney, nudging Snubby very hard indeed. 'See! I bet that's the fellow *you* were mistaken for – a regular ragamuffin! He's even got a little black dog – a mongrel poodle – and he's making for the rocks over there where *you* were sitting. Now what do we do?'

Chapter Twelve

Snubby And The Ragamuffin

They all watched the little ragamuffin go to the patch of fallen rocks where Snubby had sat. The small dog leapt about at his heels, and then sat down by him, as he settled himself on one of the rocks.

'See? He's waiting for someone,' said Roger. 'I bet he's got the *real* secret code-letter all right – the one that mad fellow thought *you* had!'

'I expect that man was told to look out for a ragamuffin of a boy, sitting on those rocks, with a black dog,' said Barney. 'And the boy would hand him a letter – secret instructions about something or other, I should think – and . . .'

'And old Snubby happened to go to that very spot, looking like a ragamuffin himself – with Loony who's as black as any dog can be expected to be!' said Roger. 'And what was more, Snubby happened to be reading a letter in code – his code and Bruce's – but how was the man to know that? He must have been certain it was his own code-letter!'

'Gosh – no wonder he was furious with me then!' said Snubby. 'He must have thought I was actually trying to decipher his secret instructions or whatever they were! You know, he might have killed old Loony, if that rock he threw had hit him!'

'I think this is pretty serious,' said Barney. 'Do we tell Miss Pepper, or not?'

'We *don't*!' said Diana at once. 'She might want to leave immediately! And it *is* so nice here! I don't expect

71

anything horrid will happen now, especially as Snubby has taken off those frightful clothes. You're *not* to wear them again, Snubby.'

'Not even the cap?' said Snubby, disappointed. 'I rather fancied myself in that.'

'*Certainly* not the cap,' said Barney. He stared round at the boy still sitting patiently on the fallen rocks some way along the beach. 'That kid will have to sit there a long time! The bearded fellow won't be back, that's certain. He's probably going slowly mad trying to decipher Snubby's code, and making it fit in with his!'

'I'm going to talk to that boy,' said Snubby, getting up. 'I might find out something.'

'Better not,' said Roger.

'Why?' said Snubby, walking off in his bathing things. 'We're sure that horrible fellow with the beard won't come back again – he thinks he's got the letter he wanted. The boy will just think I'm some tripper or other.'

And off he went with Loony, whistling a dance tune, jigging along in time to it. When he came near to the waiting boy, he suddenly remembered his Christy minstrel pretence, and began to make a noise like a banjo, pretending to strum with his fingers.

It was a very very peculiar noise and the boy looked up at once, thinking he was hearing a real banjo. He was astonished to see Snubby's pretence, and laughed.

'Twang – a – twang – a – twang – a – twang – a – twang – a – twang-a-twang-twang!' The sounds that Snubby made between his teeth were exactly like a cheap banjo!

'Hallo!' he said, sitting down grinning, 'I like your little dog. What's his name?'

'Woolly,' said the boy, running his hand over the poodle's woolly back. 'What's your dog's name?'

'Loony,' said Snubby. 'Short for lunatic. You waiting for someone?'

'Yes. A man with a beard,' said the boy. 'Got to give him a letter from my uncle.'

'Who's your uncle?' said Snubby, strumming his pretend banjo again.

'Morgan the Cripple,' said the boy, beginning to imitate Snubby. 'Twang-a-twang-a-twang! He was a fisherman, but he broke his leg – and he lets out fishing boats now instead of fishing.'

'Why didn't he *post* the letter?' said Snubby. 'Lazy fellow!'

'How do I know?' said the boy. 'I say, look at your dog and mine making friends! I do wish that man would come for his letter. I thought I was late – but he's later still. And I did want to go out in a boat with my Pa this morning.'

'All right. You give me the letter and I'll wait here for him,' said Snubby. 'And if he comes I'll give it to him, see? He won't know I'm not you, will he – we've both got a black dog!'

'Well – I'd get a fine thrashing if anyone found out,' said the boy. 'But I'm not waiting here all morning. Here – take the letter – and wait till he comes. Don't say a word about me, though!'

'Right. You go off,' said Snubby, feeling suddenly very excited. 'I'll wait about on these rocks with Loony, my own black dog!'

The boy thrust a letter into Snubby's hands and went off quickly, his poodle at his heels. Snubby sat there on the rocks, and waited, his heart beating. The man wouldn't come back, of course – but he must stay here on the rocks till the boy was out of sight!

It seemed ages till the boy disappeared. Snubby looked along the beach, to where he had left the others. They were all there, watching intently.

Snubby stood up as soon as the boy was out of sight,

73

and then he and Loony raced over the sands to the other three. He flung himself down beside them, panting.

'The boy *was* waiting for the man with a beard,' he said. 'His uncle – a man called Morgan, who hires out boats – gave the letter to him to deliver. The boy didn't say why – I don't think he knew. He's a bit simple, I think. He said he was late, and he hoped the man would come soon, because he wanted to go out in a boat with his father.'

'And so you offered to wait in his place and deliver the letter?' said Barney. 'We wondered what was happening when the boy suddenly went off.'

'Yes. And he gave me the letter!' said Snubby, triumphantly slapping his bathing trunks where he had hidden it. 'What do you think of that?'

Everyone stared at Snubby, and nobody really knew *what* to think. Snubby always did such surprising things!

'Let's go back home and examine the letter,' said Barney. 'I don't know whether we ought to or not – but it does seem as if something peculiar must be going on. Why should Morgan, whoever he is, send a letter in code to a man like the one who knocked you about so roughly? Why *in code*? If Morgan is only a fisherman, presumably *he* didn't write it – so someone else must have given it to him to hand to someone else – it was too secret and precious to be trusted to the post!'

'*Do* let's go and examine it,' said Diana. 'We might have to take it to the police, you know. But what could be going on in a dear little place like this – full of country folk and fishermen?'

'Smuggling perhaps?' said Roger hopefully.

'What kind of smuggling could go on here!' said Barney. 'No, I don't think it's that. In fact I can't *imagine* what it is. Come on – let's get back. Anyway, it's getting on for lunch time.'

Snubby smacked his lips at once. 'Ha – good cooking – very good cooking!' he said. 'Oh, by the way, I learnt something from old Mrs Jones at the ice-cream shop this morning, when I went to buy these smashing clothes. She told me that Mr Jones, who keeps our inn, is her son – and she said it's always been his dearest wish to own it, and now he does, because some rich friends he met when he was learning to be a chef in London, lent him the money to buy it.'

'And I suppose those rich friends are Sir Somebody This and Sir Somebody That, whom she told us so often came down to stay,' said Roger. 'I bet they don't have to pay a penny when they come.'

They were nearly at the inn now, and Barney gave Snubby a nudge. 'We'll go to the caravan and see your letter there,' he said. 'We've plenty of time.'

Soon all four, with Loony and Miranda, were shut in the caravan. Snubby was just about to show them the letter, when Loony barked sharply.

'I bet that's Dafydd again, with that Waddle of a goose,' said Diana, crossly, and opened the door. Yes, it was! He was up on the wheel, peering in at the window.

'Go away, you little snooper,' said Diana, half amused, half cross.

'Soon be dinner,' said Dafydd solemnly, his arm round the goose's neck.

'Well, we'll be in good time,' said Diana. 'Run away, now!'

She shut the door and they peered at the envelope Snubby took from his bathing trunks. 'It's a bit squashed, because I've sat on it,' he said, and slit the envelope. He drew out a one page sheet of paper, folded in four, and opened it out flat.

'There! It's in code, as we thought! said Barney,

excited. 'We'll never decipher it, of course. Look at all the little figures and letters!'

'No wonder he thought that Bruce's letter which I was trying to read, was *this* one,' said Snubby, staring at it. 'All this mess-up of figures and letters! Gosh – I wish we could decipher them.'

'Well, we can't,' said Barney, folding up the sheet. 'What are we to do with it? Shall we just wait and see if anything happens? The man who took *your* letter, Snubby, will soon find out that it's not the right one, because he won't be able to decode it – and if he could, he'd only read a lot of rubbish!'

'Well, I like *that*!' said Snubby indignantly. 'Bruce and I don't write rubbish, let me tell you.'

Nobody took any notice of his indignant remark. Diana spoke to Barney.

'And when the bearded man finds out that he's got the wrong letter – from a boy who wasn't the messenger after all – and that therefore someone else took the *right* letter from the fisher-boy and went off with it, what will he do?'

'Ah – what *will* he do?' said Barney, tickling Miranda under her chin. 'I think we'd better wait and see – and in the meantime, we'll keep this letter very very carefully!'

Chapter Thirteen

Two More Visitors At The Inn

Miss Pepper came to the caravan, just as the four children were getting up to go. She looked sharply at Snubby, fearing that he might be wearing his dreadful clothes – but he was still in his bathing trunks. The old clothes were on one of the bunks.

'You can throw those away, Snubby,' she said. 'See here are your own things, washed and cleaned up. Please put them on.'

'Can't I come in to lunch like this?' said Snubby, looking down at himself.

'No,' said Miss Pepper definitely. 'Diana, how brown you are getting! Did you have a nice morning?'

They went off together talking. Barney had been thinking deeply, and now he turned to Snubby and Roger. 'I think it wouldn't be a bad idea to take a walk over to the fishing jetty this afternoon and see if we can spot Morgan the Cripple, and perhaps talk to him,' he said. 'I'd like to see what kind of a fellow he is – and wouldn't I like to know what he's mixed up in!'

'Good idea!' said Snubby at once. 'Do you hear that, Loony? Walkie-walk this afternoon!'

Loony promptly went mad, and raced round the little caravan at top speed, jumping from bunk to bunk, barking.

'Er – Loony,' said Barney, 'sorry to disappoint you, old fellow – but you're *not* coming with us this afternoon!'

'Why ever not?' demanded Snubby, astonished.

'Use your brains!' said Barney. 'If that boy who gave

you the letter is there, he'd recognise Loony at once, and, even though you wouldn't be in bathing things this time, he'd perhaps recognise you if you had Loony with you. But without Loony, and wearing ordinary clothes, I don't see how he *could* recognise you.'

'Loony won't like not coming,' said Snubby gloomily. 'And he'll bark the place down if we leave him in the caravan.'

'Well – we'll get Di to stay with Miss Pepper this afternoon, and keep Loony with her,' said Barney. 'It's either that, or we leave *you* behind with Loony, Snubby.'

'Oh, Diana will have Loony all right,' said Snubby. 'Stop showing off, Loony please – we know all about your wonderful jumping – look what you've done to my bed-clothes, you ass!'

They went off to the dining-room of the inn, and found Diana at the table, and Miss Pepper at the sideboard, putting slices of cold ham on to plates. Snubby went to help her, and Loony at once sat himself exactly below Miss Pepper's right arm, hoping she might perhaps drop a slice of ham!

Barney told Diana in a low voice what he proposed to do that afternoon, and she was quite willing to stay behind with Miss Pepper and Loony. 'We could all three go for a little walk,' she said. 'Miss Pepper would like that. By the way – there are two more visitors at the inn!'

'Who?' asked Barney, looking round the table, pleased to see an enormous salad, and mounds of new potatoes. 'My word – what a fine spread!'

'I don't know their names,' said Diana, 'but look – here they come now!'

Two men walked into the room, one tall and commanding, with a monocle in his eye, and a smart, upturned moustache. The other was a short man, with a black beard and sunglasses.

Snubby turned at that moment to take two plates of ham to the table, and at once saw the two men. He jumped violently and a piece of ham leapt off one plate, and was at once snapped up by a delighted Loony. Snubby went quickly to the table and hissed at the surprised Barney and Roger, nudging them, and nodding over towards the table by the window where the two men sat with their backs to them.

The boys knew immediately what he meant! The man with the beard and the sunglasses was the one who had snatched Snubby's letter from him! Good gracious – and he was staying in the hotel!

'Has he seen Loony, do you think?' whispered Snubby. 'He might recognise him. He can't recognise me, I'm sure, now I'm properly dressed.'

'Take Loony out at once,' ordered Barney. 'Quick – before they see him. Here, stick a bit of my ham into his mouth, then he won't mind what you do with him! Lock him into the caravan.'

Snubby snatched a piece of ham off Barney's plate, picked up Loony, and put it into his mouth. Loony was so amazed at this extraordinary generosity that he didn't even bark. Snubby was able to streak out of the room with him at top speed, certain that the men hadn't seen him.

Miss Pepper was astonished to see him carrying Loony out of the room. 'Was he sick or something?' she asked, sitting down at the table. 'Poor Loony! Perhaps he swallowed too much sea water this morning.'

'You never know,' said Barney, and changed the subject at once. 'This must be home-cured ham, mustn't it, Miss Pepper. It's got a wonderful flavour!'

'It probably is,' said Miss Pepper. 'Diana, pass me the salad cream, please.'

Snubby came back, grinning. 'I'm sorry that Loony felt sick,' said Miss Pepper.

'He'd better stay behind this afternoon,' said Barney solemnly, 'and perhaps go for a walk with you, Miss Pepper – and Diana, too?'

'Yes. That's a good idea,' said Diana. 'Would you like me to go for a walk with you, Miss Pepper?'

Miss Pepper was really delighted. 'We'll go up into the hills,' she said. 'And you could take your field-glasses with you, Diana, and your bird book, and we could try to spot some interesting birds for your school essay.'

Roger winked at Barney. Everything was going along very nicely!

Snubby kept on staring at the two men, and Barney kicked him to make him stop. Who were these men? It should be easy to find out from Mrs Jones. He grinned secretly to himself to think that one of them probably had Snubby's code letter from his friend Bruce in his pocket – and had probably tried a dozen times to decode it, and failed!

Barney had a chance of finding out who the men were immediately after the meal. the two of them walked out of the room and went upstairs, and Mrs Jones came in to clear away, with Dafydd and Waddle hovering about outside in the hall as usual.

'Two more visitors, I see, Mrs Jones,' said Barney as she stopped to stroke Miranda, and give her a titbit.

'Oh, yes – they come often,' said Mrs Jones proudly. 'They are Sir Richard Ballinor, and Professor Hallinan – he's the great bird expert, you know. They are friends of my husband, he met them in London, and they know his cooking is good, very good, so they come here often, and they love the place, they love the mountains and the hills and the sea, and . . .'

The boys waited patiently till she had run on for some time, and then Barney interrupted.

'I expect they were pleased when your husband bought this place,' he said, 'it makes a nice holiday spot for them, doesn't it?'

'Ah, the good kind men, they lent my husband the money to buy the inn he so much wanted,' said Mrs Jones, in her lilting Welsh voice. 'So always I welcome them and give them my very best.'

I expect they've got that Best Room of yours then!' said Diana at once. Mrs Jones nodded.

'But that is not the room they *like* best,' she said. 'The room they always have is the room you have – with the two windows. But there – that Miss Pepper of yours is not one to change her mind, is she?'

'No, she's not,' said Roger and Diana together, remembering how many times in the past they had tried to make Miss Pepper change her mind about something! And then they heard Miss Pepper's voice at the door.

'Aren't you coming, children? Loony is barking his head off in the caravan!'

'Right,' said Barney, and they left Mrs Jones, who would certainly have chattered for an hour if they had stayed!

Miss Pepper and Diana and Loony set off for their walk in the hills, Diana with the field glasses slung over her back. Loony was rather puzzled that Snubby didn't come with them, and was inclined to stay with him – but when Snubby artfully rolled into his bunk and pretended to go to sleep, Loony at once decided that a walk with Diana was better than an afternoon in a boring caravan, with everyone shushing him.

'Now let's take our bathing things, and go all the way along the beach to the fishing jetty,' said Roger. 'We can bathe whenever we like – either before we look for Morgan the Cripple, or afterwards.'

'Better be afterwards,' said Barney. 'It's idiotic to bathe too soon after lunch.'

They set off with Miranda scampering in front of them, only leaping on to Barney's shoulder when they met a dog or a shouting child. The sun shone out of a cloudless sky, and became very hot indeed as they walked over the white sand, past the caves.

They came near the little stone fishing-boat jetty. Not many people were there. A few old boatmen sat on the low sun-warmed wall, and a woman sat knitting on a wooden seat. Barney and the others lay down on the sand nearby.

A dirty, unkempt boy in a bright woollen jersey came running on to the jetty with a mongrel poodle, and Barney sat up at once, nudging the others. 'That's the boy who gave Snubby the letter,' he said. 'There can only be *one* mongrel poodle in this little place, surely!'

They all sat up and watched the boy. He went to where a boat was being untied, and helped to push it off. It was a pretty sight to see its sails unfurling and filling with wind.

A man came on to the jetty at that moment, dressed in fisherman's clothes – a man who limped badly and walked with a stick.

'Morgan the Cripple, do you think?' said Roger, as the fisherman went to talk to some old cronies on the wall. 'Come on – let's go up on the jetty. We might be able to get into talk with him.'

But before they had got up from the sands someone else strode on to the jetty – a man with a dark beard, wearing sunglasses. He called sharply to Morgan, who got up at once. 'Here, Morgan – I want a word with you!'

'I bet there's going to be a quarrel!' said Barney excitedly. 'Let's hope we hear it. Come on – we'll get nearer to the wall!'

Chapter Fourteen

An Exciting Afternoon

'Come over here,' said Morgan to the bearded man, and took him to one side of the jetty, out of hearing of the other fishermen there. Barney and the others crawled over the sand as near as they dared, and lay down hidden by the stone jetty wall.

'Morgan – that letter you gave your nephew to deliver to me,' began the man. 'That wasn't the one you were given for me, you know it wasn't.'

'What are you talking about, Sir Richard,' said Morgan in a deep puzzled voice. 'That letter never left my pocket, and that I swear, from the time it came to me till the time I gave it to Dai this very morning. Didn't he go to the pile of rocks we arranged?'

'Yes. He was there – dressed as you said, and the little black dog too, so I knew it was the right boy,' said the beared man. 'But I tell you *he gave me the wrong letter*. I can't make head or tail of any of it!'

'That were the letter given to me for you,' said Morgan obstinately. 'Jim give to me as usual, straight from his pocket to mine it went, and all he said was, 'We'll be back Friday. Be ready,' and off he sailed again. That letter was what he give me, I tell you.'

'I don't understand it,' said the bearded man, staring at Morgan. 'Where's that nephew of yours? I'll have to question him – though how *he* could have changed the letter beats me. Morgan, if you're double-crossing me I'll pay you out in a way you won't like!'

'I'm not double-crossing anyone!' said Morgan, raising

his voice angrily. 'Do I want to double-cross myself? I'm in this as much as you are, aren't I?'

'Don't shout like that,' said the other man, looking round anxiously, afraid of the other fishermen hearing.

'I'll call Dai,' said Morgan surlily. 'He's there, watching that boat. He'll tell you it was the letter all right. Dai! DAI! Here a minute!'

The small boy and the poodle came running up. 'Yes, Uncle Morgan?' said Dai, glancing at the bearded man, and looking scared.

'Did you give this gentleman the letter I gave you for him this morning?' said his uncle sternly.

'Yes,' lied the boy. 'Yes, of course I did.'

The bearded man suddenly caught hold of the small boy, and held him in such a fierce grip that he began to howl. 'You didn't give me any letter! You're not the boy I saw! He was bigger – and his dog was a black spaniel – not a poodle.'

'Let go the boy,' said Morgan sternly, seeing that Dai was scared almost to death. 'You said you had a letter given to you by a boy – who *was* the boy then, if it wasn't Dai?'

'I don't know – I tell you, it was a boy with a spaniel – a real ragamuffin, like your nephew,' said the man, glaring at the terrified boy. 'And when I came up to him, I saw he was actually *reading* the letter! It was in code. I immediately thought it was the letter he should have delivered to me and took it, though he tried to stop me.'

Morgan laughed harshly, and turned away. 'Then you are a fool, Sir Richard. The boy wasn't the right raga-muffin, and the letter was his, not yours.'

Sir Richard grasped Morgan's arm and swung him round. 'Man, this is urgent, you know that. I've not got the right letter, I tell you – the letter you gave to Dai. Where's *that* letter? You, boy, answer me at once!'

'I – I gave it to a boy who came to talk to me,' wept poor Dai, terrified out of his life. 'I waited and waited for you, and this boy said he'd give it to you for me. I didn't know you'd already been – and gone off with the wrong letter.'

Sir Richard pushed the boy away from his with such force that he almost toppled over into the water. Morgan scowled. 'Leave the boy alone. What harm's been done? You got a letter you couldn't read – and someone else has got a letter *he* can't read. I'll get in touch with Jim and he'll send another.'

Sir Richard took out a handkerchief and mopped his forehead. he came close to Morgan and spoke in his ear, so that the three boys listening down on the sand below the jetty could only just hear his words.

'You deliver the next letter to me yourself, Morgan. If anything goes wrong, it'll be laid on *your* shoulders for thinking that idiotic nephew of yours was trustable. If Jim's letter hadn't been in code, there'd be someone else now who would know enough to spoil all our plans for Friday – yes, and for always!'

'Aw – shut up,' said Morgan rudely, and turned away.

'And if I find that boy whose letter I took – and who got *my* letter from Dai – I'll wring his neck!' said Sir Richard in such a bloodthirsty tone that Snubby, who could hear every word, felt suddenly scared. What had seemed rather a peculiar joke, was turning into something that wasn't a joke at all! Why on earth had he gone and talked to Dai and persuaded him to hand over the letter?

'I'd know the boy anywhere,' went on Sir Richard, still in the same angry voice. 'Awful ragamuffin – a tramp of a fellow in long, dirty-looking trousers, a horrible jersey, and a peaked cap too big for him – and a black spaniel. Dai is dressed much the same, but he isn't as big as this other fellow – and the black dog misled me, of course.'

Snubby was feeling distinctly uncomfortable now, and so were Barney and Roger. How maddening that this bearded fellow was staying at the inn! Would he recognise Loony? And then Snubby?

Morgan strode off, leaving the other man by himself. The fishermen on the wall looked at Morgan curiously as he passed. They had been too far away to hear anything that was said – but they knew there had been a quarrel.

'Your grand friend upset, Morgan?' called one old fellow. 'Wasn't your last catch of fish good enough for his lordship?'

Morgan didn't answer. The fisherman nudged one another and grinned as the bearded man walked after Morgan, but nobody dared to call out to him. Dai had disappeared entirely, hidden somewhere out of sight.

The three boys on the sand lay there silently for some time, and then, hearing no more voices, rolled over and looked at one another. 'Let's go and bathe,' said Barney, in case anyone was listening. He added in a low voice, 'We'll talk later. Come on.'

'Yes – a bathe would be fine, it's so jolly hot,' said Roger loudly. Snubby said nothing. He was still very shaken by what he had overheard. He hoped the letter was safe in the caravan. Had he better destroy it?

They said no more till they were well away from the jetty. Then Barney mopped his head and said 'Whew! What on earth do we do next? You've landed us into something now, Snubby – all through that idiotic code-letter from Bruce.'

'It wasn't idiotic,' said Snubby in a rather meeker voice than usual. 'Anyway, that fellow – fancy him being the Sir Richard Mrs Jones told us about – that fellow couldn't puzzle out our code. It's a jolly good one, and not idiotic as you seem to think.'

'Let's bathe,' said Barney, 'and perhaps when we feel

a bit cooler, we can think this business out. Good thing we didn't bring Loony, Snubby – that fellow might have spotted him – and us.'

'I say – what on earth are we going to do with Loony now?' said Snubby in sudden dismay. 'We mustn't let that fellow, Sir Richard, see him at all – but you know what Loony is – rushing about all over the place!'

They all splashed into the cool sea, and when they came out they felt decidedly better. They sat on the sand and talked.

'Today's Wednesday – and whatever is going to happen is planned for Friday. *I* think it's smuggling,' said Roger. 'There are only two more days to go. Do we go to the police, do you think?'

'No. No, I don't think so. If we do, they will question that bearded fellow, and whatever's planned won't happen,' said Barney, frowning. 'I'm just thinking of something we heard one of the fishermen yell out to Morgan. He said "Wasn't your last catch of fish good enough for his lordship?" Well now, what did that mean? It means that Morgan hires out a boat to Sir Richard, presumably for catching fish – but perhaps brings in *something else* – either instead of fish, or hidden in the catch.'

'Something that he wants brought here to be hidden, do you think?' asked Roger.

'Yes. Perhaps something he wants to hide for some considerable time,' said Barney thoughtfully. 'I wonder who this Sir Richard really is – and his friend Professor Hallinan, the bird expert. I think they are just *posing* as Sir Richard and the Professor – using their names instead of their own. I think I'll walk into Dilcarmock and telephone my father after tea, and ask him if he can find out.'

'They must be rich, to lend Mr Jones the money to buy the inn,' said Snubby, screwing his toes into the sand.

'I can't think *why* anyone should lend a few thousand

pounds to a fellow like Mr Jones, just because they liked his cooking so much,' said Barney. 'I mean – when you lend money, you expect to get some good return from it – the profits made on the visitors that come to the inn, for instance. But very little profit can be made on *that* inn, I'm sure. Beside ourselves there are only those two men there!'

'Well – what *does* he give them in return then?' said Snubby. 'Do you imagine he lets them use his inn as a kind of headquarters for whatever they are really up to?'

Barney sat us straight and smacked his knee. 'Of *course*! You've hit it! What other reason could there be? There's a little gang here – Morgan and Jim, whoever he is – and Mr Jones – all in some game together, and this inn is somehow the heart of it. Gosh – we *have* tumbled on to something!'

'But what have we tumbled on?' asked Snubby, excited. 'How can we find out what it is? I SAY – this is pretty exciting, isn't it? I simply can't wait till Friday!'

Chapter Fifteen

Oh, Loony

Loony was extremely glad to see the boys when they came back, and rather astonished to be shut up immediately in the caravan, when everyone went to have tea. He barked dismally, and Miss Pepper was surprised at Snubby's seeming hard-heartedness.

'I really can't see why he can't come in to tea,' she said. 'He was as good as gold with us this afternoon. We had a wonderful walk – and Diana spotted some most unusual birds with the field-glasses.'

'There was one bird I couldn't make out,' said Diana. 'A green bird with a red top-knot.'

Mrs Jones tells me that there is a Professor Hallinan staying here,' said Miss Pepper. 'A famous ornithologist, and . . .'

'A *what*?' said Snubby, astonished.

'Bird expert,' said Miss Pepper. 'So I suggested that Diana should ask him about the bird. He'd be sure to be able to identify it.'

The three boys felt extremely doubtful about this, as none of them believed that the Professor was a real bird-man, any more than Sir Richard was really a Sir Anybody! But Barney winked at the boys, and said cheerfully, 'Yes, Di – good idea. I'll come with you and listen to what he says. Might learn something – you never know!'

Snubby gave a sudden chuckle. 'No – you never know!' he said. 'Miss Pepper, we're going to walk in to Dilcarmock after tea – coming?'

'Good gracious no! I've had enough walking today,'

said Miss Pepper. 'You'd better catch a bus part of the way, it's quite a distance.'

The two men came in to tea at that moment and nodded to Miss Pepper. Diana determined to catch Professor Hallinan when he went out of the room. So she hovered about with Barney, while Snubby and Roger went to comfort poor Loony in the van.

At last the men came walking out, and made for the stairs. Diana darted to the tall moustached one, with a monacle in his eye.

'Oh please do excuse me, Professor Hallinan,' she said breathlessly. 'But I know you are a famous ornith – ornith – whatever it is, and know all about birds – so *do* you think you could help me to name a bird I saw today?'

'Er – surely! I'd be pleased to try,' said the Professor. 'Where did you see it?'

'Flying over the hills,' said Diana. 'Green, with a red top-knot.'

'Ah well, I fear I couldn't identify a bird on so little description,' said the Professor, courteously. 'It *sounds* as if might be a rare immigrant, which is sometimes seen here – Latin name *Lateus Hillimus*. Yes, it might be that.'

'Oh – thank you,' said Diana. 'I hope I remember such a peculiar name!'

Barney now entered the conversation, very politely. 'I saw a Short-Necked Curlikew,' he said, 'just outside the inn, it was. Surely that was unusual sir?'

'Very unusual,' said the Professor.

'And would you say that the Dotty Shade Warblers could be found in these hills?' asked Barney. 'I have heard they nest at times.'

'Er – well, yes, I believe they *have* been known to nest here,' said the Professor. 'Excuse me – I must join my friend.' And away he went up the stairs.

Diana stared at Barney in the utmost amazement.

'Short-Necked Curlikews! I've never heard of them in my *life*,' she said, 'and I know the names of *most* of our birds now. And who ever heard of the Dotty Shade Warblers?'

'Nobody,' said Barney, taking her arm. 'Your Professor is a fraud, dear Diana. What did he say that green bird of yours was – a *Lateus Hillimus*? Poppycock! You won't find *that* bird in any of your bird books! He's no more a bird expert than I am. I only wish I'd asked him if he had ever seen the curious nest of a Poppy Cockbird.'

Diana giggled. 'Gracious – I've a good mind to put the Poppy Cockbird into my school essay, just for a joke – and draw one too. But I say, Barney – do you really think the Professor is a fraud? He was so polite and knowledgeable too.'

'All tricksters are,' said Barney. 'And I bet that his friend, Sir Richard as he calls himself, is no more a botanist than the Professor is a bird expert! They're frauds both of them – using other people's names – pretending to be what they're not. My father knew their names – but I bet if he met them here, he would have spotted that they were bogus. Anyway, I'm going to phone him and ask him to make some inquiries, so that we can be certain.'

'Well, let's go and break the news to the others,' said Diana. 'Come on. Goodness – to think that the bogus Professor said that he thought your equally bogus Dotty Shade Warblers could be found in these hills! How do you *think* of names like that, Barney?'

'It's easy!' said Barney. 'Come on, Di. I want to be off to Dilcarmock to telephone my father. And we *must* keep Loony out of Sir Richard's sight, there's no doubt about that. He'd recognise him at once!'

They went halfway to Dilcarmock by bus, and then walked the rest of the way. Loony was delighted. Two long walks in a day – he was truly in luck!

Barney telephoned his father. 'Dad? It's Barney here. Can you hear me?'

'Yes – speak up a little though,' said his father. 'Are you all right?'

'Fine,' said Barney. 'But there's a bit of a mystery on about two men here – the famous experts that old Mrs Jones at the ice-cream shop told us about . . . Sir Richard Ballinor, and Professor Hallinan – they've arrived at the inn, and I've a feeling they're *frauds* – no more experts that I am! The Professor doesn't know one bird from another. What are they like, Dad? The real men, I mean?'

'One is tall, with an upturned moustache, and wears a monocle,' said his father. 'And the other, Sir Richard, is rather short, and has a beard.'

'Gosh,' said Barney, surprised to hear his father give such a close description of the two men at the inn. 'That pretty well describes the two fellows here, Dad – the ones I think are frauds. I say – could you possibly find out if the real Sir Richard and the real Professor are at their homes? If they are, I'll know for certain these two fellows are frauds, and we'll watch them to see what they are up to. But if you hear they're away in Wales – well – I suppose they won't be frauds after all. I think they are, though, in fact, I'm sure of it!'

His father chuckled. 'Quite a mystery!' he said. 'I'll certainly find out where the real Sir Richard and Professor are – they're both members of my Club and I can easily enquire there. I'll let you know at once whether your two men are false – or genuine.'

'Thanks,' said Barney. 'Don't telephone though, Dad – in case one of the men answers. Send me a telegram – and put just one word – "False" if the real experts are not the ones here – and "Genuine" if they are. Then I'll know what to do.'

'Right. But don't get mixed up in anything unpleasant,

Barney,' said his father. 'Let me know if there's any more I can do to help. I'll find out what you want at once, and you'll get a telegram tonight. I'll put the inn's telephone number, so that the post office will phone it through to you personally. Now don't get into any trouble – if these men aren't what they seem, they may be most unpleasant if they think any snooping is going on.'

'Right, Dad. Thanks and goodbye,' said Barney and put down the receiver. He went out of the box and told the others what his father had said. 'We'll know for certain tonight if what we think is correct,' he said. 'I *bet* we're on the right track!'

The four walked halfway back, and caught the bus the rest of the way, feeling quite tired. Even Loony decided that it was possible to overdo this walking habit! Miranda, of course, loved it all, for she sat on Barney's shoulder most of the time – and was thoroughly spoilt by all the passengers in the bus!

'You'll be sick down my neck if you accept any more sweets from people,' said Barney at last. 'Stop nibbling my ear, Miranda, you tickle!'

At a few minutes before eight, the telephone bell rang, and Mrs Jones came hurrying into the room where everyone was sitting. 'For you, Master Barney, please.'

Barney shot out, and a voice over the phone said, 'I have a telegram for you, sir. It has only one word though, and that is – *"False"*.'

'Thanks,' said Barney, and put down the receiver. 'False! Well, we guessed right. Mr Jones's rich and important friends are no more than rogues who are making money in some dishonest way with his help! Rogues who are working in disguise and using other men's names! Now we can go right ahead, and try and find out what's happening. Friday night is apparently *the* night. If only we knew what to look for!' He went to tell the

94

others. Diana wanted to tell Miss Pepper, but nobody agreed.

'But all this sounds as if it might be dangerous,' said Diana. 'And surely the *police* ought to be told those men are frauds.'

'We'll wait till Friday comes, and see if we can find out what is happening,' said Barney. 'And for goodness' sake, let's keep Loony out of sight. If one of those men spots him, and guesses that he belongs to one of us, there will be danger – because they'll know Loony's owner has got the real letter, and they'll go for Snubby at once to get the precious letter!'

'All right. Let's destroy it then!' said Snubby promptly.

'No,' said Barney. 'We might have to produce it, to show we really did get hold of it – when the police come in on the job – as they'll have to sooner or later. I'll take it and hide it somewhere safe. I'll get it now.'

He went out of the room, and down to the caravan. The letter had been put into Snubby's pillow-case, on his bunk. Barney slipped in his hand and took it out. Then he found some drawing-pins and took them and the code-letter outside the van. He crawled underneath it and pinned the letter on the under-part of the caravan, very firmly indeed.

He crept out, grinning. If anyone found it there he would be very very clever!

Loony was sitting sadly by himself in the van, wondering why he wasn't allowed in the inn. Barney felt sorry for him and left Miranda there for company. The little monkey sat close to Loony, chattering in his ear, but he took no notice at all. He was waiting for his beloved Snubby to come for him!

Everyone went to bed early that night, for they were very tired.

'What with bathing and walking, and all the rest of the

excitement we've had, I can't keep awake another minute!' said Snubby with a tremendous yawn that set all the others off too, Miss Pepper as well.

'Come along, Diana,' she said, getting up. 'You go off to your caravan, boys. Sleep well!'

They all slept very well indeed, and Diana didn't want to get up when the hot water arrived next morning, brought as usual by Mrs Jones, followed by Dafydd and the goose!

'Oh, Mrs Jones – I don't think we need have the goose in here,' protested Miss Pepper, and Mrs Jones shooed both the little boy and Waddle away.

'I didn't even know they were behind me,' she said. 'That Dafydd – he puts his nose everywhere, and that goose, he is just as bad – in my larder he was yesterday. Miss, as sure as I stand here, pecking at the scones I had made for tea. Sir Richard and the Professor, they make such a fuss of my Dafydd, Miss, he follows them all day long, they spoil him, I say, and . . .'

'Well, thank you, Mrs Jones, we'll be down in half an hour,' said Miss Pepper firmly, knowing quite well that if she didn't interrupt Mrs Jones, she would be standing there talking till breakfast time!

Everyone was punctual for breakfast for once, and Sir Richard and the Professor were at their table too. Nobody knew that Dafydd and his goose were once more peeping in at the window of the caravan – and that Dafydd was feeling very very sorry for poor lonely Loony, left there to wait for Snubby to return.

'Poor dog Loony,' said Dafydd softly, and tapped on the window. 'Poor dog!'

Loony saw Dafydd's small face peering in at the window and barked hopefully, pawing at the window-pane as he stood on his hind paws on one of the bunks.

96

'Dafydd will undo the door for poor dog Loony,' said the small boy pityingly. 'Wait, dog Loony.'

He scrambled down from the wheel he was standing on, and with his goose behind him, went to the door. It was shut, not locked, and he opened it easily.

Loony shot out at top speed, barking, and the goose fled for its life, cackling as if had laid a hundred eggs. Dafydd was cross. He had at least expected a word of thanks from Loony!

Loony tore across the slope of the hill and into the hall of the inn, the door of which was always left open. Where was Snubby? He flung himself against the door of the dining-room and scampered in, barking delightedly.

'LOONY!' said Snubby in horror. 'You bad dog! How did you get out?'

Loony threw himself on Snubby and licked him, whining as if he hadn't seen Snubby for a month. Barney glanced quickly round at the two men at the window table, with their bacon and eggs in front of them. Sir Richard was staring at Loony in amazement, and he nudged the Professor. 'That's the dog!' he said. 'I'd know him anywhere. He belongs to that boy, see?'

Barney couldn't hear what was said, but he could guess. Blow! Now the men would know that Snubby was the boy who had their letter. 'Quick, Snubby!' he said, 'let's get out of here with Loony. Buck up! Those men have spotted him – and you too!'

Chapter Sixteen

A Day Out For Snubby!

Snubby was really scared. He got up at once, and followed by Barney, left the table and went quickly out of the door. Loony went too, barking in delight. Miss Pepper was most astonished, and stared after them indignantly.

'Where have they gone – and why did they leave the breakfast table without a word to me?' she said. 'Is one of them feeling ill, Diana?'

Roger gave Diana a little kick under the table, afraid she might say something that would make trouble. 'Er – didn't you think Snubby looked a little pale?' he said.

'Perhaps it's a bit of the sun. He may have said a word to Barney about it.'

'I'd better go and find out,' said Miss Pepper.

'Oh, wait till Barney comes back,' said Roger. 'Don't leave your hot bacon and eggs! I expect old Berney will be back in a minute.'

He shot a glance at the two men sitting at the window table. They were talking earnestly, and the bearded man looked angry and troubled. Roger wished he could hear what they were saying.

Snubby was now safely in the caravan with Barney. Loony at his feet, and Miranda cuddled in Barney's arms. They were talking earnestly.

'How did Loony get out? He can't open the door himself!' said Snubby. 'I bet it was that little nuisance of a Dafydd – always snooping round! Well, *now* the fat's in the fire! Those men spotted Loony all right – and know

98

I'm the boy who took the code-letter from that fraud Sir Richard.'

'Yes – and they're certain to try and get it now,' said Barney. 'How, I don't know – but it might be jolly unpleasant for you, Snubby, if they catch you! I think the best thing for you to do is to hide.'

'All right. But where?' asked Snubby dismally. 'In the caravan? They'd soon find me here.'

'No, certainly not in the caravan,' said Barney. 'I almost think the best thing to do would be to catch the next bus to Dilcarmock and spend the day there. Unless the men happened to see you getting on the bus they's never guess you'd gone there. I'd better come with you.'

'Yes, do,' said Snubby, still looking dismal: 'But what on EARTH are we going to tell Miss Pepper?'

'The truth!' said Barney, getting up. 'I'll see if I can catch Roger's ear and tell him what we're going to do – and he can tell Miss Pepper we decided to go to Dilcarmock, and rushed out to catch the bus – and apologise for us.'

'I never finished my bacon and eggs,' groaned Snubby. 'Oh, why did I ever get mixed up with that idiotic letter?'

'I'll see if I can catch Roger,' said Barney, and ran up to the inn. He was careful not to be seen from the dining-room window, for he knew the men sat there. He went to the dining-room door and peeped in. Miss Pepper had her back to him, and he was able to signal to Roger unseen.

'Excuse me a moment, Miss Pepper,' said Roger, and slipped out of the room before she could ask him any questions. She was puzzled and annoyed.

'What *is* everyone doing this morning?' she said. 'I hope *you* feel all right Diana. I think I'd better go and see what is happening.'

'Well, have some hot toast first,' said Diana, trying to

give the boys as much time as she could. 'Take this nice brown piece.'

Barney told Roger their plans in a few words. 'We think Snubby had better clear off for the day – so we're going to Dilcarmock by bus and won't be back till supper time. Then I'll lock Snubby into the caravan, and we'll say he's tired – and I'll take him something to eat there – and perhaps have it with him, in case those men try to get him. Got it?'

'Yes,' said Roger. 'But Miss Pepper is getting very suspicious. For goodness' sake go now – she'll be out in half a minute, I know she will.'

'Right. We'll go at once,' said Barney, and went to fetch Snubby from the van. Roger watched them go racing down the slope to the village below. Would they catch the bus? It was about due now, and if they missed it they would have to wait a whole hour. He went back to the inn and met Miss Pepper hurrying out, having eaten bacon and eggs and toast very quickly indeed.

'Oh, Roger! What *is* happening?' she asked. 'Really! Leaving the table like that, one after the other, without a word of explanation! Where are Snubby and Barney?'

Roger looked round carefully before he answered, in case the man might be within hearing. 'Well, it's all quite simple,' he said, smiling brightly. 'Apparently they made up their minds to go to Dilcarmock for the day, and had to rush off very suddenly to catch the bus. They asked me to apologise to you.'

'Well – why in the world couldn't they have said just one word to me about their plans,' said Miss Pepper, still puzzled. 'Aren't you and Diana going?'

'Er – no – we thought we'd stay and keep you company,' said Roger. 'What about going out in a boat, Miss Pepper, just us three?'

'Well, that would be very nice,' said Miss Pepper. 'Very

nice indeed. But I shall have a few words to say to Barney and Snubby when they come back this evening – tearing out of the room like that in the middle of breakfast!'

The two men came out of the inn at that moment, talking in low tones, looking all round. Roger was sure they were looking for Snubby. They looked at him, and Sir Richard took a step forward as if he were going to say something. Then the other man pulled him by the arm, to stop him. Obviously nothing was going to be said in front of Miss Pepper!

'I bet they know she'd call the police if they began to make a rumpus about Snubby and secret letters!' thought Roger. He was glad to see Diana coming out behind the men.

'Di! We're going boating!' he shouted. 'Just the right morning for it – hot sun and a wind off the shore.'

'Oh *good*!' said Diana, longing to know what had happened to Snubby and Barney, but not daring to ask in front of Miss Pepper. Roger took Diana's arm and hurried her off to the caravan. 'Just going to tidy up the bunks!' he called. 'We'll be ready in ten minutes' time.'

Diana thought it was a very good idea of Barney's to go to Dilcarmock for the day. 'If only we can get Friday over, with whatever's supposed to happen then, I'll feel safer!' she said. 'Oh dear – why does Snubby *always* get into trouble? And us with him! And he never seems to mind, does he? I bet he's sitting happily in the bus now, pretending to play banjo or something, and keeping everyone in fits of laughter.

Diana was almost right in her guess! Snubby *was* in the bus – but he wasn't playing a pretend banjo, he was playing a mouth-organ – or rather, pretending to, his hand up to his mouth, making a most realistic zz-zz-zz noise, exactly as if he were playing a jiggy tune! And as Diana had surmised, everyone was delighted, laughing and egging him on. No – Snubby wasn't feeling nearly as worried as the others!

When Miranda slid down to the floor and began to dance in time to Snubby's horrible noises, even the bus driver had to look round – and the bus almost went into a ditch!

'Shut up now, Snubby,' said Barney, alarmed. 'You'll cause an accident.'

Back at the inn the others were preparing for a morning's boating. Miss Pepper insisted on large sunhats being taken, for the sun would beat down on the boat and there would be no shelter at all. They had to go and buy some at old Mrs Jones's shop, which meant an ice-cream each, of course.

While they were eating them, the two men from the inn passed slowly by, and peered in. They said nothing, much to Roger's relief, and walked on.

'I don't somehow like those men,' said Miss Pepper. 'I can't imagine why they're down here – they don't seem to fish or bathe – and look, they're in their city suits even on a day like this! If they weren't who they are I'd think they were up to no good!'

'I wouldn't be surprised if you're right, Miss Pepper,' said Roger solemnly, and Diana gave a sudden giggle.

They had a glorious morning quite far out in a boat. They took turns at rowing and steering and lying flat with a hand over the side dragging through the water. The two children bathed from the boat as well, and slowly their faces, arms and legs turned a bright red-brown. Miss Pepper was extremely glad of her enormous sunhat!

Barney and Snubby also had quite an amusing time in Dilcarmock. It was a big seaside town, full of trippers, and had a tremendous lot of side-shows. Barney, who had once been a circus-boy, used to going round with fairs, enjoyed joining in the amusements he had known so well

– hoopla stalls – dodgem cars – swings – roundabouts and so on. He even met someone he had once known at Rilloby Fair, and they had a wonderful talk which poor Snubby couldn't even share.

Miranda loved it all, of course, and Loony met so many stray dogs tearing about that he had the time of his life. He thought Dilcarmock was much more interesting than Penrhyndendraith!

'Time to get the bus back,' said Barney at last. 'We shall miss supper at the inn if we don't – even though you must have had at least a dozen ice-creams, Snubby, and goodness knows how many shrimps, and some of that awful gingerbread, and three meat-pies, and – let me see – how many cheese sandwiches was it?'

'Well, I'm beginning to feel hungry for my supper, all the same,' said Snubby. 'So don't let's miss the bus, Barney. Loony, keep to heel. I don't want to lose you just as the bus is due.'

They went to the bus stop, and the bus came rumbling along in about two minutes. They settled into the front seats, Miranda on Barney's shoulder, eager to see everything as usual. Loony lay at Snubby's feet.

'I do hope those two men won't try to get me this evening,' said Snubby suddenly. 'I'd forgotten all about them, I was enjoying myself so. Do you think I dare go in to supper?'

'Yes – you'll be all right if we're all with you,' said Barney. 'But we *must* go about together, all four of us *and* Loony, till bedtime. We can say we're jolly tired and go off early, see?'

They were glad to walk up the slope to the caravan, for they really *were* tired. Roger was there, waiting for them with an anxious face.

'I say!' he said, as soon as he saw them. 'Something's happened – the code-letter's gone from under the caravan where Barney pinned it. I think that silly, snooping little Dafydd found it. I can't find the little wretch anywhere, or I'd take it from him – and I only hope the men don't see him with it! Isn't he a *pest*?'

Chapter Seventeen

Where Is The Code-Letter?

Barney and Snubby looked at Roger in horror. The code-letter had gone? Who would have thought anyone could possibly find it, pinned so neatly to the underside of the caravan?

'Not only that – but our caravan lock was broken when I went to it after tea – and the whole place was upside down!'

'*That* must have been the two men searching it for the letter,' said Barney at once. 'Dafydd wouldn't dare to do that. He wouldn't be able to break the lock for one thing.'

'Why do you think Dafydd has the letter?' asked Snubby.

'Well, I'll tell you.' said Roger. 'You see, Miss Pepper, Di and I came back for lunch, and I went to get something out of the caravan – and I saw Waddle the goose standing by it. The lock wasn't broken then. I was surprised to see Waddle all by himself, because he's like a dog, always at Dafydd's heels . . .'

'Where was Dafydd then – under the caravan?' asked Barney.

'Yes! I looked all round for him, and couldn't see him – and then the goose stuck its head under the caravan and cackled as if to say "Buck up, Dafydd!" And *I* looked under and there was the little pest, as quiet as a mouse!'

'Did you see if he had the letter?' asked Snubby.

'No. I didn't think about the letter then!' said Roger. 'I just shouted at Dafydd and told him to come out, and said he wasn't to go near the caravan. He's too light-

105

fingered – takes anything he fancies, like a monkey. Oh – sorry, Miranda. I forgot you were present!'

Miranda chattered as if she understood, and Roger went on with his tale. 'Well, Dafydd shot off with Waddle – and then I suddenly remembered the letter and crawled under the van to have a look. And the letter wasn't there – but the drawing-pins were scattered on the ground below so *somebody* must have taken them out to get the letter. And I'm dead certain it *was* Dafydd, because if it had been the two men they wouldn't have come in the afternoon and searched the caravan for it, would they?'

'Not if they'd taken the letter in the morning,' said Barney. 'Well now, the thing is – has that little pest got the letter still? We'd find it out as soon as we can.'

But Dafydd had gone to bed! 'He is fast asleep,' said Mrs Jones. 'Such a boy he has been today, and that goose of his! Into my larder they were, and up the stairs, and into mischief everywhere, and . . .'

'Er – would he like this little clock we won at hoopla in Dilcarmock?' said Barney, bringing a gay little clock out of his pocket.

'Indeed and he would, oh indeed to goodness!' said Mrs Jones. 'But not tonight, sir, he is asleep! Tomorrow I will give it to him myself.'

'No, *I'd* like to give it to him,' said Barney, putting the clock firmly back into his pocket, and went off before Mrs Jones could say any more.

'We'll make him give up the letter in return for the clock,' said Barney. 'The little wretch! He's everywhere! Fancy crawling under the caravan!'

'Well, kids do silly things like that when they're as small as he is,' said Snubby. 'I remember thinking it was grand fun to crawl under my uncle's car when I was his age, and let oil drip on me.'

'You *would*!' said Diana. 'Ugh! Thank goodness I didn't want to do things like that.'

They had a pleasant supper, and, much to their surprise, the two men were not there.

'Have they gone, Mrs Jones?' asked Barney, nodding his head towards the window-table. She shook her head.

'Oh no, young sir. They had an early meal and have gone to see some friends. Busy men they are, sir, even when they are down in quiet Penrhyndendraith – rich men, important men, sir, and proud I am to think they like our inn – but it's the cooking, and very good cooking! You too like my husband's cooking, I know! You . . .'

'Yes, yes, Mrs Jones,' said Miss Pepper, and the cheery little woman took the hint and scuttled out of the room.

'She's absolutely non-stop!' said Snubby. 'Honestly, I never know why you stop her, Miss Pepper. I could listen to her for ages.'

'I dare say,' said Miss Pepper. 'But you and I have slightly different ideas, Snubby.'

'Don't squash me like that,' said Snubby crossly. 'Anyone would think I was an orange.'

Miss Pepper simply couldn't stop laughing, and the other chuckled. 'You *can't* squash old Snubby,' said Roger. 'We've all tried – but he's made of rubber. He bounces up again immediately.'

They all went off to bed early again, really tired with their long day. The three boys held a conference in their caravan.

'I'll nab Dafydd first thing tomorrow morning if I can, and get that letter from him,' said Barney. 'And Snubby must be very very careful not to go near the two men, in case they think he's got it on him – they know it's not hidden in the caravan, because they've searched for it – what a mess they made, the wretches!'

'How am I to stay away from the fellows tomorrow?' demanded Snubby. 'I can't *keep* going off to Dilcarmock.'

'We'll think of something,' said Barney. He yawned. 'I'm going to sleep – and woe betide Dafydd tomorrow if he doesn't give me that letter!'

The next morning they looked for Dafydd and Waddle as soon as they got up, but they were nowhere to be seen. Barney went along to the kitchen, where Mr Jones was cooking breakfast that smelt too delicious for words.

'Er – good morning. Do you know where Dafydd is?' asked Barney politely.

Mr Jones turned, scowling, holding a frying-pan in his hand. 'No, I do not. I will not have him here when I cook.'

The boys went out of the kitchen hurriedly, feeling that Mr Jones did not want them there either when he 'cooked.'

'What a dour, surly fellow,' said Roger. 'You'd think he'd be jolly cheerful, having this inn for his own.'

They kept a sharp eye out for the two men, but did not see them. Barney went cautiously into the dining-room to see if they were there – and found Mrs Jones clearing dirty plates away from the men's table.

'Oh – have they had their breakfast already?' asked Barney.

'Yes – early they were today!' said Mrs Jones. 'Sir Richard, he said they had much business to do today, and . . .'

'Oh, he did, did he?' said Barney. 'I wonder what kind of business he does in a little place like this.'

'Sir Richard owns two fishing vessels,' said Mrs Jones, 'and many other things. He . . .'

But just then Miss Pepper came in with Diana, and Mrs Jones hurried out of the kitchen to tell Mr Jones they were down.

The boys went hunting for Dafydd again after breakfast, keeping a sharp lookout for the two men, who, however, were not to be seen,. It wasn't until nearly lunch-time that they found Dafydd, wandering along with Waddle as usual. He came up to them at once.

'Mum says there is a clock you have,' he said. 'A clock for me.'

'Oh, she told you, did she?' said Barney, taking the gay little clock out of his pocket.

Dafydd gazed at the clock in delight, and rattled something off in Welsh. He reached out for it – but Barney held it away.

'Dafydd,' he said, 'if I give you this – *you* must give *me* something.'

'My knife!' said Dafydd, and dug his hand into his pocket.

'No, Dafydd – I want that paper you found under our caravan,' said Barney. 'You were bad to take it. But if you give it to me now, you shall have the clock.'

'Paper gone,' said Dafydd solemnly.

'Gone? Where's it gone?' demanded Roger.

'Men took it,' said Dafydd, pointing in the direction of the inn.

'When?' said Barney sharply.

Dafydd did not seen to know. He suddenly began to cry. 'They shout at Dafydd,' he said. 'Dafydd sit there, to make a boat with the paper,' and he pointed to a little wooden seat in the inn garden. 'And man come and say 'You give me that!' and he take it – like this' And Dafydd made a grab at the clock Barney was holding.

'Good gracious!' said Roger. 'That's a blow, isn't it! Dafydd, when was this?'

'Man hit Waddle,' said Dafydd, aiming a blow in the air. 'Bad man. Steal from Dafydd. You give me clock now?'

'No. You haven't got the letter to give me,' said Barney sternly. 'You were a bad boy to take the paper away and make a boat.'

'He probably didn't think it was ours,' said Roger, as the little boy began to cry bitterly. 'After all, you don't usually find a paper sheet stuck under a caravan! He couldn't have guessed it was so important.'

'I suppose he couldn't,' said Barney, looking at the sobbing child. He suddenly put his arm round him. 'Stop crying. We forgive you. See, here is the clock – you wind it up like this – it says tick-a-tock, tick-a-tock!'

Dafydd was overjoyed. He stopped crying at once and took the clock. He held it to Waddle's ear. 'Listen!' he said. 'Tick-a-tock, tick-a-tock.'

The goose backed away, not at all sure about the clock.

'And this is how you set the alarm bell going,' said Barney, hoping the child would understand. 'See – you wind *this* little handle – and now listen!'

The alarm bell shrilled out and the goose raced off in fright,, cackling loudly. Dafydd was entranced. He suddenly put his arms round Barney and gave him a great hug.

'You nice boy,' he said, 'Dafydd get back paper for you. Yes, Dafydd give it to you.'

'I wish you could, old chap,' said Barney. 'But it's too late now! Run along.'

Dafydd went to find his goose, and the others looked at one another hopelessly.

'No good,' said Barney. 'Those two men have the letter – and know all they want to, whatever it is – they know what "Jim" had told them to do tonight, and everything. Well, it's about lunch time. Where's Miss Pepper?'

I'll go and get her. She's upstairs,' said Snubby. 'Come on, Loony, let's go and tell Miss Pepper she's VERY late!'

And away he went at top speed with Loony, racing up

110

the stairs. But Miss Pepper was not in her room, and Snubby turned to go down again, Loony running in front of him.

He stopped dead as he saw Sir Richard coming along the landing, out of the Best Room. The man saw him and rushed at him, catching him by the collar.

'You! You pest! How dare you take that letter from that boy Dai! How much do you know? You tell me, or I'll throw you down the stairs.'

He swung Snubby over the stairway as if he really meant to keep his word. Snubby, half choked, was terrified out of his life.

He gasped out something, but the man could not understand, and shook him as if he were a rat. 'Answer me! I'll get the truth out of you if I choke you!'

Loony heard the angry voice and came tearing up at top speed. The little spaniel gave an angry snarl and flung himself on the man, nipping him sharply in the calf of the leg. Sir Richard let Snubby go, and yelled with pain, and the boy at once fled into Miss Pepper's room, and locked the door behind him.

He listened, gasping and choking and heard the man rush down the stairs, pursued by a very angry Loony Gosh – now what was he to do? He simply DARE not slip out of Miss Pepper's room – that fellow might get him again!

Chapter Eighteen

Dafydd's Discovery

Roger, Barney and Diana waited patiently for Snubby and Loony to come down with Miss Pepper. In a short while Miss Pepper appeared from the garden of the inn, where she had been sitting, reading a paper.

'Oh – are you ready for lunch?' she said. 'Where's Snubby?'

The others looked at one another. Where *was* Snubby – and why hadn't he come down when he found that Miss Pepper wasn't in her room? Barney felt suddenly alarmed.

'I'll fetch him,' he said, and went into the inn. He tore up the stairs, and came to Miss Pepper's room. It was shut and locked. Loony was there scratching at the door whining. Barney knocked. 'Snubby! Are you there?'

Snubby's voice answered him, sounding rather weak. 'Yes. Oh, Barney, is it you? I'll unlock the door.'

He unlocked it and Barney went in at once. 'What have you done to your head?' he said. 'My word, you look awfully pale, Snubby. Has something happened?'

'Yes,' said Snubby, lying on Miss Pepper's bed again. 'That bearded man attacked me – half choked me, and almost flung me down the stairs. I must have hit my head somehow – against the wall, I suppose, when he shook me till my teeth rattled! Loony went for him and bit him – good old Loony!'

'Grrrrr,' said Loony, fiercely, remembering.

'Gosh!' said Barney in horror. 'What a brute the fellow must be! You'd better stay out of his way, Snubby. He's furious with you for getting his letter from the little fisher-boy, Dai, of course. Pity we couldn't read it!'

'I'm staying up here,' said Snubby. 'I don't know what you can tell Miss Pepper, but today I'm quite definitely keeping out of Sir Richard's way.'

'I'll tell her you hit your head and hurt yourself,' said Barney, troubled. 'I'll suggest to her that you stay up here as it's much quieter than downstairs. Perhaps after to-night those men will go. Do you want any lunch? I could bring a tray up for you.'

'No thanks,' said Snubby. 'I couldn't eat a thing. My tummy feels all of a wobble.'

'Bad luck, old son,' said Barney, thinking that Snubby must indeed feel terrible not to want his lunch. 'Try to get a bit of sleep.'

'My head's begun to ache,' complained Snubby. 'Oooh, Loony, I *am* glad you went for that spiteful wretch!'

Loony leapt on the bed, and Snubby pushed him down. 'Sorry – this is Miss Pepper's bed, not mine,' he said. 'Though I dare say if I went to lie on Diana's bed, *she* wouldn't mind you coming beside me.'

Barney went downstairs and told Miss Pepper that Snubby had somehow hurt his head, and wanted to lie down quietly, and that he didn't want any lunch. Miss Pepper was quite alarmed to hear this and ran up the stairs at once. Barney quickly told the others what had happened, and they listened in dismay. Poor old Snubby.

Miss Pepper came down at last and they began their dinner. Miss Pepper was quite worried. 'I cannot *imagine* what Snubby was doing to bang his head like that,' she said. 'How very sensible of him to want to lie quiet this afternoon – of course my bedroom is just the place! Nobody will disturb him there. I'll pop up after lunch to see if he's all right, and then leave him in peace till tea-time. He says he has a most terrible headache, poor boy.'

113

'I bet he'll be all right by tea time,' said Roger, eating an enormous chunk of home-cooked meat-pie. 'I say, wasn't that little monkey of a Dafydd pleased with his clock! He must have set that alarm off about twenty times since we gave it to him. I keep hearing it trilling away somewhere or other.'

Miss Pepper went up to see Snubby after lunch, and was glad to find him fast asleep, with Loony on guard. She tiptoes out of the room, hoping that he would sleep till tea-time and then feel quite recovered.

'Wouldn't you like to bathe this afternoon?' Miss Pepper asked the three children. 'And lie out in the sun?'

'Sounds fine,' said Roger. Let's go a good way along the beach this afternoon, where there are those rock-pools. I bet some of them would be as warm as toast to wallow in.'

So they all went over the white sands, and settled down by the rock-pools. The rocks were quite high there, and the tide was going out, leaving warm, shallow pools in which swam grey shrimps.

They bathed, and then lay either in the deliciously warm pools, or on the hot sand. Miss Pepper put up a huge sun umbrella, lay down under it and fell asleep.

Barney lay in one of the pools, amused to feel a shoal of little shrimps trying to nibble his leg. He sat up to tell the others – and caught sight of two people coming along the sands, deep in talk together.

'Hist!' he said in a low voice. 'I spy Sir Richard and the other fellow coming along. Keep your heads down. I wonder where they're going?'

The two men walked quickly past on the sand, talking in low voices. 'Gone to chat to Morgan and Jim, I suppose,' said Barney. 'About the Doings tonight, whatever they are! What do you bet that one of Morgan's boats is coming in at dead of night with some mysterious "catch" that they don't want anyone else to see unloaded?'

'Look – isn't that Dafydd and his goose?' said Roger, in surprise. 'Following some way behind the men?' I wonder what he's up to? See how close he's keeping to the cliff – as if he doesn't want them to see him?'

'Doing a bit of shopping again, I suppose,' said Diana. 'You just never know where that child will pop up next!'

They all lay down again in the pool, their heads propped against convenient rocks. Diana yawned. 'I think I'd better get out and lie in the sun. I'm almost asleep, and I don't want to wake up choking in the water!'

It was a truly lazy afternoon, and the four, with Miranda too, thoroughly enjoyed it, though they missed Snubby and Loony very much. Miranda sat near Barney on a rock just above his head, sad because she could not sit on his shoulder as usual. But nothing would persuade her to lie in the pool too!

After about an hour Miranda began to chatter quietly, and Barney sat up in the pool. 'What's up?' he said. 'Someone coming?'

A small brown face, with a shock of untidy hair above it, peered round the rock at him. It was Dafydd! A long curving neck peering round as well, and Barney saw that Waddle was there too.

'Shhhhhh!' said Dafydd mysteriously, and then began to point with his finger some way up the beach, jabbing the air with it.

'What is it? What do you want to tell me?' said Barney in a low voice.

'Men,' said Dafydd. 'Two men. Dafydd see where they go. Dafydd want paper back, and follow men. Up long hole.'

'What on earth does he mean?' said Barney to Roger, who was listening. 'Do you suppose he went after the men with some wild idea of getting back that letter for us?'

'Up long hole,' said Dafydd, nodding. 'Dafydd take you.'

'This sounds interesting,' said Barney. 'Let's go with him and see what he means. Wait a bit, though – is that voices? Maybe it's the men coming back. Dafydd, come down here.'

Dafydd and the goose scrambled over the rocks and sat beside Barney, Dafydd's bare feet in the water, and the goose paddling solemnly round the pool.

'Men come back,' said Dafydd, peering over the rock. Barney pulled him down.

'Keep still,' he said, and Dafydd understood and sat quite still, swinging his feet to and fro in the warm pool.

The men passed by once more, on their way back, and were soon out of sight. Dafydd stood up. 'Up long hole?' he said, pointing over the sands. Barney and Roger scrambled out of the pool, shook themselves like dogs, and followed the small boy and goose back along the way the men had come.

They came at last to the caves that led into the cliffs, and Dafydd disappeared into one of the two marked 'DANGEROUS'. Barney pulled him back.

'No! This cave is dangerous,' he said.

Dafydd obviously didn't understand. He ran right into the cave, and the two boys followed him, feeling rather scared in case part of the roof fell.

'I suppose if the men *did* go into the cave, it can't be very dangerous!' said Roger.

'Or maybe they labelled it "Dangerous" themselves,' said Barney grimly. 'Perhaps they've got a convenient hiding-place up here!'

'Well – it's not much of a cave!' said Roger, as they came to the end of it. 'Nowhere to hide anything here!'

116

'Look at Dafydd,' said Barney. 'He's climbing up that rock – now he's running along a ridge – he's gone!'

So he had! He disappeared halfway along the ridge of rock, and Waddle the goose, left behind on the sandy floor of the cave, sent a sorrowful cackle after him.

Dafydd appeared again, beckoning. They could only just see him, outlined agaist the dark cave-wall, standing on the ridge.

'Up long hole!' said the small boy. 'You come too. Up long hole.'

Barney and Roger began to feel excited. They climbed part of the rock at the back of the cave, come to the ridge, and walked along it. Halfway along there was a hole in the wall of the rock, and it was through this that Dafydd had disappeared. He had now slipped through it again, and the two boys peered after him in the dim light, for the cave was almost dark.

'You come too?' asked Dafydd, and added something in Welsh that they didn't understand.

'Rather!' said Roger, and scrambled through with Miranda at his feet. 'Where in the world does this lead to? What a pity we haven't a torch. I say – it really *is* a long hole, isn't it – as far as we can see, anyway! Come back, Dafydd – we can't go scrambling about in pitch darkness!'

Chapter Nineteen

Very Exciting!

The two boys and Miranda climbed back into the cave where Waddle greeted them with loud cackles. Dafydd leapt down and joined them.

'Long, long hole,' he said. 'Men go up long hole. Dafydd too. Long, long, long.'

'All very mysterious indeed,' said Barney. 'Thanks, Dafydd. Did the men see you?'

'Not see Dafydd. Dafydd not get letter,' said the small boy, looking doleful. 'Dafydd make clock go Tr-r-r-r-ring, and men call out quick!'

Barney laughed. 'You little monkey! You crept behind the men, and set off the alarm! My word, they must have been scared. Good for you, Dafydd. Now you must go home.'

Dafydd set off across the sands, and the boys went to tell Diana where they had been. She was intensely interested.

'The men *must* be smuggling something,' she said, 'and hiding it up Dafydd's long, long hole.' I bet to-night there will be fresh goods to take up there.'

'Yes, quite probably,' said Barney. 'I wonder why they went there to-day, though. Perhaps to make room for the new goods? I wish we'd had a torch – we'd have gone right up the the very end of the hole. It's a steep passage really, of course, but Dafydd kept calling it a long, long hole! Funny little chap – he went up the rocky cave-wall like a monkey – well, like Miranda did, actually – with a spring and a leap and a jump! He must have eyes like a

118

cat – I believe he would even be able to see in the darkness of that passage! It seemed to go up pretty steeply, as far as we could tell.'

'Barney – let's watch to see if those men go out to-night,' said Roger eagerly. 'They'd have to pass fairly near our caravan if they did, and old Loony would be sure to bark. We could creep after them, and see what they take into the cave, if they do go there.'

'Yes. I don't see why we shouldn't,' said Barney, suddenly excited. 'Snubby can come too if he's feeling better – but not you, Di. Miss Pepper would hear you slipping out of your room.'

'I do hope old Snubby *is* better,' said Diana. 'Fancy that man attacking him like that! The sooner I hear those two men are in prison, the better I'll be pleased. Passing themselves off as a Sir Somebody and and Professor!'

Miss Pepper suddenly woke up with a jump and looked at her watch. 'Good gracious! It's tea-time!' she said 'You run on ahead, children, and tell Mrs Jones to get tea. I'll follow at my own pace.'

'Good,' said Barney, as they ran off over the sand, 'now we can slip upstairs and tell Snubby what we've discovered, without Miss Pepper overhearing.'

They found Snubby feeling much better, and began to tell him of their afternoon's excitement – but Snubby interrupted.

'Listen!' he said, 'something awfully peculiar happened this afternoon, when I was lying here, half asleep. Loony heard a noise first, and barked. I sat up, thinking those men might be coming into the room – but I hardly thought they would, with Loony barking like mad! But the noise didn't come from *outside* the room – it seemed to come form *inside*.'

'What noise?' asked Barney, puzzled.

'I don't exactly know how to describe it,' said Snubby.

'It was a – a sort of bumping and banging – and it came from that side of the room near the fireplace, but – well, as if it was *under* the room, sort of muffled.'

'Oh, Snubby!' said Diana, looking suddenly scared, 'it must have been the Noises that Mr Jones warned us about, when he said we'd better not have this room, we'd far better have the Best Room. He said that Noises sometimes came in the night – but I've not heard any so far. Miss Pepper and I thought it was just nonsense, of course. And now *you've* heard them!'

'Yes. I certainly heard them,' said Snubby. 'I didn't dare to get off the bed – and Loony began to bark his head off, and ran all round the floor, trying to find out what was making the noises.'

'What on earth *were* they, do you suppose?' said Barney puzzled. 'Is there a door behind the chest – a cupboard, or something?'

'Look and see,' said Snubby, and the three children peered round the back of the great chest. But no door was there, only the stone wall.

'It's a mystery,' said Barney. 'But I say, we'd better not stay up here discussing it. Miss Pepper will wonder what's up again. Are you coming down to tea, Snubby?'

'Rather. I feel jolly hungry – and I don't particularly want to stay alone in this room of noises any longer,' said Snubby. So down they all went, to find Miss Pepper patiently awaiting them, and a very fine tea on the table.

The four children, with Miranda and Loony, went to have another talk after tea, in the caravan. They shut the door and spoke in low voices. Barney told Snubby of their idea to follow the men, if they went out that night, and see if they went up the 'long, long hole.'

'I'd like to come – but I don't think I will,' said Snubby. 'I feel a bit shaky now I'm up. I'll tell you what I will do, though – when you have left the caravan to follow the

120

men, I'll nip upstairs and lie on the couch in the room next to Diana's and wait till I hear them come back – and report to you as soon as you reach the caravan.'

'Righto, if you want to,' said Barney, understanding quite well that Snubby wasn't particularly anxious to stay all by himself in the caravan that evening!

'Better find our torches,' said Roger. 'We shall certainly need them. Do you mind if we take Loony with us, Snubby?'

'Er – no,' said Snubby, wishing he could say yes, he did mind! He knew he would feel much safer with Loony somewhere near him!

They found their torches, and then put on warm jerseys, for the wind had changed and now blew cold. They went to join Miss Pepper, and set off for a short walk in the hills behind the inn. A bird flew up as they walked over the heather, and Barney pointed to it solemnly.

'Is that a Crazy Corn-Crake, or a Yellow Black Bird?' he said. 'We'd better ask the Proffessor when we get back!'

They all began to feel excited when they were back from their walk, and had had supper.

'It's not dark till about ten,' said Barney, 'so we'll have a game of cards, shall we? Anyway the men are still here, so we needn't worry about them slipping off without us seeing them!'

The two men were walking up and down outside the window well in sight. At about ten they came indoors and went upstairs.

'Getting ready to go, I expect,' said Barney. 'Come on, we'll be off to the caravan and keep watch. We'll say good night to Miss Pepper now.'

Miss Pepper and Diana went upstairs to bed. 'Good luck!' Diana whispered to the boys, as she left. Snubby went off to the caravan with Roger and Barney, who

121

slipped on their warm jerseys again and put their torches into their pockets. Snubby began to wish he was going too, but they wouldn't let him.

'You still look groggy,' said Barney.'We don't want you fainting, just as we go up the long, long hole, and watch for the men. They won't guess we're watching, so they'll probably come straight out of the front door.'

The caravan was in darkness, and the three boys peered out of the window, Miranda too. At about half past ten they heard footsteps, and by the light of the half moon saw the two men coming down the slope.

But wait – there were *three* men, not two! Barney nudged Roger sharply. 'See who the third man is – Mr Jones! I *thought* he was in this, didn't you?'

'Wait till they've gone round the bend, then we'll follow,' said Roger excited. 'Gosh! Fancy Mr Jones going too!'

They slipped out of the caravan with Loony as soon as the men were round the bend, leaving poor Snubby alone. He didn't like being on his own and shot up to the house, creeping up the stairs and going to the room next to Diana's as he planned. He lay down on the couch there wishing heartily that he had Loony with him.

Meanwhile Roger, Barney, Miranda and Loony were stalking the three men. They were now down on the beach, making their way to Merlin Cove, where the caves ran back into the cliffs. The moon gave enough light for the men to be clearly seen in front of them, and the boys were careful to keep out of sight by walking close to the cliffs.

'Tide's coming in,' said Roger, 'and its going to be pretty high tonight, with that strong wind blowing off the sea. Hallo – look! Is that a boat coming ashore?'

They stopped, keeping close to the cliffs, and watched a boat being rowed ashore. Two men were in it, and the boys felt sure that the man rowing was Morgan. Who was the other?

'Jim, probably, whoever he is,' said Barney. 'I can't see that they have much in the boat – if they are bringing in goods they have smuggled in a fishing catch.'

The three men did not go down to the boat when it grounded on the sands but waited while it was pulled up on the beach by Morgan and the second man. Then Morgan and his friend began to lift what seemed to be big packets out of the boat, and went up to the caves with them.

The men took them and disappeared into the cave marked 'Dangerous.'

'The one we were in this afternoon, of course!' said Barney.

Then Morgan and his friend went back to the boat and staggered up the beach with more packets, evidently the last ones for they, too, disappeared into the cave. One of them came back and pulled the boat right up to the cave entrance, making it fast.

Then he too went into the cave, and it seemed as if all of them had gone to some hiding-place where the packets were to be placed.

The two boys and Loony went right up to the cave and stood outside, listening. Not a sound was to be heard except the little waves breaking on the sand as the sea came in.

'Come on,' said Barney. 'Into the cave we go, and up the wall at the back on to that ridge. Maybe we can hear the men if we listen at that hole that goes up and up,'

They went in quietly, not switching on their torches at first, for the moon shone into the cave and lighted it.

'Up we go!' said Barney, leaping up the wall on to the ridge, and pulling up a most surprised Loony. 'And don't let's make any noise, for goodness' sake. Loony, not a growl or a bark from you, or you may put us in danger. Here's the hole, Roger. I'll lead the way!'

Chapter Twenty

The 'Long, Long Hole'

The two boys shone their torches up the hole.

'It goes up and up and up!' said Barney. 'It's rather like a shaft, only not so steep, of course. I can't hear a thing, can you?'

'No,' said Roger. 'The men must be a good way up – come on!'

They began to clamber up the long, steep passage, switching on their torches every now and again to show them their footing. Not a sound could they hear until at last Loony gave a little growl of warning. They snapped off their torches at once.

'Voices!' whispered Barney. 'Voices some way in front. We'd better be careful now. Shade your torch with your hand, Roger, when you switch it on. Come on – they're a long way ahead yet. Quiet now, Loony!'

They went on again, listening for any sound from above, but could hear nothing. Either the men had now gone beyond hearing, or were being very quiet. The boys came to a very steep part indeed, and discovered that rough steps had been cut there. They climbed up them, and came to what seemed to be a small cave in the very heart of the cliff. They sat down to rest for a moment, panting with the long, steep climb. Loony ran round, sniffing here and there.

'Loony! Miranda? Where have you gone?' whispered Barney, switching on his torch and shining it round the little cave. '*Now* where are they, Roger? I can hear them, but can't see them!'

He got up cautiously, and went farther into the cave. He found the two scraping about behind a big rock, unearthing the bones of some small animal. 'Leave that alone!' whispered Barney. 'Come with us. We're going on up the hole.'

Miranda leapt on to his shoulder and Loony reluctantly left his find. Once more they all scrambled up the steep passage, which was, in truth, more like a 'long, long hole,' as Dafydd had said.

'Have you any idea of the direction we're going in?' asked Roger.

'No – except that we seem to slant to the left all the time,' said Barney. 'We must have got beyond the cliffs by now and be burrowing up the hills at the back of them.'

They heard noises again a little later, and stopped to listen. The noises went on and on, and sounded as if goods were being moved or stacked.

'I bet they're opening those packets and stacking the contents somewhere,' said Roger. 'Shall we go any nearer?'

'Yes – but I think perhaps only one of us,' said Barney. 'You stay here with Loony and Miranda, and I'll go as near as I dare. Keep your hand on Loony's collar.'

Barney went on up the steep passage, and soon the sound of voices was quite loud. Counting was going on – '100 – 200 – 300' Barney heard. He looked up the passage, which was not so steep here, and saw a bright circle of light not far ahead.

'That's where the passage stops and the hiding-place is,' thought Barney. 'They're all up there together. I can hear Morgan's deep voice now – I wish I could hear what he's saying – but I hardly dare creep any closer.'

He stayed for about ten minutes, listening to the sound

of goods shifted about and stacked, and voices arguing. Then suddenly he got a shock.

The men were coming back, and the lamp or whatever it was that he could see shining some way up the passage, in the hiding-place, was suddenly switched off. The beams from torches appeared instead! Barney scrambled back to Roger quickly, finding it much easier to go down than it had been to climb up!

'Roger – they're coming down!' he whispered. 'Pretty quickly, too. Come on. Where's Miranda?'

'She slipped off,' said Roger. 'I didn't see her go. She's probably gone down again.'

They went down farther, hoping to see Miranda waiting for them, but she was nowhere to be seen. Loony didn't like slithering down any better than he liked scrambling up! They came to the little round cave where Loony and Miranda had unearthed bones. 'There she is!' said Barney, exasperated, shining his torch on the little monkey.

She leapt up to a jutting piece of rock and chattered at him. 'Come here at once,' ordered Barney in a low voice, but Miranda chose to be annoying, and sat up on the rock, swaying about and chattering all kinds of nonsense.

'We'll have to go on, Barney,' said Roger. 'I can hear the men getting quite near.'

'Well, I'm not leaving Miranda,' said Barney. 'Come on – let's hide behind that rock where Loony unearthed those bones. The men will never guess anyone is here – they don't know they were followed.'

'All right,' said Roger, feeling uneasy as the men's voices became louder and louder. He and Loony went quickly to the big rock and stood silently behind it, Loony pressing against his legs. Miranda at once dropped on to Barney's shoulder and put her tiny paws down his neck.

The voices came very near, and the sound of the men's

feet was almost deafening as they slipped and slithered down the steep rocky passage. Loony couldn't help giving little growls as they passed the entrance of the small cave in which the boys were hiding.

Roger tapped him sharply, afraid that the men would hear, and stop to investigate. But mercifully they didn't, and soon the sound of their voices and feet grew less and less, until finally the boys could hear no sound at all.

'It's all right now – we can go,' said Barney, relieved, and switched on his torch. 'Miranda, take your hands out of my neck, you tickle terribly. And stay on my shoulder, or I'll never bring you out on an adventure again!'

The boys went down the hole, slithering over very steep parts, making far more noise than when they went up! They came at last to the end of the hole, and stood on the ridge of rock on the wall of the big cave. The moon shone into the cave – and what a shock the boys had!

The moon now shone, not on white sand, but on heaving water! Water that was already as high as the ridge they stood on! It caught the moonlight at the entrance, and then shimmered in the light of the boys' torches, at the dark rear end of the cave.

'The tide's come in to the cave – *right* in – and it's still coming!' said Barney in horror. 'I never thought of that. It's swept into this cave – and all the caves, of course – and the wind is piling up the waves high enough to swamp the lot. What shall we do?'

'I reckon the men only just got away in time,' said Roger. 'But, of course, they had a boat. Look out – that wave will sweep us off the ridge!'

They leapt back a little way up the hole just in time to avoid being swept away as an enormous wave splashed right over the ridge. They retreated back up the hole, scared.

'Well,' said Barney, 'it certainly looks as if we're going

to be penned up here for some time, because the tide isn't full for an hour or two. It's that strong wind that's making it so high. Blow! Snubby will be waiting and waiting for us to get back – and he'll be worried stiff.'

'I say – let's go back up the hole and see what the men have hidden in that hidey-hole, or whatever it is, right at the top of the passage,' said Roger, excited. 'Come on – it's a fine chance for us, Barney! We know the men can't come back, because they wouldn't be able to get through the water in the cave.'

'You know – that's an idea!' said Barney, delighted. 'A really good idea! If we find out what's hidden there, we can go to the police tomorrow, and tell them, not only about the men, but about what they've hidden, and where it is! If only we hadn't to make that wearisome climb all over again!'

'Oh, come on – it won't seem so bad this time, because we don't need to be afraid of the men hearing us,' said Roger, and Loony barked all the excitement in his voice.

So back they all went again, up the long, shaft-like passage – and certainly this time it did not seem so long, for they could go as carelessly as they liked, and not be afraid of making even the slightest noise! They let Loony bark, and allowed Miranda to scamper ahead as much as she liked.

They came to the last part of the passage, which was steeper than ever.

'There's a rope-ladder here, at the very end,' panted Barney, shining his torch in front of him.

Roger saw a strong rope-ladder stretching up from the end of the rocky passage to the entrance of the hiding-place. He held Loony while Barney went up the rope with Miranda. Then he went up too, leaving Loony below.

The boys stared round at the hiding-place. It was about eight feet square, a natural hole in the rock that someone had made into a kind of cell by chipping the walls smooth, and the floor level. It was stacked with oblong packets, marked with numbers. Except for a few empty bottles which had held drink of some kind, and a couple of old rugs, there was nothing else to be seen.

'Gosh – what a wonderful hidey-hole!' said Roger, looking round. 'I wonder who first discovered it. Barney, what do you suppose is in those packets?'

'I think I know all right!' said Barney. 'They're packets of stolen bank-notes! Bank-notes that can't be passed for some considerable time, because the numbers are known – but which could be shipped across to Ireland easily enough, perhaps from this Welsh coast – or stored till the hoo-ha and excitement has died down, and then used some time in the future!'

'I *say*! But there must be millions here!' said Roger, amazed. He patted a big packet. This will be about the only time in my life that I shall ever be able to say I have laid my hands on hundreds of thousands of pounds! Barney – *now* I can see why those men got Mr Jones into their power – they badly wanted some good headquarters down here on this coast – where they could bring their goods by boat and hide them, and take them away again by boat – over to Ireland, perhaps, as you say!'

'Yes. Or help themselves to a packet or two when they knew they could get rid of the notes undetected in London, or some other big town!' said Barney. 'Do you remember the last bank raid, Roger – where the thieves ambushed the driver of a bank van – and drove off in the van with hundreds of thousands of pounds? Not one note has been traced so far – and I wouldn't mind betting it's all here!'

Roger's heart began to beat fast as he glanced round at the stacked packets again.

'Could we open one just to see?' he said.

'Better not,' said Barney. 'We'll tell Miss Pepper tomorrow – and I'll telephone my father. He'll get on to the London police. The village policeman here couldn't possibly deal with it.'

Roger sat down on a pile of the packets. 'To think I may be sitting on half a million pounds!' he said. 'Oh, Barney – I *wish* we could get out of here and tell everyone! To think we're penned up here for hours because of that high tide.'

Barney glanced all round the little room, and then happened to look upwards. What he saw so astounded him that he stood as if turned into a statue, staring, staring. Roger was quite alarmed.

'What's the matter?' he said, and looked upwards too. He was as amazed as Barney at what he saw.

'A *trap-door*! A wooden trap-door! Set in the roof of this funny round hole. BARNEY! Let's open it and get out and see where we are. Quick, Barney!'

Barney was as excited as he was, but more cautious. 'Wait a bit, wait a bit! We don't know where the trap-door leads to, ass. We might walk straight into trouble! Shut up, Loony, shut up barking! Gosh, we've excited him now, too, and he'll bark the place down. I'd better go down the ladder and drag him up here. Perhaps he'll be quiet then.'

They stacked up the packets high enough to reach the trap-door, and then mounted them. Both boys raised their arms, and pushed at the wooden trap-door, which fitted closely into a square of the roof. But it would not budge.

'Must be fastened the other side!' panted Barney. 'Oh, *blow*! Try again, Roger!'

They tried again, banging at the trap-door in their impatience, making a tremendous noise.

'I expect it opens into some deserted cellar or pit,' said

Roger. 'Probably nobody will hear us, Barney. Try again! Oh, Loony, DO be quiet!'

'I suppose the men prefer to use the cave way when they bring the money in,' said Barney, taking a rest, 'because it's so easy to bring it by boat. Nobody would suspect a boat going out by night, and Merlin's Cove would be quite deserted then. But the men don't need to help themselves to the money by way of the cave and the hole. When they want it, they've only to open the trap-door and drop neatly down, collect what they want, and go back through the trap-door again. Very clever!'

'Let's try the trap-door again,' said Roger. 'We might use one of the packages as a battering-ram – they're solid enough! Do stop barking, Loony – it's quite deafening in here!'

The two boys stood on the packages – and then they suddenly leapt down in fright. Loony growled fiercely, making Miranda jump in fear on to Barney's shoulder.

'Someone's opening the trap-door!' said Roger. 'I can hear noises up above. Oh, gosh, Barney it's not those men, is it? We're trapped if it is. We've no getaway at all!'

Chapter Twenty-One

The Trap-Door Opens!

And now how was Snubby getting on, lying alone in the little room next to Miss Pepper's, missing Loony very much – listening anxiously for the two men to return to their room nearby?

He was quite determined to creep behind the big couch he was on, if he heard so much as a footstep! But he heard nothing at all for what seemed like hours, and at last fell asleep very suddenly indeed.

Diana too, in the next room was fast asleep, but Miss Pepper was still reading a book. At last she yawned, shut her book and blew out her candle. She was just going to sleep when she thought she heard a little noise. She opened her eyes and listened – no – it must have been an owl outside.

She fell asleep, and then awoke again some time later. She sat up. What had awakened her? she listened intently. There – a noise – it came again and again. It almost sounded as if it was in the room!

Miss Pepper was not easily scared, but her hand was trembling a little as she lighted her candle again. Diana woke up, as the light flickered in the room.

'Are you all right, Miss Pepper?' she asked, sleepily, thinking it was the middle of the night, although she hadn't really been asleep very long. 'Ooooh – what's that?'

'I don't know,' said Miss Pepper, puzzled. 'I heard noises – but there doesn't seem anything to cause them.'

'Oh, Miss Pepper – they must be the noises Mr Jones

told us about!' said Diana. 'He didn't want us to have this room because of them – nor did Mrs Jones.'

'Oh yes,' said Miss Pepper. 'But I really thought that was only a bit of nonsense. There – did you hear that? A deep-down sort of noise – bump!'

'Yes,' said Diana, scared. 'I don't much like it. Where's it coming from, Miss Pepper?'

'I don't know,' said Miss Pepper, getting out of bed, and holding the candle into every corner. Diana thought she was very, very brave! Bump! Boomp! Bump!

'It's coming from the old chest!' said Diana, with a little scream.

'No, dear, no,' said Miss Pepper. 'Don't be silly. There's nothing in the chest but our clothes. You know that.'

Miss Pepper went to the door of their room and opened it, looking out, holding her candle up to make sure that the three boys were not playing some sort of a silly joke in the middle of the night to scare her and Diana. They could be very annoying at times!

But no – no one was there. She noticed that the door of the next room was a little open, and went to it. Was anyone hiding in there?

She had the surprise of her life when she saw Snubby fast asleep there, sprawled on the big sofa, still in his day clothes! What on *earth* was he doing there? She went over and shook him. He awoke in a hurry, scared stiff, thinking the men had got hold of him!

'Why are you here, Snubby? Did you hear any noises?' asked Miss Pepper, wondering if by any chance she could be dreaming it all.

'Ooh – you *did* frighten me,' said Snubby. 'What noises? No, I've heard none – but I did hear some when I was resting in your room today – bump – boomp – bump!'

134

'Yes – that's what *we've* been hearing, Diana and I,' said Miss Pepper. 'Come and listen, Snubby.'

So Snubby joined Diana in the next room, and they all listened. But they could hear absolutely nothing at all now.

'Funny!' said Snubby. 'Not a sound to be heard. Can I sleep on your couch at the foot of the bed, Miss Pepper – to – to see that you're safe, you know.'

Miss Pepper smiled a little. 'Of course, Snubby – but now tell me why you were sleeping in the next room, instead of in the caravan with the others? What's happened? Have you quarrelled?'

'I can't tell you just yet, Miss Pepper,' said Snubby awkwardly. 'Tell you tomorrow, perhaps.'

He snuggled down on the sofa, with a blanket thrown over him, and Diana and Miss Pepper got into bed again. The candle was blown out, and they all lay in darkness, hoping to goodness that there would be no more disturbing noises. None came, and one by one the three fell asleep once more.

Some time later Snubby woke again, and sat up, astonished. He heard a MOST surprising noise – so surprising that he thought he must have been dreaming. But no – there it was again – wuff-wuff-wuff! It was Loony barking!

'Miss Pepper! I can hear Loony barking!' he cried, shaking her awake. 'But it can't be! Di, wake up! Can you hear Loony?'

Now they were all awake and listening. Wuff-wuff-wuff! Yes, that was Loony all right. But where was he? The barking sounded near, and yet muffled.

'This is really mysterious,' said Miss Pepper, worried. 'Where in the world can Loony be?'

Then loud noises came – bang! Bang-bang-bang. They sounded almost as if someone was knocking at a door somewhere, very fiercely indeed.

135

'The noises *are* coming from the chest,' said Diana, almost in tears.

'Let's move it out,' said Snubby. 'I thought the same myself this afternoon, when I heard them. Come on – help me, both of you – it's most FRIGHTFULLY heavy!'

It certainly was – but they managed to shift it at last – and there, where it had stood, was a wooden trap-door, shut tightly down!

'Gosh – look at that! No wonder they didn't want you to have this room!' said Snubby. 'This trap-door must be used for something secret – for whatever dirty work those two men are doing! There – I can hear Loony again! AND Barney's voice – listen!'

'But – but who put them down there and shut the trap-door on them?' said Miss Pepper, overcome with amazement. 'I never heard of such a thing in my life! Can we lift up the trap-door, Snubby? Oh dear – I feel as if this *must* be a dream!'

'Can't be,' said Snubby. 'It's much too noisy. Gosh, they're banging at the trap-door again. They couldn't open it while the chest was standing on it, of course. Hey, wait a bit – I'll pull this handle – ah – UP she comes!'

And the trap-door gradually lifted as Snubby and Diana pulled at the iron handle!

Down below, there was great consternation of course. Barney and Roger were absolutely horrified to see the trap-door being raised from the other side! They at once thought that somehow the two men were there, and that now they would be discovered – and properly trapped. They ran to the rope-ladder and began to climb down it. But Loony wouldn't come. He began to bark excitedly as the trap-door opened, and he heard Snubby's beloved voice.

'Hey!' called Snubby, taking the candle from Miss

Pepper, and sticking it down the hole. 'Loony! What on earth are you doing there! LOONY!'

Loony nearly went mad, trying to jump as high as the trap-door and failing miserably. Barney and Roger and Miranda paused when they heard Loony's happy barking, and heard Snubby's voice.

'That *can't* be Snubby opening the trap-door!' said Barney amazed. 'But it's his voice! Quick, let's get back into the little room and see.' So back up the rope-ladder they went – and saw Snubby peering through the open trap-door, waving a candle, and Loony almost mad with joy.

'SNUBBY! How did you get there?' yelled Roger. 'Where are you?'

'In Miss Pepper's room. Under the old chest,' said Snubby, getting muddled in his excitement. 'But I say – how did YOU get down there? Gosh, this really MUST be a dream. Hand Loony up, will you, before he goes stark raving mad!'

Loony was handed up, and promptly did go completely mad, tearing round and round the room, leaping on the beds, and barking at the top of his voice. Miranda leapt through the trap-door too, and poor Miss Pepper's bedroom became a complete madhouse, as the two animals chased round and round.

Barney and Roger climbed through the trap-door, helped by Snubby, and were soon sitting on the beds, laughing and most relieved at their extraordinary escape.

'*Well*! To think that passage from the cave led right up to Miss Pepper's bedroom!' said Barney. 'I never even dreamed it would go to the inn – but of course, now I think of it, it went so very steeply up a slope and veered this way all the time right to the hill that rises up against the back walls. So easy to make a secret entrance! Everything fits in beautifully now – the men staying here – and wanting this bedroom – because it's the entrance to their hidey-hole – and . . .'

'I simply cannot *imagine* what you are talking about,' said poor Miss Pepper. 'Will you kindly enlighten me?'

'Oh, don't go all starchy, Miss Pepper darling,' said Snubby hugging her. 'We've had a secret from you – listen.'

And he and the others poured out their strange story to the amazed Miss Pepper. She could hardly believe it.

'Why didn't you tell me anything of this?' she demanded. 'I would have taken you all away from here AT ONCE.'

'That's just why we didn't tell you!' said Roger. 'We couldn't bear to leave in the middle of something mysterious like this. Isn't it *exciting*, Miss Pepper?'

'It's certainly *exciting*,' said poor Miss Pepper, quite overcome. 'I wonder why it is that I can never go away with you children without getting mixed up in something really undesirable!'

'But Miss Pepper – don't you think it's *desirable* to catch thieves?' said Barney. 'Those two men must be two of the cleverest rogues in the country – and we've found out! Oughtn't we do something about it at once?'

'Oh dear – in the middle of the night?' said Miss Pepper. 'Well, perhaps we ought.'

'Roger, you and Snubby see if you can get some of those packages up into the bedroom,' said Barney. 'And I'll go down quietly to the telephone, and wake up my poor father – and tell him to inform Scotland Yard – or his local police if he thinks it's best – of our discoveries.'

So, while Snubby fetched a rope from the caravan to fix to the strong handle of the trap-door, and then slid down it to pass up packages to Roger, Barney went quietly down to the telephone, woke up his astounded father and told him the news. He kept an ear open for the two men to come back, but not until he had put down the receiver and gone upstairs again did he hear quiet footsteps.

He slipped into Miss Pepper's room, shushing the others, and listened until he heard the men's door quietly shut. Then he slipped out again, and came back looking so triumphant that Miss Pepper was astonished.

'What have you been up to now, Barney?' she said. 'Nothing much,' said Barney. 'The men left the key of their room outside in the lock, so I just slipped out, and locked them in. They will have to wait there till the police come and let them out – because I've got the key in my pocket!'

It was very late when at last the three boys, with Loony and Miranda, went down to the caravan to get a little sleep. Diana and Miss Pepper crawled into bed, but could not go to sleep for a long time, because they had to talk and talk and talk!

'It will be an exciting day tomorrow!' said Diana – and it certainly was! Two cars arrived about nine o'clock, full of plain-clothes police, and poor Mr Jones had the shock of his life when they appeared in his kitchen!

The two men also had a terrible shock when they found their door well and truly locked on the outside – and were faced by four sturdy policemen when at last it *was* opened!

'What's the meaning of this!' blustered Sir Richard angrily – but he calmed down at once when an inspector reached out and tugged off his beard!

'Ah – George Higgins,' said the inspector. 'I thought so. You look more like yourself now, George. You and your friend took some fine-sounding names, didn't you! Would you please come with us – and your friend too. Don't worry about the bank-notes – we'll take care of those!'

And within twenty minutes the police cars had gone,

taking with them the false Sir Richard and the equally bogus Professor, both of whom they had been looking for for some considerable time. Alas – Mr Jones went with them!

Poor Mr Jones! As Mrs Jones said. 'He's not bad is my Llewellyn, not wicked at all. It was those men, with their lies and their promises. They tempted my poor Llewellyn, they lent him money to buy the inn. How was he to know they were bad men – a Sir and a Professor! And his cooking, it was so good, so very good cooking!'

Morgan and Jim were also paid visits by the police, and disappeared from the little village of Penrhydendraith for a long time.

Mrs Jones, in tears, begged Miss Pepper not to leave. 'I have no money!' she wept. 'Stay here with the children, and let me have your payment. What else shall I do? My cooking is fair, not very good cooking like Mr Jones's, but it is not bad. Have pity on me, Miss Pepper.'

'Well, we don't *really* want to leave,' said Miss Pepper. 'We can none of us go home at the moment – and I'm very very sorry about all this, Mrs Jones. We'll stay for another two weeks at least. And let's hope it will be a *holiday*, not a peculiar mystery to be solved, with noises in the night and all the rest of it!'

And a holiday it is, with sunny days, blue seas, white sands – boating, fishing, bathing, walking! All the four are as brown as berries – and they have been joined by another boy, small and just as brown. Dafydd has tagged on to them, with his faithful goose Waddle – and his precious alarm clock!

Everyone knows when the five are coming down to the beach. Wuff-wuff-wuff! Chatter-chatter! Cackle-cackle-hiss! R-r-r-r-r-ring! R-r-r-r-r-ring! R-r-r-r-r-ring!

'Somebody ought to write a book about those children and their doings!' said old Mrs Jones, as they go by.

Well, Mrs Jones – somebody has!

Have you read all the "Secrets" stories by Enid Blyton?

The Secret Island

Peggy, Mike and Nora are having a miserable time with unkind Aunt Harriet and Uncle Henry – until they make friends with wild Jack and discover the secret island. £2.75

The Secret of Spiggy Holes

On a holiday by the sea, Mike, Jack, Peggy and Nora discover a secret passage – and a royal prisoner in a sinister cliff-top house. The children plan to free the young prince – and take him to the secret island. £2.99

The Secret Mountain

Jack, Peggy, Nora and Mike team up with Prince Paul of Baronia to search for their parents, who have been kidnapped and taken to the secret mountain. Their daring rescue mission seems doomed to failure – especially when the children are captured and one of them is to be sacrificed to the sun-god. £2.99.

The Secret of Killimooin

When Prince Paul invited Nora, Mike, Peggy and Jack to spend the summer holidays with im in Baronia, they were thrilled. By amazing luck, they find the hidden entrance to the Secret Forest – but can they find their way out? £2.75

Have you read all the adventures in the "Mystery" series by Enid Blyton? Here are some of them:

The Rockingdown Mystery

Roger, Diana, Snubby and Barney hear strange noises in the cellar while staying at Rockingdown Hall. Barney goes to investigate and makes a startling discovery...

The Rilloby Fair Mystery

Valuable papers have disappeared – the Green Hands Gang has struck again! Which of Barney's workmates at the circus is responsible? The four friends turn detectives – and have to tackle a dangerous criminal.

The Ring o' Bells Mystery

Eerie things happen at deserted Ring o' Bells Hall – bells start to ring, strange noises are heard in a secret passage, and there are some very unfriendly strangers about. Something very mysterious is going on, and the friends mean to find out what.

The Rockingdown Mystery	**£2.99**
The Rilloby Fair Mystery	**£2.99**
The Ring o' Bells Mystery	**£2.99**

Order Form

To order direct from the publishers, just make a list of the titles you want and fill in the form below:

Name ....

Address ....

....

....

Send to: Dept 6, HarperCollins Publishers Ltd, Westerhill Road, Bishopbriggs, Glasgow G64 2QT.

Please enclose a cheque or postal order to the value of the cover price, plus:

UK & BFPO: Add £1.00 for the first book, and 25p per copy for each addition book ordered.

Overseas and Eire: Add £2.95 service charge. Books will be sent by surface mail but quotes for airmail despatch will be given on request.

A 24-hour telephone ordering service is avail-able to Visa and Access card holders: 041-772 2281